CALVIN COBB
Radio Woodworker!

CALVIN COBB
Radio Woodworker!

A Novel With Measured Drawings

Roy Underhill

LOST ART PRESS
FORT MITCHELL, KENTUCKY

CALVIN COBB: RADIO WOODWORKER!
Copyright © 2014
by Roy Underhill

All rights reserved. No part of this book may be reproduced in any form or by any electronic or mechanical means including information storage and retrieval systems without permission in writing from the publisher, except by a reviewer, who may quote brief passages in a review.

First printing.

ISBN: 978-0-9906230-2-1

Publisher: Christopher Schwarz
Editor: Megan Fitzpatrick
Book design and production: Linda Watts
Cover: Jode Thompson
Distribution: John Hoffman

PUBLISHED BY LOST ART PRESS LLC IN 2014
26 Greenbriar Ave., Fort Mitchell, KY 41017, USA

WEB: http://lostartpress.com

THIS BOOK WAS PRINTED & BOUND IN THE UNITED STATES OF AMERICA

For Dad.

OTHER BOOKS BY THE AUTHOR

The Woodwright's Shop: A Practical Guide to Traditional Woodcraft

The Woodwright's Companion: Exploring Traditional Woodcraft

The Woodwright's Workbook: Further Explorations in Traditional Woodcraft

The Woodwright's Eclectic Workshop

The Woodwright's Apprentice: Twenty Favorite Projects from the Woodwright's Shop

Khrushchev's Shoe and Other Ways to Captivate an Audience of 1 to 1,000

The Woodwright's Guide: Working Wood with Wedge and Edge

ABBREVIATIONS

Calvin Cobb: Radio Woodworker! takes place during the spring and summer of 1937. Some help on the alphabet agencies of the New Deal may prove useful.

AAA – Agricultural Adjustment Agency
CCC – Civilian Conservation Corps
FRC – Federal Radio Commission
FSA – Farm Security Administration
GAO – General Accounting Office
WPA – Works Progress Administration

SATURDAY MORNING, JUNE 11, 1937

Fearful of Maryland cops, the cabbie dumped Calvin at the gate of the Beltsville Agricultural Experimental Station and raced back toward the D.C. line. Without the workday ant-parades of lab-coated scientists lacing between the brick buildings, the concrete paths of the station seemed cold as tombstones. Calvin stood listening. Over a background of bleating goats, an engine roar echoed from a far hill and he took off running.

The laboratories gave way to hog pens and turkey houses as he ran. He came to a rough pasture and saw at the far end a gray tractor, headlights flashing, headed straight for a herd of boys, scattering them and sending some leaping over a board fence. The tractor spun around without slowing and chased a small group, corralling them in a corner of the field as they threw up their hands in surrender. The scream of the tractor engine drowned out the cheers and taunts of the other CCC boys closing in behind it.

Seated at a card table at the edge of the field, a woman was watching the business through field glasses. Calvin came up behind his alleged subordinate and called her name in angry voice. "Linda!"

She spun so quickly that the empty sleeve of her dress made a ghostly grab at him. "Chief!"

"So what's so special about this test that you couldn't tell me about it?" He lifted the field glasses and surveyed the action across the field. The tractor roared and the cornered boys made a sudden dash, sweat cutting pink streaks through the dust on their backs. The tractor bolted in pursuit, looping and jigging to chase the whole sunburned herd into the field. The tractor swerved to the left to chase three mavericks, running over a dropped fatigue hat and sending it flying in a long arc. A quick reverse drove the running boys back into the pack, forcing them all into the far corner where they threw up their hands in cheering surrender. The driver of the tractor gave a few bounces on the iron seat and waved her hand in victory.

Calvin handed the field glasses back to Linda. "She's gonna kill someone!"

Linda inhaled a draft of summer morning air. "She has to keep 'em busy or they'll wander off."

A green pickup truck turned into the lane and pulled up beside them. Ellen, sitting in the passenger seat beside the pimply CCC boy at the wheel, rolled down the window as Calvin walked over to her.

"Morning Chief!" She glanced quickly at Linda and back at him. "Nice to see you." She winced, struggling against her back brace, unable to turn away from Calvin's lowered eyebrows.

Dozens of bobbing white enameled kitchen scales surrounded Ellen's wheelchair in the back of the truck. Linda pushed past him to lean in the window. "Any word from Anne?"

"She's on her way," said Ellen. "Had to take a taxi from 14th Street."

The distant tractor screamed. "Better take the scales and tally sheets out to the boys before Verdie kills 'em," said Linda.

Ellen nodded to the grinning CCC boy and they drove off toward the roaring tractor at the distant end of the field, leaving Calvin and Linda swathed in oily exhaust. The tractor engine howled and flame shot from its exhaust stack. Calvin pulled Linda's field glasses back to his eyes. "Sounds like it's going to blow." The scream from the tractor echoed off the buildings behind them. "What the hell is that thing?"

Linda waited for the roar to ease. "Some guy at Ford designed it. It's got very good steering." She pointed at the light green leaves of a distant oak grove. "I think the wind is dropping."

Calvin ignored her diversion. "But what's that whine?"

No answer came.

"Linda?"

"It's…the supercharger. It's very special and we only have it for today."

"A supercharger?"

Linda flipped through the pages on her clipboard. "This is the same way we've done our tests for years."

"No, we've never tried to pull a spreader so heavily loaded that it needs a tractor with a supercharger!"

Linda began to speak, but only inhaled and looked up at the trees.

"Oh, no!" He leaned around to face her.

"The front wheels ride way out. It's plenty stable!"

"Oh, hell no!" He slapped the field glasses on the table and started across the field. "What the hell are you thinking!"

She followed him. "It was Verdie's idea! She's had it up to sixty just fine!"

"Sixty! Who the hell needs to spread manure at sixty miles an hour?"

"We're only going up to fifty, tops!" She swung her one arm

wildly to keep her balance as she followed him across the rough ground.

"Absolutely not! We're not going to get Verdie killed for a stupid spreader test!"

She punched his arm hard enough to make him stop and almost hit back. "We're not testing manure spreaders! We're testing Little Shirley! We're testing her!"

He stood seething, rubbing his arm.

Linda pointed back toward the city. "There were stiffs in the building, Chief! Guys in monkey suits prowling around on Tuesday. Burroughs men. They're after her!"

"Linda, this is nuts! You want Verdie to die for that stupid machine?"

"She's not stupid!" She punched him again in the same place.

"Stop that! I can't hit you back!"

She squared off to him. "Oh, I wish you could! Go ahead! Let's see just what the hell you can do!"

"Oh, for crying out loud! Stop it! This is no way to run a government office." He tried to put his hand on her shoulder but she jerked away.

"Probably not!" She fixed him with red eyes and jutting chin. "But look, she's growing. She can do things now she could never do before! You saw what she's been doing with your radio scripts! You need her too!"

"Not like you do."

"Yes, we need her. So what's wrong with that?"

From across the field, Ellen's command voice echoed, ordering the CCC boys into line to receive their tally sheets and scales. She was speaking to the boys, but both she and the woman driving the tractor were looking back across the field at Calvin.

He saw them watching him. He shook his head, looked up at the breeze in the trees and blew a jet of air from his puffed cheeks.

"Oh, Chief, thanks!" cried Linda. She wiped at her eyes and looked up at the trees. "You can help, too. Anne's bringing your lady friend's little RoBot camera to get sequence shots of the plume."

"Kathryn Harper's in on this?"

"No, she's not *in* on it. Anne just borrowed her camera, just to try the spring motor drive. She'd love it out here, with the grass and the horses. She's from Kentucky, ya know."

"Anne?"

"No, Kathryn! Whisky money! Her father moved their business to Europe during prohibition. Don't you read *Radio Guide?*"

"Guess I'd better start," he said, as they turned to walk back to the table.

"Well, you know you're supposed to take an interest in other people. That makes them interested in you."

Calvin shook his head. "How's the rest of the manure?"

"Excellent! Mostly pig, but the moisture is dead on. They did a really nice job."

A taxi turned into the lane and stopped by their table, Anne's hand waving from the passenger seat. The two women briskly updated each other while Calvin extracted the heavy surveyor's tripod from the back seat. As he stood with the tripod balanced on his shoulder, watching the women talk, a breeze swept back Anne's long hair, momentarily revealing the moonscape of scars that passed for the left side of her face. Calvin turned away to look out at the long field, rolling ground randomly dotted with hundreds of bright aluminum cake pans.

"Morning Chief!" said Anne as she joined him to walk to their camera position at the far end of the field. "Thanks for toting the tripod." She reached down to flip a grasshopper out of a cake pan as they passed.

"Where did you find four hundred cake pans?" he asked.

"They had 'em here," she answered, as she skipped ahead

of Calvin. For a person just in to middle age, her step was as happy as a calf let free in bright meadow.

They set up their position at a gap in the fence at the far end of the field. Calvin stood up the heavy tripod and Anne adjusted the settings on the tiny camera. "I'm going to kick in the green filter and see if that doesn't punch up the brown."

Calvin stifled the urge to suggest that a number two filter might be more appropriate. Through the field glasses, he sighted Ellen directing the boys as they linked and safety-chained the boxy John Deere Model E Spiral Beater Spreader to the streamlined grey tractor. In the high seat, he watched Verdie pull on a gas cape, goggles, gauntlet gloves and finally a steel doughboy helmet. She dropped into her seat, almost out of view behind the engine, and the tractor's headlights flashed twice. "Verdie's ready. How you doin' there?"

"Just a minute. Give 'em the slow flash," said Anne.

He sighted through a little signal mirror and swept slowly between Verdie's and Linda's positions.

Anne stepped back behind the camera and sighted through the finder. "Okay, I'm ready."

Calvin picked up the red and white semaphore flag. "You sure?"

"Yep. Keep the stopwatch right there." She indicated a spot two feet ahead of the camera lens. "When the flag goes down over there, hit the button. Okay, give 'em the fast flag."

Calvin waved the flag rapidly back and forth overhead and then held it steady. The lights on the distant tractor flashed, a flag went down and he hit the stopwatch. A flock of blackbirds unrolled onto the edge of the field but the roar of the engine sent them flying. Viewed straight on across the field, the only noticeable motion was a slight jiggering about as the tractor and spreader accelerated. In seconds, though, the little train grew a dark peacock's tail as the manure hit the spiral beater.

The supercharger's whine grew constantly louder as the distance between them closed, quickly drowning out the clicks and whirs of the camera as Verdie climbed upward through the gears. The bouncing spreader came into view above the tractor as she reached a slight downhill section. The brown aura now spread in an arc full ten yards wide and equally high.

A sudden spurt sent the brown plume upwards in a starburst-fingered pattern. The front end of the spreader bucked frantically upwards in protest.

"Was that the harmonic?" called Calvin.

"Yes!" shouted Anne. "Yes! Oh God, it has to be! She was right! I can't believe it!"

A new sound — deeper, shaking — reached their ears. The supercharger screamed over the ten raging cylinders. Rooster tails of dirt flew from the tractor tires, cutting through the manure rainbow like brown galaxies in collision. Calvin had a half second to ponder the implications of this intersection before the bucking front end of the tractor caught his eye. He glanced at Anne, still transfixed as the roaring juggernaut bounded straight for them. Now a coarse spray reached them, stinging their faces like tiny bees.

The tractor was upon them in a brain-rattling roar. Anne stood implacable — ill-served at this moment by her proven ability to remain calm, even at the approach of a walking artillery barrage. Calvin, however, stood his ground only through slowness of reflexes, so when the steel wheels of the spreader hit the bump and the machine transformed into an exploded-parts diagram, it was actually his earlier attempt to dodge the tractor that saved them. He threw himself at Anne, carrying her and the camera below the trajectory of flying wheels and gears. A length of drive chain whipped through the air, smacking Calvin's shoulder like cannon shot.

The tractor, now pulling only a towbar, flew past them,

followed by a catalog of cast iron spreader parts plowing waves of dirt from the turf. The tires rocked hard from side to side as Verdie jumped on the brake pedals and the grey monster slowed in backfiring, whining complaint. It turned back toward them, almost tipping over and finally stopped. Verdie jumped from the seat and limped fast toward them. "Oh my God, are you all right?" she shouted. Pulling off her goggles left her eyes in white raccoon bands — the rest of her all brown.

Calvin, heart pounding, staggered to his feet, wincing from the mile-a-minute slap of the flying drive chain. He probed gingerly at his bruised shoulder. "Anne, are you okay?"

"I'm alright. That was amazing! Look at the spreader! Nothing's left!" Anne pointed at one of the spreader wheels still rolling toward a distant fence.

Verdie examined them for bleeding and breathing, shaking her head. "I couldn't brake evenly and if I'd tried to turn I would have flipped. All I could do was keep going."

"It's my fault," said Calvin. "I set us up too close to the path." He spat straw from his mouth and wiped at his face. "I didn't think how fast you'd be going."

Verdie laughed. "You look like you've been dipped in shit!"

He spat again. "You should talk!"

Anne brushed dirt from her stocking. "I've hardly got any on me. Chief, you're a regular Sir Walter." She waved to the approaching pickup truck that was now halfway across the field. A line of CCC boys fanned out on both sides of the truck, recording the weight of manure in each aluminum cake pan, dumping out the contents and tossing the empties into the truck. "I'm going to run and look at the numbers! I'm sure we got it!" she called, already jogging away.

Verdie wiped at the brown ring below her eyes. "Come on Chief. I'll give you a ride back." She rubbed at her right eye and winced.

"Are you all right?"

"I'm fine! My stump is just a little sore from jumping on the brakes." She shook off his concern with a laugh. "Hurry up now! You gotta get cleaned up for your big date." She wiped at the pig manure on her chin. "And we've got four hundred cake pans to get back to the home-economics lab."

SIX WEEKS EARLIER

Calvin Cobb dodged through the morning stream of pedestrians on Pennsylvania Avenue, ready to spring up the gum-dotted steps of the old Post Office building. In the gleaming, Ionic-columned forest of 1937 New Deal Washington, entering this grimy castle was best done quickly — like pulling off a bandage. Today, though, he paused and glanced back at the odd behavior of the sidewalk crowd. Men and women who should have been hurrying to their own offices were, instead, holding onto their hats and squinting straight up at the clock tower high above him. In a flash, Calvin threw himself flat against the granite column framing the doorway. It took a few seconds of peering upwards into the shadows of the clock tower for him to realize that it wasn't a jumper they were looking at — it was a painter working on scaffolding suspended halfway down one of the gigantic clock faces. Calvin now shuddered with a new fear as he reasoned in Washington logic. *They're retouching the clock on the iceberg — the wrecking ball can't be far behind!*

He was still looking up at the painter when, next to his own office on the eighth floor, a window opened, sending snowflakes of loosened paint glittering in the sunlight. A faint chattering racket echoed down into the street and he dropped his head back against the stone — the girls were already at work, and their boss was late again. He spun around and pushed at the door, but the heavy oak swung grudgingly at its own pace. He strode past the useless elevator cages and sprang up the stairs, two at a time. At the fourth floor landing, a cigar-chewing workman was piling cardboard file boxes onto a hand truck. The careful labeling of the boxes told Calvin that these were the files of the saved — another tiny tribe striking out for their new offices in the white marble city, another lifeboat pulling away.

At the sixth floor landing, Calvin swung around the newel post of the stairwell and almost collided with the south end of a northbound "Eskimo." Too polite to race on around him, he was now forced to match the man's slow climb. Courtesy was all he could offer. At twenty-nine with an engineering degree, Calvin could still make a fresh start — but some of these old pencil pushers had worked at the same government job since the McKinley administration. Now they'd been abandoned in the building like ancient Eskimos on the ice. When the man finally shuffled out the landing to the seventh floor, Calvin grabbed the handrail and pulled himself springing up the final steps, three at a time.

The chattering sound meant that his staff already had their cobbled-together, punch card calculator running at full tilt, so he took the long way around the atrium to his office — a counterclockwise path that avoided the pebbled glass window of the machine room. Better that the girls discover their boss in his office than see him arriving late.

The coat tree by his door wobbled under his hat and jacket. Calvin steadied it and went back out to look over the railing into the pit of the atrium, eighty feet below. The old Post Office was an odd building, designed like an empty square box with offices in walls of the box surrounding a huge atrium that was covered by a steel-trussed skylight roof. The glass roof was now patched with tin and covered with dirt that yellowed everything beneath it. Even on the sunniest days, peering at the building's turreted clock tower through this gigantic skylight was like a view upward from the bottom of a filthy harbor.

Looking down into the pit of the atrium, Calvin stared for a moment at the prime oddity of the building—a second glass roof covering the ground-floor level, seven stories below. Now dust-gray and spotted with waste paper, this lower glass roof had a practical purpose before the Post Office moved out and the building became transient quarters for a dozen different federal agencies. It was originally intended to muffle the noise of the 1890s-vintage mail sorting equipment on the atrium floor, while still letting the postal higher-ups observe their underlings laboring below. The designers never considered that the laboring underlings could also look back up.

Calvin took a shallow breath and stared up at the narrow iron trusses of the skylight above him and imagined suddenly finding himself transported there, clinging to a thin iron spandrel high above the cavernous pit. The frightening image worked— a shivering thrill began below his ears, converged in his spine, and broke up into a million rivulets in his legs. He had charged himself with his full morning dose of adrenaline—just as the one-armed woman patted him on the back.

"Morning, Chief! Nice weekend?" Linda's flickering smile betrayed delight in making him jump. She stuck her pencil into her massive bun of graying hair and fanned through the corners of the papers held under the stump of her left arm.

"Very nice, Linda, thanks!" He tried to smile, but the tall woman's energetic asymmetry made him dizzy and he backed away from the railing. The clatter of the machines spilled out of a quickly opened door as Ellen—shrunken and red-eyed in her cane-backed wheelchair—poked her head out and sneezed. She tried to speak, but squirmed and gagged and finally made a running gesture with her fingers followed by a thumbs-up. Linda returned the thumbs-up and Ellen rolled back in, struggling with a handkerchief and leaving behind the smell of ozone and soldering flux.

"We've got some-thing-to-show–you!" said Linda in sing-song rhythm as she motioned him to follow. She caught him rolling his eyes and changed her tone. "Now you be good. The girls have been working all weekend."

He raised his hand in surrender and Linda opened the door to a room dominated by black machinery and bound by webs of wires. Verdie, her brown coveralls blending with her gray-flecked red hair, glanced up at them through a rising column of soldering flux smoke. She grinned, pulled off her motorcycle goggles and, using her detached prosthetic leg as a crutch, hopped to her foot. Calvin worked his way around a stack of Monroe calculators toward Ellen, who had rolled her wheelchair to sit before a motor-driven Burroughs 031 keypunch machine. Although it sounded like a street full of jackhammers, the black steel cabriole legs of the machine and the formal posture imposed by Ellen's back brace made the scene resemble a piano recital.

As Ellen typed numbers from a notebook into the keypunch machine, Anne examined the ejected cards. Unlike the other women, who wore their hair either in modern curls or pinned up in a Gibson girl roll that was twenty years out of date, Anne wore her brown hair long. The right half of her face was strikingly attractive, and her long hair covering the left half gave her a mysterious, movie star look. At forty-one, she had a figure and graceful beauty that wrenched men's heads around. Stomachs wrenched when her curtain of hair swung open enough to reveal the horror-show of pink rubber band burn scars lacing the left half of her face. She turned quickly and loaded the cards into a black Burroughs 601 multiplying punch, announcing each with its title. "VELOCITY…MASS…VOLUME… IMPELLER ANGLE."

Calvin pointed to a drumming bank of machines beside the open window. "CAN WE SHUT THAT BUNCH OFF?" he shouted, holding his hands over his ears.

Verdie stuffed her goggles into the side pocket of her coveralls and shouted too loud into his ear. "IT'S THE STEPPING RELAYS. THEY'RE VERY NOISY."

He rolled his eyes and threw up his hands. "THANK YOU. YES, THEY ARE!"

Linda knuckled him on his shoulder. "WE'RE JUST GOING TO RUN A SHORT ONE FOR YOU." She patted a rack that held dozens of large semi-circular stepping relays that sparked and hammered back and forth in a spasmodic reshuffling with each punch of a key. "THE OLD TELEPHONE RELAYS FROM THE BASEMENT. THEY CONTROL THE PLUG BOARDS! THAT'S HOW SHE DOES DIFFERENTIAL EQUATIONS!"

Calvin squinted to read the nameplate on a Burroughs 405 tabulator. "Is this—NEW?"

"THIRD FLOOR," said Linda. "Agricultural Adjustment Administration LEFT IT."

Calvin shook his head. "THESE BURROUGHS MACHINES ARE ALL LEASED. SHOULDN'T YOU ASK SOMEONE BEFORE MOVING 'EM UP HERE?"

Ellen rolled back to face him. "IF WE HAVE TO SHOVEL SHIT, I THINK WE'RE ENTITLED TO COME UP WITH A BETTER SHOVEL." She turned to avoid Calvin's blush. "EXCUSE MY FRENCH."

The other women laughed and Verdie passed the cocoa tin

to receive Ellen's nickel. Verdie shook the tin to gauge its contents, but stopped when Anne suddenly held up her hand. The women glanced at each other, eyes wide, stock-still, listening. Slight movements of their hands, fingers, heads, synchronized with a rhythm emerging through the racket. *TIGA-TIGA-TIGA-THUM. TIGA-TIGA-TIGA-THUM.* Verdie closed her eyes and dropped her head. Calvin called out, "WHAT IS IT?" Linda shushed him, jerking her head to listen, pencils wiggling in her hair bun.

TIGA-TIGA-TIGA-THUM. TIGA-TIGA-TIGA-THUM.

"SHE'S IN A LOOP!" said Linda.

The rack of relays rocked with the hammering rhythm. *CACK-CACK-THUM! CACK-CACK-THUM!*

"SHE'S GONNA CRASH!" cried Anne, as two tall racks slammed against one another.

"NO!" called Ellen, rolling forward in her wheelchair too late to catch a falling clipboard of tattered papers.

All the telephone relays now marched in lockstep synchrony. *CACK!-CACK! CACK!-CACK! CACK!-CACK!* Flecks of plaster dropped from the ceiling.

"PULL THE PLUG!" called out Linda. "DAMN!"

Back at his desk, Calvin listened as the girls argued about who had said what particular cussword and how many nickels each violator owed to the cuss-pot. Linda rapped at the glass on the half-open door. "Sorry about that, Chief," she said.

"What made it do that?"

"Roaches, probably. They get caught between the relay contacts. Sometimes it sets up a looped connection that—kind of spreads—like a cold. " She glanced around at the papers stacked on his office floor. "I hope you're not eating in here."

"No, of course not." He arched his eyebrows and nodded at the door.

Linda pushed it closed and perched on her accustomed corner of his desk. "Any word?"

He drew in a breath and shook his head. "Nothing good. We're not on the Beltsville list, that's for sure."

She picked up a triangular scale ruler and poked among the papers on his desk. "Moving us out to the research station *would* make too much sense, now, wouldn't it?"

Calvin nodded at the window. "So maybe it is South building, after all."

She bit at her upper lip. "I've been all over the floor plan. There's nothing labeled Broadcast Research." She grasped the stub of her left arm with her right hand.

"Well, if they don't know about us," he tapped three times on his desktop, "then they can't cut us, either."

Linda nodded up at the ceiling. "You saw the angel of doom up on the tower, didn't you?"

"Ah, they've been chipping away at the iceberg since—forever. They sure as heck won't budget to tear it down this year." He pushed the "Year of Recession or New Depression?" headline on the previous Friday's *Evening Star* into view.

Linda tugged the corner of the newspaper. "Cuts both ways, Chief. Hard times makes hungry watchdogs."

Calvin leaned forward to conceal a shiver. "I expect the GAO has bigger fish to fry than the five of us." A bang on the door brought him back upright as if a General Accounting Office auditor had been listening in.

The footrests of Ellen's wheelchair battered the door open. "Found it!" She held an envelope towards Linda. "Relay bank five."

Linda pulled the envelope from Ellen's quivering hand. "Bank five, huh? That makes sense." She passed the envelope to Calvin and stared at the window for a moment. "Bank five. Okaaay."

Calvin studied the cockroach in the envelope, punched through in its middle and burned black by the sparks. He began to pass the envelope back to Ellen, but she was frantically wiping her drool from her lace collar. He turned and pushed the envelope at Linda. "Okaay. Relay bank five." He nodded knowingly, as if the words meant something to him.

Ellen shivered and gave a sudden cry. Her wildly squirming body slid lower in the wheelchair as she struggled to push herself back up. Linda dropped the envelope and tried to steady the wheelchair for her. Calvin rose and grabbed her under her arms. "Don't touch me! Let me go!" Ellen punched out at Calvin with a spastic left hook to his throat. He fell back. Linda lost her grip on the wheelchair as Ellen spun it about and forced it banging out the door.

Calvin felt his throat and swallowed. "How long has it been?" he gasped. Ellen's moaning echoed in the atrium.

"Four days." Linda closed her eyes and took control of her breathing. "Withdrawal doesn't seem to kick in when the work is going well." She picked up the envelope from the floor and shook the cockroach into the trashcan. "We'll get her back on thirty milligrams for a while." She set the empty envelope on his desk and pounded it flat with the end of her fist.

"She was going to fall on the floor."

"I know." Linda gave him a flat smile as she backed out the door. In the hall, Anne and Verdie were already arguing softly with Ellen—the black leather roll of syringes and morphine vials perched in her lap like a demon puppy.

As the voices withdrew, Calvin sat back down, closed his eyes and rocked slowly from side to side. He pulled at the arms of his chair, working the play in the joints—there were plenty of other chairs left in the building if he wrecked this one. He leaned across his desk and probed beneath the newspaper for his box of Ritz crackers. He stuffed one in his mouth and pulled a cloth roll of spiral auger bits to the front of his desk. The gleaming steel bits made a soft ascending *clink, clink, clink, clink, clink* as he unrolled them. He stopped chewing long enough to savor the soft chimes, but through the wall he heard Ellen's cries as the muscle spasms wrung her like a dishrag. The light morphine injections dulled Ellen's self-control before they reached her pain and she would loudly engage God in a dialogue on the ironic justice of her injuries. In her four months as an aerial photo interpreter in northern France, she had spotted where dozens of German officers were quartered by finding the circular paths left in the grass from when they exercised their horses after dark. By the time she herself was hit, she'd directed artillery fire right onto the pikelhaubes of twelve of the Kaiser's finest, and, as her CO liked to boast back then, "the horse they rode in on."

Calvin swallowed and slid the roll of auger bits back across his desk—none of them needed sharpening. A rustling in the corner of the office echoed the clatter of the bits. He sat still as little scratching sounds announced his friend's arrival up the radiator pipe. The rat, brown and white like a movie cowboy's horse, crept in fits along the asbestos-wrapped radiator pipe, sniffing and wary. Calvin pretended not to watch the rat follow the path along the ledge and onto the bookshelf, hiding in shelters made from map tubes and books. The rat's final dash through a miniature souvenir life ring and down a wide wooden ruler led to her inevitable fall into the glass Prince Albert tobacco jar.

"Now I've got you me pretty!" growled Calvin softly as he wiggled the end of his necktie at his captive.

"Oh Captain Blood, I am your captive once again!" he said, now in trembling falsetto. "Be merciful Captain!"

"I shall have mercy my fair Christina, but first you must dance for me." He joggled the jar balanced on his knee.

"Dance for you my captain?"

"Yes, me lovely! You must dance the dance of the seven whiskers!"

"Oh Captain, I shall dance, I must dance, I…"

Three knocks came on the frosted glass window of his office door.

"Curses, me proud beauty!" he rumbled quietly to his captive as he rose from his chair. "We are…interrupted." With the jarred rat in his left hand, he opened the door.

"Hello," said the pretty woman in the hallway. "Boy, they've got you way up here, don't they? I wondered why they hadn't moved you over to the new building, but I guess you get better reception up here."

Calvin froze.

She glanced up and down the corridor. "I'm sorry to just drop in on you, but I thought I'd stop in and see how we're doing. I mean if that's possible."

The rat skittered in the jar. Sweat dripped under his arm. "Certainly, certainly, just let me put something…papers away." He darted away from the door, put the jar on the shelf and leaned a manila report folder against it. "Come on in."

"I'm sorry if this is a breach of protocol for me to just drop in on you. But you know how long it can take to get any information around here. Agriculture is so big and we're so spread out." She held out her white-gloved hand. "We haven't met. I'm Kathryn Dale Harper."

"Calvin Cobb." He jerked his hand free too soon and shoved a pile of books off a chair for her.

"Thank you." She sat. "You are…head of Broadcast Research?"

"I'm section chief. Smallest section in the Department of Agriculture, that's why we work so hard!" He seized a small cork board covered with polar charts, tables and grids and held it for her to see. Her clover honey curls poured across her shoulders as she leaned forward. She squinted at the charts with eyes the color of Delft china seen through the thinnest drop of milk.

"These are all from last year," he explained.

Relieved, she leaned back and her hair cascaded over her shoulders again. "Do you have anything from this year that I could look at?"

"Ah, sure." He turned to his desk to search for the data on the wet weather performance of an experimental McCormick front-end manure spreader. "We're constantly updating here at Broadcast Research. These are just raw numbers here, but we'll have something soon." He handed her a folder of dotted grids, punched cards, and paper tabulation tapes. "I've got aerial reports from last spring, too — if you'd like to see them."

"Thanks, no, I just want to..." She thumbed through the papers in the folder, her face smiling, frowning, squinting. Calvin marveled at the mobility of her face. Her expressions stilled so rarely that her soft symmetry flashed like glimpses of a hummingbird's scarlet. "You do break your research down into specific programs, don't you?" she asked.

"We test programs, practices and equipment. Obviously how you use the equipment often determines its effectiveness. Then we report to the decision makers."

She bit her upper teeth into her lower lip for an instant and leaned forward. "What do you have on *Homemaker Chats*?"

"I'm sorry, *Homemaker Chats*?"

Her eyelids flickered and she drew in a breath. "*Farm and Home Hour*...? 12:45...? Every day...?"

"Every day...?" he echoed.

Her eyes grew wide, her voice louder. "USDA Radio Service...?"

"Oh, on the radio!" He grinned. "Oh, I understand! No,

we've never had anything on the radio! But that would be great! That's swell!"

She looked at him in wide-eyed silence for a moment and then quietly asked, "This *is* the Broadcast Research Section?"

"Yes."

"Yes, so, what, exactly, does the Broadcast Research Section do?"

Grinning, he started to reach toward his desk.

"No. No. In English, please, what do you do here?"

He leaned toward her. "We study the effectiveness of broadcast seed, nutrient and amendment distribution technology and practice. And you know a really great angle? With this dust-bowl, with the floods along the Ohio, and all these hills stripped bare by mining and logging — aerial seed broadcasting of ground-cover crops is really important right now!"

She stroked her fingertips on her forehead. Recovering with a quick exhalation and shake of her head, she gestured at the graphs pinned on the corkboard. "So these reports are on… manure spreaders?"

"This one is." He shot his eyes back and forth between the charts and her growing look of amusement. "The tables are for drop spreaders and the polar charts are for rotary broadcasters."

"So you actually study what happens when the…" She arose from her chair, chuckling and shaking her head.

"Yes, when it hits the fan — our work begins." Calvin hoped to share the joke, but she turned away, pretending to take in the view out his window as she struggled to compose herself.

"I'd better let you get back to it then." She turned back to him, smiling and shaking her head, but her eyes darted away toward the scratching sound on the shelf. "Mr. Cobb?"

"Yes?"

"Did you know there is a mouse in a jar above your desk?"

"Oh yes, ahh, I think it's a rat. I mean, a stray lab rat." He turned to take the jar. "They used to do nutrition research down on the fourth floor. I catch them, now and then." He held the jar to his side, shielding it with his body. "You're not afraid of them are you?"

"Oh please. Let me see the little cutie." She leaned forward to look in the top of the jar as he held it. "He's a little cutie!"

"I think it's a she. Named Christina."

"Christina?" She looked around the office and then at him with narrowed eyes. "I thought I heard a radio show when I was waiting outside — something about pirates."

Heat rose in Calvin's face.

"My mistake, I guess." She smiled and looked up at the water-stained ceiling. "Did you know that peanut butter makes a more effective and economical mouse bait than cheese?" She did not give him time to answer. "You would know that, if you listened to *Homemaker Chats*." She started for the door. "Thanks for your time Mr. Cobb."

"I'll sure be listening from now on." He followed after her. "When would you like to do this story on us?"

"Oh, we'll be in touch. Thank you Mr. Cobb. Good-bye Christina — me proud beauty." She winked at the rat and laughed when the rat seemed to wink back. Calvin's toes grasped at the floor.

"I'll look forward to hearing from you, then. Thanks for stopping in!" He watched her walk confidently down the hall to the elevator. "Good-bye, " he said in Christina's quiet voice.

In the wake of her footsteps, heads cautiously poked out of office doors, then full bodies emerged, all looking at the receding figure. Calvin stepped to the brass railing and leaned around a column. Across the atrium, he watched her emerge from the corner and continue down the hall to the one working elevator. As she passed behind the columns of the Gothic arches, he quickly conjured the fantasy of a princess walking.

She could be in the Alhambra. The iron trusses of the gigantic skylight now became a huge Arab tent. An English lady, no — an American lady, visiting his desert palace. And he was the Sheik of Araby.

Linda came up behind him. "Who on earth was that?"

He didn't turn. "I thought she was a GAO inspector, but she's with the department radio service."

"Radio service?"

"Yeah. She does *Homemaker Chats* or something."

Linda peered at the distant figure and then burst out, "*Homemaker Chats*! Holy cow! Was that Kathryn Dale Harper?"

Anne heard her. "It's Kathryn Dale Harper! We could have met her!" She waved into the machine room. "It's Kathryn Dale Harper! She's still at the elevator!"

Linda and Anne took off after her, pushing Ellen ahead of them. Verdie stayed behind, shaking her head in disgusted amusement as she adjusted the fit of her right leg. "She's a swell pick for the voice of the American housewife." She twisted her leg sharply clockwise. "Not even married." She held her fingers to her mouth in mock embarrassment. "Oh, did I say house*wife*? I meant to say home*maker*."

Voices echoed across the atrium as the women shook hands. The elevator door opened and a chorus of good-byes followed Kathryn Dale Harper as she quickly stepped inside. The rat in Calvin's jar began a furious scratching at the glass. Verdie's eyes narrowed at the jar. "God, I hate those things!"

"Oh, you know she's harmless," said Calvin, holding up the jar.

"Yeah? Well, they don't wait until you're dead to start in on you." She turned and clumped back into the machine room. Calvin winced at yet another reminder that while these four women were knee deep in the slaughterhouse, he was still a Boy Scout collecting tin cans.

Linda and Anne rolled Ellen back from the elevator. "Had to be a Schiaparelli!" said Linda. "Those brisk lines and all."

"Oh no. Schiaparelli's still doing that military look," said Anne. "I've got my old uniform if anybody wants that!"

"Molyneux," said Ellen, weakly.

Linda leaned down. "What dear?"

"Her suit. Molyneux. Classic."

Linda patted Ellen's shoulder and let Anne roll her back into the machine room. She joined Calvin at the railing. "I can't believe how young she is! On the radio she sounds like the voice of experience, but she's got to be about your age. What on earth was she doing up here?"

"She asked if Broadcast Research had ever been featured on *Homemaker Chats*."

"You're kidding!"

"No. I said I thought the aerial seeding program would make a great radio story."

Linda's expression of delight dissolved. "Well that's not a very good way to lie low — go on the radio and tell everyone we're here."

Calvin leaned over the railing in hopes of one more glimpse. "They're gonna find us sooner or later. They're not going to put us on the radio and then dump us. So, why not tell everybody about the good work we do?"

"Not put us on the radio and then dump us? That's like saying they'd never send painters to work on a building if they knew they were about to tear it down." Linda rolled her eyes to look down into the atrium. "Look." She pointed to the third floor and a line of gaping doors to empty offices, "That's the entire inland aquaculture section — out. Gone! They're not moving anyone anymore. Now they're just cutting." She reached out and plinked the jar in Calvin's hands. "But I see you've already started puttin' by food for hard times." She waggled her head and her eyes went wide. She threw her hand up to her hair. "Oh hell! Can you believe I had a pencil stuck in my bun! The whole time we were talking to her!"

Calvin turned to his office and motioned for her to follow. He closed the door, tipped the Prince Albert jar on the floor by the radiator pipe and watched Christina disappear down the hole. "I think this could be really good. Let's clean up the offices, get some stuff on the walls that looks really interesting, put the reports in order, maybe revise some of the old bulletins."

"Chief, the thing about radio is…you don't have to clean up." She spotted the box of Ritz crackers on his desk and picked it up in triumph.

"I might have something interesting in the tower," said Calvin, pretending not to see the bright red and yellow cracker box in her hands. "Some of the spreader models."

"The spreader models? My God, Chief, a federal agency that studies manure spreaders is a perfect target for the anti-New-Dealers." She dug in the box for a handful of crackers. "Just give us a little time and we'll have something to really impress people."

"Your machine?"

She narrowed her eyes at him. "Yes, our crazy machine." She organized the jumble of crackers in her hand into a stack. "I hope you understand what we've got next door."

"A bug killer?"

Dust dropped from the crackers in Linda's fist. "Listen chief, if we could rebuild the Fourth Division's telephone exchange in six hours, under fire, by candlelight, *while* wearing gas masks, then I *think* we can fix the cockroach problem!" She dropped a broken cracker back in the box and exchanged it for a whole one. "When we're done, we'll be able to make a mathematical model of any farm machine that you can imagine and test it on a completely mathematical field." She nibbled at a cracker.

"Any kind of manure you can imagine too!"

Calvin rubbed his fingertips together, choosing his words carefully. "Linda, I think the calculating machine may be just…a little too far from what we're supposed to be doing."

"Sir, as far as I can tell nobody knows we're even here, much less what we're *supposed* to be doing!"

"Well, Miss Kathryn Dale Harper apparently knows we're here."

Linda reached across her chest in a gesture that would have been crossing her arms if her left sleeve had not been empty. "Chief, if you go on the radio and talk about building better manure spreaders, the Hooverites'll have us out on the street by rush hour."

"So, you'd rather I say that, while we were supposed to be improving farm machines, we just happened to knock together a Buck Rogers electric brain." He nodded his head from side to side in mock consideration. "Linda, I might as well say that we've invented a death ray!"

Linda glared at him. "I wish I *had* a death ray." She sprayed her imaginary ray gun around the room, then the building, then the world, finishing on Calvin and herself. She spun around and walked out, slapping the empty sleeve of her dress against the door casing.

cack-CACK! cack-CACK! The machine began another of its clamorous sessions, a process as foreign to Calvin as the girls' overheard complaints of flashes and phantom pain. The pebbled glass in his door rattled with the slamming banks of relays. The glass had SECTION CHIEF painted on the outside, but on the inside, he was a FEIHC NOITCES. He rested the back of his head lightly against the rattling glass and pondered the empty chair where perfect Kathryn Dale Harper had sat. He glanced up at the window, but she would be out of sight by now.

Banging buckets echoed down the hall from the clock

tower entrance. The painter was done for the day. The stacks of ordered papers on Calvin's desk no longer made sense, and he gathered them into a single pile.

"I'll be up in the lab," he called into Linda's office as he escaped down the hall. He drummed up the stairs to the ninth floor and walked to the door squeezed between two empty storerooms. He crouched slightly as he passed down the short corridor that led into the square base of the clock tower, but once he emerged into the room, he could stand twenty feet tall if he wanted. Four huge frosted glass clock faces crowned the upper walls of the chamber. Four shafts driving the clock hands converged overhead with bevel gears that doled out the seconds from the clockwork on the floor above. Visitors felt tiny beneath the giant clock faces — smaller than mice in a grandfather clock. But the sense of being inside something intentional, something measured and deliberate, appealed powerfully to Calvin.

Slit windows in the walls, narrow like archer's loopholes in a castle, gave views of each compass point. Calvin peered through the east window by his workbench. With the trees not fully leafed out yet, he could still see the mottos chiseled into the facade of the new Justice Department building up the street. In large letters under the window of the FBI director's office were the words "No Free Government Can Survive That" — a disturbing statement if you missed the subsequent "Is Not Based on the Supremacy of Law" that continued around the corner.

Those FBI men up Pennsylvania Avenue were, in part, responsible for the stack of golden-hued, white oak boards leaning against the wall beside Calvin's workbench. He had salvaged this mellow timber with growth rings as tight as a deck of cards from the demolished cabinetry on the atrium floor far below. The cabinetry had all been purpose-made in the 1880s as specialized organs to digest the United States mail — oak cubby-hole kidneys for insufficient address, oak hopper-table livers for postage due. But after the postal operations moved out in the summer of 1934, the FBI moved in, waiting for the completion of their new building up the street. They demanded uniform desks in uniform ranks and broke up the oak woodwork in the atrium with fire axes and stacked it for the dump, exposing embarrassing rectangular outlines on the marble floors where ten thousand nightly moppings had left fossil seashores of filth. Calvin, staying late in the evenings, had rescued as many planks as he could and given them sanctuary in the tower.

He unlocked his wall-mounted tool cupboard and took a plane from the shelf. The cabinet had belonged to a European master stamp engraver and some of his old prints were still tacked to the doors; Dürer's the *Knight, Death and the Devil* on one, and on the other, an unknown eighteenth-century engraver's *Virtue Fleeing from Décolletage*, showing a young man pursued down a flight of stairs by a quartet of busty young beauties in spectacularly low-cut gowns.

This afternoon, with everyone else ready to slip from the iceberg, he lifted a plank still bearing shreds of varnish and deeply stained with purple ink, and laid it on the workbench. He took up his jack plane and went to his compulsive work. The old surfaces — stabbed by angry clerks, passed over by millions of love letters, bank orders, Christmas cards, draft notices, invitations and regrets fell in corkscrew shavings to the floor. He finished planing the long board and resumed his work on a glass-fronted wall cabinet for Linda's stacks of punched cards. He cranked his bit-brace auger, turning the center bit into the oak to rough in a mortise. "Why do you choose a center bit for this work Mr. Cobb?" he asked himself in a high and barely audible voice.

"Well, Miss Harper, for a shallow hole, a center bit actually cuts faster," he answered himself. Tan shavings wound outward in an unbroken spiral. The central pike of the bit poked through the far side of the plank. He turned the plank over and inserted the center pike into the hole, and bored down again until the bit pushed into open space, carrying with it a speared button of oak.

He worked until the sunlight rectangles cutting through the slit-windows of the castle grew rust-red. Out the dusty west window, a deep sun fired diagonal rows of clouds into scarlet furrows that left the Washington monument in stark silhouette. A bunt of his hand knocked the shavings out of the rabbet plane and he locked it and the other tools back in the cabinet. Closing the cabinet left him facing the old engravings tacked to the door faces. He stared at one of the lusty women in *Virtue Fleeing from Décolletage*. He would find a set of colored pencils. He would color her eyes Delft blue.

If it had not been Tuesday, he could have listened to her voice on *The National Farm and Home Hour*, but today meant lunch with girlfriend Amanda in the café on the top floor of the *Evening Star* newspaper building across the street. At least today he would have the news of the upcoming radio interview — or, rather, the offer of an interview that he would have to refuse. He shuffled his assembled reports, studies and recommendations between different piles until quarter to noon, and then went to the washroom to comb his hair.

He needed some good news. Two years of "I'm waiting for you, Calvin" heard the tone devolve from the offer of a reward, to loyal dedication, and finally to a nagging scold. For the first year of their weekly lunch dates, they would stop in front of Galt's jewelers to look at the sparkling engagement rings. He was often startled by their reflections in the window. He and Amanda were the same age, but she looked so much older standing beside his grinning, all-American Boy-Scout face. In that first year, they would neck and grapple furiously on the elevator ride to the top floor of the *Evening Star* building. Now she just met him at the table.

Crossing the street, he steeled himself for the contrast between the old Post Office and the *Evening Star* building. The two buildings had faced each other across Pennsylvania Avenue for almost fifty years, but the smaller newspaper building was literally on the sunny side of the street. He meandered through the infectious excitement of the dining room, catching bits of the unfiltered news of Washington and the world: Sit-down strikes at beauty parlors in New York. A Negro father and son lynched in Indiana. Ten or twelve strikers shot by police at Republic Steel. Firing squads in Spain. Jews lining up for racial registration in Germany.

He found a table for two by the window and sat down. Across the street, scaffolding hung on the clock face of the tower, but no workman was in view. Noon now. He looked for Amanda and spotted her already seated with a guest by the wall near the cash register. He closed his eyes and shook his head. These days, she often invited various brothers, cousins or friends, and Calvin reluctantly gave up his table to join them.

The wide-smiling dapper man at Amanda's table was holding forth on how if all the Chinese jumped off of chairs at the same time on a command given over the radio, then they could send a tidal wave crashing over Japan and wipe out the invaders — just like that.

"They don't even have food and you want them all to have radios?" asked Amanda, dismissing Calvin's arrival with a glance.

"People will give up food before they'll give up their radios," said the man.

"They don't even have chairs! How can they jump off chairs if they don't have chairs in China?" she asked, twisting her lips.

"They can jump off walls then. You know they've got walls. They've got the Great Wall don't they? And what, there's 500 million of 'em. Each of them at 150 pounds. They could make one heck of a bump!"

"They're all starving, they don't weigh 150 pounds," said Amanda, holding Calvin off with a quick wink.

"All right 100 pounds, that's still...fifty thousand million pounds...twenty-five million tons, accelerated over, say, five feet. With just one direct appeal to the sub-literates, you could knock the earth out of its orbit! Or at least have the Chinks give the Japs a bath. That's why they call it the Yellow River, you know!" Amanda laughed as the man gestured high with his hand, and then brought it down to offer to Calvin. "How do you do? You must be Calvin. Have a seat my friend!"

Calvin started to sit as commanded, but Amanda stopped him with her hand. "Calvin, this is Randoph, the gentleman who is building the free-flight aviary at the zoo."

Half-crouched, Calvin nodded at the dapper man. "You're the guy who buys all the pencils." Amanda had frequently mentioned this entertaining builder who made daily visits to the Cathedral Heights artist's supply store where she worked. The waitress came and asked for Calvin's order. He had yet to look at the menu so he just asked for his usual order of fish. Amanda shook her head at his lack of imagination, but he rallied and counterattacked. "You were talking about radio programs. I'm going to be...I was asked for an interview on the *Farm and Home Hour.*"

She paused and then turned to face Randy. "Well...I don't suppose it could have been the Jack Benny show!" She stirred her tea, dinging her spoon against the sides of the cup.

Randy laughed, "Good-o, Cal! Radio needs more talk about manure spreaders! Hey, isn't that redundant?" He laughed again at his joke and said he was just kidding, but Calvin was too dismayed that the man knew that he studied manure spreaders to be offended.

"The farm news!" said Amanda. "Let me know when it'll be on so that I can miss it!"

The builder eyed a passing waitress admiringly. Amanda traced his gaze but he snapped his attention back to Calvin and said in a mock radio voice, "I understand there is a paradox in assisting farmers with the purchase of mechanical equipment, such as tractors, in that it allows for increased production — but also creates a decline in farm employment. A boon for the owners, a bust for the workers."

"Well, sort of," said Calvin.

The birdcage builder traded glances with Amanda. "Oh boy! You gotta do better than that on the radio!" He rubbed his hands together. "Here's what you do. Answer any question with an analogy that relates to their field. If they ask about tractors and laborers, you answer that it's like radio cutting into record sales. That makes 'em think you're really interested in them."

Calvin frowned, struggling with the logic. "You mean, why would anyone spend money on records when they can listen to the radio for free?"

"Yeah, but forget that! The important thing is to make the other guy, in this case, the interviewer, feel important."

Calvin's plate of soggy breaded fish arrived. He looked at Amanda's plate and for the first time it registered that they had already finished.

The builder tapped the table. "I was thinking of the tractors 'cause we use a lot of colored CCC boys down at the zoo. We do everything with shovels and wheelbarrows just to keep 'em busy."

Amanda yawned and looked around. "Keeps 'em out of trouble."

"Hey, I saw that folding bookstand you made for Amanda. Very nice!" said the builder. "So how'd you come up with that?"

"It's an old design from a French cabinetmaker's book. It's just one piece of wood." Calvin poked at the fish. "Say you're an engineer, maybe you know." He set down his fork. "I use a lot of old oak planks to make research models. You'd think that the dust and the dirt in the old boards would dull the planes and the chisels, but every time I go in to work, it seems they're sharper than ever."

"Maybe the dust is somehow sharpening the tools as you work," offered the builder.

Amanda waved the subject away. "I've got something for you to read, Calvin." She pulled the latest of her Calvin-improvement tomes from her handbag. "I've wanted you to read this for months, but I just got it back."

The builder tapped the cover of *How to Win Friends and Influence People* as she passed it to Calvin. "You'll like it. It's a real easy read."

"Thanks," said Calvin. The dust jacket was torn, giving the photograph of Dale Carnegie a mocking white leer. He studied the face and nodded, smiling back at the master of manipulation, glad to share his growing joy. In Amanda's last side-by-side suitor-comparison luncheon, Calvin had defeated a balding Southern Railway dispatcher. Today, he was clearly the loser, and he had never been happier in his life.

Calvin dodged streetcars back across Pennsylvania Avenue and pounded up the sixteen flights of steps. He emerged from the stairwell back onto the eighth floor, but it was too late to get to the radio in the clock tower. It suddenly occurred to him that Kathryn Dale Harper, now that her show was done for the afternoon, might call his phone and he quick-stepped down the hall to his desk.

All afternoon, like an Egyptian ruin in the desert, the copy of *How to Win Friends and Influence People* was buried and exposed under shifting dunes of papers as Calvin dug through old reports. He rubbed his art gum eraser at smudges on graphs and tables and shot sidelong glances at the telephone. A proper interview — and you never knew when that might happen — called for something tangible, something farmers would appreciate, but that wouldn't give the FDR-haters more ammunition. He dug into the piles beside his desk, poked beneath his old boss's yellowed photos of shipboard Thanksgiving dinners held under battleship gun barrels — searching for a good story about the Broadcast Research Section helping farmer Gray or advising John Deere. Under a bundle of his old boss's Christmas cards from harbors in Cuba and Hawaii, he came across the framed photograph of eight young women in uniform. *So that's why the girls are acting crazy*, he thought. *Good Friday, 1918, so I missed the…the 19th anniversary.* He tossed the bundled cards back on the desk. *So what the hell do you give your staff for disfigurement day?*

Through their half-open door, he could hear them buzzing around their machine and tossing around prime numbers like beach balls. He had once tried to figure how many whole bodies the four of them made up — what with all the missing arms, legs and faces. The math was easy enough. The Germans had been firing their Paris gun at the city for two days — but nobody knew it. Hidden seventy-five miles away in a forest, their first shots went eleven miles past the city because they didn't allow for the rotation of the earth during the shell's three and a half minute passage through the upper atmosphere. Compared to this complex problem of trajectory, the rest was plain subtraction. Forty thousand American women volunteered for overseas military service in the Great War. Rigorous, some say sadistic, testing culled this lot down to the three hundred smartest, fastest, toughest. On Good Friday, March 29, 1918, at 4:27 p.m., twenty-six of these women were on leave, sitting in pews listening to an organ recital in a Paris church when the Germans got their math right. The quarter-ton Krupp shell hit above the second pillar on the north side of the church of St.

Gervais. The explosion collapsed the stone vaulting, crushing the women under a mountain of marble mixed with white-hot steel. Nineteen years later, here in the top corner of the old Post Office building was the remainder — three and one eighth.

"Miss Harper is in rehearsal right now," said the chirpy voice on the phone. "But if she was expecting you, she'll be off the air by 1:15. Were you coming to watch her broadcast?"

"I'd like to. Yes. I'm supposed to," Calvin half-lied easily.

"Where are you now?"

"Old Post Office building."

"Where? I can hardly hear you over that machinery!"

"I can find you, don't worry!"

"Well, she doesn't go on until 12:45, and you might catch her between rehearsal and show time. Do you know where we are?"

"Sure, New South."

"We're in the New South Building. Ask at the desk just as you come in the wing one entrance. They should be able to help you find us."

Calvin snatched up his folder of reports and dashed out his door. He skidded to a stop and made an about-face. The reports wouldn't be enough — he needed props! Even if she was going to postpone the interview, he still needed to make a good case for not abandoning the idea. He ran up the stairs to the tower and snatched spreader models and process testers off the shelf, packing them roughly into a pasteboard bank box. *This makes good sense!* he told himself as he drummed down the marble stairs. He pushed out the 12th Street doors and hustled under the gatehouse of the new IRS building. *We can't do the interview just now, Miss Harper, but do keep us in mind!* Across Constitution Avenue he trotted, across the muddy Mall, passing between the museum and the long greenhouses where the lilies were in full perfume. He half-ran across B Street and around the agricultural administration building. Now he confronted the tawny brick of New South building, the largest office building in the world that still had no place for them. He put his head down and pounded up the steps of the wing one entrance. The guard called him back and insisted that he look at a map. The five interior wings and four wings of the perimeter created nine possible basements, with the radio studios in the center wing basement to cut out as much traffic noise as possible.

The receptionist was flustered when she saw him. "Miss Harper is busy now. She'll be contacting you. No, she's coming out. Wait just a minute."

Kathryn Dale Harper wore a trim blue skirt with an immaculate white blouse and scarf. "Mr. Cobb, how nice of you to drop by! Come step into my office. I have to go on in just a minute, but do step in!" She glanced behind Calvin several times as she led him down the hall into a small room with streamlined furniture and sconce lamps on the walls. "Sit down. Please. So nice to see you again!" She closed the door and leaned against it.

He sank into a chair, the box in his lap weighing him down. "Thanks. Thanks."

"Remember when I came to speak to you about the interview yesterday, about your work?"

The leather upholstery squeaked beneath Calvin's writhing.

"Yes. But I just wanted to tell you that I, that we really…"

"Yes, well, I was very interested in what you do, and it all seems very important. But, it really was an error on my part, you understand. You see, I was hoping to gain a better understanding…and when the secretary told me there was an office of broadcast research over in the old…"

A knock at the door made her jump. She opened the door and a broad-smiling man with a head like a battered cue ball intruded. "Kathryn, we need you in the studio." He glanced at Calvin. "Whoa! What happened to you? Did you come here by sewer?"

Calvin looked down and saw that his shirtfront was dark with sweat. "I ran down from the old Post Office building."

Harper inhaled deeply. "Mister Hattersley, this is Mister Cobb. He was just stopping by."

The man waggled his smoke-yellowed index finger at Calvin. "Are you the guy who does the voices, with the mouse?"

Calvin flushed as he struggled up out of the chair.

"Hey, no law against it!" said the man. "And I thought all the nutty people worked with us already." He reached out his hand to Calvin and shook it enthusiastically.

"Mister Cobb, this is Mister Larry Hattersley, chief of the department radio services." She held her gathered papers to her chest. "Mr. Cobb studies farm machines and he was just stopping by."

Hattersley extracted a group of stapled-together pages from Kathryn Dale Harper's bundle and glanced at them. "Ah, so you have a real job! Are you going to do a talk for us?" he said absently.

"I just came by to tell Miss Harper that…" Calvin's dry mouth made it hard to form the words.

"Kathryn said she overheard some guy putting the moves on a mouse up in the old building, but I didn't make the connection with an interview. You're not on today's show are you?" Hattersley pulled a dented gold watch from his vest pocket and stared at it as if he had never seen it before.

"No, I just came by to see…"

"Well, if you wouldn't mind sitting with the engineer, you can watch the broadcast and then pick up where you two left off. Come have tea with us!" He pulled a briar pipe, missing its stem, from his vest pocket and stared at it. Kathryn Dale Harper shot an exasperated glance at Hattersley, but he was checking his pockets and even looking behind himself as if the missing pipe stem was hovering just out of sight. She shook her head and backed out the door. Calvin hefted up his box of models and followed them down the hall. Hattersley pointed to a thick glass window. "Just wait in there with the engineer and we'll see you after the show."

Calvin thanked him and pushed through the gray metal door.

"They told me to sit in here," said Calvin to the man seated before the bank of dials.

"They always do," said the man, the resignation in his voice twisting into an upbeat note on his last word. The voice was familiar, as was the broad, olive-toned face now looking at Calvin's reflection in the long window into the studio. The man turned in his chair. "Calvin! Holy cow! What the hell?"

"Holy cow, Bubby, what the heck! I had no idea you worked over here. Good to see you!"

"Damn! Calvin! How'd you find me? I've always wondered what happened to you."

"This is an accident. I thought you were in Chicago. I had no idea I'd run into you, but this is great!"

"Well sit down, man, we're just about to go on!" Bubby turned his attention to a voice on his headphones. He pushed a switch and spoke into a microphone. "Right. Washington ready. Thirty. On the floor, thirty to Chicago and the top." He turned back to Calvin with a smile. "Long way from the Western High School Cat's Whisker Club, eh?" He quickly wheeled back to check the meters on his console. Through the glass, Calvin watched Kathryn Dale Harper as she stood before her microphone, her script flowing down almost to the floor. She slowly rolled her head in racehorse-at-the-gate circles. Bubby reached for the microphone again and said "Fifteen to Chicago and the top." Kathryn Dale Harper nodded at the glass. Bubby pushed the left headphone tighter to his ear and wheeled back to the microphone. Keying it, he said "Washington ready, thank you Chicago."

As he turned a dial on his console, a warm, resounding voice came from the speaker on the wall. *"The National Farm and Home Hour!"* said the voice, and a band began to play the *Stars and Stripes Forever*. The voice continued. *"Greetings again good friends and neighbors. This is the National Farm and Home Hour, the nation's bulletin board of agriculture, brought to you courtesy of the National Broadcasting Company in cooperation with the United States Department of Agriculture. It's a beeauuutiful day in Chicago! Well, the temperature is 39 degrees and it's cloudy, but here to bring you plenty of sunshine is Walter Blaufuss and the Homesteaders playing..."*

"That's Chicago?" asked Calvin.

"I can tell you're a fan."

"I'm usually working when the show comes on."

"At lunchtime? Hey, it doesn't bother me. Bores me to tears."

"The band is okay," said Calvin.

Bubby shook his head. "If you want to swing, this ain't the show for you, brother."

"How long before she goes on?"

"Harper? She's on at 12:45, has to do the whole half hour now. Chicago does fifteen, we do thirty, they do fifteen and we're gone."

As Bubby fiddled with the controls, Calvin read the thoughts betrayed by his old friend's darting eyes. With civil service positions like air pockets in a sinking ship, Calvin knew that Bubby was waiting for his "old-pal-that-just-happened-to-drop-by" to start hinting for a job or a loan. He nodded toward the studio. "She was going to interview me."

"Interview you?" Bubby laughed.

"I'm with Agriculture too — a section chief."

Bubby raised his eyebrows and nodded, half in relief and half in recalculation of their relative status. He slipped the headphone back over his ear and placed his left hand on the big Bakelite knob. "Hold on." The music finished. Harper kept her eyes on Bubby as he raised his right hand, holding up a pointing finger.

The voice on the speaker said *"Thank you Walt, and now Farm and Home friends, we take you to Washington, D.C., for Homemaker Chats with our very own doyenne of all things domestic, Miss Kathryn Dale Harper."* Bubby's hand came down to point at her.

Kathryn's voice was warm and sophisticated. "Thank you Everett and hello everyone. It's still cherry blossom time here in our nation's capital and a lovely time of year to look at new curtains. Of course...."

Bubby slipped the earphone back off of his left ear and twisted a small black knob reducing the volume on the monitor to a barely audible level. "If you can believe it, we're feeding to the entire Blue network right from right here."

Through the glass, Calvin watched Kathryn Dale Harper as she engaged the microphone as if it were a favorite child. He eased closer to the monitor so he could faintly hear her explaining how dry cotton batting was your best choice for cleaning places that soil more quickly, places like walls over registers, radiators and stoves. She did sound older than she looked, but only in an eternal sense, as if she would think nothing of looking up from a bubbling apple pie to see a thousand ships crossing the Aegean to take her back to Sparta. A shiver ran from his ears and he reached up to rub the back of his neck. Kathryn Dale Harper looked up and, still smiling, managed a frown with her forehead. Bubby slowly rotated the shade on the lamp above them, darkening the control room.

"Don't make any big movements while she's on. She's pretty easily distracted."

They watched quietly for a while. A twist of the dial brought Harper's voice listing the new electrical appliances, such as washing machines and even dishwashers, made possible, and practical, through Rural Electrification. "The old cry of '*votes* for women' is now '*volts* for women!'"

Calvin nodded carefully. "So it's all farm news and home-making?"

"Now it is. Biological Survey used to have this spot," said Bubby quietly. "What are they now?"

"Who?"

"Biological Survey. We lost 'em to Interior and they changed the name to something else." Bubby turned back the dial. "Boy, this is killing us. Thirty minutes is just too long. We've had five stations of the Blue network drop us already." He twisted the volume all the way down. "So, what are you doing?"

Calvin exhaled a long sigh. "Well, Bubby, I run this lost little section that studies seed and manure spreaders." He pulled a model cyclone spreader from his box and set it on the mixing console. "Just me and four forgotten girls still stuck up at the old Post Office building."

"I didn't think there was much call for manure spreading expertise in this town — not outside of Congress."

Calvin had heard this jibe and every variant many times before, but he laughed and nodded.

Bubby peeked in the box of miniature machines made of wood and tin. "So you get to make models and fool with girls? Sounds like my kind of job!"

"Oh I wish. They're all…they're all in their forties, all war veterans, all kind of hard luck cases."

"That's what Harper said!" Bubby spun back in his chair. "Said it was like the reverse of Snow White—this guy up in the old Post Office with these seven dwarf women. So that was you!" Bubby turned his attention to a voice coming through his headphones and checked his stopwatch against the studio clock. Calvin glanced into the studio. Kathryn Dale Harper stood with Hattersley going over papers spread atop a grand piano. A distant voice rattled off the price of hogs, corn and soybeans from Bubby's headphones.

"Yeah, well, there's only four of 'em. My old boss hired 'em back in…"

"Fish and Wildlife Service!" Bubby spun in his chair and swung back the light shade.

"What?"

"Fish and Wildlife Service! That's what Interior changed Biological Survey's name to! We lost 'em because some genius decided to do a feature on bird banding and figured a way to involve the listeners out in the boonies. So he says on the air, 'The next time you see a crow or raven, see if it has a band on its leg, and you'll see your USDA Washington Biological Survey at work!' So these yahoos out in the sticks start shooting crows, and there's this band on their leg reading 'USDA • Wash • Biol • Srv' on them. The hillbillies read this as cooking instructions: wash, boil, serve! So word hits the papers that the New Deal food relief program consists of putting cooking instructions on crows. That's all Interior needs and they're on 'em like a dog on a pork chop."

Bubby glanced at his stopwatch and turned up a dial. The

voice from the speaker said *"and the march today is Sousa's Washington Post March!"* He stood to attention and marched in place. The voice faded back in over the music, and he mouthed the words as they came out. *"So ends the two thousandth, eight hundred and tenth broadcast of the National Farm and Home Hour. Aired daily by the National Broadcasting Company with news and features from the United States Department of Agriculture. Join us again tomorrow as we bring you more for the Farm and Home. Until then, we leave you with these words from a wise old man, 'Never speak back to your Pa — unless you're defending your Ma!' Good-bye and lots of good luck...everybody. And now, our national anthem."* Bubby faded down the monitor. "You'd better hurry if you want to talk with her."

"Well, come on with me. Hattersley invited me to tea. I could use a friend."

Bubby gave his head a quick shake. "Engineers don't dine with talent."

"I'm an engineer." Calvin poked at a pair of headphones lying on the desk.

Bubby handed Calvin his box of models. "If you're talking instead of doing, then you're talent. Come on back after you're done."

Hattersley's amused look re-emerged as they rode an elevator up to a private dining room off from the massive cafeteria on the top floor. Calvin tried to explain that he had known Bubby in high school, which caused further confusion until everyone realized that Bubby, Bobby and Robert Nezarian were all the same person.

"I thought we had three engineers for a moment!" said Hattersley. "I hope I haven't made any comments about Jews around him," said Hattersley as he led them into a small dining room.

"He's not Jewish," said Kathryn quickly. "Armenian is orthodox Christian. Kind of Eastern Orthodox."

"Well, I sure don't want to insult anyone."

A white-aproned waitress brought in a tray of sliced beef sandwiches and coffee. Hattersley pulled a sheet from his case and turned to Kathryn. "Changes over at CBS. They're still leading in with the poetry man, and then an hour of Hummert soaps; *Helen Trent's Romance* is still at 12:30, but they've got a new one at 12:45, *Our Gal Sunday*."

"A new Hummert show? That's an oxymoron," said Kathryn shaking her head at the list.

Hattersley pulled a copy of *Radio Guide* from his briefcase. "Here's the problem. If we go up against CBS with women's programs, we're fighting them head to head." He opened the magazine to a weekday schedule. "I mean, this is midday, the men have been out working, they've come in from work, the woman has been listening to the radio all morning. She's had *Betty Crocker* at ten, followed by *Ma Perkins*, *Today's Children*, *Backstage Wife*, *Big Sister*, and then *Girl Alone*. When the man gets in for lunch, it's his turn to listen. Our entire half hour can't be directed to women — can it Calvin?"

Kathryn shot a quick smile at Calvin, leaving him stunned as she turned quickly back to her boss. "So what do you propose?"

"*Uncle Sam's Forest Rangers* gets a consistently high male rating. What about putting *Rangers* on twice or three times a week."

"Well, Larry that's fine, but we'd have to pay NBC for production costs, and it would make us even more dependent on them." Kathryn put her sandwich back on her plate. "I want to move beyond recipes and interviews as much as you do."

"Yes, but we can't get too highbrow. It's still farm radio. Men love those forest fire adventures." He pointed at Calvin as evidence for his assertion.

"I didn't know we got to bring our own cheering sections today." She patted the cover of *Radio Guide* with both her hands. "I just think we can do better than countering a soap opera with a smoke opera."

Hattersley sighed and turned to Calvin. "So you do animal voices — with the mouse and everything? Boy, if we had someone doing animal voices and sketches, that would be swell!"

"How about a pest control series?" offered Kathryn with the slightest glance at Calvin.

Hattersley picked up her thread. "Good idea! So Calvin, can you do a boll weevil?"

"Perhaps a corn borer?" said Kathryn. "It's *Parasite Parade*, with Bobby Blow Fly!"

Hattersley picked up the copy of *Radio Guide*. "Seriously, if a ventriloquist's dummy is the biggest thing on the radio just now, we can be pretty creative here. *Vic and Sade* had a sketch just this morning about a restaurant with an anesthetized pig out back where they just cut off what they needed for each ham sandwich. It was great!"

"I love *Vic and Sade*," said Calvin, wondering if he should have a sandwich too.

"The guy who writes it is a total nut," said Hattersley with enthusiastic admiration. He chose another sandwich from the platter and took a nibble off its corner. "So Calvin. What is it you do now? You've got a farm animal act? That might work!"

Calvin inhaled, but Kathryn spoke first. "Mister Cobb actually studies the machines that spread…stuff out on the ground."

Hattersley frowned. "What section are you in?"

"I'm actually the chief of the section, Broadcast Research."

"Broadcast Research?" said Hattersley. "Wow, I think we could use some of that around here! Find out how our program ratings are. Wait! So you broadcast hay seeds, and we do hayseed broadcasting!" He laughed. "Are you out at Beltsville?"

"No, but we work out there a lot. Aerial distribution," said Calvin. "It's really interesting. We section a field into a grid, we set random distributions of flypaper around the field, and the plane flies over and spreads its seeds. Then we gather up the flypaper and count the seeds on each of them and from that we can determine the effectiveness of the dispersal method. I was telling Miss Harper that with all the floods and erosion, this is very important for seeding big areas."

"So you bomb hillsides with seeds to stop floods?" asked Hattersley, chewing.

"Well, no, other people do that. We study the effectiveness, the evenness. It's a lot of math."

Hattersley shook his head. "Boy, who would ever think there'd be a job counting seeds on flypaper? Don't you ever get to fly in the plane?"

"Oh sure, I get to fly."

"You fly the plane?" asked Kathryn.

Calvin squirmed and flushed. "Well, if the regular pilot is sick or something, somebody has to fly the plane, and I'm there."

"That must be very exciting. What kind of plane is it?" she asked.

"A Curtis." Calvin reached for his empty coffee cup. "They've got a bunch of different ones. Sometimes we use an auto gyro."

"So you're a regular Alfalfa Earhart," said Hattersley, smiling. "We could take one of those little Presto disc cutters out there and record you as you fly over. Get the prop noise and the sound of the seeds landing."

Calvin put his cup back on the tray. "I brought something to show you, if I may." Hattersley nodded, and Calvin reached in his box to extract a heavy, glass-fronted picture frame. "This is a normal distribution modeler. You turn it upside down and the ball bearings go into the hopper at the top. When you turn it over again, they flow down one at a time and hit the array of little hickory pins." He turned the frame over and the balls streamed down one by one. "See? Each bounce off of a pin is a fifty-fifty chance for the ball to go to either side of each pin. But since the balls all start in the middle, to get to the edge, a ball would have to do the equivalent of flipping a coin and having it come up heads six times in a row. A few balls do make it to the edges, but most stay toward the middle, and the pattern we get," he said, as the last of the balls rattled into their slots, "is this smooth mound called a normal distribution."

Hattersley washed down his last bite. "Very nice Calvin." He pointed to the low shoulder of the ball bearing mound. "That explains how we got out here on the fringes of American society!"

Kathryn Dale Harper tapped her finger on the middle of the pile of balls. "The problem is we're losing the cities. Our mandate from the Secretary is to build unity between the farmer and the factory worker."

"The harvester and the haberdasher," chimed in Hattersley.

"The plowman and the plumber," she continued. "Americana — folk music — that's what they all have in common." She inverted the box and the balls rattled back into the reservoir."

Hattersley shook his head absently. "So maybe another farm machinery interview is not what we need right now."

Calvin hopped a bit in his seat. "Well, that's why I came over here to ask you to postpone the interview until, maybe the fall or winter, when we'd be better prepared."

But Hattersley wasn't listening. He reached for the oak frame of Calvin's model. "Where'd you get this?"

"I made it. We make lots of scale models like this to test full-sized spreaders."

"It's very nicely done. You made this?"

"Well, I've always made things. Since I was a kid."

"You know," he said, tapping the varnished wood, "we do farm programs about growing food, and then Miss Harper's program about how to prepare it. We do the Forest Ranger program about growing trees, but we don't do anything about using them, about using the wood."

"We've done wood stories," said Kathryn. "Two months ago, remember? We did *Lignin: Enigma of the Forest*."

"No, I mean something regular, once a week, about the different kinds of wood and things like that. How to know good wood from bad."

"You mean like naughty pine and his evil ways?"

"There really is bad wood, and people don't know," said Calvin.

Kathryn shot a who-asked-you look at him. "Well, we've done it. Everything from preserving to polishing."

"What we haven't done is a program on making things. Men like to make things," said Hattersley. "Woodworking is very big these days."

"You mean a regular program on woodworking?" asked Kathryn. She laughed and then looked at the two men in turn. "Think about it, gentlemen, wouldn't you need television for that?"

"How'd it go?" asked Bubby, searching his lap for a dropped screw.

Calvin rolled his eyes. "Awful. I told this lie about flying a plane. They saw right through it."

"Shame on you!" The big man's hands worked quickly, stripping wires in a microphone head.

"Bubby, what's the word on television?"

"Like prosperity—just around the corner!" A tiny plume of smoke drifted up from within the microphone as he soldered.

"Television is the biggest secret in the industry. I saw the RCA tube system in Chicago. Beautiful! Disc scanners are dead. No more mechanics, it's all electronic." Bubby pushed his soldering iron back in its coiled wire rest and tugged at the new connection.

"So, are we talking next year or what?"

Bubby shrugged. "Probably '39 before they're ready. But you won't hear a peep about it until the entire system is in the stores, ready to buy, with programs to watch. They've had wire-line television in Germany since the Olympics, and they've just gotten broadcast television in England, but it almost destroyed their radio industry." He brushed dried spittle out of the microphone screen before replacing it over the ribbon capsule. "The BBC announced they'd have television within a year, and radio sales completely crashed. Everybody was holding out for a television."

Calvin banged his head slowly against the thin steel walls of an equipment rack.

Bubby glanced up from his work. "And how was tea?"

"I don't know. I was too wound up to eat."

Bubby tightened the last screw in the brushed aluminum case of the microphone. "Listen, let's walk over to the Tidal Basin and I'll buy you a hot dog, what d'ya say? I'm parked over there anyway. Leave your box of toys here and you can pick it up later."

Bubby flipped switches in the control room, darkening both it and the empty studio. As they made their way out of the building, he gave Calvin a running commentary on the jobs of the occupants of each bustling office. Calvin recognized many as former friends and daily associates at the old Post Office. Earlier, in the studio, he had envied Bubby's proximity to Kathryn Dale Harper. Now he realized how much he missed the competition and pipe-puffing jokes of other men his age — none of whom smelled like rosewater, incontinence or ulcerated stumps. By the time they emerged into the sunlight, Calvin felt hollow, scooped out like a pumpkin. They walked in silence, south past Printing and Engraving. "So you really liked Chicago?" Calvin forced himself to ask as they crossed the bridge over the black water of the Washington channel.

"Ox butcher to the world! The city of big shoulders! Ever been there?"

Calvin watched for a lone cormorant to resurface after its dive. "Chicago? No."

"It's a great place to break into radio, better than New York. They've just doubled the wattage on WLS. You can pick 'em up easy here at night." A skipjack, high in the water after unloading its oysters, raised its sails with a squeal of pulleys. "Ever hear the *WLS Showboat*?"

Calvin shook his head.

"It's a variety show, like *Make-Believe Ballroom*. The sound of the showboat was just me doing sound effects — blowing a steam whistle and cranking an eggbeater in a bucket of water, but you wouldn't believe the mail we got! Thousands of people wanting to know when the showboat was coming to their town!"

Calvin laughed. "Won't be able to pull that off so easily when people have televisions."

Bubby considered this seriously for a second. "No, but you could do it like a stage play, or something. I don't guess we'd be able to pull off your old specialty either. No more 'Calvin Cobb the man of a thousand voices' doing all the parts."

Bubby paid for the hot dogs, waving off the change from the vendor on the beach at the south end of the Tidal Basin. Immense wooden staging behind the sand showed visiting dignitaries what the view would be like from the level of the proposed Jefferson Memorial. A policeman talked with a bedraggled family who had camped under the staging to avoid the fee at the East Potomac park tourist camp. Calvin and Bubby climbed the wooden stairs and looked north as the last clouds of April drifted through the blue. Above the pale pink of the remaining blossoms, a few of the larger trees were turning the full deep green of spring. Calvin studied the tip of the Washington Monument, the scaffolding-shrouded Cathedral on the distant hill and the White House dead ahead — seeking any visual anchor to distract him from the new Agriculture building that they had just left.

"It's a nice spot," said Bubby. "Sorry to lose the bathing beach, though." He pointed across the water to the corridor cleared through the trees. "I didn't realize it was straight out from the front door of the White House."

"You know what really happened." Calvin looked about in exaggerated caution. "Franklin D had the opening cut through the trees so that he could watch the girls in their swimsuits. He has to build this Jefferson memorial thing as cover after Eleanor caught him with his telescope."

Bubby laughed, threw the end of his bun to the seagulls and gestured for Calvin to walk on. A breeze put pink petals in the air like snow that swirled and leapt and then rested in windrows. They rounded the downwind quarter of the Tidal Basin where the jagged waves of the dark water became soft pillows as they swept under the pink blanket of floating blossoms. They ducked under the branches of a huge holly tree and climbed the abutment onto the tide gate bridge, then turned to watch as a bright metal DC-3 flew low down the Potomac toward them, dodged the power plant smokestacks and landed at Hoover field across the river.

Bubby toed a bit of broken mortar off the edge of the bridge so that it fell onto the jumble of flotsam below. "So where'd this airplane story come in?"

"Aw gee, I'm such a nitwit." Calvin toed at a cigar butt, trying to push it over the edge into the water but the breeze rolled it back onto the roadway. "The work is ninety percent manure, but I said I flew the plane that spread the seeds over the hills. I once did a study on aerial broadcasting of winter wheat over soybeans, but I made out like I was the Lindbergh of limas!"

"Whereas you're really the Einstein of excrement."

Calvin nodded. "The Michelangelo of merde."

"So who does the DaVinci of dung report to?"

"The Gauguin of guano reports to no man."

"You report to someone. Who's your boss?"

"No boss. Not any more." Calvin flung a stone into the Potomac and nodded across the river toward Arlington cemetery. "He's up there on the hill."

"Well, who'd he report to? That's who your boss'd be now."

"Well, the Commander was an old Navy pal of Franklin D's, so probably straight to FDR."

Bubby grinned. "You're shittin' me."

"Well, we used to shoot the shit, that's for sure." Calvin grinned and tossed a stone in a high arc that plopped in the river with a tiny black splash. "After the war, my boss got this 'swords into plowshares' idea. Figured if they could restore the forests around the Mediterranean, it'd give folks new places to live and forever end the cause of war. So once Franklin D gets in the White House, the Commander sells him this idea of repacking old poison gas shells with seeds and fertilizer and shootin' 'em at the barren hills around the Adriatic."

"Is this another one of your stories?"

"Oh no! This guy was the Navy's top guy in shore bombardment, he took this real seriously." Calvin pointed out into the broad river. "Wanted to have battleships cruising around the Mediterranean, bombarding the mountains with old gas shells filled with pinecones and horse shit. Called it 'Trees from the

Seas.' FDR must have owed him a favor or something, 'cause they took him in, stuck it under Agriculture and renamed it Broadcast Research. He'd met the girls during the war so he tracked them down them to do the calculations. Hired me to cut up Jap fireworks and make models of these reforestation shells. After he killed himself, we found all these letters in his desk from Deere and Moline and all these ag-equipment manufacturers asking for help, so we started helping them — just kept working."

"He killed himself? I mean, I know he was crazy."

Calvin waited as a family with picnic baskets passed. "It was an accident. They let him work up at the old testing grounds up at American University. There was this old mustard gas shell he's working on, trying to convert into one of his turd bombs, and he opens it in his office. Doesn't even make it out the door. A week later they take everything in his office, the papers, the old shells, everything and bury it all in this valley behind the labs. That's the end of him and the end of 'trees from the seas.'"

Bubby leaned hard against the pipe railing, making it vibrate. "So now you're the boss?"

"Well, I don't know! All the departmental records of the Broadcast Research Section are buried in this creek bank out Mass Avenue. So I'm still deputy section chief. We still get paid, we still have a budget and we still spend it. But nobody lays claim to us. We're too small to be noticed under the department budget, and we're not under anyone, so we just keep working."

"The lost section."

"The lost section." They walked on, working their way around photographers fussing to get branches of blossoms to frame their images of pretty girls. Calvin glanced back at the Post Office tower. "And we do great work, but nobody needs it.

Now they're going to tear our building down, so unless we set up shop in one of the parks — I don't know."

"So you asked K.D. Harper to do an interview?"

"No. She just showed up at my office yesterday morning. I didn't even know who she was." A couple walking arm in arm shot Calvin a dirty look when he threw a stone into the water too close to them.

Bubby shook his head. "Well, her ratings are slipping. I thought she was going to try this folk music angle, so I don't know why she thought a story on your Broadcast Research section could help." Bubby grabbed a branch as they passed and shook down a shower of brown-tinged petals. "Cal, I'd try to get you a shot at this interview if you think it would help, but I'm just the engineer."

Calvin kicked a fallen branch out of the path. "I can't do an interview now anyway. We need to lie low until the girls finish this machine they're working on. We didn't even discuss an interview. Somehow we got onto an idea about a separate show on woodworking."

Bubby laughed. "Woodworking on the radio?"

"Yeah, I know. It's too visual. That's why I was asking you about television."

Bubby knuckled him on the shoulder. "I'd love to do another show. We've got stacks of sound effects records, new mixing boards, studio disc cutters — and they all just sit there." Bubby looked at his wristwatch. "Listen, I'm driving up to meet some pals from WLS to see a new Presto cutter. Why don't I see if they have any job leads?" He pointed at a row of parked cars. "I'm parked down here."

"You're driving back to Chicago?"

"Nah, just New Jersey. The Hindenburg is coming in and Herb and Charlie are flying down to Lakehurst to cover it. I'm going to drive up tonight and catch up with 'em tomorrow.

This is a heck of a machine they've got, size of a big typewriter case, but cuts a 15-minute record." He strode quickly up to a parked Cadillac and opened the door, then closed the door and laughed. "Gotcha!" He wheeled around and opened the door of a Ford delivery van.

"What's the story? You pick up laundry after hours?"

Bubby climbed in and rolled down the window. "It's my camera truck. I'm going to do free-lance event coverage for the newsreels — soon as I get a camera."

Calvin grabbed the lower rail of the van's roof-mounted platform. "Got the rope and the anchor, now all you need is the boat."

"You got it! Hop in. I'll give you a lift home."

But Calvin had seen Bubby's worried glances at the growing traffic. "My stuff is back at your studio. You go on, I'll catch up with you when you get back in town."

"Great, thanks! And listen, I'll do what I can — if you decide an interview might help. But, you know — a government agency that studies manure spreaders? That's just the kind of thing the Hooverites would love to get in the headlines."

"Yeah, that's what we figured." Calvin squinted up as another gleaming DC-3 began its turn off the river. "So, what if we had a death ray, or an electric brain?"

"Oh! Now *that's* radio!"

Calvin watched him drive off, then slowly turned to walk back to the basement studio. He walked against the tide of workers flowing from the stone boxes, frustrated that he couldn't avoid walking past the damn swan boats on the north side of the Tidal Basin. He turned his head, but the splatter of the paddlewheels and happy chatter of the passengers carried across the water to him. He fought off the memory of scowling Amanda sitting beside him as he pedaled furiously against the wind in the pathetic, painted-plywood *swan* boat. Randy the brilliant builder would have known to choose a *row* boat so he could smile randily at Amanda as he faced her and rowed her along with powerful strokes. Calvin winged a stone into a floating drift of cherry blossoms, opening a black hole in the pink for longer than he expected.

The late April day was slipping toward evening, but at South building, crowds gathered in the entrance hall. He made his way through the departmental orchestra gathering for a rehearsal, passed the archery club assembling for its business meeting, and pounded down the first set of stairs he came to. The stairs led to the wrong basement hallway, but they were the fastest escape from the happy banter. He walked the length of a hall, watching each reflection of an overhead light in the linoleum until he passed over the bright pool and then looked ahead to the next one. He walked until the sound of bonhomie was replaced by the fundamental hum of the building. Only then did he look for numbers that might guide him to the studio.

He found the door and walked in, searching for a light switch before realizing that he was in the studio rather than in the control booth where he had left his box of props. He froze. Illuminated behind the glass of the control room, like a department store window display, a head of curly hair banded by a pair of black headphones bobbed gently. The woman's eyes were closed and her brow furrowed with concentration. A large black record spun on the turntable in front of her. She looked up and Calvin's gut tightened. He swallowed, but she turned her head to rest it in her hand and closed her eyes again. She had not seen him.

He backed deeper into the studio and watched as she responded to the sound in her headphones. A rectangle of light from the door splayed across an opened record-shipping box atop the studio Steinway. He could just read the hand-written label: *Cher Katrine, Musique pour cordes, percussion and célesta: Bartók Bela-Bâle, Dec '36.* He lifted one of the webbed canvas straps of the hardboard shipping box and felt the empty interior.

Monitoring the bobbing curls, he scuttled below the line of sight to find the studio panel in the dark back corner of the room. As he slowly turned a black knob on the console, the speakers filled the studio with modern, disjunctive music. First the sound of cellos under attack by a piano and a kettledrum. Then the string section made a furious pizzicato counterattack. Now came silence, broken by a sound like a golf ball bouncing in a glass goblet. The kettledrum moaned. Angel flights of bells tried to rise but were drowned by a crescendo of drums. The needle scratched off the record and the figure in the studio slowly stood.

She opened the door into the studio. Still concealed by darkness, Calvin thought for a moment he had the wrong person. She was now wearing yellow, flared slacks and a gray sweatshirt with a jaunty Mickey Mouse saluting from the folds, but there was no mistake. Even as she walked in silence, he could see that the music was still playing in her head. She eased the white record sleeves into the shipping box and drummed her fingernails on the piano top. He held his breath for her to leave, but she slid onto the piano bench and lifted the fallboard. Shoes fell from her feet and her bare toes curled as they touched the cold bronze pedals. The delicacy of her wrists and ankles made the rest of her seem fuller by comparison.

She began to play — a light, walking dance, formal but with winks of peasant abandon. She eased closer to the piano, her body swaying and her head punctuating the notes. She played, and icy spring water cascaded from her fingers, coursing crystalline over green moss. Her arched wrists rose and dove like sea birds feeding on ancient, black-keyed Gypsy notes. Reflected in the fallboard, her long fingers dug and fluttered. The shiver began in Calvin's neck and raced to his fingertips. She stopped and spun about.

"Who's there?" The falling damper silenced the last note.

"Calvin. Calvin Cobb. We were in the meeting today."

She rose from her bench. "What the hell are you doing, hiding in the dark?"

"I left my box of…stuff. Bubby said it would be okay to pick it up."

"My God, you scared the hell out of me!" She closed the fallboard over the keys.

"I'm really sorry. I was…That piano, your playing was wonderful."

She fumbled with the lid of the record box. "You shouldn't sneak up on people."

"I didn't mean to. I'm sorry." He glanced back at the knob on the studio panel, but left it and made for the control room to retrieve his box. She was buckling the straps on the shipping box when he stepped back into the studio. He paused with his back to the door. "I've never heard Bela-Bale before."

"Bela-Bale?"

"Maybe that's not how you say it." He pointed at the record box.

She squinted at it. "Oh!" She laughed. "Bartók!" She stifled another laugh that escaped in a snort. "Bela Bartók! Bela is his first name. Bâle is the French for Basel, Switzerland. That's where this was recorded." She dabbed at her eyes with her sleeve.

He breathed in deeply. "Well, that piece you just played, it really got to me."

"The Rumanian Folk dances? Well, they're supposed to get to you. Old sentimental, nationalistic stuff—profoundly visceral." She stood regarding him with a lip-biting smile, suppressing her laugh. "But we've all moved beyond that now." She covered her mouth as she yawned to un-pop her ears from the stifled laugh. "Oh my. Bela-Bale!"

"Sorry." With a flat grin frozen on his face, Calvin turned and left too fast to see her wave her hand to stop him. He strode straight down the hall and bounded up the nearest steps onto the street. The moon cut a white fingernail in the fading light over the Arlington hills, but walking north across the Mall, he did not even look for bats in the darkening sky. The notes of the piano kept playing in his head. From his box, the ball bearings in his normal distribution modeler laughed at him, maraca-like, with every step. He wanted to toss it, but it was government property.

Thursday morning, midway across Pennsylvania Avenue, Calvin heard the siren approaching. He quick-stepped out of the crosswalk as a motorcycle whipped around a streetcar and tore through the intersection. None of the other pedestrians bounding out of the path of the pursuing squad car could see that the motorcyclist was a woman, but Calvin knew exactly who she was, and he smiled. At least this morning, with the police chasing Verdie, he might make it to the office before her.

In front of the old Post Office, a tourist family impatiently studied the dingy granite turrets while listening to the guidebook commentary of the father. As Calvin started up the front steps, the mother called out, "Excuse me! Excuse me! Do you work here?"

"Sure do!"

The woman held her hat as the breeze fluttered the veil. "We want to see the cat and the dog. The book says they're in the walls by the 12th Street entrance, but all those doors are locked."

"They're probably just stuck. Come on in this way. I'll show you."

"Thank you! Thank you!" they chorused and joined Calvin climbing the steps under the gray granite arches.

Once inside, the mother swept her fine, kid-gloved hand along the black and green veins threading through the creamy stone wainscot of the hallway. "This is all marble?" she asked.

"Marble inside, granite outside, but the building is actually steel framed, very innovative for the 1890s." Calvin enjoyed playing the tour guide.

"Oh my goodness, steel framed," said the mother, flashing her right eyelid. She tilted her head just enough to give her smile a teasing, flirtatious edge.

Calvin was instantly flustered. He had yet to catch on, but his regular-guy looks and ready smile made him a handy but harmless fulcrum for women who needed to lever their husband or boyfriend back into line.

The father's lower teeth pushed out beneath a trim moustache and a cocked Tyrolean hat. He eyed Calvin's old brown herringbone jacket and gave a tiny snort. "There's supposed to be a cow figure in the wall too," insisted the father, waving the just-published WPA guide to the city as if Calvin was somehow responsible for this fact.

The demand brought him back onto confident ground, as he knew every chance configuration in the stone Rorschach test of a building. "You're right, but the cow has been covered over with the demolition." He led them down the dark hall, their footsteps echoing. "They wrote that book in '35, so the information is a couple of years old. They're going to tear the whole place down as soon as they find the money. They call it the 'old tooth,' and figure they need to 'extract' it. We call it the iceberg." Calvin pointed into the gloomy atrium with its two greenhouse-glass roofs. "That's where the mail sorters used to work."

"Because it's so cold?" asked the daughter. She was wearing

the current vestment of innocence and optimism — a Shirley Temple dress with short puffed sleeves and pleats from the neck to the knees.

"No, because of the light." Calvin saw her frown up at her father. "Oh, the iceberg! I'm sorry, no, it…it just makes us think of an iceberg, kind of adrift in the new linoleum sea."

The motorcycle engine roared by on 12th Street, the police siren close behind. Calvin quick-stepped ahead to glance through the open door of an empty office to see the chase, but they had already passed by.

"Why the heck are they re-painting the clock numerals if they're going to tear it down?" asked the father.

Calvin smiled and shrugged. "Welcome to Washington!" He noticed the little girl taking in his words, so he added; "Actually, I'm sure there's a very good reason for it. It seems to be the pattern. Anyway, people are moving out of here to their new buildings pretty regular now."

They continued down the hall around the atrium. The mother gently corrected her daughter when she rattled a pencil along one of the radiators. They passed three more serendipitous figures in the veined marble walls — figures that weren't in the guidebook. Calvin checked off the Bear Dancing With the Teapot, the Two Fat Chickens, and the Naughty Dutch Girl, but knew from experience that few others appreciated them. As they passed an open door in an area recently vacated by Interstate Commerce, two hunched-over Eskimos glanced pitifully up from their desks. Calvin led the family on to the 12th Street entrance hall and stopped. "All right," he addressed the children, "the cat and the dog are in plain view. Can you see them?"

From his guidebook, the father knew where to look right away and pointed out the figures to the mother. The daughter took a few seconds and cried out "I see it! I see the cat."

"Where? Where's the cat?" said the little boy.

"Right there!" said the daughter. "On the wall, right beside the door. The dog is on the other side. The dog is not so good."

"Where? I don't see it!"

"The cat's easy to see, honey," said the mother, tapping the marble wall. "See? This pattern looks like the face, and here's the body."

The father picked up the little boy and held him, but he cried—frustrated, angry. "I don't see the cat!"

"We're going to leave if you can't be quiet," said the father. "People are trying to work here."

The boy cried, the girl pointed. Calvin pulled a file folder from an abandoned box of papers, drew an oval on it and wrote within it the words "Hello, I am Calvin the Cat!" He tore the edges off the oval shape and walked up to the wall. "Here, look," he said to the little boy who was alternately looking and burying his face in his father's shoulder. "Do you like the funny papers?"

The boy sniffed. The police siren wailed in the distance.

"The nice man asked you a question, Andrew. You like the funny papers don't you? *Popeye?*"

The little boy sniffed and nodded. Calvin slipped the cardboard speech balloon under the edge of the door casing to the left of the elusive image. "Look. See, just like in the funny papers. He's saying 'Hello, I am Calvin the Cat!'"

The little boy looked at the wall and his smile grew. He looked away and back and smiled even brighter. The mother turned to Calvin. "He sees it! Thank you. You are so kind to take time from your work to help us! And you're with the government?"

The police siren grew steadily louder. Calvin sidled closer to the door and listened at the crack. The motorcycle sound shifted from a distant reverberation to a clear, hard note. He threw his shoulder against the door while giving its bottom a hard kick, pushed out the door and held it open. The motorcycle and rider jumped the curb and bounded up the steps, whipped past Calvin and skidded into the entrance hall. Verdie spun her motorcycle to a stop and cut the engine as Calvin pulled the door closed. The siren Dopplered by and kept on going. Calvin turned back to the family, now cowering against the wall. "Sorry. Uh. Yes m'am. Department of Agriculture."

Verdie rolled her motorcycle back onto its rear kickstand and swung stiffly off. She pulled off her goggles and leather helmet and let out a "Whooh!" Her lively eyes and grin cancelled out the aging effects of her lined face and paprika hair. "Thanks, Chief. I owe you another one!"

"You're lucky I was down here. I was showing these folks the cat and the dog."

"Oh!" She stepped towards them, but something seemed to give in her right leg. "Are you all here for the cherry blossoms?"

The cowering family worked up a general nodding. The motorcycle clicked as it cooled. Verdie backed up against the radiator and shook her right leg, pinching and twisting through her brown coveralls. "Well, I hope you enjoy your stay in Washington." Her leg seemed to develop an extra knee joint at mid thigh. "It is so beautiful this time of year." She slid down to sit on the floor, yanked off her artificial leg and pulled at a steel bar on the back of the thigh. The bent leg sprang vigorously straight.

The girl screamed and the little boy cried "Momiee!"

Calvin held out his hands. "Verdie!"

"Sir?"

"Could you wait to get to the office to do that?"

"Oh! Sure. Sorry chief." She slipped the too-pink artificial limb back into her coverall leg and accepted Calvin's hand to stand upright again. "The roller cord broke."

"Not the pulley?"

She grasped the side of her thigh through the fabric. "Pulley's fine." She began to reach inside her coveralls between the buttons but glanced at the wide-eyed family and thought better of it. "I'll just hold it from the side 'til you can look at it. I think the spring needs a boost too."

"It's probably the T-joint caps. I'll be right up."

She pulled a small briefcase from under a cord on her luggage rack and smiled at the cowering quartet. "Enjoy your stay!" she called as she limped off like a movie cowboy.

Calvin rubbed his toe on the black skid marks across the marble floor. "That's Verdie. If the police aren't after her, it's her ex-husband."

The father unstuck the 12th Street door by kicking furiously at its bottom. Calvin watched the family hurry off. He leaned at the crack in the door to steal a final glimpse of the mother. She had a pretty face, but there was even more beauty in the patient way she guided her children with glances and hand gestures. As the family reached the end of the block to turn the corner, Calvin vaporized the father with a blast from his imaginary death ray.

Climbing the steps of the old building, he heard the sorters, relays, cardpunches and printing bars already running. Linda stepped into the hallway, sliding two punched cards against one another and holding them up to examine the patterns in the holes. She spotted Calvin and waved for him to hurry in. "We're going to run one! Now you'll see!" She took Calvin's arm and guided him through the maze of humming wires, squeezing past the other women, deep into the room. Verdie passed a stack of cards to Anne, who loaded them into the far corner of a Burroughs 601 multiplier at the left end of the mechanical tangle.

"Let the Chief start it!" said Anne.

"Right there!" said Ellen as she spun her wheelchair back from the keyboard and pointed to a toggle switch lying free on the desk. "Don't touch the bare wires!" she said.

Verdie pulled a bent punch card from the wastebasket to serve as insulation as she held the switch hard to the table. "Just flip the switch. I'll hold it down."

Calvin flipped the cold toggle. The machine on his left began an impatient ingestion of the stack of cards. The counter wheels of the five accumulators on top ticked off a cryptic score. Banks of relays in the huge steel racks shifted, sometimes in small increments, sometimes in wholesale repositionings that were followed by mutterings within the multiplying punch machine on the right. Calvin's eyes fixed on the exposed sparking relays and were only occasionally distracted by the arrival of a new card in the hopper.

When the machines went quiet, Anne reached out and decorously removed the stack of cards from the 601 multiplier and held it aloft. Faint murmurings came from all around as she handed it to Verdie who passed it on to Ellen who added a small bundle of cards to the bottom of the stack and placed them all back in the feed hopper of the 405 tabulator. The machine was already taking in cards, jerking the banks of telephone relays into a hammering shuffle. Slowly, the 405 began chugging out a wide teletype paper from its mouth of type bar teeth that rose and fell and rearranged themselves into a different miniature city skyline for each pulse. As the paper emerged, the women leaned forward to examine it. The elation in the room rose with the lengthening paper.

Calvin looked at the paper too, but could not comprehend it. The emerging paper was almost three feet long now and covered with upper and lower case Xs, Ms, and Os in a field of periods. Cheers erupted as the paper grew longer. Faces turned to Calvin for his response. Seeing his incomprehension, hands began tracing arcs like a cartoon frown across the paper. The paper chugged on a minute more and then moved out several blank lines and printed a line of text before the machines stopped. Linda tore the long paper from the tabulator and presented it to Calvin. All eyes were on him as he read the bottom line: "Acceleration 0 To 65 Mph, Deere Model 'E' Spiral Beater Manure Spreader."

Ellen reached out and tapped the arcing dark band across the page. "The pattern! Look! See the density change! Heavy bands here at 28.6 and here at 51.2 miles per hour! Chief, we predicted the harmonics and didn't even have to leave the building!"

Calvin looked at the paper, nodding. He reached in his pocket, looked around at his audience, said, "Damn!" and dropped a nickel into the cocoa tin. "Good work! Really impressive!" He studied the long paper. "Changes everything, doesn't it?"

"It really is new!" said Verdie.

"She's a wonder!" said Anne.

"And she's all ours!" said Ellen.

Calvin held the paper high in both hands and looked it up and down. "This is just tremendous! I'm going to take this. I'm going to study it. And I'm going to contemplate it!"

The women went happily back to their cards. Linda followed him back into his office

"They were so excited. You know..." said Linda, "it would help if you looked in on us more often."

Calvin covered the *How to Win Friends* book on his desk with the roll of paper. "I guess I need to take a more genuine interest in others."

Linda pushed the door closed to contain some of the noise. "What do you mean, others?"

"Just something I read."

She glanced out the window at graying skies and distant

rumbling thunder. "Do you want us to put together an explanation of the computing machine? This is a new way to calculate, totally new. You just saw a little of what she can do."

"It looks like Frankenstein's castle in there."

"Chief, we've found pulsing distribution at two speeds in one of the most widely used spreaders in the country."

"At 28 and 52 miles an hour?"

"Right, and I know what you're going to say." She held up the flat of her palm.

"What am I going to say?"

"That horses can't pull a loaded manure spreader faster than four and a half miles an hour."

Calvin nodded in mock seriousness. "But if they could…"

"But if they could…then we'd know."

"So if Seabiscuit and War Admiral get harnessed to a John Deere Model E spreader — we'll have that covered, so to speak."

Linda pulled a pencil from her hair and tapped the desk. "Sir, I know you get this." She looked at him with squinting eyes. "I know you're plenty smart enough to understand what we're onto here."

Calvin leaned back in his chair and fiddled with his triangular scale rule, "No, Linda, I'm not."

She looked long at him. "Okay, so you don't get it. But listen, I don't think there's any one of us who understands the whole thing. But you grasp the potential of what we've created, don't you? There's never been anything like this!"

He pulled himself up in his chair. "You really think you've got something?"

"I do, Chief. It's really…It's like it's beautiful and scary at the same time." Her eyes glistened.

Calvin rapped on the arms of his chair with his knuckles. "So how long do you need — before you're ready to show this thing to the big wide world?"

"Well, that's just it. We need her to make a huge splash. Another few months, maybe." She slid closer down his desk. "Stiffs in monkey suits have been snooping around downstairs. They've gotta be from Burroughs. If they pull these machines out on us now — it's all over. We've got to get her to the point where she's so impressive that they won't be able to steal her from us."

"They won't do that."

"You know they would! But she's ours and I'll be damned if they…"

"Linda, I understand." He rolled back in his chair and crossed his arms, suddenly cold. "We'll lie low until you're ready. And nobody's taking your machines away. If they try, we'll stop 'em." He managed a quick snarling look for emphasis.

She sensed the frustration underlying his mock ferocity, but she didn't know what to say except a faint "Thank you," as she eased back out the door.

Late hurry-home traffic squeezed into the streets, and the ozone drifting up from the streetcar power rails put a dizzy edge on the dampening air. He needed something to read, but both the library and Brentano's were closed. A magazine from Peoples Drug then, anything. He stared at a Norman Rockwell *Saturday Evening Post* cover of kids at a fishing hole. Was that what Kathryn Dale Harper meant by visceral appeal? But she said "visceral" not "infantile" appeal. *US Camera* had an abstract Edward Weston nude on the cover. He flipped it open and stared at a spread of disjointed pictographs by Moholy-Nagy. *What an idiot I am. Bela-Bale!* He dropped it back in the rack and picked up the new *Life* magazine with a gigantic dam on the cover and carried it back to the lunch counter. He flipped through it as he waited for his Salisbury steak and green beans, begging distraction from the photos of New England debutantes, pudgy prizefighters and dead Spaniards. He flipped the page from a story on an underwater wedding and ran smack into an advertisement for *How to Win Friends and Influence People*. Amanda's copy of the bible of success was on his desk. He ate, left the copy of

Life behind and walked back down to Pennsylvania Avenue to retrieve the book.

As Calvin entered the old Post Office, the atrium echoed with dustpans banging on cans, with mop buckets clicking over joints in the marble floor. Most of the Negro janitors were also Great War veterans and sometimes took turns chasing the loneliness with French soldier songs. As he entered tonight, the song *Au pres de ma blon-de* rattled the transoms. The janitors were all male, but sometimes, very late at night, people heard an extraordinary woman's voice. Calvin had thought her a myth until he once heard her singing *Swing Low, Sweet Chariot*. Hers was always the last voice heard, and it could put standing waves in the inkwells of every office on every floor.

He padded silently up the stairs, flight after flight. The building still made its own electricity at night, but the forty-year-old generators connected to the heating plant in the basement were now so worn and ill-adjusted that the lights wavered like torches. The janitors had developed a system whereby the trash and sweepings, the mops and buckets, moved downward from the top floor as each was cleaned. Operating an elevator while it was powered by the generators usually caused it to stall and the lights to go brown, as governors slid clutch belts to idlers, opening circuits, over-speeding the dynamos so the lights suddenly went purest white and sometimes popped like flashbulbs.

He set his heavy briefcase on the floor by his desk, sat for a moment, then stepped back out to the railing and looked down into the pit of the atrium. Such a hole. Were the atrium sunk in the ground, it would be a terror — an abandoned quarry with wrecked cars and old stoves rusting in the water at the bottom, with snakes and poison ivy and tales of foolish divers paralyzed by striking hidden rocks. Below he heard the echoing bang of trashcans. He stepped back into his office, left the door open and quietly dug down into the left-hand stack of papers on his desk for *How to Win Friends and Influence People*. "It's all about relationships," ex-ladyfriend Amanda had told him. In the light from the door, he flipped the book open and saw a pencil-underlined passage.

"Learn everybody's name and take an interest in them." Calvin sank in his chair. He was terrible at names, but only because fear of getting a name wrong made him freeze at the critical moment. He glanced up at the old photograph of the girls in his office in their uniforms. It took him over a year to build enough confidence to use their names without choking. Now there was Verdie — she was good at names. Her own nickname came from the French soldiers at Verdun. "Ils ne passeront pas!" shouted the *poilus* when she shot by on her motorcycle. No one could pass her as she raced between temporary morgues and opulent military headquarters, trying to give names to another batch of leather-belted skeletons.

He flipped to the next penciled underlining in the book and read. "Be a good listener." He had listened once to what passers-by said when they caught a glimpse of the scarred half of Anne's face. He would not do that again.

"Smile!" Now the girls were good at that. Fiendish screening tests ensured only the least panic-prone women volunteers made it to Europe. They couldn't have paralyzed men trapped flat on their stretchers see a woman panic when a German artillery barrage came stomping toward them in the night. One rain-soaked November, the girls had to build their field telephone exchange next to a line of soldiers buried alive in their trench by an exploding shell, leaving only the tips of their rusting bayonets at the ends of their rifles exposed. The sight was considered too demoralizing for regular soldiers — but not for them. "Smile!"

"Show respect for the other man's opinions." Well, Randy (got your name right!) this looks like your goddamn underlining here. "Make the other person feel important." Seems my former girlfriend gave me your old book underlined with a pencil she sold to you. "Appeal to their nobler motives." So do the world a favor, Randy-jerk (as good to call names as learn them!) and drop the hell dead!

Calvin tossed the book on his desk and sat perfectly still, listening to the voices in the building, the evening traffic in the street. In a moment of random silence, he heard another noise, a more solid, familiar, "pocking" bang. He rose and went to the doorway. Voices arose from below and a distant door squeaked and then slammed. The pocking noise came again, from above him now, from the tower.

He slipped up the stairway to the ninth floor and down the hall to the tower entrance. The door was propped open by a pasteboard box from inside. Before he reached the door, he heard the slap of a board within and realized that one of the janitors must be in there now. He was turning to leave when he heard the distinctive shearing sound of a plane. He walked silently down the corridor and stuck his head in just enough to see a young black man working at his bench. Calvin's tool cabinet was open and the doors, removed from their hinges, were leaning against the wall, the padlock and hasp still joining them. Beside the bench, virtually complete, but still the greenish-brown of unfinished walnut, was a low cabinet with rounded, streamlined corners. The man was planing with Calvin's jointer in fast, steady runs down a narrow length of walnut held edgewise on Calvin's bench. He stopped to check the board with his try square, turned and saw Calvin's face staring at him.

"Excuse me!" said Calvin, half for interrupting and half in indignation.

The man raised his head but said nothing. He turned back to the bench, smiling and shaking his head from side to side.

"Excuse me. You're not supposed to be in here," said Calvin, holding to the edge of the door.

The man still said nothing, but kept shaking his head as he bunted the mouth of the plane with the palm of this hand, popping out the shavings in a small explosion and returned it to the wall cabinet. With his left hand he lifted the walnut strip from the bench and placed it on top of the unfinished casework on the floor. In the same motion his right arm swept the workbench clear of shavings. He stood now, looking down at his work.

The dust in the air made Calvin sniff. "This is our laboratory, and we use these tools in Government research. You can't be coming in and messing them up."

Only now did the man look up. Younger than Calvin, the man looked straight at him with a pitying smile. "I am not messing them up." He turned back to the wall and bent over to pick up the doors to the tool cabinet.

"I'll get those," said Calvin "And you don't need to clean in here any more. I can do it."

The young man turned and leveled his eyes at Calvin again. Now, quickly, he smiled, shook his head and bunted his hand against the center divider of the walnut cabinet, reached around and pulled it out the back. He slapped the top from underneath and it came free, revealing hidden dovetails in its underside. The sides came free from the base and he quickly laid the pieces in a stack, took them in his arms and walked toward Calvin.

"Excuse *me*," said the man. Calvin stepped back and glanced down at the heavy load under the man's arms, surprised by the pink flesh that showed through the fingernails on the dark-skinned hand. The man noticed Calvin's reaction, looked down and saw the source of the white man's surprise. He shook his head with a disgusted smile, hooked the tower door with his foot and bumped it open with the end of his boards.

"No!" said Calvin, not knowing what it was that he was denying. He stepped in and held the door open, but the man had already passed through.

Galloping thoroughbreds dragged Calvin around a racetrack in his dream. The laughing Negro jockey whipped his horse faster and faster. They circled Calvin's rooming house as his landlady called to him from the stands. "Mister Cobb! It's landalady! Landalady! Man has emergency!" Suddenly she was pounding on the door and he was awake. He drummed barefoot down the cold stairs in his pajama bottoms and undershirt. Mrs. Costaggini opened the front door. Bubby's eyes were bloodshot, his trousers streaked with ash and sand, reeking of fuel oil and fire.

"Calvin! Thank God!"

"Bubby, what the…What happened?"

"There was an accident. I need to come in."

Mrs. Costaggini held the door against him. "Trouble with the police?"

"No! No! It was a fire! I have to store some government equipment in a safe place for tonight." Bubby turned and pointed to a black, leatherette-covered case beside him. "I just need to leave this here tonight. It's my typewriter. I'll get it tomorrow, I promise!"

Calvin could see that it was not a typewriter.

"Stolen?" demanded Mrs. Costaggini.

"No Madam! I am trying to keep it from being stolen."

"It's all right, Mrs. Costaggini. He's okay, really!" Calvin pushed the door open as Bubby picked up the case and stepped in. "I'll let him back out. Thank you, Mrs. Costaggini."

The landlady's head twitched as if trying to shake a fly off her nose. "I smell the fire on you. Where was this fire?"

"Beltsville, out in Beltsville." Bubby looked back out into the dark street.

"Don't wake anyone," she barked. "Don't make my walls dirty!"

Bubby barreled ahead of Calvin, carrying the black case up the stairs. He saw the open door to Calvin's room and went right in. Calvin came in behind and closed the door. Bubby had already set the case down and flopped back on the bed.

"Are you all right?"

Bubby whispered. "Your landlady is Italian. I couldn't talk in front of her. Is she political?" He looked to see if the shades were pulled down.

"Political?"

Bubby sat up, provoking a chorus of popping bedsprings. "Has she got pictures of Mussolini all around?"

"I don't think so." Calvin looked at the case. "What were you doing at Beltsville?"

"It wasn't Beltsville, it was Lakehurst! The Hindenburg! I've driven for four hours. I've got the recorder! Did you hear the radio?" He waved at the Philco on Calvin's beside table.

"God, yeah. They said what happened on the ten o'clock news flash."

"I was there! I was right there! We were recording it just as it happened. We've got the whole thing recorded on discs. They're trying to get them back to Chicago right now. I'm just the bait. I've got the recorder, and just the blank discs." Bubby nudged the case with his sandy shoe. "I had to tell the police who I was before I could leave. One of the Nazi guys was right there taking down addresses. I'm sure they'll have people waiting for me at my place, so I came here. God, I know I drove a hundred miles an hour!"

"What happened to your hands?"

"I tried to help lift—some girder or something. I'm okay. I'm okay." He stared at the window shade. "We waited all day in the rain for the Hindenburg to come in and then it burns. God, it burned…" Bubby's face drew wide and flat. "Oh Christ, I saw this little kid with his legs broken and swollen up like sausages. All these people with nothing but their belts and shoes left, all their clothes, all their hair burned off. Women burned, on fire, blind and still trying to walk. You can't touch them because all their skin is burned." Bubby began to choke. "God almighty! Their lips and ears burned off!"

"Shhh, shhh. Let me get you some water," said Calvin, and he slipped out the door to the bathroom. He could hear Mrs. Costaggini arguing with her husband in Italian below. Bubby took the glass and held it between red, blistered hands.

"Oh my God! Bubby, you're really burned."

Bubby drained the glass. "It hurts like hell. God, it was so quick. The motor fuel caught fire and poured down on everyone. I was right there by the mooring tower. Charlie and Herb were with the recorder by the hanger, and they were recording all through it. The explosion knocked the needle out of the track, but they got it all on the discs, the whole thing!"

"Shhh, shhh." Calvin took the empty glass.

Bubby flopped back on the bed. "God, it stinks. It just stinks. I'm on the phone to NBC in New York to tell them what we've got, and the idiot operator hangs up! She says there's a disaster in New Jersey and no calls are allowed in. I said we were with

WLS and we were at the crash, and the stupid cow says, 'WLS is the Chicago station, so what would WLS be doing in New Jersey?' and she hung up!" Bubby looked at his wrist but he had no watch. "What time is it?"

Calvin looked at his alarm clock. "Two-twenty."

"God I hope they made it!" He turned to the clock and tried to calculate, but shook his head in frustration. "These Germans tried to take all the cameras away, and then one guy realizes what we've got and he starts arguing with me and Herb. He wants the discs. Herb tells him to go to hell and the Nazi goes off to get help. So I get the Presto machine here and the blanks and make a big argument and distract 'em while Herb and Charlie scram with the four cut discs."

"Do you want something for your hands? I've got some butter downstairs."

"No, just sleep." Bubby lay back and pulled his feet onto the bed. "Look, I'll just…Get me up early tomorrow, don't let me sleep."

Calvin sat as Bubby's breathing overcame the occasional moans. He pulled an old quilt from his trunk and spent the night on the floor in miserable, sputtering half-sleep, filtering the reek of burned oil, aluminum and flesh through a dirty shirt.

Bubby shook Calvin awake. "Holy cow, you're still asleep! What time do you have to be at work?"

Calvin tried to rise to look at the alarm clock, but his neck hurt so badly he fell back. "What time is it?"

"Almost ten. Listen, I called Chicago. They made it! Two big Nazis were waiting for them out front of the studio, but they went up the fire escape. They've already played the discs on WLS and they're going play them on both NBC red and blue networks tonight! It's incredible! Charlie said you could hear everything!"

Calvin was dully stunned to see his friend clean-shaven, dressed and his hands newly bandaged with white gauze. "How'd you get all fixed up?"

"Your landlady. She's great! I love her! She let me use her phone too." Bubby knelt by the black case on the floor, popped it open, looked inside and fumblingly re-latched it. "Okay, I'm on my way over to the *Star* building. They want to interview me for tonight's paper, so can you do me a big favor?"

"Sure. What?"

Bubby stared blankly into space for a moment and then

jerked himself back. "Take the recorder over to your place and then bring it over to the *Star* building at one. They want to get a photograph of me with it. I've got to run back to the studio, talk to Hattersley and then race back over your way for the interview."

Calvin looked at the heavy black case and thought about carrying it eight blocks to the old Post Office. "Sure," he said.

"Swell! Here. Two bits for a taxi," said Bubby. He attempted to reach into his pockets with hands wrapped like boxing gloves.

"Bubby, I got it. You go on!"

"Thanks pal. Good thing you're the boss and can show up when you want to." He ran down the stairs.

Props were always handy when you're late, and this time Calvin had a doozie. As he rode the bouncy elevator up to the eighth floor, Calvin pondered taking the recorder to the tower, the better to defend it from attacking Nazi hordes. He was well into retelling Bubby's eyewitness account of the tragedy to the girls, when the eyes of his audience reminded him of their personal connection to burning horror. Linda hushed him by giving him a copy of the morning *Post*. He read details of the disaster as the women examined the disc cutter. All of the women had red, puffy eyes. He cringed at his idiocy.

Calvin was ready to leave for the *Star* building at twelve-forty, without even a gesture at routine work. He swung the machine ahead of him as he walked, riding the bowsprit of history, feeling sorry for the luckless drivers rushing by on Pennsylvania Avenue on their insignificant assignments. In the lobby of the *Star* building, Bubby stood talking to a reporter, a black case by his feet. He spotted Calvin and called out, "All right! Let's eat!" He touched his bandaged hand lightly to Calvin's shoulder. "The drugstore in the Trans-Lux building has a lunch counter. NBC's in the same building and we can drop off the Presto. It's only a couple of blocks."

"I thought they wanted to get a photo of you with the disc cutter."

"They used a Graflex box instead. Had to get the photo in the early edition."

"Don't you have to be back at work?"

"Look at my hands. I ain't turning no dials with these!"

Calvin portaged the heavy case on his shoulder as Bubby told details of the interview. They walked under the marquee of the Trans-Lux, slowing to take in the lobby cards of coming attractions. At the Peoples lunch counter, Bubby freed his thumb from the bandages enough to hold a hamburger.

As they ate, Bubby glanced around at their fellow diners. A dark man sat at the counter, finishing a milkshake and examining in turn a half-dozen souvenir-of-Washington key chains with horoscope inscriptions. Bubby studied him, then swiveled on his stool and looked at a woman reading a storybook to a little girl seated on her lap. He watched for a few seconds and swiveled back around to the counter. He put his hamburger down, set his elbows on the counter and buried his eyes in his bandages. He turned and whispered to Calvin. "These people around us? The woman with the kid behind me?" Calvin glanced at them and nodded. Bubby looked up at Calvin. "They're just sitting there like nothing happened, and it seemed so strange to me." His face was racked flat. "I thought something was wrong with them. I just couldn't imagine feeling like them, just sitting there, normal—but, for a minute, I couldn't remember why."

Back upstairs at NBC there were more photographs and questions. Through the double glass windows separating the hall from the studio, Calvin watched Bubby tell his story again. Smart-looking girls with red lips and clipboards and stopwatches that bounced against their sweaters rushed about. Men in sharp jackets carried scripts and leaned into each other's offices, or conferred in front of glass-brick walls. At four-thirty they all packed into the green room to hear the network feed from Chicago. They glanced at each other and squirmed as Herb Morrison's voice described the slow approach of the doomed airship—tormented by their helpless anticipation, ashamed of their inability to turn away.

The story in Friday morning's *Post* had more interviews from Bubby: "Local Man Helped Victims & Recording." Calvin still held the paper open as he sat down at his desk, but folded it when he saw the drafts for the new extension service bulletins waiting for his re-writes and layout. He started at the sudden loud voice in the hall. "Calvin! You'd better—be up here!" Bubby's voice came between labored breaths. "God almighty—I think you're—trying to—kill me!"

Calvin opened his door and stepped out into the hall. Bubby hobbled toward him as the door of the adjoining office opened and Linda poked out her head.

"Holy cow," huffed the big man, tugging at the sticky wool of his trousers. "Calvin. This is—ridiculous. What's with the—elevators?" Bubby leaned on the brass rail and looked down into the atrium. "That's a long way down! Hey, it echoes!" he called, and the reverberant *"hos! hos!"* came quickly back.

Linda stepped into the hall and Calvin tugged Bubby around to face her. "Linda, this is my old friend Bubby. Bubby, Linda Cole, assistant deputy chief, Broadcast Research Section,

USDA." He peeked around her at Ellen's empty wheelchair in the hall. "Something wrong?"

"I had her lie down in the office. Anne's running up to the Soldier's Home to get some more…supplies." She placed her papers under the stump of her left arm and offered Bubby her hand but just patted his wrist when she saw his bandages.

Bubby looked past her into the room and sniffed at the soldering flux. "What's all the equipment?"

Linda waved her hand at the door. "It's kind of an integrated electro-mechanical…"

Verdie's voice came from within the room. "It's our baby!"

Calvin rescued a pencil about to fall from Linda's hair. "They've wired together some old Burroughs machines from Social Security. Got 'em doing differential equations."

Verdie stepped into the doorway. "We're down to single TURD."

"That's a Theoretical Unit of Rectal Debris," explained Linda.

"We work closely with Brown University," said Verdie.

"That's how they mathematically model different spreader designs," said Calvin. Used to be we had to go out and run the manure spreaders over a big piece of canvas and then gather sections and weigh it. The girls prefer this new method, I think."

"It leaves us flushed with pride!"

"Thank you, Verdie, I think he gets the picture!"

Bubby nodded thoughtfully, then brightened and poked his hat at Calvin. "So you guys actually study what happens when the…"

"…shit hits the fan!" they finished the line for him in unison. Calvin rattled the change in his pocket and winked at Linda. "I'm buying." He stretched out his arm to his friend. "Ladies, Bubby here works with Kathryn Dale Harper. We've known each other since third grade."

Linda tapped her pencil on her thigh as if it were a swagger stick. "You were at the Hindenburg."

"God, that was awful," said Verdie.

Bubby nodded at the floor. "Yeah, really bad, you can't imagine." He looked quickly up, sweating now. Linda caught his eye and exchanged a glance with Verdie. Bubby dropped his eyes to stare at the floor.

"It takes time," said Linda.

Calvin broke the silence. "Why don't I give Bubby a quick tour of the place?"

Bubby was already walking ahead, not knowing where he was going. "Pleasure to meet you, ladies!" he called back.

"Pleasure's ours," they chorused as Calvin caught up and led him into the stairwell.

"Jeese, Calvin." Bubby shook his head. "They put cripples up here on the top floor? Whose brilliant idea was that?"

"They prefer it."

"They're vets. Can't they get pensions and stay in a home or something?"

"No, they're women. They're supposed to get married."

"That's not what I hear about Army gals."

Calvin stopped on the landing and turned to face him. "Bubby, please."

"Oh, they can't hear me!" He held up his hand in surrender. "Listen, I'm hot stuff now. I had my picture taken with Hattersley and the Presto. I told him you were my friend and how you had helped me. Cal, I got you a shot at a show!"

"Bubby, right now a radio interview is the last thing…"

"No, no, no! Not an interview, a show! We still have contractor money in buckets. You need to be at today's lunch meeting with a proposal."

"A proposal for what?"

"For your radio show, on wood! Your own show! Fifteen minutes a week."

"But they knocked woodworking out of the picture."

"Because it's too visual?"

"Needs television," said Calvin. He turned to continue up the stairs. "That's what Miss Harper said."

"Well, she'll be at the meeting, so you'll need to acknowledge that somehow. We just need to find the right angle."

Calvin pulled his head back. "You're saying stick with the woodworking idea?"

"Absolutely! Politically, it's perfect. Interior's trying to get the Forest Service away from us now, so a forest products series would really put a feather in Hattersley's hat."

Calvin stared at him for a moment. "Come look at the workshop." He led Bubby through the corridor into the clock tower. He had avoided the place since the encounter with the young black man and was glad of Bubby's company. The shop was just as he had left it—walnut shavings still matted on the floor.

"This is where I make the test models." He patted the bench and swept his foot through the shavings.

Bubby turned about, looking up at the huge clock faces, two of which glowed bright yellow with the morning sun. "What a weird place to work." He looked out the slit window down to Pennsylvania Avenue. "So, you finally got to be a mad scientist in a tower." He picked up a wooden leg in the corner and stroked it. "This one of your test models? Nice work Doctor Frankenstein!"

"That's Verdie's. Lost her right leg."

Bubby picked up another leg from the stack. "Boy, how many does she need?"

Calvin stared for a moment, entranced by the spokeshaved willow-wood sculpture. The leg in Bubby's hands was actually shaped after Anne's. Calvin couldn't mentally flip the contours of Verdie's left leg and Anne volunteered her right one as a model. "Took me a while to get it right."

"Kinda like-a Pinocchio, cept-a you make-a nice-a girl!" Bubby's eye latched onto the brass acorn finials on the looping iron top of a large intricate clockwork-looking machine. "Wow, what's this?" He swept a trail in the dust across a brass plaque and squinted at the Cyrillic lettering.

Calvin gave the treadle of the lathe a push, setting round leather belts and grooved drums into motion. "Peter the Great supposedly used it to decorate snuffboxes. The Post Office bought it to engrave all those interlacing rosettes that make stamps harder to counterfeit. They sheared some of the fancy gearing, but I just use it to make parts for the girls." He spun the lever bar on the transverse feed and blurted out, "I solved a mystery the other night. I found out why my tools were always sharp. One of the janitors was working in here on nights and weekends. I guess he started off slow, just cleaning up until I got used to it."

"These old colored fellas can be very clever when they want to. Did he take anything?"

"No, and this guy was our age, younger, actually. He was getting into the tool cabinet by knocking the pins out of the hinges. Left all the planes sharper than I ever do. Making a record cabinet, I guess, modern style. Very professional. I've thought about it ever since, what's he doing working as a janitor?"

"Ask him."

"I chased him off. I feel like a jerk."

"You know that's bad luck," said Bubby as he poked his mitt approvingly at the engraving of the busty French girls. "You violated the gleaning covenant. It's the elves in the cobbler's shop story. You chased off one of the elves!"

"Please!" Calvin looked up at the ceiling. "I certainly don't need more bad luck."

Bubby laughed. "Well, it's bad luck to be superstitious, so don't be."

"Really. This guy was good."

"Okay. Then we'll put *him* on the radio. You're sure not showing much enthusiasm for this opportunity." Bubby looked up at the catwalk and steps leading upward. "Can we go all the way up?"

"Sure." Calvin pulled a long, fat pole from behind his bench and stood it on end, its top leaning against the catwalk.

"We have to climb that?" asked Bubby.

"Easy!" said Calvin. He gave the pole a bump on the floor. As if it were split down the middle, one half of the pole swung down parallel to the other half, rungs pivoting out from pockets carved in the facing halves. It was a perfect ladder.

"Will it hold us? I don't want it to fold back up while I'm on it."

"It'll hold me. I don't know about you." Calvin climbed half way up, jouncing the rungs as he went.

Bubby pointed at the disassembled section of iron stairway that lay on the floor against the far wall. "Why'd they pull out the original steps? What'd you have? Jumpers?"

Calvin climbed back down and hopped from the last three rungs. "Yeah."

"Really?"

"Yeah. Really. I'll hold the ladder. Don't land on me if you break it."

They emerged through the trap door in the uppermost reach of the tower. Bubby beamed at the view, but held back against one of the columns. He leaned carefully out to look down at the street far below. "Whew! I see why they took the stairs down." He pointed northwest. "See the radio tower up there at Tenleytown? That's right where my house is, up on River Road." He stepped back and over to the west archways. "Alright, I see now. You got the new Post Office, Interstate Commerce…" He swung a counter-clockwise panorama at the roofs of the surrounding new uniform buildings of the Federal Triangle. "…Internal Revenue, Justice. Yeah, this place is coming down."

"I know!"

"So, all right. So you need a job, and you sure need to get away from this dump." He pointed across the Mall at South Building. "We'd better get moving if we're going to make that meeting!"

"Bubby, I can't. I'm really grateful, but I've got obligations, here with the girls." Calvin bent at his waist to stretch his back.

"Don't do that! You make me dizzy." Bubby stepped back to the trapdoor and began to descend. "Well, listen, Radio Services always needs clerical help. Answering letters and stuff."

"They do?" Calvin followed quickly after him. "Oh, they'd do great for you! I'm serious! Linda—she just got her one arm but she's still the fastest typist on earth. They're all of 'em geniuses. They've all had radio and telephone experience. And they're all qualified nurses too."

"Gosh Calvin, I just said we need the help, not that we have any jobs for sure." He worked his way gingerly down the folding ladder with his bandaged hands.

"They're obsessed with this calculating machine they've been working on. You think Radio Services could use an electric brain?" Calvin closed the collapsing ladder and slid it behind his workbench.

Bubby stared at him. "Oh, man, we have *got* to get you out of here." He turned and hurried through the shop and back out into the hall over the atrium.

Calvin followed close behind. "Well, if talking about a show gets a foot in the door for us, it might be worth it." He ran his fingers back through his hair. "So, a radio show idea." He led the way to the stairwell.

"Just something simple," said Bubby, "trees and wood and

with a story." His voice vibrated as they drummed down the stairs.

"Like Paul Bunyan."

Bubby stopped to catch his breath on the fourth floor landing. "Paul Bunyan is strictly out. We did a Paul Bunyan story years back and some clown writes their congressman that we were supposed to be planting trees, not cutting them." They pushed out the 12th Street exit onto the street, squinting in the sunlight. "Then the *Daily Worker* weighs in with some crap about how we're showing Paul Bunyan as a dictator when he really represents the progressive spirit of the people."

"The ox is blue, but Paul's a pinko?" Calvin's voice echoed under the portico of the IRS building. "So what kind of woodworking show do they want?"

"They don't know. That's your job." Bubby stopped to catch his breath again, supporting himself on a park bench midway across the mall. "All you really have to do at the meeting is know everybody's name and then pretend you're interested in them."

"Oh, not you too!"

"Psychology is the magic key to success!" He poked his hands at the ground for emphasis, the white bandage mitts making him look like a begging pup. "Just make whatever you want seem like it was their idea." He started walking again. "Okay. You met Larry Hattersley. I think he's a baseball nut."

"I don't know a damn thing about baseball."

"You don't have to." He pantomimed swinging a bat. "Just fertilize the soil of relationships and the ideas will emerge."

"Well, the woodworking show idea really was his to begin with, anyway. And Kathryn Dale Harper?"

Bubby puffed out a breath. "Well, psychology doesn't work as easily on women."

Calvin glanced down at his armpits. "God, I make a total ass out of myself every time I've seen her."

"Remember the Shakespeare gal fell in love with the donkey. You'll be fine!"

"She drops him when the magic wears off."

"Well, you just make it work long enough to get your show on the road."

Calvin cupped his hands to smell his breath. "And the whole comedy of the play is the mismatch between them!"

Bubby stepped ahead and, walking backwards, shook his bandage in Calvin's face. "And I'll be laughing from the front row, but for now, we'll just take this one dream at a time, okay?"

Calvin refused to meet his friend's "gotcha" gaze. "Ah, Puck you," he finally said.

"What?"

"I said, Puck you!"

Bubby grinned and fell in beside him. "Well, Puck you, too!"

Calvin reared back as Bubby led him down the stairs to the basement hall. "We don't have to meet in the studio, do we?"

"We're late." Bubby checked the tuck of his shirt as he strode along and Calvin did the same. "Everything'll be fine. Just remember the psychology and think of them as frien..." He glanced in the window in the studio door. "Crap!" He pulled back to flatten against the wall and rolled his eyes up to the ceiling. "Brockwell's in there."

"Who?"

"Brockwell. I don't know what you call him. He plays this fancified folk music."

"John Brockwell? The pianist?"

Bubby glanced in again. "You've heard of him?"

"Sure, he's famous. What's he doing here?"

"Working on a weekly spot on the *Farm and Home Hour*. He's your competition."

Calvin leaned over enough to glimpse the top of Hattersley's bald head nodding in rhythmic response to a tilted-back shock of thin gray hair. "What the heck is a high-class composer going to do on farm radio?"

"This guy? Whatever the hell he wants." Bubby swung his head to the window again. "Damn! They saw me. Okay, here we go."

Hattersley beamed gratefully at their arrival. "Welcome! Welcome Bobby!" He stared at Calvin as some mnemonic device retrieved his name. "Welcome…Calvin!"

Kathryn Dale Harper seemed choked by the ruffed white collar flouncing out from her chalk-striped suit jacket. She untwisted her hand from the strap of a handbag covered with large multicolored wooden beads that rattled softly to rest as she set it on the padded props table. "Delightful to see you again Mister Cobb."

The man at the piano pushed back his bench with an agonizing scrape. "Cobb?" He squinted at Calvin. "Did you say Cobb?"

"Yes sir," said Calvin. "Pleasure to meet you, Mister Brockwell, sir."

Brockwell moved with a slow command of space as he smiled at Calvin. "Perchance the Cobbs of the Eastern Shore?" He pronounced the final word as 'show-ah.'

"We're, actually, North Carolina—so, Virginia, I don't know—unless it was way back."

The man smiled, intrigued by Calvin as though he were a dog of perplexing breed. "Cobb is a very old, Anglo-Saxon name. Old-stock American. A pedigree of honor!"

Kathryn reached for Bubby's wrist. "How are your paws progressing?"

"Better. But I sure am ready for these to come off!"

Calvin wished he had bandages on his own hands.

Hattersley compared the time on his pocket watch with the big studio clock. "What a world!" He glanced about, counting the chairs. "The butcher at the A&P told my wife that someone fired at the Hindenburg with a death ray."

Bubby shook his head. "There was a bunch of newsreel cameras there, so I expect we'll see it by this weekend."

Brockwell eased the fallboard over the keys. "If we were in Berlin, we could have seen it already."

Hattersley nodded. "They'd have to ship the newsreels over first, though, of course."

"Not at all," said Brockwell. "During the Olympics, I watched us win the backstroke gold, all on television, all in the comfort of my hotel lounge — just as it happened."

Calvin waited for the others to comment, but no one did. "So — with a long enough wire?"

"Exactly!" Brockwell beamed at Calvin, opened his mahogany writing box, extracted a pen and wiped its nib.

Hattersley watched Brockwell settle in. "If...if you need to keep working, Mister Brockwell, we could move our meeting upstairs."

Brockwell unscrewed his ink bottle and dipped his pen. "No, no, no. You won't bother me."

Hattersley took a long breath and sat. He turned to Calvin and waved for him to sit. "So, Bobby, I'm sorry, *Bubby*, says you have a program idea."

"Yes, uh, Larry, it's not as, uh, interesting as some things. But it could be about, say, making a bat. How they make baseball bats."

"So, you got a wood turning program? *Tune in to Turning?*"

Calvin spoke too loud. "Great idea, Larry. And you've also got selecting, sawing and seasoning." He glanced at Bubby, who was shifting his eyes over to indicate Kathryn. "Miss Harper, I expect you use seasoning of a different sort in your work." His breath came in short gasps. "The cooking, I mean."

"Seasoning, yes, in cooking, of course." She laughed quietly as she slid a stack of photographs back into a yellow box. "The spice of life."

"And if you like variety, there's all the woodworking joints too. Mortise and tenon, dovetails, tongue in groove," said Calvin.

"Really?" She leaned forward, crossed her legs and waggled her foot.

Hattersley goaded the table with a pencil. "We've been thinking. Why hasn't there ever been woodworking on the radio before? It's obvious why music, news, drama and homemaking work on radio. They give you relevance, tension and sensual appeal." He counted off the features on his fingers. "But woodworking is just the same material with lots and lots of numbers for the dimensions."

Calvin slipped back in his chair. Kathryn leaned to console him. "You see, Calvin, we already have hog and corn prices, so we don't really need more numbers."

Calvin nodded. "So — if we could tell how to make a chair by saying 'Take three pounds of birch, add a half pound of pine, two fresh hickory limbs and a dash of locust, saw until smooth and dovetail for thirty minutes in a moderate drill press — then we could do woodworking on the radio."

Hattersley worked his hand in a circle as though stirring a pot. "How to bake a chair?"

Kathryn laughed. "Sounds tasty!"

Across the studio, Brockwell cleared his throat. "You know, looking at this sheet music, I was trying to imagine a wood crafting book without pictures. You'll find hundreds of cookbooks without pictures, but handicraft is just too visually dependent."

Calvin felt the heat rise in his face. "Well, sir, that's just the problem we're trying to solve."

"I'm not trying to be critical, now," said Brockwell. "Just trying to understand. Music, food, stories — all work on radio because they are better perceived with the eyes firmly closed!"

Kathryn released a held breath and turned to Calvin. "'O for a muse of fire!' eh, Mr. Cobb?"

Calvin nodded, flattered.

"In music, there's the variety of instruments, tonalities, as well," said Brockwell.

Calvin turned slowly to him. "You know, Mister Brockwell. That's a great idea you just had!" He tapped his knuckles on the table and stood. "In cooking, the interesting variable is the ingredients. In music, it's the instruments as well as the notes. In woodworking, it's all the different tools!"

Hattersley brightened. "Tools? So, saws and planes and chisels?"

Calvin stepped toward the piano and turned back to face them. "Tools! Yes, sir, Larry, I think that was what Mister Brockwell was going for! All the different tools and how to use them, that gives you the variation. Then you're away from the measurements problem." He held his hands out as if the idea was in a box.

Bubby piled on. "Right! We could put some characters in it, too. Human-interest stories, like a father and son, and the father teaches the son! They're just solving problems around the house, or the farm, and the father teaches the son how to use the tools."

Hattersley pushed out his lips and nodded. "Two characters. Simple story lines. Things people need to know. That's not bad!" He rubbed his knee. "Calvin, you know if you could come up with something that unites urban and rural interests, that's precisely what the Secretary is pushing for." Calvin nodded and inhaled, but Hattersley continued before he could answer. "Listen, we need to get on this, pronto, if we're going to have anything ready for the summer season." He sealed the deal with an auctioneer's rap of his hand on the table. "Calvin?"

"Sir?"

"Calvin, I'm going to ruin your weekend. I'll need a sample script by Monday's meeting. Keep it simple, now, just tools and teaching."

Calvin reached out to shake his hand. "Thank you…Larry."

Hattersley smiled and gathered his papers. "And you're sure your section can spare you?"

"Oh, sure! I'll make it work."

"Okay, then. Good man!" Hattersley tapped Calvin on the shoulder with his papers. "See you all Monday then. Mister Brockwell, we'll see you again on Tuesday. Kathryn, don't forget your Banana Board interview. I expect there's a *bunch* of 'em in the press room already." He grinned and made his exit.

Kathryn shook her head. She turned to speak to Calvin just as the studio door pushed open again. "Miss Harper," said the receptionist, "the banana people are *appealing* for your presence in the press room."

"Oh, I'll be right up!" She gave a nod to the men. "Gentlemen, I must away."

"We understand," said Calvin. "Wouldn't want the banana people to think you're *yellow*."

"No." She sighed and pushed out the door.

Brockwell jerked his head back to throw the hair from his face. "Mister Cobb?"

"Sir?"

"A word with you before you go?" He peered at him through steel-framed glasses with lenses as thin as watch crystals.

"Certainly." He glanced at Bubby, who signaled that he would wait in the hall.

Brockwell held his eyebrows high until the studio door closed. "I think our Mister Hattersley's testing you." He scooted down the piano bench towards Calvin and smiled conspiratorially. "This folderol about keeping it simple is just a test to see if you have the big vision. If you came in Monday with that father and son script, wouldn't that say you don't have any ideas beyond what was discussed?"

"Well, that was just a starting point."

"Good, good. People don't understand that Americans need larger-than-life heroes these days. But light-hearted, too. Everybody loves to laugh." He leaned toward Calvin. "I've always said that the man who can write a good parody of Bible tales will rule the world. People love to see these lofty types brought down to earth. And, you're dealing with this midwestern audience. Literally, barnyard humor is what you have to use. Like Noah and the Ark. Think of the mess with all those animals!"

Calvin nodded and backed toward the door. "Well—lots of work to do, then."

"Excellent! 'Make no little plans.' That's a motto to live by. Take it far, be unafraid, and don't forget those Bible stories!"

"Thank you, sir. I'll keep all of that in mind." Calvin pushed out the door and quickstepped to join Bubby at the end of the hall. "What an idiot I am!" He gave his head a wet dog shake as they strode down the labyrinth of hallways.

"What? You did fine!" said Bubby. "You did great!"

Calvin mock-pounded his head back against the wall. "That yellow banana gag. I can't believe I said that."

"Ah, don't worry about that! But the correct term, I believe, is tongue *and* groove, not tongue *in* groove."

"I didn't say that!"

"Oh yeah you did! And taking an interest in someone doesn't mean staring at their legs."

"Oh, Jesus!"

"Still" Bubby grinned. "She threw you a bone! Pretty encouraging considering she's been working on Brockwell's music program." He nodded back into the studio. "What did he want?"

"He suggested I write something like that Adam and Eve sketch that got Mae West banned from NBC."

"Well, if he's trying to sabotage you, just take it as flattery."

"Nice to be taken seriously."

"So, you need a fifteen minute story. Tough to write a starting script in just two days. Can you have one of your girls type it?"

"I…This would be hard to explain to them. I mean, the radio show…doesn't include them."

Bubby clicked his tongue. "Well, it should be simple anyway. Just some grandpa telling some kid how to build a birdhouse or something." He boxed a bandaged fist on Calvin's shoulder. "You can do it! Time and the tide!"

Calvin walked fast across the Mall with his best man-of-destiny strut and his chin jutting like Mussolini's, singing the Hoosier Hotshots song.

I don't like your peaches,
   they are full of stones.
I like ba-nanas,
   because they have no bones!

But Kathryn Dale Harper had thrown him a bone…

Don't give me tomatoes.
   Can't stand ice cream cones.
I like ba-nanas,
   because they have no bones!

…and famous composer John Brockwell found him enough of a threat to try to sabotage him. He admired the ivory luster of the Capitol dome against the blue sky as he walked. An image floated in — Calvin building the ark as Kathryn, dressed in her rosy toga, admired him with her blue eyes and handed nails to him. He could not recall staring at her legs, but knew that he could carve every contour. Had he really made the "tongue in groove" Freudian slip, or was Bubby just teasing? Between the third and fifth floors, the perfect defense drifted into his brain; "Sometimes a tenon — is just a tenon," and filed it away for future use. On the final steps, he happily repeated Hattersley's words under his breath. "Keep it sim-ple. Just tools and teach-ing. Keep it sim-ple. Just tools and teach-ing." He continued the chant as he walked down the hall, tapping the rhythm on the wall. "Oh, for my muse by the fire!" he said as he dropped into his chair. "With a loaf of bread, a jug of wine…" A large brown envelope registered in his vision, the return address; *General Accounting Office*.

Linda stood in the open door, face grim. Calvin pushed the brown envelope a few inches away across his desk. "When did — this — come in?"

"Ninety minutes ago." She had difficulty speaking.

Calvin stared at the flat envelope, wishing it away. "Ninety minutes," he echoed.

She nodded and bit into her upper lip. "Inspector showed up with lots of questions that *I* couldn't answer. Wants our section reports for the last three years."

He fingered the envelope. "So, was everyone busy?"

"We were when he came in, but then Verdie had to go racing up and down the street looking for you. Anne went running up and down the tower. And I'm stalling, saying you'll be back any minute."

Calvin slowly unwound the string and button closure of the envelope and half-extracted the questionnaires and folded charts. "How the hell did they find us?"

"God knows, but you need to hand deliver the whole thing to GAO on Monday at one. They want internal clients, external clients, functional reporting charts…" She exhaled and shook her head. "This is probably our last chance. We've already started pulling vouchers. I'll bring you what we have so far."

"Okay." Calvin's stomach tightened at the smell of his own sweat. "I'll be right here." He splayed the GAO papers on his desk in a purposeful exhibit and studied the external clients questionnaire. He kicked himself that it was now too late in the day to mail last-minute test reports to manufacturers. Still, if he mailed them Saturday or even Monday morning he could claim them on the audit. He stood and stared at the ream of GAO audit forms fanning out across his desk. Slipping the papers back into their envelope made an immediate improvement. He stared out the window towards the White House for a moment, but the envelope was still on his desk when he looked back.

Saturday passed under shuffled piles of payroll records, expense vouchers, research papers and extension reports. All written evidence of their worth went into a file box on Calvin's desk. For the first weekend in months, the girls' computing machine sat silent.

Calvin tried to manifest a reassuring presence, working confidently at his desk all day. When they finally headed home, Jupiter shone bright in the darkening sky. They would be back on the job early the next morning, but Calvin carried on. He boldly inked in "Broadcast Research" on the functional chart under the division of Agricultural Engineering. He cleaned a drawing of the wooden shell casing for the fourteen-inch naval gun that could pack a half-ton of seed and fertilizer and enough explosive to cover a sixteen-acre circle. He brushed off the crumbs of the art gum eraser and added the drawing to the pile. He typed a new cover sheet for Ellen's ingenious design for a miniature radio transmitter and receiver to fire the dispersing charge at a precise proximity above the ground. Anne's cartoon-like drawings showed the safety features of shell-rotation arming using electrolyte mixing and quick-charging capacitors to prevent premature detonation. Full darkness hung at the window now. Calvin stood and surveyed the papers spread over his desk, the overflow on the floor. All the brilliant, useless work they had done. Now, after the bombing of Guernica and the slaughter in Ethiopia and China, nobody was going to be shooting mountains with pinecones and horseshit.

Night came on. He exhaled deeply and closed his eyes, listening to the janitors already at work on the floors below. When this building was gone, where would they go? Where would whiskered Christina go? He shook himself back into focus and was bounding up the stairs to the tower workshop before he knew it. He could clean up the shop and order his mind. A bit of physical labor to nourish the muse.

Wind whistled in the hands of the western clock face as Calvin shoved the curled walnut shavings into piles with the side of his shoe. He contemplated metaphors comparing wood grain to broom straw. *Ya see, Sonny, rip saws are like chisels and crosscut saws are like knives.* As he swept his foot beneath his workbench he hit something buried in the shavings — a pencil-yellow box. He reached with his toe to pull it out, but it was too heavy and spun in place. Squatting, he swept the shavings away and revealed a black "Stanley" logo on the lid and "No. 45" on the end. He brought it to the bench top and looked inside at the nickel-plated and rosewood-handled multi-plane — a Civil War surgeon's toolkit of a plane.

Calvin set the silver skates of the main body of the plane on the bench. He fitted the fluted stocking-top sockets of the rosewood-knobbed fence on the gleaming arms. They slid down effortlessly to click against the cam stop. In the boxes of cutters, a few of the plow and dado irons were bright-polished from sharpening, but most were still purple-edged bronze-yellow from tempering. He grasped the handle of the chilly contrivance, not noticing that the slitting cutter had been reversed rather than removed. He lifted the plane and the blade sliced deep into his knuckle.

Blood dripped on the bench. He held shavings against the cut and pummeled down the stairs to the eighth floor, trying to remember where Linda's first aid kit was. Approaching his office, he heard banging trashcans and a man singing.

"Adieu la vie. Adieu l'amour. Adieu toutes les femmes."

The old janitor's arms reached out from Linda's office door to dump a wastebasket into the large rolling trashcan in the hallway.

"C'est bien finis, c'est pour toujours."

Calvin looked into the trashcan blocking his way, as if he might find a suitable cloth for a bandage amid the papers and dirt.

"De cette guerre infâme," sang the janitor. He turned and saw Calvin. "Hello! Hello! All done! All done!"

Calvin nodded as his blood dripped on the floor. He moved his hand over the trash can and smeared the drops on the floor across the linoleum tiles with the tip of his shoe.

"You all right?" asked the old man.

"Just cut myself. Need to get to the first aid kit."

"Let me get this out of the way." He rolled the trashcan to the side.

Calvin stepped in and almost took a fall as he slipped on a sheet of paper lying beside the can.

"Careful now!" said the janitor, watching him.

Calvin nodded again and found the first aid kit fastened on the far side of Linda's desk. He flipped the single spring latch on the metal box and the contents spilled out onto the floor. He spotted the gauze and tore open the blue paper package with his teeth. The janitor watched him as he fumbled and dripped blood onto the floor. Calvin missed the end of the roll and tugged the gauze into an hourglass shape. The janitor suddenly swooped down into his face and said, "Would you like me to help you?"

The black man's angry eyes startled Calvin. "I can't find the end."

The janitor snatched the roll of gauze in his hands and began unwrapping it. "Trying to do this yourself," he muttered, "with me standin' right here." He took up a small pair of scissors and cut a short length, wadded it up and thrust it into Calvin's hand. Calvin cleaned the blood from around the cut. The janitor was ready with the glass applicator from a bottle of iodine. He stopped, watched the dripping blood and recapped the iodine. "Let that bleed a minute." He pulled a zippered leather pouch from his pocket and tore out a big pinch of brown tobacco and set it on the table. "Better'n iodine," he said as he turned to fumble in his coat.

Calvin picked up the sticky wad of tobacco and squeezed it on the cut. His blood flowed into the cold shreds. The sting came like a hornet and he called out.

The man turned back, pipe in hand. "What the hell are you doing?"

"It stings!"

"You put my damn tobacco on your cut!"

Calvin released his grip and cupped the brown mass in his hand. "I thought you said it was better than iodine."

"Bleedin' is better than iodine! Damn, that's good jamb o' the fence!"

"I'm sorry. I misunderstood."

"You got you a good tattoo now. Well, put it back on, see if it works. I know it's good on bee stings."

Calvin remembered. His old boss liked talking with this man. The girls too, would share catch-phrases and conversations in French that left them all laughing and shaking their heads. His boss had said to Calvin. "Damn, this old boy spends two years fighting the Huns, comes back and asks Congress for a little help and gets gassed and bayoneted again right out here on Pennsylvania Avenue!" What was his name? Old Willie… something, his dead boss called him, although he was probably the same age as the Commander.

"I was working in the laboratory in the tower," explained Calvin.

"Uh huh," said the janitor, repacking the contents of the first aid box. "You almost broke this." He held up a glass vial of morphine. "Then you *would* have a problem."

"I found a tool a man left."

"Uh huh," said the man, looking toward the back of the room without focus.

"Do you know who it might belong to?" asked Calvin.

"No, I don't," he said, seeming to count the blood splats on the floor.

"There was a man, a young man working there, the other night, and I told him he couldn't work there anymore," said Calvin. "I wanted to tell him it was all right. He can come back and get his plane and work any time he wants. I was just…I just didn't know he was going to be in there."

"Startled you?" He nodded at the brown wad. Calvin lifted it and saw the red line of the gash. The bleeding had stopped.

"He did, yes. So, I'm trying to find him and let him know he has my permission. It's okay for him to come and work when he wants."

"Uh huh. So, what do you want me to do about that?" The man took his hand and wrapped gauze tight around his finger.

"If you knew who it was, you could tell him."

"I'm not a messenger boy." He snipped the gauze from the roll, tore the end in two and jerked the ends into a too-tight knot.

Calvin remembered his last name. Valentine, old Willie Valentine, or Captain Valentine, they called him. "I don't…

I'm just trying to do right. Really, he was taking better care of things than me."

"Uh huh!"

Calvin pushed at the bandage. "Stuff works! Fence jam, huh? And you can smoke it too!" He looked around for a cloth to wipe up the blood on the floor. "You used to talk with my old boss." Valentine pulled free a rag from a wire loop on his trash can and handed it to him. "Thanks." He wiped at a blood splat but left a brown outline. "You were in the army, right? Harlem hellcats?"

Valentine squinted at Calvin. "Hell-*fight*-ers!" He shook his head, and repeated quietly. "Hell-*fight*-ers." He tossed his broom into the rolling trashcan. "How about the First Separate Battalion, Three Hundred and Seventy-second Regiment?" He was breathing hard now. "And it ain't 'fence jam,' it's 'jamb o' the fence.'" He stared at the night-filled window. "So, you want us to start cleaning up the tower again?"

"No. Sir. I just wanted to say it's all right for anybody to work up there if they take care of the place. And I want to get that plane back to the man who was working. I know it was expensive."

Valentine squinted at him over the bowl of his pipe as he packed it. "All right then."

Calvin nodded at the pipe. "Jamb o' the fence. Can you get that around here?" he asked, thinking of buying some as a peace offering.

"You can't buy it. The name tells you that." Valentine took a match from a nickel-plated cylinder and lit his pipe. "I'll bet you never even seen a snake fence — split rails all stacked up?"

"I have, sure." Calvin interlaced the fingertips of his two hands to make a right-angle intersection.

Valentine poked at the interior angle formed by Calvin's hands. "Right in there. That's the jamb o' the fence. That's the place where they can't plow and the pickers pass by." He struck the match on the side of the trashcan. "That's the wild place." Match light glowed on his his face as he drew the flame down into the pipe.

"Thank you Mr…" Calvin held up his bandaged finger. "*Captain* Valentine. Thanks." With his left hand he offered back the rag.

"Keep it," said Valentine.

The woman's voice sounded in the atrium,

'A band of angels comin' after me,

Comin' for to carry me home."

And Captain Valentine eased back into the hall in a trail of smoke.

Calvin's eyes opened just enough to decipher his alarm clock in the beam of the alley light. Four thirty, bed sheets thoroughly rucked. His eyes closed again to the soft pulse of his electric fan.

Abraham Lincoln was in Calvin's dream now, looking over at Thomas Jefferson and shaking his head. Calvin's pen just wouldn't write—it ripped the paper, poked through holes down into hollows in the desk. Grant chewed his cigar. General Lee shot a sidelong glance at his huge blue ox that glared at Calvin with bloodshot eyes. Grant buckled on his sword, then snatched Calvin's paper away, crumpled it and threw it to the floor. Lee stuck his tongue out at Calvin. Grant stormed out the farmhouse door, slapping clouds of dust from his uniform. Sounds of fighting and moaning came from the front yard. Horribly wounded men came crawling in the door, accusing Calvin with their bloody, torn guts. Angry Paul Bunyan's axe came swinging towards Calvin's legs.

He started awake again. The moaning was coming from the yard. He let up the window shade and blinked into the morning light. A small crowd had gathered under the white-blossomed apple tree in the backyard of his rooming house. The moans came from a huge Persian cat, tied by its feet to a board so that the landlady and her sister could give it his Sunday-morning bath. They chattered soothingly in Italian to the howling cat and laughed with the passers-by attracted by the spectacle.

Calvin rocked on his bed and contemplated his bookshelf. *Uncle Remus*, *Two Little Savages*, *The Boy Mechanic*. His eyes lit on a copy of *How To Work With Tools and Wood*. He pulled it from the shelf, lay back and opened it at random. The difference between a rip and a crosscut saw. What was he thinking? That might make an interesting fifteen minutes of radio — *if* it were part of a hand-sawed human sacrifice.

A fifteen-minute script? What was that on paper? One hundred and forty words a minute, so fifteen times that is... twenty-one hundred words? About a minute a page — so fifteen pages. And where was the GAO report? What more was there to do? He dressed as the howling continued. Some of the audience sang a mocking cat's lament to the tune of *O solo mio*. Church bells rang in competition with passing fire engines — the Capitol Cafe would be open soon. How long did writing take? If he gave it ten minutes a page, fifteen pages would be a hundred and fifty minutes. The GAO report came first, but he could at least think about the script as he ate. He snatched a notebook and hurried down the stairs. Passing the grocery on the corner of 18th Street, he peered in the window, wishing he could he just go in and buy some pages of radio script off the shelf.

He opened his notebook beside his bowl of chicken broth and dumplings. He always tried to sit by the window so they would give him a bigger serving to impress passers-by, but this time it seemed to be just extra dishwater. He smeared a grease spot on the paper with the side of his hand. The dreams had to mean something. He pulled back the bandage on his hand, expecting to see that the gash had been magically healed by the old black man's wonderful jamb 'o the fence tobacco, but the cut was still red and weepy. Captain Valentine hadn't been in his dream, but such dreamlike encounters had to mean something. He stared out the window, across the street at Ford's Theater. *Lincoln was in the dream! Lincoln the rail-splitter, Lincoln, what did he use? An axe? No, wedges and a big mallet.* He shook out his pen and wrote on the top of his page *"With Mallets Towards None."* That deserved another cup of coffee.

At the next table, a bearded man in a knit watch cap and plaid flannel shirt worked his way into a huge mound of mashed potatoes, his lack of teeth requiring exaggerated chewing motions. The man's watery eyes gleamed with pleasure as he processed each mouthful, and primed his fork with the next load. Calvin looked back at his page and wrote: *"The young man was as tall and angular as a hornbeam tree — the same material from which his unsplittable wedges were carefully crafted."* He looked up and realized that he could hear the man gumming the mashed potatoes. The man's plate was mounded higher than ever. How could there be more potatoes? Calvin tilted his own empty bowl, made himself smaller and stared at his page, but the *yap, yap, yap* of the mashed potato man gripped him. He folded his notebook, paid the bill and left.

As he approached the old Post Office building he could feel the GAO report just waiting to whack him with a rolling pin for being out so late. Climbing the stairs, the whole idea of a Lincoln the rail-splitter script seemed stupider with every step. Agricultural Engineering had published a half-dozen bulletins scorning split rail zig-zag fences. They wasted land with every zig and zag and weed-filled jamb 'o the fence. Besides, nobody split fence rails anymore. Soft voices came from the machine room. He stepped quietly past the windows, slipped into his own office and eased into his chair.

With scissors worn from too much sharpening, he trimmed the rat-nibbled edges of overlap field trial results on the Deere-Burpee model A-3 spreader and slipped it into the pasteboard box. The GAO audit required everything going back to April 1934. Through the afternoon, he worked backward through his files. In the bottom drawer, he found his original presentation to the Naval Ordinance Bureau in Norfolk on the reduced bore erosion predicted if wood-cased reforestation shells were used as practice rounds in the Navy fourteen-inch gun. He tossed it in the box with the other papers.

That trip to the Navy base with the Commander had been a hell of humiliation. The Captain of the *West Virginia* politely allowed the Commander to make his case, but just as politely refused to allow their "shit-shells" on board his vessel. Calvin and Linda had followed dutifully along behind the Commander, carrying tables showing how to convert the lightweight reforesting shell trajectory into the arc of the standard 1,600 pound armor-piercing shell. The sailors on the battleship hid their smart-ass comments from the Commander and from Linda — their military bearing demanded respect — but Calvin was fair game. During the courtesy tour, even the contractors installing a test-model anti-aircraft gun on the battleship deck made amusing scatological comments for Calvin's benefit. He tried to ignore them by concentrating on the beautiful sweep of the teak splinter deck, and contemplating that the Bofors gunners, should they ever have to use this new weapon in a last-ditch defense against torpedo planes or dive bombers, would do so with their butts cupped in plain old John Deere iron tractor seats.

Linda knocked at his door. "That's it for the vouchers. All present and accounted for." She set a pile of papers beside the box on his desk. "There's a bunch of the Extension Service bulletins to add to the pile, though."

Calvin fingered through them. "I think I got 'em all. Already in there. But I want to go through it all one more time."

"Whew!" Linda fell back against the doorjamb. "You should get some sleep so you'll be fresh tomorrow."

Calvin shook his head. "If I'm late tomorrow morning, just add any last-minute stuff to the box. Okay?"

"Okay." Linda rubbed her exhausted face with her hand, her left arm stub moving in sympathetic synchrony. She batted at the rim of the box. "You know, this sort of represents everything we've done together."

"Seems small, doesn't it?"

"Well, it doesn't have your models in there."

"No, and it doesn't have your calculating machine either."

"No, it doesn't." She lowered her voice and settled on her accustomed corner of his desk. "Chief, what's the best we can expect?"

Calvin bit his lip. "Well, at the very least, I'll stay out of jail."

"But once the GAO finds out we're — disconnected, we're bound to get reassigned."

"I'm afraid so."

She shook her head. "We're not leaving Shirley behind."

"Who?"

She waved her hand toward the machine room. "Shirley, we call her Little Shirley, after, you know…Shirley Temple."

He shook his head. "You call who Shirley?"

"The machine! The computation machine. We call her Little Shirley. We're not leaving her behind."

"Linda, that thing weighs a couple of tons!"

"I know, sir! We haven't figured it out yet, but I'm sure we could hide her up in the tower."

Calvin leveled his eyes with hers. "We'll do what we have to do," he said, too tired to argue practicalities. "No one left behind, that's your Marine ethos, isn't it?"

She grinned. "Semper fi, chief."

"Semper fi."

As Linda's receding footsteps echoed in the atrium, Calvin stared out his window at the red lights, slowly, hypnotically blinking at the top of the Washington monument. He stretched, yawned and started back on the GAO questionnaire, inking in the final tentative pencilings. He kept slouching lower in his chair and finally had to stand at his desk to sort the contents of the box. The required vouchers were right on top, followed by the ordinance modifications and fuse diagrams, then equipment test reports and extension bulletins — enough to choke a storm drain.

He slid the box into a safe niche behind his desk to ensure that no janitor would mistake it for trash, dropped back in his chair and closed his eyes. Audit tomorrow afternoon. Before that, he would have to track down Bubby and apologize. Brockwell will sure be happy that he had come up empty. There'd be no chance for an interview now either. After the audit, there would be no more Broadcast Research section.

The gigantic pencil-shaped George Washington blinked slowly at Calvin with two red eyes. Inside the giant pencil, Linda and the girls scurried up the winding staircase pushing a fat Shirley Temple ahead of them. The giant George Washington kicked out ponderously with his black leather riding boots, shaking off the tiny Hessian soldiers pursuing them. Calvin bolted upright, stopping only to snatch a big pinch of fresh typing paper before pounding down the stairs.

Eight o'clock and Calvin had refilled his pen twice. He padded into the kitchen where the water was just beginning to jump into the glass watchtower of Mrs. Costagini's aluminum coffee pot. Starving. Crackers and cheese. He rummaged in her kitchen drawer for a knife. *But they can't logically have tools in a Hessian prison!*

He lay back on the bed, staring at the bookcase. *Boy's Complete Book of Indian Crafts.* Oh my faithful Indian companion! Just in time!

Now he was typing. *Okay to listen to Jack Benny? No listen radio, Kemo-sabe! Write radio!*

He needed the kicker for the end. Anything. *Who turned on that damn radio? Later, and then only for the Charlie McCarthy Show. No more coffee! Lower your standards and keep going!*

To muffle the clack of his little Underwood, he set the typewriter on his bed, turned his chair over on it and tented it with the quilt that still reeked of burned airship. He sat cross-legged on the bed, typing into the night as, over the radio, W.C. Fields traded jibes with Edgar Bergen's wooden puppet.

"Ah, yer father was a gate-leg table," said Fields.

"If he was," said smart-ass Charlie McCarthy, "then yer father was under it!"

"You meant Washington didn't you?" Hattersley peered over his reading glasses at Calvin. "It says 'Washimtom.'"

Calvin leaned over to look at the page. "Washington…is correct."

"Thought so. But it's right at the start so I didn't know if it was intentional." Hattersley took his pencil and corrected the errant spelling. "You know it's usually better to stay away from Washington and Lincoln. Some people have no sense of humor."

Calvin glanced across the table. Bubby crossed his eyes. Kathryn eyed Hattersley sideways, her fingertips lightly on the table, piano-like.

Hattersley shook his head at the script. "Where it says 'sound of auger,' that's a sound effect?"

"Yes sir."

"Always needs to say SOUND in the character line and type the whole thing in capitals."

Calvin blinked to focus on the manuscript. He tried to guess at the rate of Hattersley's reading and follow along.

"Need for you to put three spaces when the character changes." Hattersley flapped the script to the table. "Do you have copies of this?"

"No sir, just the one."

"Always make carbons. How many parts are in this? Unless it's a series that everybody knows, you always need to put a cast of characters at the start."

"There's, I guess, six character voices."

"That's a lot." Hattersley tapped the eraser of his pencil on the table. "We need to decide this today. Can you read it?"

Calvin picked up the script. "Just read it?"

Kathryn laughed. "Don't want to put any pressure on you!"

"Just read it for us. The length looks right. Just read it like you think it should sound. On a new concept, it's much easier to get the writer's intention if you can hear them read it."

"Okay." Calvin licked his lips. "Any time?"

Hattersley nodded. Calvin inhaled and read.

```
         George Washimtom and the Liberty Ladder
                      --ooOoo--
               Sound of auger.
TIMMY:         Hi Grandpa! Wha'cha makin?
GRANDPA:       Why hello Timmy, I'm making a ladder
               for the barn. Just boring the holes
               for the rungs.
TIMMY:         Boring? Yeah, I'll say it's boring!
GRANDPA:       You think this is boring, why, if it
               weren't for a famous ladder, we'd
               all be wearin' red coats today. Yes
               sir!
TIMMY:         Oh Grandpa, is this another one of
               your ...
```

"Calvin?"
"Sir?"
"Not necessary to say 'Timmy' or 'Grandpa' before the line. That has to be clear on its own."
"Sorry."

	Oh Grandpa, is this another one of your stories?
GRANDPA:	Well. let's see, it was back in the winter of 1776. The imprisoned patriots had never known such cold. Every morning saw another patriot die, his frozen body carried out for a crude burial under the mocking glare of the cruel ~~Prus~~ Hessian Guards. Suddenly, ~~at~~ from the gates of their stone prison came the clanking of chains and the creaking of doors that announced the arrival of more American prisoners. More prisoners that meant fewer men to fight for liberty, and more mouths to ~~divide~~ share the starvation rations.
GUARDS:	Ja! More schwein fur der sty!

Calvin glanced up at Hattersley. "Do you want me to do the sound effects or just read the description?"
"Just read the description."
"Okay."

> Ja! More schwein fur der sty!
> (grunts and groans as the men are

	pushed down the stairs, laughter from the guards and clanking and creaking as the door is locked behind them.)
GRANDPA:	There were two men, one normal sized, the other was a man of extraordinary stature. Colonel Watson went over to look at him.
COLONEL:	Well soldiers, welcome to ... hunnh?
GRANDPA:	The colonel gasped as he recognized the tall man
COLONEL:	General Washington! Not you! Captured!
WASHINGTON:	Best be quiet son, they don't know it's me.
COLONEL:	But how did they capture you, General Washington?
WASHINGTON:	The doctor and I were returning to our camp at Valley Forge with medicine for the troops when a marauding gang of Hessians burst upon us in the road. I began to draw my sword, but one of them came up behind me and clubbed me over the head.
DOCTOR:	Knocked him cold! Which was a good thing, too, if you'll pardon me saying so General. Had he been conscious, they would have quickly discovered who he was, simply by asking him!
PRISNRS:	That's right! He can't tell a lie, never has, never will!

DOCTOR: So I pushed my Doctor's bag under the General's arm. They think that he is the doctor and that I am his assistant.
WASHINGTON: That was quick thinking Doctor, but now we must escape.
DOCTOR: That's right! We have to get the General out of here before they question him again.
WASHINGTON: More important, we have to get that medicine to the troops at Valley Forge. Colonel, what is your escape plan?
COLONEL: Well General, we have a tunnel, just narrow enough for a man to squeeze through. It comes out behind a p rain barrel in the courtyard, but ...
WASHINGTON: But what son?
COLONEL: We can get into the courtyard all right, but once we're there ...
WASHINGTON: Yes?
COLONEL: Well, General, there's a wall. A wall too high to climb. These men are too weak to climb a rope, we need a ladder, but ...
WASHINGTON: But what son?
COLONEL: Well General, the tunnel is just too narrow and twisty. We'll need at least another month to widen the tunnel so that we can fit a ladder through it!
DOCTOR: A month! Those men at Valley ~~Ford~~

	Forge can't hold out that long! Besides, the minute they discover that they have captured General Washington, why, the revolution is over!
COLONEL:	There is always the chance that a few of the stronger men could rush the wall under cover of darkness, boost each other up, make sort of a human pyramid. Well, the strongest ones could make it!
WASHINGTON:	Only the strongest ones could make it? And leave the others behind? If we chose that path Colonel, tell me, what are we fighting this revolution for anyway?
COLONEL:	I'm sorry General, I just ...
WASHINGTON:	Now don't be sorry son. We've just got to think. Why don't you show me the tunnel.
COLONEL:	Right men, pull that water tub out of the way. (scraping sound) Follow me General. (Voices echoing) You see General, the tunnel has to twist around these giant blocks of stone. A man can bend and snake his way through, but a ladder has to be straight and strong.
WASHINGTON:	You could get a single pole through. What about making a ladder in pieces and assembling it once you are into the courtyard?
COLONEL:	General sir, we thought of that,

we even made the rungs and side pieces, but we have only a few seconds to get over the wall before the guard comes back. Here, let's crawl on a little further, I'll show you. (grunting as they crawl) (whispering) See General, the guard paces back and forth, regular as a cuckoo clock, you know how methodical these ~~Prussians~~ Hessians are. That leaves us only a few seconds to assemble the ladder, get a few men over, then hide the ladder while the guard comes back, and ... gosh General, its just got us beat.

WASHINGTON: Don't say that Colonel. Where free men put their minds and hearts to a problem, why nothing can hold them back. I remember something that Thomas Jefferson once said ... Why of course, Jefferson! Colonel, let us return to the cell. We have work to do!

- music interlude -

DOCTOR: Well of course General, I remember that ladder! Jefferson was so proud of it he kept showing it off and folding it up and unfolding it and making me climb up and down it to show how strong it was. I believe Ben Franklin gave it to him.

WASHINGTON: That's good Doctor. Now, do you think you could make a drawing of it

	so that these men could make one?
DOCTOR:	Yes sir, General, I'll get that drawing ready right away!
COLONEL:	Begging your pardon General, but how can you make a ladder that folds up? How could the sides be strong enough?
WASHINGTON:	The side pieces are unbroken, and so are the rungs. The trick is to make the connections between the rungs and the side pieces pivot. Here, soldier, hand me that gridiron from the fire.
SOLDIER:	Here you are, General.
WASHINGTON:	Thank you son. Now, see how this gridiron is like a ladder with two straight sides and lots of parallel cross pieces like the rungs of a ladder? Now to make it fold all we have to do is to pull back on one of the straight sides and push forward on the other and (grunts) it collapses.
SOLDIER:	Hoppin hickory nuts! He bent that with his bare hands!
WASHINGTON:	See? Like this it becomes no wider than the thickness of the two side pieces. Looks just like a single pole, but spread it out again, and (grunts) you have your ladder back again. Here son, finish breaking this gridiron apart, the iron rods will make excellent pivot pins for

	the ladder.
SOLDIER:	(grunts) I can't budge it! Here, somebody help me!
WASHINGTON:	All right men. We've got a job to do. How many of you are woodworkers?
SOLDIERS:	(off) I am General, why back on my farm ... Me too General, I'm a cabinet maker from the city, I make the best ... I'm a wheelwright General ... I can make anything General ....
WASHINGTON:	All right, men, all right! I should have known, you're all woodworkers ... because you're all - Americans! The Doctor here has a drawing.
DOCTOR:	We'll need tools too General. We need gouges. I suppose we could sharpen spoons.
SOLDIER 1:	It won't work Doctor, our spoons are all pewter. They're too soft to cut wood.
SOLDIERS:	(off - groans and moans of despair)
LONE FEATH:	Ugh! General! No needum gouge!
WASHINGTON:	Who is that? I recognize that voice!
COLONEL:	Why it's Lone Feather, General, one of our Indian scouts.
WASHINGTON:	Lone feather, eh? Son of Two Feathers?
LONE FEATH:	Ugh General. You fought-um bravely against my father and the French king. Now we and the French are allied with you in ~~the~~ cause of liberty for all men.

WASHINGTON: Your father was a brave and noble warrior, Lone Feather. But what do you mean that we don't need gouges? How can you hollow wood without gouges?

LONE FEATH: Gouge is white man's tool, but Indian long time useum crooked knife. We makeum crooked knife, we makum ladder plenty fast!

SOLDIER 1: I'm a blacksmith, I can make them crooked knives!

SOLDIER 2: Yeah! A lot better'n he can make a straight one!

WASHINGTON: All right men. No time for that! Let's get to ...

Kathryn shook her head. "I'm sorry. You said a 'crooked' knife?"

"They're like a hoof knife, but a lot smaller," said Bubby.

Hattersley grinned as he leaned back and turned to her. "North woods Indians use 'em. They've got a curved tip so you can hollow with 'em." He tilted his glance knowingly to Calvin.

Calvin nodded. "They have some on display at the Smithsonian—just before you get to the tipi." He lowered his script as if he was ready to walk over there right now and show them to her.

She raised her hands. "I'm surrounded by Boy Scouts!" She patted Calvin's script. "Sorry to interrupt."

Calvin found his place again.

WASHINGTON: All right men. No time for that! Let's get to work. Our comrades at Valley Forge are counting on us! Our

	whole nation is counting on us!
SOLDIER 2:	(moving off) Ain't that sumthin'. Prisoners havin' to rescue the Army!
WASHINGTON:	Colonel, if you can supervise the work, I'd like to visit the men who have fallen sick.
DOCTOR:	General, shouldn't you be gettin' some rest? You've been up for days!
WASHINGTON:	First things first. Doctor, first things first ...

- music -

DOCTOR:	Well, Colonel, how's the work going?
COLONEL:	Ah just listen to 'em Doctor. Working with wood really boosts their spirits.
DOCTOR:	And, I hope it boosts their bodies as well, over the wall that is.
COLONEL:	Doctor, they're going to town! Listen to 'em work! Those crooked knives are really doin' the job of hollowin' out those ladder posts. (sound of loud sawing) Say, that man sawing, isn't he too loud? Surely the guards will hear him!
DOCTOR:	That's not sawing Colonel, that's the General! he's finally fallen asleep. I figure his snoring will cover the sound of the men working!
COLONEL:	If that don't beat all! The General's helpin' even when he's sleepin'!

- music -

WASHINGTON: What? What time is it? How long have

	I been asleep?
DOCTOR:	Just long enough for us to finish the ladder, General. It's just before dawn. We'll have to make our break pretty soon.
WASHINGTON:	Good work Doctor. Colonel, are the men ready?
COLONEL:	Ready and rarin' to go, General, I've got healthy men paired off with the weak and wounded. Every man knows his job. ~~We8re just waiting~~
WASHINGTON:	Good work, Colonel. Now, I want you to lead the way. Get all the men over the wall and away from here on foot. The Doctor and I will go last and get the wagon with the medicine and follow after. That way the guards won't hear the noise of the wagon until the men have had a chance to get away.
COLONEL:	Pardon me General, but shouldn't you go first? I mean, after all ...
WASHINGTON:	No Co^{l}onel, let the men go first. And get them away from here as quickly as you can. If something should happen, and the guards start shooting, the men already over the wall must escape with the wagon. The medicine must get to Valley Forge or all is lost.
COLONEL:	Yes sir, General, see you in Valley Forge! All right, first group, into the tunnel! ~~Wait~~ Remember, wait for

>
> Lone Feather to give the signal that the guard is out of sight. That will give enough time for six men to rush to the wall, open the ladder and climb over. The last man needs to close the ladder and pull it against the wall so that it will look like a rain ~~gutter~~ downspout. ᴿeady? Now go!
> (noises of men moving and shuffling into tunnel)

WASHINGTON: Well Doctor, this is it.

DOCTOR: General Washington, I have got to say that it is mighty brave of you to be the last one up the ladder and over the wall.

WASHINGTON: Nothing brave about it at all Doctor. I am the biggest man here by a long shot. If my weight were to cause the ladder to break, why none of us would make it.

~~COLONEL:~~ ~~Well, your turn's comin up. there goes~~

DOCTOR: General, that ladder won't break! The men made the rungs from the best second growth hickory, and the post from yellow pine with rings as tight as Ben Franklin's belt buckle! Look, there goes the last group of six. We're next General.

WASHINGTON: Here we go. unhhh (crawling) There. All right. We're the last ones. I see the ladder all folded up where

	it should be against the wall. We'll just wait for Lone Feather's signal. (low bird whistle) There it is! Go Doctor! Good. Unfold it and pull it out from the wall. Good. Hurry up now, it's getting light! Go on Doctor! Lone Feather is whistling again! Hurry! Something's wrong! Hide at the top while I fold the ladder again!
GUARD:	ALT! VAS IST DAS? WHO IST? SCHPEAK OR I SCHTICK YOU MIT MY BAYONETTE!
WASHINGTON:	Who ist? You ask who ist?
GUARD:	JAH! WHO IST?
WASHINGTON:	Why I am General George Washington, commander of the Continental Army and I am leading an escape of my troops from your evil prison with the aid of this folding ladder.
GUARD:	WASHINGTON? JAH! HA! HA! HA! YOU ARE GEORGE WASHINGTON UND I AM ... OOMPH! OOOOH! (sound of club and falling to the ground)
WASHINGTON:	... a ladder that also makes a handy bat! Hang on Doctor, here I come.
DOCTOR:	Gosh General, sometimes it pays to tell the truth.
WASHINGTON:	Doctor, it always pays to tell the truth.
DOCTOR:	And to carry a big stick!
WASHINGTON:	You can say that again. Now let's get this medicine to Valley Forge!

- music -

GRANDPA: So, Timmy, that's how Thomas Jefferson's ladder saved the day, or rather, that's how American woodworkers saved the day.
TIMMY: Gosh Grandpa, that's a great story, but wasn't it Teddy Roosevelt who said speak softly and carry a big stick?
GRANDPA: Well, I reckon it was, but now you know where it came from. Well, gotta get back to work now!
TIMMY: OK Grandpa, BYE!

Hattersley looked at his watch and took in a deep breath. "Well, it's got a certain…buoyancy that I like. He turned to Kathryn. "It's not *Fall of the City*, but that's not what we need. As for having Washington snoring — presidential body functions? I don't know. But it really supports the story." He tapped the script with his pencil. "And, it's buoyant." He drummed his fingers on the table. "So, Kathryn, what do you think?"

She spoke through her hand that she held poised beneath her nose as if ready to stifle a sneeze. "I've got to say I liked the feeling of it. But it still has people with foreign accents as the enemy."

Bubby interrupted. "But they're, what, Hessians? Who the hell is a Hessian?"

Kathryn started to answer, but Hattersley spoke first. "Oh that aspect's fine. You gave the American prisoners all different accents, and even threw in an Indian." He reached across the table and patted the script. "But what do you learn? It doesn't teach you how to make this ladder thing. You simply couldn't do it from listening to this program." He nodded and cleared his throat. "Somehow, the whole thing about learning how to use the tools got lost since our last meeting."

"It was very imaginative, Calvin. It really was," said Kathryn. "You paint a nice picture of the kitchen, even if you don't give the recipe."

Bubby circled his bandaged hand on the table. "But the radio story is entertaining, and those that want 'em can write in for the plans." He turned to Calvin. "That's what you were thinking, right?"

Calvin nodded, exhausted.

Bubby sat back triumphantly. "And we get audience information to boot! We'd find out who's listening and where."

Hattersley leaned forward. "Boy, we sure could use some hard audience data to show the Secretary."

Bubby turned to Calvin. "Little books of plans, like you see in the backs of the magazines are, what, twenty-five cents each?"

"If that," said Calvin.

Hattersley rocked in his chair. "Kathryn, how many Aunt Sammy's Radio Recipes do we send out?" He shook his head and leaned back. "No, never mind. What do we have, five weeks? We couldn't get a whole booklet together in time for summer season. They can't turn around something like that at the printing office."

Bubby tapped his pencil. "So just let 'em ask for one drawing at a time. That would give us better program response information anyway."

Hattersley cleared his throat. "That's a lot of clerical work to do that." He turned to Calvin. "What are some of your other program ideas?"

"Well, I thought, perhaps, Lee can't surrender at Appomattox because they don't have a table to write on. So they have to make one. And we do the same thing for all these other turning points in American history."

"Just don't have Robert E. Lee snoring, *that* you dare not do." said Hattersley, shaking his head.

Bubby leaned in. "But still, they're all stories told by an old guy in his workshop. And this kid keeps coming in and bothering him. And he tells these stories to shut him up."

Kathryn tapped a pencil. "Kind of…Scheherazade with a hand saw."

"Munchausen with a mallet!" said Bubby.

She rolled her eyes to Calvin. "So each week you get a story where the problem is solved by a woodworker hero and you get him making something and…"

"…and if they want to make it for themselves, they write for plans," said Bubby. "They can just enjoy the story or they can get the plans and make the project of the week."

"Now someone, I suppose, has the money for this," said Hattersley.

"For printing? It's just one sheet of paper," said Bubby.

"A popular item can generate at least 20,000 requests," said Kathryn.

Hattersley interlocked his fingers and tapped his thumbs together. "Well, we could charge. We charge for the recipe book. What would this cost?"

Bubby was bouncing as if he had to pee. "Nothing for postage. So, two or three cents apiece for a mimeographed page. Have 'em send in a three cent stamp for every drawing and it can pay for itself."

Kathryn shook her head slowly. "Printing's not the big expense. It's handling all the correspondence. We also have to consider talent. We'd have to audition and then try to hire performers."

"Oh, Calvin has the clerical staff, and he can do all the voices," said Bubby. "You just heard him do that, and I've done sound effects for hundreds of shows."

Hattersley turned to Calvin. "That wouldn't be fair to you. Say you suddenly freeze up and leave us hanging with dead air."

"I'm sure you could still write them," consoled Kathryn.

"What if..." Bubby bounced his bandaged hands on the table in an alternating rhythm. "What if we could guarantee you a perfect performance from Calvin every week? Guarantee it!"

"Guaranteed perfection? I'd like some of that," grunted Hattersley.

"So would I," said Kathryn.

Bubby opened his hands as much as his bandages permitted. "We simply record Calvin's shows ahead of time with one of the new disc cutters. We get it right on disc, and then play it back at air time!"

Hattersley snorted. "You know that's not permitted. The networks don't allow recordings to go on the air."

Bubby bit at the loose end of his left-hand bandage, pulling it tighter. "That's right, they didn't! Not until the Hindenburg! Not until last week!"

Calvin struggled to pull his watch from his pocket as he plotted his course for the exit. He called back to Bubby. "I gotta scram! Thanks so much! Wish you could go to this audit with me!"

Bubby called down the hall after him. "You're getting audited? Yow! Well, break a leg, man! But I think you got this in the bag!"

Calvin trotted back across the mall and pumped up the stairs to the office. Linda met him in the hall with a shaking head and a new folder. "Anne retyped the Allis-Chalmers front end reports. But I couldn't find that box of yours."

"Good work," puffed Calvin, panicking for instant. "I hid it behind the desk." He leaned over his desk and saw the box sitting safely where he had left it.

"Where have you been? We were getting worried."

"Taking care of loose ends. Listen, time's getting tight, could you call a cab?" He had plenty of time to walk to the GAO in the old Pension building, but this changed the subject.

Calvin lifted the box of evidence from behind his desk, and was surprised to feel its weight actively shifting in his hand. He looked in and saw that this box was filled with a fluffy, white mound of finely shredded paper. Wrong box. He looked under the desk, beside the desk, but there was no other box. He reached in the box and pushed the white fluff aside. Christina looked back at him with proud, sparkling eyes, her tiny babies wriggling beside her. Calvin folded the fluff back over her.

"I looked out front. Street's full of cabs so…" Calvin's white face stopped Linda cold. "What? What happened?"

Calvin pointed to the fluff where all their records for the audit should be, and pulled it back to reveal Christina.

Linda's hand flew up over her mouth. "Oh my God! Is anything left?"

He lifted a handful of fluff. He pushed more fluff to clear an edge, reached in and pulled at the side of the stack of reports and vouchers. He could see the sides of the hole filled with the wriggling ratlets shift, so he moved his pinch deeper. Again, his pull made the bottom of the hole shift like a cigar cutter, but he kept pulling and extracted the bottom quarter inch of the deep stack. Some early manufacturer correspondence remained intact, but all the Extension Service reports, the vouchers, and the radio fuse and barrel erosion tests were shredded into a beautiful rat's nest.

"Okay, okay," said Linda. "I've got copies. I have carbons on the letters in my files. And any of the Extension Service material that we had duplicated is still in the stacks."

"Can you pull 'em fast?"

"Sure. Oh God, I hope you have the voucher carbons."

Calvin slapped at his pockets. "I do, but not here, I mean, I hope I do. Everything from '34 and '35 is in the Van Ness office. The ground proximity fuse designs are there too."

"At the Bureau of Standards? You know they've thrown all that stuff out by now!"

"It was there in October!"

"Ask GAO guy for an extension."

He rolled his eyes. "What am I going to tell him? The rat ate my homework? That's good for a train ticket to Leavenworth." He set the box on his desk. "All right, this time of day I can be up there and back in thirty or forty minutes. You get everything ready here and have someone out front with it. I'll grab it and head straight to the hearing."

"You're cutting it awfully close!"

Calvin flipped through the short stack of papers in his hand. "If the voucher carbons aren't still at Van Ness, I'm going to jail anyway." He tossed the stack on his desk. "See what you can save. Out front. Thirty minutes!"

He pounded down the stairs and out the front door, ran into the intersection and into the back seat of a westbound cab before the driver could even turn around to look at him. "Bureau of Standards, Connecticut and Van Ness!" Calvin jerked his hand to his inside coat pocket and confirmed his billfold. "Two bucks if you can make it in ten minutes." He slammed against the back seat as the Plymouth jumped forward. The cabby laid on his horn and careened through the red lights down E Street past the White House and up 17th and they were on Connecticut Avenue before he knew it. Only when they were spinning around Dupont Circle on the two right wheels did the cabby call out. "What's the hurry?"

"Gotta get a report to the GAO by three. I want you to wait for me when we get to the Bureau of Standards and then get me back to the old Post Office and then to the old Pension building. Another two bucks if we make it by three!"

"You're on!" The cabby raced around the right of a grimy red oil truck. They heeled into the angle at Kalorama Road and screeched to a stop behind a concrete truck. The cabby pulled out to the left to pass, but pulled back in as a stream of bumper-to-bumper traffic approached. "They're working on the bridge. It's down to one damn lane."

"Well we gotta go next."

"Yeah, I just..." the cabby turned to look out the back window. "Damn."

Calvin turned to look. Another cab and a long line of stopped traffic blocked them.

The cabby craned his neck, ground his gears and jumped the clutch as he laid on the horn and forced his way in front of a cream and blue Hudson ragtop. "All this damn construction!" They crept across the bridge and through the stoplight.

Calvin reached for his watch. Twelve twenty-eight!

The driver glanced at him in his rear-view mirror. "Hey, how long is it going to take you at Standards? You ain't gonna have but a minute."

"This is it! Pull in right there! Second building!"

The cab whipped around and bounced up the drive, jerking to a stop in front of a long building of snot-yellow brick. Calvin had the door open the instant the cab stopped. He sprang from the seat, but a hand grabbed his jacket and pulled him back in.

Red eyes on a stubbled face with a busted nose glared at Calvin. "That's two bucks mister. I'm not falling for this one!"

"We weren't here in ten minutes!"

"Like hell! Two bucks, pal!" The man released Calvin's jacket and snatched the dollars as Calvin withdrew them from his billfold.

"Wait here!" Calvin jumped out and slammed the door. He dashed up the steps and through the door. He ran in and slid into the receptionist's desk and had to push off to make his left turn down the hall. "Hi! How ya doin?" he called as she yelled after him. He slid to a stop at the last door on the right and burst into a laboratory full of all varieties of waffle irons attached to huge banks of meters and wires wound in spiraling coils. He scooted past two men in white lab coats to reach a bank of green filing cabinets.

"Can I help you?" called one of the men.

"No thanks!" Calvin pulled open the bottom drawer and yanked out a bulging brown file envelope from behind the hanging files. He pulled a hanging file from in front, glanced at another and dropped it back.

The bald man was behind him. "You need authorization to be in here!"

"I left these here when we moved downtown. It's all right," said Calvin. He set the files on the table and jerked through them. "Yes! Yes! Yes! All right!" He clutched them to his chest.

"This is government property and you need some kind of author…"

The door opened and a guard looked in, the receptionist behind him. She pointed at Calvin. The guard closed in as the men in the white coats backed off. Calvin bolted. The receptionist hit him with something as he passed, but he tore down the hall and out the front door.

The cab was gone.

He skidded down the loose gravel in the driveway. His legs tore down the sidewalk. The sound of a motorcycle came right behind him. There was a siren and someone calling "stop!" He unwound his pace, heart pounding. It was over.

Verdie's motorcycle jerked past him. "Get on!" she yelled, and flapped her hand at the luggage rack on her rear fender. "Put your feet on the frame!" She snatched his papers and stuffed them in a leather dispatch pouch on her chest.

"The cops are after me!" He jumped on and grabbed the strut of her saddle seat.

"They're after me too!" She sped down the sidewalk. "Hang

on!" She shot between cars onto southbound Connecticut Avenue just as two D.C. motorcycle cops roared past heading north.

"Crap! They saw me!"

The policemen turned and sirens blared again.

"Can you outrun 'em?" Calvin's neck snapped back as Verdie jerked the gearshift lever back between her flapping skirts.

"Cops ride Chiefs!" She whipped around a milk truck making a left into the Park and Shop center. "This is just a Scout!" The sirens gained on them. "Gonna hafta lose 'em!"

They shot across the Klingle Bridge and hammered through a pothole, wrenching Calvin's lower back. The sirens were right behind but Calvin was afraid to look. "Hang on!" shouted Verdie. The bike skidded sideways, regained traction and smoked across the street and between the bronze lions and into the National Zoo. They lay down into a hard right turn, smoked up a concrete path and the sirens receded. The free-flight cages shot past—toaster-shaped, wire-covered dirigible frames. Now the sirens seemed in front of them, but they were just screeching birds. They scattered a school group as an elephant bellowed on their right. Sirens came nearer. They roared down the hill sending families scampering behind the lizard-capped columns of the reptile house. Men in uniform ran out in front of them.

"Cops!" yelled Verdie. "Where the hell are they when you need 'em?" The back wheel skidded again. "We'll go around the bears!" The engine roared and Verdie stood on the footplates to better see a brown bear pacing for peanuts. "I love bears!" She threw her body sideways to bring the motorcycle back on the path after they bounced down a short flight of stairs. She snatched at her prosthetic leg. "Damn! The roller cord again!" The sirens were hard behind them at the crest of the hill. She turned the bike onto a path angling steeply down the valley and fumbled with her leg for a moment, then pulled it free and tucked it between her bottom and the seat.

They wobbled over the stone bridge and onto Rock Creek Parkway. Verdie's hair lashed at his face and into his mouth, gagging him as he shouted, "Where are they?" Water sprayed out in wings as they plowed through the ford across Rock Creek.

"Maybe ahead of us!" she called back. Their engine note reverberated under the huge vault of the Calvert Street Bridge. "I warned you about that goddamn rat, didn't I?" They flew down the center of a freshly paved lane of the new parkway, passing bewildered workmen left and right, laying down on the curves, losing the sound of the sirens. Verdie shifted up again as they shot below the daffodil-dotted slopes of the cemetery.

As they flashed under the Indian bridge a siren came up behind them again. The policeman on his more powerful Indian Chief was quickly beside them, siren wailing, leering at the stocking top and garter strap on Verdie's exposed left leg, pointing for them to pull over. She turned to yell at him and her prosthetic right leg popped out from beneath her. Calvin grabbed at it and hooked it in his arm so hard that the foot kicked him in the teeth. The cop looked up and saw the second bare leg where one should not be. A horn blew in front of them. The cop looked up at an asphalt truck dead ahead. His tires smoked, his bike wobbled and he dropped back behind them.

They sailed under the streetcar trestle and buzzed across the plank-covered bridge beside the old stone lime kilns. As they approached the river, the sky opened out and the cool air offered a quick catalog of industrial stinks. Sirens grew loud again, enveloping them on the straight stretch by the brewery as two cops overtook and sandwiched them. Verdie tried slowing and surging ahead, but the cops converged and blocked the way. She pushed left onto a feeder road of the parkway, but the cops saw she was trying to make a break cross-country for the Mall and they forced her slower and slower until they stopped in sight of the top of the Lincoln Memorial.

Calvin's ears rang so badly that all he could hear was barking from the policeman. He forced his grip loose from the seat strut so that he could raise his hands—just as Verdie popped the clutch and the bike shot forward. His legs flew up as he hinged back and almost catapulted her from her seat, but then the bike stopped and seemed to stand on its front wheel for an instant, throwing him upright and slamming against her back. "I told you to hang on!" she shouted.

They shot through the cool blackness of an underpass and skidded sideways out into the sun. The concert barge flashed behind in his peripheral vision. The instant that their forward motion stopped, Verdie popped the clutch and gunned the bike to climb, bumping up the broad marble stairs of the Watergate. The angle of the climb put Calvin's ass in the air and trip-hammered his nuts into the luggage rack on every fourth step.

Verdie wove through traffic circling the Lincoln Memorial and then tore down the path between the reflecting pool and the Munitions buildings. Drifting blossoms zipped past them like bullets. The shadow of the Washington Monument was the blink of an eye. They skidded down the dirt path between the greenhouses on the Mall and turned onto 12th Street. The girls were waving from the corner at Pennsylvania Avenue. Linda held out the fat brown envelope. Verdie snatched it, tucked it under her dispatch pouch and fired off down the sidewalk to their receding cheers.

Calvin closed his eyes and tucked his head down behind Verdie's back. He heard horns and roars and shouts, felt flashing sunlight and shadow as he floated deeper into a world of dull red and ringing tone. The motion stopped and Verdie was shouting. He opened his eyes to the red mass of the huge brick

Pension Building with its frieze of endlessly marching Yankee soldiers. She shook the bike from side to side to hurry him off. He stood and eased off the rear of the bike, but could not straighten up. Calvin heard her shout "Gimme the leg!" He shook his head, uncomprehending. She shouted again. "Gimme my damn leg!" She had been jerking at it but he would not let go. She slapped the envelopes and folders into his hand.

Calvin waddled toward the steps, hunched in pain. Verdie shouted after him, "Fix your hair," but the words made no sense to him. He turned. She was brushing at the top of her head. He nodded and brushed his hand across his head. He could not recall the last time he replaced the hard maple pressure caps in the T-joint of Verdie's knee. With a jolt, he remembered where he was.

Calvin pushed through the huge door into the cacophony of a thousand GAO clerks clacking at a thousand keyboards. Three desks with busily typing clerks lay between him and the first wall of partitions. He hobbled forward, but a guard appeared and directed him to the tall man at the second desk. The man at the desk took Calvin's manila envelopes and glanced at the numbers on the back. Consulting a table, he added another set of numbers and slid the corner of the envelope into a machine that stamped a red circle with a stubby arrow pointing at the time of day. He thrust the envelope back into Calvin's hands and called out, "Go up around to the right! Up the stairs! First desk!" He returned to his typing.

Calvin stumbled up the wide marble staircase and found a desk and a female clerk at the top of the second flight. She had a face that seemed to be all in the same flat plane. She stared at his hair for an instant as she took his envelope. There was no chair in front of her desk. Was standing part of the trial? The woman did not open the envelope but looked instead at a large grid map on her desk. He dully realized he was at another way station. Below the railing, a sea of typists tapped at rank upon rank of gray machines. Eight colossal Corinthian columns dwarfed the phalanxes of accountants. White partitions, buttressed at their intersections by filing cabinets, divided the huge floor like a chocolate box with a vanilla man or woman in every square.

The clerk waved the envelope at Calvin to get his attention while keeping one finger on the map. "G nineteen!" She tapped one finger on the drawing and pointed over the railing into the ocean of clerks. "Down the stairs, go right to the end, go left up to aisle G, then back to desk G nineteen. If you get lost, please do not interrupt anyone. Just come back here."

Calvin eyeballed his course, nodded to the clerk and took back his envelope. Working his way down the corridors, he stepped aside for hustling, folder-toting clerks, weaving a path through the beaverboard maze. The walls were oddly free of the ubiquitous WPA posters instructing citizens to BRUSH YOUR TEETH, EAT A BALANCED DIET, or MAINTAIN MACHINERY PROPERLY. The assault of noise from slapping keys, totalizings and carriage returns peaked at every breach in the wall on his way to aisle G. Not a single head on either side glanced up from its typing, sorting, counting or examining as he passed. Ahead on the right he could see G nineteen and a man's hat and coat hanging on the tree by the opening. Calvin squeezed his fat envelope and felt a painful quiver in his lower back.

The man with the tiny black mustache introduced himself but the words never reached Calvin's brain. He sat and watched the man pull the contents from the envelope. What was that tactic from *Win Friends and Influence People?* Calvin's eyes searched the office for a clue, a photograph, something that he could compliment or show an interest in, but the walls of the open-topped office were as bare as those outside. The man pulled an iridescent pen from his vest and tapped it at each line of the questionnaire. He went through each page, tapping with the unopened pen. When he reached the final page, he set it carefully on his blotter and took up Calvin's folder of supporting material. Flipping through it, he asked Calvin if this folder contained the entirety of his accounting including all vouchers, warrants, invoices and receipts. Calvin nodded and choked out a yes. The man then told him he was going to number each item with his stamp and that Calvin was to initial each one to the right of the number and then place it face down on the desk to maintain the order. Calvin nodded and the man added the thump of his automatically advancing numerical stamp to the roar of the building. Calvin took each item and penned in his CC.

When he initialed the last document — a draft of a pamphlet instructing farmers how to calculate manure overlap with spiral beater spreaders — the examiner passed a single-page document across the desk. He explained that providing false or misleading information to the General Accounting Office was a felony and that signing this document was his confirmation that the information provided in the questionnaire and all attachments were true and accurate and to sign right here. Calvin signed and the examiner placed the certification in a separate folder of similar documents.

"All right sir! Let's take a look at your file," said the man, sounding like a too-happy dentist. The examiner pulled a folder from his in-box, opened it and stopped at what he saw inside. "Oh!" The examiner's face paled. "You've been flagged."

"Flagged?"

"Yes." The man rose from his desk and looked up at the giant columns as if they were watching him. He fussed with his hair and tie, gathered the folders from the desk and said, "You need to stay right here. Do not leave this office until I return."

"Can I…" said Calvin, not sure what he was asking for.

"No, just stay right here," said the man. He cleared some

papers from his desk and placed them in a filing cabinet and closed the drawer. "Wait until I get back. Just stay right here."

Calvin shivered in his sweat-soaked clothes as he stood and watched the man hurry off with all his reports under his arm. Sharp new pains wrestled with the dull ones in his back. Was there a jail under the marble floor of the Pension building? Were they even now herding the girls into the elevator? Was Verdie clubbing away with her leg at the cops in a last-stand-at-the-Alamo scene? His left shoulder ached and a ringing began in his ears. He stood with effort and raised up on tiptoe enough to look out at the tops of heads bobbing down aisles like coconuts in hidden rivers.

Far away, beyond the giant columns, behind the railing on the second floor, he glimpsed his inquisitor. The man held Calvin's folders against his chest as he nodded at the words of a woman who was looking, not at the examiner, but directly at Calvin. The woman saw him look, shook her head, and turned back abruptly to his inquisitor. Her dark hair was as stiff and curly gray as George Washington's wig in the schoolroom painting. It moved as a unit when she tilted her head back and patted the folders in the examiner's arms. She took a final, dark look at Calvin, gave her head a shake and stepped back out of sight. The examiner followed.

Calvin doubled over with a sharp pain in his lower back, knowing he would pee blood as soon as he reached the prison. He eased back down into his seat and wondered how much money he had in his pocket.

The examiner swung back in the door. "Well, that saved us a lot of time!" He clicked his tongue and placed a new brown file hanger on the desk. He glanced down at Calvin and laughed, "I guess it saved you and yours a heck of a lot more!" He took all Calvin's documents and piled them on the open cardboard sheets. "All done!" The man closed the file folder, took out his pen, hesitated in thought a moment and then drew a heart shape on the subject tab.

"Who was that? That woman up there?"

The man glanced back up to the second floor and tidied the papers that remained on his desk. "Section chief." He spun about in his chair and placed Calvin's bulging file in the lowest drawer of his filing cabinet. "She's the one who flagged your file."

"So 'flagged' is good?"

"In this case, you bet! In other cases — not so good." The tilt of the man's head hinted at severe understatement.

"So why did we get…good flagged?" Calvin's mouth was so dry he could hardly speak.

The man shrugged as he drew a line through Calvin's name on a list. "Maybe your folks made some kind of positive impression. Probably looked productive to the visiting examiner. You know, everybody typing away. No chitchat. Anyway, that's it for now." He whipped his pen back into his pocket and reached out his hand. "Thanks for coming by."

"Nice…" Calvin tried to swallow. " Nice pen."

"Thanks! It's a Conklin! Birthday present!" said the man, tossing a smile down at his shirt pocket. "Think you can you find your way out?"

Calvin nodded enthusiastically. He could have slashed his way out of the building right now if he was the last man standing against the entire Mongol army.

Calvin hung by his right hand from his coat tree as the women prodded the story of the audit from him. "All the man said was that we must have made a good impression on the inspector."

Anne laughed. "I told you that lamb's blood on the door was a good idea!"

Calvin grimaced and twisted, his testes aching. "Well, apparently, pounding the keys is all the lamb's blood we need. He said there must have been lots of typing and not a lot of chit-chat going on when the inspector looked in."

"That was just dumb luck then," said Linda. "We were hand-checking the last simulation run when the guy looked in."

"Well, if looking busy saved us, then we're going to need a lot more of that regular clerical work going on around here."

The women squirmed in silence. Good as they were at it, typing and filing was the equivalent of ditch-digging for female military officers.

"Clerical work?" Verdie sneered out the word.

Calvin leaned over, distracted by a noise behind his desk. "Maybe Radio Services could use some help with listener mail."

Christina's box on the floor shook as the nursing rat mother scratched an itch.

Linda set her fingertip on a cracker crumb on Calvin's desk and pressed it into dust. "That's pretty low-level labor considering what we're on to with Shirley."

Verdie swung her wooden heel banging against the desk, snorting in disgust. "You want us to answer mail for the cookies and curtains department?"

Calvin linked his hands behind his lower back to stretch, but the pain in his kidneys stopped him. "If we help Radio Services then we can probably count on them to keep looking after us."

Anne gave her head a shake. "So you think the radio section had an angel at the GAO?"

Calvin made a painful shrug. "I don't know who it was. But if helping Radio Services wins friends, and if punching typewriters influences people, we'd better do both."

Linda spoke quietly and quickly. "Sir, maybe you don't realize how close we are to making a breakthrough with Shirley."

"You said it'd be another two or three months."

Linda nodded, but Anne turned to her, frowning. "We're going to need more than that if we really want to shift her to binary."

Calvin held up his hands. "Well, whatever you decide, until your Shirley machine is ready for her debut, we need our little corner of the iceberg to look busy. And I mean normal busy, not..."

Ellen jerked her wheelchair. "So what, precisely, do you want us to do?" she almost shouted. "There's nothing to test anymore!"

For a long moment Calvin surveyed the eyes looking at him. Without knowing the end of his sentence he began, "That's an interesting idea, Ellen — increase the precision."

"Of what?" said Linda. "Of Shirley?"

"Why not? You all work so fast anyway. So what if you work on precision instead of speed for a little while? What if you add one or two more decimal points of precision to the John Deere overlap series?"

They looked back blankly.

"I just want us to increase the amount of keyboard work for a while."

Anne pulled at her hair. "But who on earth needs manure distribution calculated down to a tenth of a TURD?"

"*We* do," said Ellen. She reached over to Calvin's desk and pulled his copy of *How to Win Friends and Influence People* onto her lap. "This book says so. If people only like people like themselves, then we'd better camouflage ourselves to look like a regular office for a while." She turned to Calvin. "If you want, Shirley could take it down to three decimal points."

Linda shook her hair bun. "A *thousandth* of a TURD? Ellen..." She surveyed the faces of her colleagues. "We'd have to re-key all the truncated John Deere data. Do we even have that?"

"I kept the raw sample weight tallies. I suppose we could," said Verdie. "Precision could be traded for speed later on, I guess."

Calvin moaned as he straightened his back. "Three decimal places then. Just for camouflage until we see if radio services needs any help." He supported himself on the edge of his desk, working toward his chair. "Thank you, ladies, thank you."

Linda stayed behind as the others filed out, hesitantly discussing strategies for the new task. She pushed the door closed after them. "What's going on, chief?"

"I saw what a regular office looks like over at the GAO. I didn't see anybody over there sitting and gossiping about numbers as if they were soap opera characters."

"But that's how this sort of work gets done! This kind of math is nothing but relationships!"

"Well, if we're not careful, our mathematical relationship to the U.S. government payroll is going to end up being one big zero." He eased his way down into his chair. "And where else are these girls going to work?" He winced as his bruised buttocks brushed the chair arm. "Tell me, who's gonna give Ellen a job if she loses this one?"

"Don't worry about Ellen! If it weren't for you, we'd have bought a summer camp up in the mountains, or a chinchilla ranch on the Eastern shore, or something." She nodded at the sound of the machine coming through the wall. "But we've stumbled onto something new in there, and we can't give up on it just to impress a bunch of GAO saps."

He pushed his elbows against the desktop to take some of the pressure off of his ass. "That's why I want a compromise. Just a little more typing to keep the wolf away from the door. You still get to keep working on your Shirley machine."

She glared at him, silent for long seconds before pulling the manila envelope from under the stump of her arm. "I'd be a lot more impressed with your sense of sacrifice if your friend with the eyebrows hadn't dropped this off." She flopped the envelope on the desk. "I looked inside, in case it was something you needed at the audit."

"Thanks. I…" He glanced into the envelope and quickly closed it.

She tapped at it. "There's a note on the first page of your little radio script there. Says 'Get the dwarfs to handle the mail and you got yourself a show!'"

Calvin eased his weight onto his elbows again. "Look, I agreed not to do an interview, but this show idea just happened. Maybe it already paid off if it got us a reprieve."

"And I suppose you're Snow White." Linda looked at him and then at the script for a long moment, shaking her head.

He covered the script with his hands. "Oh, you didn't read it did you?"

"Oh, hell yes, I read it. So, this is what you're going to do? Goofy history sketches?"

He flipped the pages. "I didn't think it was that goofy."

"Oh, it's goofy, no question. And it's pretty transparent too." She eased slowly to sit against the corner of his desk. "So, what's Miss Kathryn Dale Harper really like? Us dwarfs get curious about real people, ya know."

Calvin startled himself with how quickly he turned to answer her. "I'm not sure yet." His face was slowly overtaken by an unstoppable grin. "But I sure want to find out."

She looked at him with a face full of things to say, but she bit her lip and gave her head a slow shake. "Well, I've got to retype this thing for you." She tugged the script from his grasp. "It's an embarrassment. And I'm just talking about the typos."

He pulled back at the papers. "I can retype it at home. It's not really part of our work here."

She rolled her eyes. "It'll take me three minutes. I can't let something this sloppy come out of this office."

"Understand me now. I don't want you to stop work on the Shirley machine. We just need to pay attention to appearances."

"No, I understand. And precision is actually not a bad idea. We can trade it for speed later on." She slid the script back into its envelope and shook her head absently. "We can re-key all the John Deere data back to the model 2, and then start on the old Kemp & Burpee if that runs out. Three more decimal points'll keep us punching keys for a good while."

"Great!" Calvin rubbed his nose against a drip. "Just so we look normal."

Linda tucked the script back under her stump. "Too late for that."

16

Across the studio, behind a grove of microphones on stands, the piano sat silent under a quilted cover like a sleeping racehorse. Calvin leaned forward in his chair staring at it, trying to strike an intense, artistic pose as Bubby read over his script. A figure in the hallway passed the small window in the studio door and Calvin whipped his head up painfully quick. He glanced at the clock. Bubby said they would have the studio to themselves until four. The chair creaked as he leaned back, shifting his pose to one of relaxed confidence — which would do just as well if Kathryn Dale Harper should happen by. But this pose quickly grew tiresome as well, and he leaned forward again to poke quietly at the saws, augers and gouges in his pasteboard box.

Bubby finally handed the script back to Calvin. "Okay. You need to write an introduction. You need to say who you are, what you're doing, and who it's for. You need say the title and set the stage. And you have to state that it's a transcribed show at the beginning and at the end. That's a federal regulation."

"Do you want me to write all that now?"

"Nah, its just boilerplate to me. Same on every show,

time-wise. Like the ending, it'll be something like —

> If you would like a measured drawing to make your own folding ladder of liberty, handy around the farm and home, just write to Grandpa Sam's Woodshop of the Air, care of the National Farm and Home Hour, US Department of Agriculture, Washington 25, D.C. Be sure to include a three-cent stamp to cover the cost of duplication. This has been Grandpa Sam's Woodshop of the Air, transcribed from Washington, D.C.

"So 'Grandpa Sam's Woodshop of the Air,' that's the title?"

Bubby pinched at a weeping blister on his left hand. "Hattersley's suggestion, so I'd go with it, if I were you."

"I thought it had a certain buoyancy about it!"

"Thought you'd like it." He grinned at his friend. "Okay, after the close, you need a signature sign-off. Something that will stick with 'em."

Calvin leaned over toward the sound effects table in the center of the studio as he thought. "How about:

> This is Calvin Cobb wishing that, as you slide down that banister of life, all the splinters go in your direction!"

Bubby nodded enthusiastically. "Believe me, that's not too corny."

Calvin rubbed the canvas cover of the wind machine. "Nah! You know we can't end each show with a Confucius-say joke about splinters in the ass."

"Well, it's borderline. So, got any theme music?"
"Not yet."
"This is very psychological, now. You need some old music that's gone out of fashion, but that still has positive associations. Gotta pluck the right strings."

Calvin stared at the piano and flipped through mental images of tattered sheet music. *Willow Weep for Me?*

Bubby shook his head. "It doesn't have to have a wood reference."

"Something by Bela-Bale, maybe, then." He waved away his comment. "Sorry, uh, how bout *Nola?*"

Bubby hummed the tune to himself for a second. "It's bouncy."

"Yes, but is it buoyant?"

"Buoyant enough for government work. Okay, *Nola* for now, and your first sound effect is what?"

Calvin looked at the script. "The auger, I guess."

Bubby wrote the cue on a notepad. "Right, okay, I'll do peanut shells in a meat grinder for that."

"I brought over an auger and a brace," said Calvin, rummaging in his box of tools.

"Wouldn't sound right. Okay, you got sawing here too. Let me hear you saw."

"Rip or crosscut?"

"Both. And I'll do Washington's snoring since you'll be doing the character voices over it."

Calvin pulled his five-and-a-half point Disston No. 9 from the box and rip-sawed down the length of a pine plank spanning two sawhorses. Bubby made snoring sounds, striving for a comic asynchrony. He signaled Calvin to stop. "You know, if this was a union job they'd have to give me actor's pay for the snoring. Alright, lets hear the crosscut."

Calvin changed saws and began cutting across the grain.

Bubby snored while studying the bouncing needle on a meter. He shook his head. "Get a thinner board so it's a little crisper, and I'd better do the sawing too. I can make it funnier."

"Right! Tell me how you can saw funnier than me." Calvin plunked the saw blade with his thumb, making it ring with a "boing" sound.

"It's all in the timing. And that 'boing' you just did is a perfect rimshot for the punchline." Bubby reached with his toe to level the gravel in a big shallow box on the floor. "So, here's your Hessian on guard duty." He stepped in the box, marched in place for a few steps, then swiveled and marched in place again. "We're going to be making history, you know that."

"Well, it's not very good history."

Bubby frowned at him for a second, then grinned and slapped at Calvin's script. "No, not your story itself! Just that it's going to be the first recorded program ever on the networks."

"You mean the second. You did the first. And what's the big deal, anyway?" said Calvin, trying to shift the subject. "Unless there's a scratch or a skip on the record, you can't tell if it's recorded or live — or is that the problem?"

"Oh, that's what they say, but it's just money." Bubby leveled the sound effects gravel with his toe. "It's like Rockefeller oil. Once you control the pipeline, you can strangle the little guys. NBC and CBS put all this dough into their wire networks. But if anyone bypasses them by mailing out shows on disks, there goes the hegemonic power of the dastardly duopoly." He laughed. "I sound like Kathryn Harper."

Calvin glanced at the window and stretched his arms over his head in an exaggerated show of nonchalance. "Are you suggesting that the voice of the American homemaker is a red?"

"Oh, she's very in with that Popular Front jazz." He tossed his head back, regarding Calvin through narrowed eyes. "Are you surprised?"

"Well, it is kind of an odd fit — slip covers and surplus value."

Bubby shrugged. "Lots o' radishes out there still — all stylishly red on the outside but white underneath. But me? I've got you some surplus value right here." He reached into his jacket pocket and handed Calvin two blue tickets.

"Holy cow! Tommy Dorsey! How'd you get these?"

Making a show of adjusting his collar, Bubby affected a hoity-toity voice. "I'm a celebrity now, don't you know? Such things come my way."

"But don't you want go?"

Bubby shook his head slowly. "The dance is out at Glen Echo, right next to the roller coaster. I've heard all the screaming I need to hear for a while." He blew out a breath and sat on one of the sawhorses. "I just burn my hands trying to pull some stupid girder and the next thing you know my name is in the paper and everybody's being nice to me!" He stood, taking control of his breathing before reaching into a bag beneath his table and pulling out a head of cabbage. "So here's when your Kraut gets clubbed." He whacked the cabbage with a short billy club, let a half second of silence pass and grunted "Unhh!" A sequential flopping of his elbow, forearm and fist onto the tabletop made the sound of a body hitting the ground. "Trust me, it's perfect when you can't see it." Bubby nodded slowly as he looked in his little spiral-bound notebook. "Okay, we got the prison door." He leaned over and patted the chain-festooned iron firebox door standing on a short wooden frame. "Got the tunnel." He patted the empty trash drum beside him. "Got your wood gouges, creaking gridiron and unfolding ladder."

Calvin took up the challenge and pointed to a yellow balloon on the cart. "All right. Thumb dragged across the balloon for the creaking gridiron. Where's the folding ladder?"

Bubby picked up a short cedar box with a paddle-shaped cedar lid. He held the lid handle and rubbed it down the edge of the box to make a squeaky opening and closing sound. "Its a turkey call."

Calvin nodded appreciatively. "And the gouges?"

Bubby took up a serving spoon and swept it repeatedly across the tabletop, slowly rolling its point of contact from the bowl of the spoon to finish the sweep with its edge. He bounced his eyebrows in happy triumph and popped Calvin on the shoulder with the spoon. "We're going to be on a tight schedule, so I'm going to give you a production calendar for the whole summer. Enjoy the dance, 'cause you sure won't have much time for a social life once we get going." He glanced up at the wall clock. "Ah! Let's get this place cleaned up."

"I thought we had until four o'clock!"

Bubby crossed the studio to retrieve a broom. "When the piano man speaks, all must obey. He wanted to start at three."

Calvin held a sheet of paper on the floor as Bubby swept the sawdust onto it. "Is Brockwell privy to Miss Harper's pink persuasion?"

"Couldn't be. He's the bone they had to throw over the right side of the fence." Bubby removed the quilted cover from the Steinway grand and began rearranging the microphones. "Some of his stooges in congress invoked the public interest provision of the Communications Act of 1934. As a balance to talking about social security, they say we have to let Brockwell share his helpful hints about blood, soil and *der volk*." He handed the piano cover to Calvin and nodded toward the props table. "He's been trying to get his own radio program for years now."

"What's been stopping him?"

"Stay and listen."

Calvin finished tidying the props and wandered slowly to the booth. He let himself in and began thumbing through the record collection in the dark corner.

Bubby, still in the studio, switched on a microphone so that his voice came on the speaker in the booth. "You may be stuck here for an hour or so," he warned. "We're going to rehearse and then we'll cut one." He made a farting noise. "Or maybe two." He made another.

Calvin found the squawk box switch and keyed it. "You get actor's pay for that?"

"Speaking of breaking wind. Take a look in the back corner there, the long fuzzy thing."

Calvin turned and saw a furry yellow column about five feet tall.

"Pull off the cover," came Bubby's voice.

Calvin unbuttoned the sheepskin at the base of the column and pulled it off. Long polished aluminum tubes sparkled in the windows of the control booth.

Bubby stepped in the booth door, grinning. "You're looking at the new Western Electric D-99089 Tubular Array Directional Element Microphone, manufactured under license from yours truly."

Calvin held the spiral of tubes cradled in his arms. "It looks like a Buck Rogers shotgun."

"That's what everyone calls it—a shotgun mike." Bubby gently polished a smudge from his creation with his sleeve. "Sixty tubes, from sixty inches long down to one inch. Each tube resonates with a different wavelength of sound, and then they all come together at the microphone here at the back. It's like a telescope for sound."

"It's great!"

Bubby shook his head, obligated to conceal his pride. "Problem is, wind makes the tubes resonate like five-dozen coke bottles. The fur coat helps a little."

Calvin aimed the Gatling gun spiral of shiny tubes at his reflection in the window. "Probably makes it a lot less intimidating for whoever you're pointing it at, too."

Bubby nodded, beaming as Calvin slid the microphone back into it sheepskin cover. He pulled a big, glossy acetate-coated aluminum disc from a case and set it on the machine in front of him. "They'll be here any minute." He leaned to peer into the tiny microscope attached to the cutting head over the spinning disc. "Lemme show you how to set up the disc cutter." He turned a small knob as he spoke. "Adjust the needle depth to cut the groove twice as wide as the land."

Calvin was about to look in the microscope when Kathryn opened the studio door and held it for Brockwell. At Bubby's glance, Calvin hunkered back into the shadows of the booth and made a small "don't worry" sweep of his hand.

Kathryn and Brockwell chatted as they laid their coats carefully on chairs. Brockwell was older and smaller than Calvin recalled from their last meeting. Thin, sandy-gray hair occasionally fell across his forehead to touch the tops of his wire-rimmed glasses. As he eased into place at the piano, he swept back his hair and his vest flashed bold diamond patterns from under his straw-colored summer suit. He ran a glissando down the keyboard.

Bubby eased out into the studio and stood at a respectful distance until Kathryn asked him to reposition a microphone so she could sit facing Brockwell. Brockwell threw his head back to clear a fallen lock of hair and saw Bubby moving the microphone stand. He redirected her seating so that she was behind him and then returned to arranging his music on the piano.

To Calvin, all of this was a silent scene played out behind the double-walled glass separating the big studio from the booth. He shivered, remembering Kathryn's toes on the bronze pedals as she played the Bartók folk dances. He didn't like looking at her now, with so much tension in her face. He slowly slid down from his chair and eased out flat onto the floor, pulling a small metal toolbox under his head for a pillow. Bubby returned to the booth, shook his head at the sight of him, and sat ready before his controls. Kathryn's voice came on the overhead speaker. "Bubby, would you like to do a sound check now?"

"Any time, Miss Harper." He put on his headphones and adjusted knobs on his console.

Brockwell's voice drawled over the monitor with an odd mixture of Virginia rhythm with an exaggerated English flattening of vowels. There was also an unpredictable punch of words, as if he was being hit on the back at random intervals. "I know a land of Elizabethan *ways*, an America of *cavaliers* and curtsies. In the southern *highlands* of America we find our *people* of the purest pedigree, and their music too, is unsullied *by any admixture* of jazz. The music of the *true* American folk, of our Anglo-*Saxon* ancestors is the true music of America!"

Calvin rolled on his side and looked up into the slotted vents of the humming amplifiers, drawing in the smell of hot electronics. Inside, ranks of tubes glowed red and lavender like a futuristic city. Calvin blinked his eyes and his imaginary rocket pack let him hover and swoop between the glass towers. He rode his dolphin-sized rocket from atop a black transformer and slalomed between metal-jacketed condensers. His ray gun blasted goose-stepping fascists as they emerged from the intermeshed blades of the variable capacitor. As he hovered over their bodies, Bubby, brave leader of his Armenian allies, awarded him with Tommy Dorsey dance tickets. In her revolutionary red kerchief, Kathryn Dale Harper hopped on Calvin's rocket in front of him.

He could not tell how long he had dozed on the floor, but Bubby was still there, resting his forehead against the control room window. With his headphones on, Bubby made a tempting target for a poke-in-the-ribs surprise. Calvin rose but quickly changed his plans when he saw Kathryn and Brockwell still in the studio. He heard the SCREEE of the stylus cutting into the acetate on the spinning aluminum disc and he tensed as if there was a cake in the oven. He eased into a chair. Bubby turned, moving slowly, his eyes serious and tired. He twisted the dial on the console and the voices from the studio came over the speakers.

"...as in your composition *Plantation Concerto* where you bring in the old Negro spirituals," came her tired voice.

Brockwell's energy was undiminished. "Of course! Even there! You hear the Negro's *Walk all Over God's Heaven*. That, of course, is *simply an* imitation of the old Anglo-Saxon camp meeting song, *To Range the New Jerusalem*. The music has changed *but the* words clearly show the origin. And *Swing Low, Sweet Chariot*, again, a crude imitation *of the* original Anglo-Saxon song which goes:

'His Grounding Chariot Shakes the Sky.
He makes the clouds his home
There all his stores of lightning lie
Till vengeance darts them down'

So you see how *much more* satisfying and beautiful the original is. But now meager and *monotonous* jazz infects even now the pockets of pure Anglo-Saxon *culture that* managed to survive unsullied in our southern highlands."

Kathryn read quickly from her script. "You have said that 'Just as the ocean is in the drop, the drop is in the ocean.' Now if the spirit of the folk is in their music..."

Bubby was staring at the spinning disc when the SCREEE of the cutter stopped and the cutting head lifted. He turned down the booth monitor, shook his head and lifted the disc from the turntable holding it like a lottery ticket that was just one number off. "Take six," he said through his teeth, barely audible.

"They're recording their shows too?" asked Calvin.

"We've started a trend."

Kathryn opened the door and stepped into the booth. "How

far did we get?" She did a surprised double-take at Calvin.

Bubby spoke through clenched teeth. "Drop in the ocean."

"We'll cut another half page."

"Cutting isn't going to help if he's going to keep adding in. The pace is dropping every time you redo it. I've only got three more discs."

"He's used to concerts," she turned to Calvin, tilting her head quizzically, "not radio."

Bubby waggled the wasted disk, shooting a reflection into the studio that made Brockwell blink in irritation. "Well, until they make a machine with a bigger disc, he's the one that's going to have to adapt."

Kathryn sighed and turned toward the door.

Calvin rose from his chair. "Listen, Miss Harper, do you want me to floor-manage?"

She eyed him narrowly. "Is that something you know how to do?"

"He's the best!" said Bubby. "He's floor-managed probably two hundred radio plays."

"Really?" She smiled at Calvin. "Your busy flying career left time for that?"

Calvin flushed. "It was back in high school."

"You've got Calvin Cobb right here, the man of a thousand voices." Bubby shook the reflection of new disc through the window into the studio. "Why don't you have him do Brockwell's voice and get us the hell out of here?"

Kathryn laughed and shook her head. "He'd have to do Brockwell's words, too." She pushed the stopwatch into Calvin's hands and held them cupped in hers for a long second. "If you can get us out of this, just your own voice will be plenty."

Calvin followed her into the studio, shooting a grin at Bubby as he passed out the door.

The few cars passing far below on Pennsylvania Avenue splashed noisily through the Saturday morning rain. Wind-whipped spray found its way into the tower as Calvin took bites from his Chik-O-Lunch candy bar and stared at the relentless one-show-a-week production calendar for *Grandpa Sam's Woodshop of the Air* tacked on the tool cabinet. They got the *George Washington's Liberty Ladder* show on the second take, so he could cross that off. To allow time for duplication and distribution, each subsequent weekly episode had to be recorded thirty days ahead of the broadcast date. That left today and Sunday to finish the script for *The Sawhorse That Saved Thanksgiving*. He tapped his finger on Tuesday; they would record the sawhorse show that afternoon, assuming Brockwell didn't show up and monopolize the studio for hours.

He unlocked his tool cabinet, took a moment to admire the clipping from the *Post* tacked to the inside of the door: "Daring Daylight Robbery at Bureau of Standards," and tucked the Tommy Dorsey tickets into the groove of the panel frame. He opened the other door. There, on the second shelf, sat the Stanley 45, now joined by a shiny black iron fillister plane. He stared at the new arrival for a moment, half irritated and half pleased. He had to groove the poplar boards for the triangular box for the third show, and the night worker's tools would do the job easier than his wooden plow plane. He could glue up the box today and insert the dovetail pins into the corners tomorrow.

He retrieved the double boiler glue pot and alcohol lamp from the low shelves at the end of his workbench. The glue pot felt lighter than it should, and he looked in at the freshly scoured cast iron interior. The midnight worker was apparently above using old, stale glue. Calvin set the pot on its iron stand atop the cabinet, poured in enough amber granules of glue to cover the bottom and then poured in too much water on top of them. He lit the alcohol burner and slipped it under the pot, shaking his head as an imaginary voice nagged him that the glue should soak before heating.

The gamy smell of the heating glue filled the tower as Calvin dug into the stack of oak and walnut planks and retrieved a vaguely remembered length of tulip poplar. He cut off a three-foot length, dogged it onto the face of his workbench and planed its edge until the shavings flowed from his long wooden jointer in an unbroken green ribbon. He flipped the board flat on the bench, jammed the end against the stop and planed the tan faces until their under-surfaces lay green and glinting.

Now the plank needed a lengthwise groove to hold the bottom board. Like loading a pistol, he dropped a quarter-inch-wide blade into place in the Stanley 45, locked and adjusted it with clicks and twists of the nickel-plated thumbscrews. A perfect, narrow shaving zipped from the board with each stroke of the plane.

Planing the groove went too quickly with the night-worker's tools. Calvin looked at the finished board on the bench and then toed at the pile of curled green shavings. He usually counted on this laboring time to think—or rather—to not think; a time to let answers drift in. His story idea for the dovetailed triangular box was lame—Ben Franklin struggling to make a box for his tricorn hat? Too thrifty to have a box with an unused corner? Franklin was already too witty for parody.

The new tools had forced Calvin's stuff to the right end of the cabinet, and he had to search for a moment to spot his brass-backed saw on the top shelf. Everything was clean and in good order, but shifted around. He glanced about, briefly panicking until he found his grandfather's copy of *The Handyman's Book* standing between the black volumes of *Audel's Guide*. A walnut shaving peeked from the top of the book, and Calvin reached for it to see what page the man had marked. The book opened to a library chair that was hinged so that it converted into a stepladder. In quick succession, Calvin thought, *that can be a show*, and, *I need to get this guy an extra key to the cabinet.* Wind shot a squirt of cold spring rain through the clock face above him and a cascade of droplets hit the back of Calvin's neck. He returned the book to its place and stared out the slit window at wind-whipped wavelets of rainwater coursing down the tiles below a downspout. What was that poem?

"*Summma's nice wif sun a shinin'—spring is good wif greens and grass*
An' deys sumpin' nice bout wintah,—tho it brings de freezin' blast"

His breath fogged the glass as he faintly mouthed the words.

"*But the time dat is de finest—whethea field is green or brown*
Is when de rain's a porin'—An dey's time to tinker 'round."

Steps echoed in from the hallway, women's shoes. He squiggled two fingers through the mist on the glass, drew in a deep breath and belted out loud.

"*Den you mends de mules' ol harness,—and you mends de broken chair!*"

His voice reverberated in the tower. Linda cautiously poked her head in the door.

> *"Hummin' all de time you's workin' — some ol common kinda air."*

She entered, followed by Anne, smiling as she carried a looped-over length of paper. Linda eyed him sideways to acknowledge his harmless madman act. Calvin stretched out his arms to present them with a view of the rain-rattled window.

> *"Evah now and then you look out — tryin mighty hard to frown.*
> *But you cain't, you glad its rainin' — and deys*
> *TIME TO TINKER 'ROUN'!"*

"Bravo, Chief," said Linda. "Your writing's improving."

"It's not mine, housekeeper we had used to recite that."

Anne spread the long scroll of paper on the workbench. "Well, we've been tinkerin' round too. Look here."

Linda placed her hand flat on the paper. "Those changes you've been making on your script are so small, but if you add words and push it on to a new page then I have to retype the whole darn thing to the end, so here's what Anne came up with."

Calvin looked at his words perfectly typed on the long roll of tractor-feed paper. "You typed the whole thing on one long sheet."

"No," said Anne, "Little Shirley did it." She pulled a stack of cards held together with a rubber band from a pocket in her flower-printed work apron. "Linda typed the whole thing in on these punch cards. Now when you make a change, any one of us can just shoot through to the card with the change, fix it, and then Little Shirley sends the whole thing to the printing tabulator." She held up the top end of the scroll. "And that'll give you this."

Calvin shuffled his hands to move through the script. "No

page-turning noise." He nodded approval and both women smiled. "Can you make carbons?"

Linda shook her head. "We'll just run it twice. So this is okay?"

"It's fine with me. I'm sure they'll be impressed at radio services, too. How's the three-point precision going?"

"Fine." Linda smiled and tapped at the script. "Listen, speaking of punch cards, Anne has a punchline for this sawhorse story if you want it."

Calvin groaned and cradled his face in his hands.

"What are you groaning at?" said Anne. "You haven't even heard it yet."

"I'm just embarrassed for you to read this stuff."

Linda flattened a rumple in the paper. "Well you should be. It's beyond silly. I mean, for cryin' out loud, the Pilgrims can't have their first Thanksgiving because they can't make sawhorses to support planks for extra tables? It's just dreadful."

Calvin wiped his eyes. "I know. It's terrible. So what's your punchline, Miss Parker?" He turned to Anne, but she was pointing up at the four converging clock shafts above their heads.

"You know," said Anne, "we do have two of those alphanumeric tabulators. There's no reason we couldn't run both of them off the same 601 machine."

"Oh! We could try it," said Linda, looking up. "If we could fix the teletype machine we could use that too — print three scripts at a time."

"Ladies, please," said Calvin. "All this is great, but do set some mannequins down in front of the machines so it always looks like somebody's working around here."

Anne cast her gaze around the tower workshop, shaking her head at the stacked boards, benches and dust. "Have you seen the record cabinet Gabriel's making for his mother?"

"Who's Gabriel?"

"Gabriel Valentine. You know. He's been working up in here at night. Captain Valentine, our janitor — that's his son."

"That's Captain Valentine's son?"

"Gabriel, sure. "I wanted him to make one for me. And we got to talking about functional design and dynamic balance."

"You and Gabriel?" asked Calvin.

"Sure. There's plasticity…but there's a formula for artistic value. Order over complexity. A Chinese Chippendale piece has lots of complexity, all the little holes and fretwork, so you need a lot of order, like geometrical repetition to control it."

"How's his court case coming?" asked Linda.

"They dismissed charges."

"What charges?" says Calvin. "What did he do?"

"Nothing!" says Anne, defensive against Calvin's alarm.

Linda steps in. "The kids at Howard are all worked up about Ethiopia. Gabriel joined in on a sit-down to block the ROTC building and somebody threw a bottle."

"Thank God, the judge dismissed charges," says Anne. She shakes her head, marveling at something. "They were going to kick him out of Howard, but since he's got the lead in the *Wild Duck*, they reconsidered."

"He's an actor too? You're sure this is the same guy that works up here at night?"

"Gabriel? Oh sure! He learned cabinetmaking at Hampton, but he can do anything!"

"Helloo," came a voice from the corridor. "Hello, anybody here?" Kathryn Dale Harper leaned through the door, wearing brown coverall slacks, a Filson jacket and oiled silk scarf. "Hello! The janitor said you all were up here."

Calvin jumped up from half sitting on the bench. "Gosh, Miss Harper, hello."

She untied the knot in her scarf and pulled it from around

her neck. "Oh please, Calvin, call me Kathryn. Let's see, it's Anne and Linda, am I right? We met when I was here last time. Hope I'm not interrupting again." She half winked at Calvin.

He grabbed at the script and began rolling it up. "Well, Kathryn, what a surprise."

She glanced up at the big clock faces. "Nice place you got up here."

"Needs curtains," said Linda and Anne simultaneously.

Kathryn laughed and pointed up to the clock face and the shadow of the hands cast by the emerging sun. "That can't be the right!"

Calvin smiled. "Time runs backwards when you're inside the clock."

She made delighted head cocking movements. "I should spend more time up here."

Calvin glanced quickly around the tower for something resembling a chair, but there was only a sawhorse. "This is our research lab. Where we make our test equipment." He knocked away the half-eaten candy bar on the workbench. Anne and Linda traded glances at his clumsy eagerness.

"Well, I won't hold you up. I just wanted to drop off some photographs and things for you." She unbuttoned her jacket and pulled out a yellow enlarging paper box and set it on the bench. "Looks like its brightening up out there." She nodded toward the window. Steely light made quicksilver of the droplets on the glass. Calvin jumped to help her as she removed her jacket. "Thanks. Oh, be careful please! My camera's in the pocket." She retrieved a stubby chromium camera from her damp jacket. The shutter clicked and the camera whirred. "Oops. Hope I got you with a smile!"

"Oh, it's a RoBot!" says Anne. "May I see it?"

"Sure," says Kathryn, handing it to her. "It's wound up, so

don't touch the shutter button unless you want to take a bunch of shots real fast." Anne lifts the gleaming steel handful to her eye, turns and looked through the viewfinder at Calvin.

"Anne used to be Signal Corps," explains Linda.

Anne's light brown hair fell back from her face as she pointed the camera up at the clock faces. "It's heavy for being so small."

"That..." Kathryn began, but the sight of the rubber-band scars on the hollowed left side of Anne's face made her gasp, "...that's the spring motor that's so heavy. But you can use it with one hand."

"That'd be handy for me," said Linda. "How are the pictures?"

Kathryn spread her damp scarf to hang over the end of the bench, carefully straightening out the wrinkles. "For snap shooting it's great. Has an f2 lens in the 40 millimeter, but no range finder."

Anne showed the exposure counter ring to Linda. "See? RoBots shoot square pictures so you get fifty on a roll—more than with a Leica."

"It's fast, but it's a trade-off," said Kathryn. "I'd prefer a Contax, but an old admirer gave this one to me."

"Nice boyfriend," said Anne, studying the arc of specifications on the lens ring.

Kathryn shook out her hair and stretched her arms up at the clock gearing. "He probably got it cheap. Every refugee coming off the boat has four Leicas around his neck."

Anne handed the camera back to Kathryn. "Well, I'm ready for a new one."

Kathryn smiled at her. "What, a new boyfriend or a new camera?"

Anne laughed. "Oh, a new camera. Either a Leica or a RoBot like that."

"Not so fast," said Linda. "A robot boyfriend might not be so bad!"

The three women stifled laughter. Kathryn bent over to straighten the wet cuffs of her coverall legs. "Well, listen, you're all working on a Saturday morning and I'm just barging in." She glanced at the scroll of paper on the workbench. "Oh, you were working on a script."

Anne clapped her hands. "Oh, I forgot to tell you the punchline!" Her eyes sparkled. "At the end, when the Indians get angry because there's no place for them to sit and eat, and the Pilgrims are still fiddling with formulas and protractors to figure the angles on the legs of the sawhorse, have the Indian chief say 'Typical paleface, always putting *Descartes* before the horse.'"

Calvin put his hand to his mouth and pulled at his nose.

Linda grinned at him. "Get it? The Pilgrims get all tied up in the geometry calculations and can't make an intuitive leap."

"Oh I get it." Calvin closed his eyes. Ancient Fred Allen gags were fair game.

Linda popped him on the shoulder with the bundle of punched cards. "Give it time, it'll grow on you." She picked up the scroll-script. "Come on Anne, let's get to work on that robot boyfriend of yours." The door closed behind the two women.

Kathryn put her hand to her head. "Oh, I can't believe I made that comment to Linda about using the camera with one hand."

"Gosh, don't think a thing about it. They joke about it all the time."

She shuddered and wrapped her arms around herself. "So listen, I acted like a sap when we first met."

"No you didn't! Besides," he grinned and pointed up at the clock faces, "time runs backwards up here."

She looked up and nodded approval. The glue pot atop the alcohol lamp suddenly sizzled as the water boiled over. "Your soup's on." She wrinkled her nose.

He turned the alcohol lamp down, and considered making a joke, like "It really sticks to your ribs," but he just smiled and stirred the amber granules to blend with the hot water. "It's glue."

She squinted past him at the Dürer engraving tacked to the cabinet door and stepped over to look more closely at it. "That should be in a museum." She glanced around the room. "But maybe it already is." She picked up her yellow enlarging-paper box and flipped it open. "I've been going through some FSA photos for the rural life exhibit. I pulled out the wood-crafting shots — thought they might give you some inspiration."

Calvin stood beside her and took the top glossy photograph from the box — an elderly black man seated between two large heavy workbaskets. He was pulling a thin strip of wood across his knee while scraping it with butcher knife. Calvin pointed to wood strip. "White oak."

"You can tell from the photo?"

"That's all it could be. That's how the *Uncle Remus* book begins. He's making a white oak fish trap at the start of the book."

"Really? Well, anyway, that's Bayard Wooten's photo. Most of these are Doris Ulmann's." She pulled another photo from the stack, beautiful sepia of a barefoot young woman in a bonnet and simple dress holding a dulcimer with four heart-shaped sound holes in its face.

"Nice," said Calvin.

"Fake," said Kathryn. "Look." She pulled out a photograph of a man seated before a fireplace, also holding a dulcimer. "See, it's the same instrument in both shots. It belongs to this guy, who is actually a conservatory-trained musician, and incidentally the photographer's long-time paramour."

Calvin compared the two photographs, wondering if he'd ever heard the word "paramour" used in conversation before.

"So who's the barefoot beauty in the first photo?"

"A medical student on summer break that looked the part of a poor mountain girl." Kathryn laid another photograph on top of the pair. "Here she is again, this time with a spinning wheel. I guess the real mountaineers weren't so reliably photogenic. Folklore and fakelore, it all gets blended up."

Calvin flipped slowly through the photos in the box, stopping on a photo of a grizzled man whittling the figure of a sleeping fox. "Lots of ideas here. Thanks so much." He wanted to look at her instead of the photos, but she was studying his reactions too closely.

She snapped open the black leather camera case that hung around her neck. "I brought these too. I put them in here because they looked so fragile. These doo-dads." She spilled a jumble of wooden whimsies out onto the bench top. "All these wooden chains and things."

Calvin extracted a looped chain whittled from basswood that could be worn like a necklace. He whistled in admiration of the dangling cage containing three free-moving spheres — all carved from one piece of wood. He placed it in her hand. "Do you know the story about how these were all made entirely with an axe?"

"These tiny things with an axe? A tree-chopping axe?" She squinted at the half-inch square by two-inch long cage.

"Yeah, there's an old country story about how you get a hoop snake to come rolling down the hill after you, rolling with his tail in his mouth."

"A hoop snake?"

"They're called hoop snakes 'cause they grab their tail in their mouth and roll downhill after you. Hoop snake doesn't have any teeth to bite you with, just has the venom in his tail stinger that makes you swell up big and soft so he can gum you to death."

"Because it has no teeth."

"Exactly. So you tease 'em and get 'em to roll down hill and sting a stick of wood instead of you. Something the size of a broomstick will swell up to the size of a streetcar. Then you chop out whatever pattern you want with your axe and then toss some turpentine on it to make the swelling go down and…" he picked up the carving from her hand, "when it shrinks back," he shook the balls in their cage. "…this is what you get."

"Where'd you hear that?"

"Old colored man that worked for my grandparents. Full of all those briar patch kind of stories, knew all these remedies and nature signs and stuff."

"Old colored man, huh? They do the same thing with the gypsies."

"What's that?"

"They attribute miraculous powers to those they deny real power."

Calvin wasn't sure who "they" were. "Wish you could have met him."

She looked up at the now brightly sunlit clock faces. "Well, if I stay up here long enough with time running backwards, maybe I can." She slid the leather case around her camera and retrieved her scarf. "Looks like it's clearing up."

He wiped at the raindrops from his bench top with his sleeve. "Are you…on assignment?"

"Just for myself. I was shooting some old brick makers working out in Alexandria but the rain got too bad." She cast her eyes down at the yellow clay clinging to the edges of her shoes. "They're the real thing—unbroken tradition." She paused and considered him. "They start firing the bricks next Saturday. You might find it interesting, if you want to come along."

And no sunlit clock face could have shown brighter than his.

Calvin let the broadcast debut of *Grandpa Sam's Woodshop of the Air* pass unheard by himself. The sacrifice of any celebration was the least he could make in return for living in this stolen season. But then came the first stamps in exchange for the measured drawings — this was joy forced upon him! He swept the half-dozen three-cent stamps from his desk and dropped them into the glass Prince Albert jar and closed the lid. At some point he had to walk them over to the Post Office building for an eighteen-cent credit. A tin letter box by the door held the six government envelopes containing the six measured drawings that he hand-addressed to the six listeners. He retrieved them and typed a record of the six addresses, taking pride in the strike of each key on the paper. If more than six people were listening to *Grandpa Sam's Woodshop of the Air*, the evidence would be waiting for him across the Mall at South Building.

Calvin stretched and arched his back as he walked. He turned sideways to let the sun reach muscles cramped from nights spent hunched over his drawing board, still delighting in the challenge of condensing the plans for each of the projects down to a single sheet. Just as each program had to fit into fourteen minutes and forty-eight seconds of time on a disc—each isometric drawing (with step-by-step instructions) had to fit into eight and a half by eleven inches of space on a paper.

At the Radio Services receptionist's desk, there waited a dozen or so more requests for the folding ladder plans. Calvin offered the bored girl his box of Beechies as he admired the framed magazine clippings of stories on Kathryn Dale Harper. "Nice day for it," said Calvin, trying out a jaunty demeanor.

The receptionist took one of the chewing gum tablets and pushed it to the corner of her blotter. "Boy, I'd love to get out of this basement and find that out for myself." The intercom on her desk buzzed. She flipped the toggle with her left hand. "Yes, Mister Hattersley?"

"Cobb's coming over to get his mail. Ask him to come see me when he arrives."

She raised her eyebrows at Calvin. He nodded. She fingered the toggle. "He's standing right here. Shall I send him in?"

"Yes," came Hattersley's voice after a long pause.

Calvin stopped in the doorway when he saw Brockwell seated in front of Hattersley's desk. Brockwell swept his hair back from his face. "How is your postal response coming?"

Calvin, easing into a chair, said. "Coupla dozen, I guess."

Hattersley dismissed the number with a wave. "Well don't worry. Everything takes a while to catch on. Has everyone been helpful?"

"Very much so. Thank you. I really appreciate it."

Hattersley's eyes darted about the room. "Good. Now, Calvin, I know you're interested in television too." He spoke slowly. "You may know that Mr. Brockwell here was in Berlin for the Olympics. While he was in his hotel, he was able to watch the events on the German national television system."

Brockwell held up both his hands to make a picture frame.

"It was a glimpse of the future!"

Hattersley picked at his thumbnail. "Since you won't be able to do soap operas or comedies on television, Mr. Brockwell very wisely wants to stockpile cultural material for eventual television broadcast."

Calvin rose to the bait. "Why can't you do soaps and comedies on television?"

Brockwell smiled. "Because of the scripts! It might interfere with believability to see the Lone Ranger carrying his script around. You certainly can't have actors memorize a whole new show every day."

"I never thought of that," said Calvin.

Brockwell crossed his legs and leaned forward like a constipated gargoyle. "Yes, but you have to think ahead, Calvin Cobb. Television receivers will be so expensive they'll only be available to the successful, and they won't transmit for any real distance, so they'll only be available close to the cities. Unlike American radio, American television is going to be a very highbrow affair."

Calvin nodded, suddenly tired. *Grandpa Sam's Woodshop of the Air* was anything but a highbrow affair.

"You record your next program tomorrow?" asked Hattersley, making quick glances at Brockwell.

"Show number four." Calvin wondered if this was good or bad.

"I hate to have to ask you this," said Hattersley, "but we need you to move up the next studio date to Saturday afternoon." And for your next two programs," he studied the calendar on his desk, they'll have to be recorded this coming Saturday afternoon."

Calvin's mouth fell. "Two shows?"

Hattersley looked at the floor. "It's a scheduling problem. Mr. Brockwell is going to need the studio for the next few weeks."

"We can record next weekend, maybe, but two shows a week!"

"Mr. Brockwell needs next weekend. He needs…the studio, Calvin."

Calvin's mouth tasted like tinfoil. "I can't come up with another program overnight. Wouldn't it be better to just find a time and squeeze it in, rather than have to slam something together?"

Hattersley began to speak but Brockwell cut him off, waving a dismissive hand. "Young man, don't underestimate yourself. In fact, I hope this will free up more of your time so you can work with me. You were a God-send the other day."

Hattersley rose in his chair, as if to take charge, but backed away instead. "I explained to Mr. Brockwell your unusual relationship to radio services — that you are working on detachment from your own research section."

Calvin struggled to his feet against an invisible weight. "Well, that's right! This radio work is already more than I should be doing, and I've got other plans for this Saturday."

He had addressed his words to Hattersley, but Brockwell answered. "This seems hard now, but it is so much better for you in the long run. Calvin, trust me."

Calvin avoided Brockwell's eyes by turning to Hattersley, but the man was biting his lip and looking at the papers on his desk. "I'd better get to work, then. Does Bubby know?"

"He's already got you scheduled," said Hattersley, without looking up.

Bubby's head poked around the corner at the end of the hall. "So you got the word?"

Calvin followed him into the booth. "Yeah, what the hell?"

"Calvin," Bubby imitated Brockwell's drawl, "we ah goin' to need your help in our great work."

"Really, what the hell is going on?"

Bubby gestured into the empty studio. "Brockwell must have something on everybody. We've got congressional offices calling to make sure we're taking care of him." He shook his head at Calvin. "He lit into Harper about something."

"What? What about?"

"I don't know, but she let him have it right back."

"At least someone's standing up to him." Calvin rubbed his forehead. "So is this just vindictive, or do we have to do two shows just because he wants a personal recording studio available when ever he wants it? How am I supposed to come up with a new program so fast?"

Bubby shrugged. "Ah, the guys who write *Lum & Abner* crank out a script in two hours flat, every day."

"Well, it's a hell of a lot easier when you know all your characters and have a few hundred old situations to draw on. I'm just getting started!"

Bubby rolled a screwdriver back and forth between his palm and his bench top. "Imitation is the sincerest form of radio."

"You want imitation?"

"I don't want anything! I'm just saying you don't have to come up with something entirely new. You know lots of stories. You've made lots of things. See if there's something you can match up."

Calvin's eyes narrowed. "You don't seem very upset. This show is pretty important to me!"

"It's important to me too, but it doesn't have to run everybody's life. Look, we do two shows this weekend and you're off for two weeks and I get a few days in Chicago."

"I'm not off! I still work. And I've got other things I need to do."

"Look, he's just treating you like a pro. It's June. America goes on vacation! Hattersley's trying to get away too. It's easier than you think." Bubby spun about and retrieved a manila envelope from his desk. "Here, Kathryn left these for you."

Calvin opened it. More photographs. A hillbilly carver standing by a fence with a bundle of twisted walking sticks at his feet. Another old man making the rim of a basket. An old woman operating the spiral-screwed wooden shaft of a rifling machine

"So how are you and Miss Harper getting along?" asked Bubby. His black eyebrows bounded suggestively.

Calvin slipped the photos back in the envelope. "She's hard to keep up with. One minute she's Emily Post, the next minute she's Emma Goldberg."

"God save us from the uncertainty of Hisen-babes." Bubby shook his head in mock seriousness. "Once you figure out what she wants, she's already moved on."

Calvin backed out into the doorway. "So, it's impossible?"

Bubby sat back at his bench and plugged in his soldering iron. "Just solve for the constant. For you, mister woodworker, that would be Planck's constant." He flipped a vacuum tube-studded metal box on its side, snipped out a flat, brown capacitor and tossed the dead component in the trash. "Just so she doesn't get Bohr-d with you."

Calvin stood, watching for a second, gathering thoughts, taking stock. The mail still waited on the receptionist's desk. The envelope under his arm held Kathryn's photographs. "What time does everyone arrive for tomorrow's show?"

"*Farm and Home Hour*? Nobody's here before ten, if you want to get one of those shows out of the way. Is that what you had in mind?"

"No, not just one," Calvin bounced the door open with his butt and stepped into the hall, "both of 'em."

WPA GUIDE

TO OUR BEAUTIFUL NATION'S CAPITAL

Washington, D.C.

INCLUDES MAP OF PROMINENT LANDMARKS AND MONUMENTS

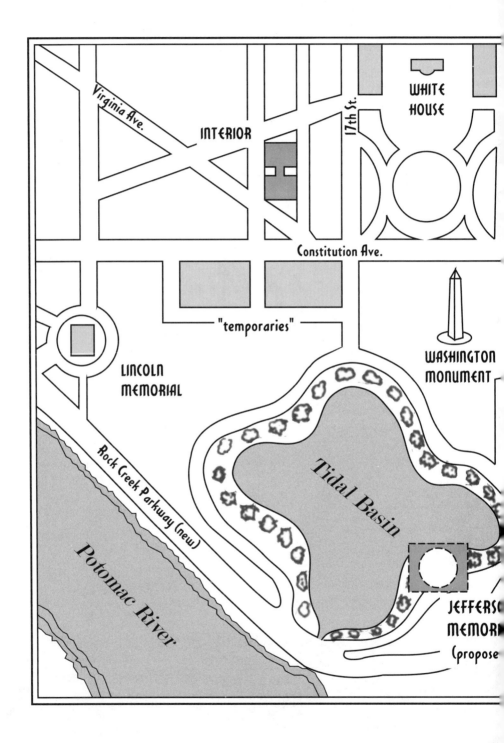

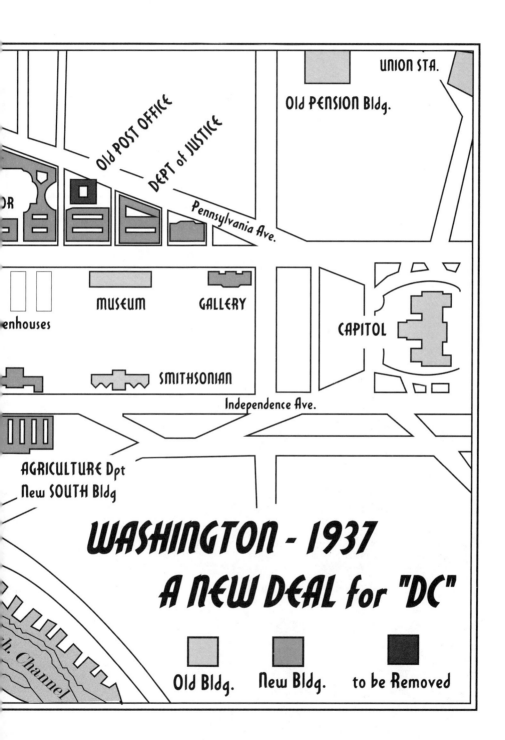

Yet another Federal building scheduled for demolition is the Old Post Office on Pennsylvania Avenue. The massive clock tower has been a beacon for Washingtonians since the 1890s. Although outdated, it is an architectural curiosity well worth seeing!

The clock face gleams like the moon when seen through the skylight of the great atrium of the Old Post Office at night. The lower glass roof of the atrium kept noise from the old mail sorting equipment from disturbing workers in the upper floors.

WPA GUIDE TO WASHINGTON, D.C.

Among the delights of the Old Post Office are the accidental figures in the marble sheathing of the first floor. Here, the "cat" greets visitors at an office near the 12th Street entrance hall.

Three hundred feet above Pennsylvania Avenue, the old Post Office tower clock gets its annual cleaning and touch-up. Combining the art of the painter with the agility of the steeplejack, these men are just two of the many thousands who have found meaningful employment under the aegis of the Works Progress Administration.

The Department of Agriculture's Radio Extension Service brings farmers daily advice on modern methods of soil conservation and fertilizer application. Even in the farthest reaches of rural America, citizens can tune in to edifying programs produced by experts in everything from sewing to soybeans!

The Old Pension Building is another relic of a grander time. With the expansion of government services under the New Deal, workers from the General Accounting Office have made their home on the floor of the great hall.

The U.S. Marine base at Quantico, Virginia, preserves relics from the "Halls of Montezuma" to the Great War. Oddities abound, such as this photo of the first Marinettes of 1918! Watch out, Kaiser Bill!

Nearby Maryland offers amusements just a streetcar ride away! Glen Echo Park provides thrills on the coaster dips — and on the dance floor of the beautiful Spanish ballroom!

Farther afield, the Virginia mountains host summer folk festivals that celebrate our musical heritage from the days of yore!

Jamb o' the fence tobacco smoke still lingered in the air as Calvin walked up the dark corridor to the tower. He had just finished counting twenty-nine three-cent stamps into the Prince Albert jar. Little purple George Washingtons, a smattering of violet Mother's Day commemoratives and the occasional oversized purple NRA emergency. But now he stretched his back and sang.

"*When I gets to heabn'*
gonna get out my tools,
gonna work all ober God's heabn',
heabn', heabn.'"

Now, with the night coming on, Calvin was ready with two shows.

"*I got tools, you got tools,*
all God's chillun got tools."

The second show should time out just right. He could do all the characters and sound effects by himself. All Bubby had to do for this second show was cue the theme music and drop the cutter into the spinning blank. His rip saw coursed down through the poplar for the one-piece bookstand, slowing as it approached the pockets chiseled halfway through the plank.

"When I get's to heab'n
gonna saw down my plank.
Gonna saw all ober God's heab'n."

He probed the pockets with his knife, slicing through into the sawn gaps.

"Gonna slice all ober God's heab'n."

The Atwater-Kent warmed up to someone playing *Ain't Misbehavin'* on a concert harp. Calvin sang along with a variation.

"*I'm happy* with *my shelf.*"

He reached to tune another station, but stopped when the announcer said, "The International Night Swing Club is now in session!" The house band began playing "that ultra-jazz impression — *Powerhouse!*" He slipped a framing square into the upper kerf in the poplar board and his ripsaw into the lower one. Gently twisting them both, he levered the two kerfs open until the few remaining fibers holding the joint snapped and the legs spread to make the bookstand. He savored the sound.

An upbeat swing version of *Am I Blue* provided the accompaniment for chiseling off the rough edges. The inane announcer came back to say that CBS was now going to make a live, shortwave connection to Paris and the 'Stef-a-nee' Grappelly Quintet at the Hot Club of Montmartre. Certainly Kathryn would love a trip to Paris. Calvin knelt to crank up the volume so he could hear the muffled, exhausted voice of Ed Murrow over the wind outside the tower. Between the wind, the weakness of the shortwave and the microphone held too far from Reinhardt and Grappelly, Calvin could barely make out *Djangology* amid the café clatter.

He found a cardboard box and packed the saw, mallet and chisel for the sound effects for the Jefferson's Bookstand and Nutcracker show, then decided to leave the box and pick it up in the morning, lest the midnight worker should need the tools before dawn. He placed the finished bookstand on top of the tool cabinet and began chopping down the blank for the nutcracker of springy hickory. With the radio at full volume he could faintly hear them playing *Limehouse Blues*. He called into the echoing air of the tower, "Mayday! Mayday Montmartre! Music's muffled! Make Murrow move the mike! Mayday!" As his turning saw danced through the hickory, the ionosphere over the Atlantic drifted just enough higher to reflect the Paris radio waves smack onto the CBS antennas. The sounds of the gypsy guitar and fiddle flowed clear and full into the tower — just as the wind outside rose to cancel out the improvement.

In the quiet after Calvin switched the radio off, he heard another voice singing. It was the haunting woman's voice echoing in the halls below. The spiritual, *Joshua Fit the Battle of Jericho* rollicked with sweet power. The moonlit clocks showed eleven — which meant one in the morning. He quickstepped to the corridor as the last note echoed. A good omen. An unseen door fell shut far below and a few moments later, a car pulled off outside.

Calvin reset the props and microphone for the second show as Bubby spot-checked the finished recording of the bookstand/nutcracker show. He refused to let Bubby know what he had in store for the second program — except to say that it was Munchausen meets the Kingfish. Bubby locked a fresh disc on the Fairchild studio machine, and the SCREEE of the cutter began. Bubby dropped his finger. Calvin punched his stopwatch and spoke to the RCA 77 as if it were a bunch of kids sitting on the edge of an old front porch.

Announcer: And now, it's Grandpa Sam's Woodshop of the Air. Join us again in that little country woodshop where a visitor has arrived and waits for Grandpa Sam and little Timmy.
Uncle Dan: Oh ah come frum Alabamy wid my ...

Calvin tipped a tomato can of nails on its side and then let the contents spill on a board.

Uncle Dan: Durn, ah dun knocked ober Mr. Sam's can ob nails! Reckon ah bedda jest sit an whittle a bit til Mr. Sam gits here. Kain't jest be doin nothin!

Calvin hummed *Oh Susanna* as he opened and closed the little prop door.

Hello dere Mister Sam, I was ... Oh, it's little Timmy! How you be doin? Waitin fo yo grandad too?
Timmy: I guess so.
Uncle Dan: Why, Timmy, Yo got yo a face longer dan a tapeworm's suspenders!
Timmy: Oh Uncle Dan, it's my friend Conrad, he has all the tools he needs to make everything he wants. He's even getting an electric drill!
Uncle Dan: Well Timmy, I rekon dat Rural Lektrifikshun is lowin folks to be makin all kinda things dey couldn't make befo, but ~~you kin do a lot wid jest what you got!~~ fact 'tiz, de best ting ah eva made wuz wit mah ol' axe -- an wit de help ob an ol' hoop snake!
Timmy: A hoop snake? What's that?
Uncle Dan: Lowd Timmy, de hoop snake is de deadliest ting in God's creation. You know how yer reglar snake has dem fangs t' bite ya wid?
Timmy: Sure, and the fangs on many snakes

	have deadly venom in them.
Uncle Dan:	Dat's right Timmy ~~aldo sanitation id de bestest way to control de vermin, some snakes are also beneficial in controling de rodent population,~~ but de hoop snake ain got no fangs, no, de hoop snake jest got gums in its mout, but it hab a terrible poison stinger in his tail.
Timmy:	Gosh, and it stings you! Why is called a hoop snake?
Uncle Dan:	Causn dats how it hunts. De hoop snake waits at de top ob de mountain, ~~wid his back slithered up in the bark ob a tree, an he waits der~~ lookin wid dem little snakey eyes for sumpin ob de mammalian persuasion to eat to pass by. Den, it casts itself forward and grabs its tail in its mout, and rolls ~~on~~ down de hill in de form ob a hoop, hence de name hoop snake. When hit gets up de speed, de hoop snake straightens out wid his tail to de front and, in a deadly vector ob venom, it sticks dat stinger in de passing prey.

The sight of Bubby's face straining with suppressed laughter almost cracked Calvin up, and he had to struggle to keep his place in his script. He regained his full concentration only when he came to the end of a new sub-plot added to his old hoop-snake story — a contest where the best wood carver got to marry the King's daughter. He signaled frantically for Bubby to get ready to boing the saw blade at the upcoming punch line.

Timmy: They gave you the prize, Uncle Dan?
Uncle Dan: Sho nuff. Evebody look inside dere and see de liddle axe marks in dere and dey say. "Lowud he dun it! He dun dis whole liddle ball-in-de-cage wid his big ole axe! Seein is believin! He gots to be de bestest carver der is!"
Timmy: So that's how come you got to marry Aunt Edith! You won the carving contest!
Uncle Dan: Yes sir, I won de contest, but jest lak you, I didn't get ebyting I wonted.
Timmy: What didn't you get? You won the right to marry Edith!
Uncle Dan: Well, der wus dis constellation prize. Dis beautiful cake dat Edith had baked fo de second bestest carver. I wanted dat cake too. ~~All dat work a choppin had built me up a powful appetite,~~ so I begged fo dat cake, I pleaded fo dat cake. But de king sez, "You hab got enuff. You got my dautter Edith, dats all you gonna git! Only de greediest man would want to hab ... dis cake -- and Edith too!

CALVIN COBB: RADIO WOODWORKER!

Bubby boinged the saw.

Announcer: Well, maybe that's not the way it really happened, but whittling is a fun and inexpensive hobby. And you know what they say: homemade fun costs less, and lasts longer. If you would like to receive instructions on how to whittle a chain with a ball in a cage out of one piece of wood, without using a snake or an axe, just write to Grandpa Sam's Woodshop of the Air, care of the National Farm and Home Hour, U.S. Department of Agriculture, Washington 25, D.C. Be sure to include a three cent stamp to cover the cost of printing. Grandpa Sam's Woodshop of the Air is written and performed by Calvin Cobb and presented in transcription by the Radio Service of the United States Department of Agriculture.

Bubby and Calvin watched in silence until the cutting needle lifted automatically from the disc. Bubby puffed his cheeks and blew off the acetate shavings. "Two in one blow!" He grinned at Calvin.

Calvin stared into the booth. "So this was okay?"

"This was great! Two down in one day, and you're still alive."

"What about the first one?"

"It's fine, but this was by far the best show yet!"

"Do you want another take on the first one?"

Bubby waved him off like a mosquito. "No! It's fine! It's done! Life moves on!"

"Because I could do it again."

"Stop! It's good enough!"

"'Good enough' is not good enough."

"By definition — it is."

"You're sure?"

"I'm sure."

"Okay."

"Okay."

"But if you want…"

"*AIEEEEEEEE!*" Bubby clapped his hands over his ears and tumbled out the door.

Smoke flowed up from the clay-plastered, ziggurat of bricks, thirty feet long and half as high. Beside rows of unfired bricks, a horse walked a muddy circle around a wooden pug mill at the end of a long wooden sweep arm. Kathryn ducked down as the sweep passed over her, laughing with a large black man who stood waist-deep in a pit at the base of the mill, slamming the extruded clay into wooden molds.

Calvin sat on a stack of half-moon shaped bricks and watched her working, springing from one position to another. Every few seconds she lowered her camera to consider the position of the circling horse relative to the fires in the kiln, timing her shooting to frame them in her image just as the man in the pit slammed a loaf of clay into the six-brick mold. A quick conversation, and the man held the clay until she gave the cue.

Kathryn thanked the man in the pit and slipped money into his huge hand. He pointed toward a canvas-roofed drying shed where a white lady was talking with a black taxi driver. She laughed and shook her head. The molder came up out of the pit, unhitched his horse and led him along to make greetings down the row of cars and people. She turned and saw Calvin.

"Is there really something to eat in that bag?"

Calvin grinned and rumpled it. The ground was still too wet to sit on, but there were plenty of stacked bricks within reach of the warmth of the kiln. Kathryn inventoried the food, apportioning thin wooden sporks and paper tubs of potato salad, waxed paper-wrapped drumsticks and cornbread. With his rooming house key he pried the caps off of little cola bottles.

He nodded toward the molding pit. "Are you satisfied?"

She thought he was referring to the food and nodded happily.

"I mean with the brickmaker."

"Oh! Third generation. Yes! With all this restoration work they've got all they can handle. They've done a bunch for Williamsburg, and they're going out to Mount Vernon when they finish here." The cloudless evening sky pushed out its first star. Boys carted split oak logs to the sides of the kiln, eased back sheet-iron covers on the fire tunnels and tossed the wood in as far as they could, sending sparks jetting through the iron-gray smoke. She swept her arm across the vista. "So what do you see here?"

Calvin leaned back on his elbows. "Two things. Comrades joined in the brotherhood of labor. I also see…" he pointed to a man in a dusty DeSoto who was speaking with the molder in the drying shed, "a hell of a lot of moonshine getting sold."

"Well, two points for you! I didn't know until he offered to sell me some."

"And you didn't buy any?" Calvin rose into the radiated heat of the kiln. "Wait here." He walked over to the canvas shed and returned with a pint jar, stopping short, stunned by the moon rising behind the pines. He shook the jar in the moonlight and watched the silvery beads dance half out of the surface. "It's good." He unscrewed the lid and handed it to her.

She sniffed it and jerked back her head. "Oh! So you say!"

"Trust me. My first job out of college was surveying for the railroad. They'd dump us off with all our transits and poles and chains and expect us to lug it all back to camp." He took a sip and forced it down with closed eyes. "Moonshiners would drive by in these big cars and figure all our equipment would be good camouflage, so we never had to walk. That's also why parts of the Seaboard Coast Line train track weave like a roller coaster."

She reached for the jar. "So this…is considered good?"

He dipped his finger in it and held it up. "It didn't dissolve my fingernail."

She tilted the jar to her lips, drank, and gasped for air. "Ooh! It's like bad slivovitz!"

"Did you catch that really acrid taste?"

"Yeess."

"Good corn liquor, one should always be able to taste the feet of the man walking when he plowed the corn."

She punched him and he banged his teeth on the rim of the jar. He sniffed some of the stuff up his nose and sneezed violently, his jerking hand sloshing some of the whiskey and she struggled to rescue it from spilling. He regained his breath and released the jar to her. "Most people think good whiskey is supposed to be aged, but we left some to set a whole week and it wasn't a bit better."

She sipped, grimaced and let out a *"Whoo-ee!"* She laughed, buried her face in her hands, sat up and let out a bellowing *"cO-O bO-Oss! cO-OO-O bO-Oss, cO-O, cO-O."* She collapsed laughing.

"What the hell was that?"

"That," she sat stiff again, "was my realm of scholarly inquiry, for my degree, from Vienna. But, specifically, that was Tennessee. Hear how it's short for 'come home bossy'? Listen. In North Carolina it's *'lO-Oke stE-Er kwO-O!'*"

Across the brickyard, in the kerosene lantern-lit drying shed, men answered back with *"YeeOOW!"* and *"WhO-O!"*

"See it works! Now, little piggies, they like *'Pig-pig-pig PO-O-ie, pO-O-ee, pig-pig!'*" Her laughing teared her eyes. The moonlight caught her teeth and hair. "Except again in Tennessee, where it's *'Whee-gy, Whee-gy, Pig-pig, Wutts, wutts, wutts!'*" She punched him gently. "Now you try."

"What, pig or cow?"

"Anything but sheep."

"*Co-ho-boss! co-ho-boss!*"

"No! No! You're not buying stamps! You calling your herd in from the hills! It's got to echo!"

"*CO-HO-BOSS!*"

"No!" she grabbed his wrist. "Consonants don't matter, they're just to get the vowel sound going. Like *'HO-O-y, SOO-OOO-wE-E.'*"

Men from the canvas shed called back and laughed. Kathryn struggled to regain her breath. One of the boys opened the eye of the kiln directly before them, exposing the slow-motion blue flames from the coals. The bricks glowed in a single yellow mass, barely discernible as individuals. He launched in a heavy stave of wood, sending sparks flying out the top of the kiln.

"So, you went to Vienna, Austria to study Tennessee pig calling?"

She lowered her eyelids. "Considering what it is you study, you'd be wise not to laugh!" She grasped the air to catch the silk of a spider suspended in midair between them.

"You know why I keep the radio on in my shop?"

She shook her head. Against the blue-black sky, tall pines swept their needles through the smoke and grasped at the sparks like children snatching lightning bugs.

"Because, 'Music hath charms to smooth the salvage beech.'"

She rolled back on her elbows. "You are a rude mechanical, thou Snug." She sat back up and took another sip from the moonshine jar. She eyed him over the rim with crossed eyes, drops glistening on her lips in the amber firelight. "Thy drugs are quick!" She pushed the jar into Calvin's hands. "No more of that!" She stood and brushed herself off, reached out for Calvin's hand and pulled him up. It was time to go.

Calvin set the jar of moonshine on a pile of bricks as they walked from the world of firelight and shadow toward the lights of the road. "So listen, those tickets to the Tommy Dorsey dance are for next Saturday."

"Dorsey's music is…kind of businessman's bounce, isn't it?"

"It's not Satchmo, but you could make it part of your research. Study the ceremonies of the bouncing Babbitts."

She shook her head. "Can't anyway. Brockwell has a concert at the DAR hall."

"Of course. That's important." He nodded too vigorously. In a few blocks they would reach the main street. He walked ahead and turned back to face her.

She plucked a leaf from Calvin's jacket. "I could tell him that my grandma died. But Glen Echo Park — that's like Coney Island. And, if it's next Saturday, the diplomatic corps is talking about making a holiday of it. All my embassy friends will be there."

"There'll be a lot of people around, sure," he raised his eyebrows and gave his head its best persuasive tilt, "but won't all of Brockwell's crowd be at his concert?"

Kathryn considered this and then shook her head sadly. "Poor grandma."

22

Linda rapped gently on Calvin's partially opened office door and peeked around the edge. Calvin pointed to the telephone at his ear, opening enough of a gap that Linda could clearly hear Hattersley's voice fairly shout, "What the hell *were* you thinking?" Linda, eyebrows raised, withdrew, pulling the door shut.

"I wasn't thinking of insulting anyone, I just had to come up with something quick."

"Dialect humor? You thought you'd do a minstrel show 'cause you couldn't come up with anything else?"

"You haven't heard it. It was a story done like *Uncle Remus*, and the guys who do *Amos 'n Andy* are white. Everybody loves them!"

"Not everybody, let me assure you!"

"Listen, I didn't mean to insult anyone or steal jobs from Negro actors. I don't even know any Negro actors."

"I share some of the blame for pushing you on the schedule, but Bubby should have known better."

"It's not his fault. I just sprung the show on him on his way out of town." He waited for him to speak. Silence. "Listen, I don't even know who Mary Bethune is."

Another silence and then, "Mary Bethune heads the Federal Council on Negro Affairs, the black cabinet. The call came straight from Mrs. Roosevelt's office."

He fumbled for an aspirin bottle in his desk drawer. "Well how the hell did that disc get to her? It hadn't even gone to duplication yet."

"Well, who knew about it?"

"I'll bet Brockwell knew. He knows everything about everyone."

"Brockwell? Are you kidding? I don't think he's the kind of guy who would object to your *Amos 'n Andy* routine! You two seem to think along the same lines. You're lucky he's got everyone out at Mount Vernon today. At least you have time to come up with a plan."

"I'll call Bubby."

"Bubby. I'm sorry, I forgot it was an hour earlier out there."

"It's okay, I'm awake." A stifled yawn crackled through the wires. "Listen, we're not going to let that bastard beat us."

"So you think it was Brockwell?"

"Had to be," said Bubby. "So what does lady Eleanor want you to do?"

"They want to know why we denied the job to a Negro actor. Apparently there's guidelines."

"Tell 'em we'll do a different show. Aw crap, and that was a great show, too."

Calvin snapped a chip of paint from the window frame with his fingernail. "We can't cancel. Then we'd be guilty of closing shop rather than letting a Negro do it."

"Then get a colored actor! Tell 'em that was just a rehearsal recording, and that you're doing the real one today. Could you do that?"

"Maybe." He stared out the window toward the White House. "Brockwell has everyone out at Mount Vernon for some damn thing, so the studio's empty."

"Call Kathryn. She had to do field recordings in Palookastan or wherever. She can run that disc cutter good as anyone."

"I just spoke to her this morning. She is not happy either." He rubbed a bit of paint chip lodged under his fingernail, forcing it deeper.

"She had a lot riding on your show. She's been fighting to get you this time slot."

Calvin had to let that sink in. "How's everything else up there?"

"Got the camera. Sound on film! Completely portable. We'll play with it when I get back."

"Okay. Thanks Bubby. I'll come up with something."

He put the phone down and Linda pushed the door open again. "Chief. You look beat."

"Maybe not yet. How's it been going here?"

"We're keeping up." She set a box of letters on his desk. "It's really an eye-opener, all these weird people that listen to your show."

"Thanks." He dug under his fingernail with a paperclip, the physical pain a welcome distraction.

"No, I'm sorry. I don't mean weird, I mean, just all types, all over. You just get so curious about all these lives that you had no idea were out there. It's a heck of a lot more interesting than the spreader work. And Shirley, she's running like a champ."

Tar smoke from distant roofers blew into the open window. Linda fanned her nose, but the sulfurous fumes seemed appropriate to Calvin. "Would you ask Anne to come see me?"

"Sure."

Anne came in fanning her nose. "Whew! We must be in the eddy. You wanted to see me."

"Yes. Anne. Remember that colored guy, Gabriel, who was working in the tower?"

She turned her head and eyed him sideways. "Yes."

"You said he was an actor."

"He is."

"Do you have any idea how I can get in touch with him?"

"Something wrong?"

"I may have an acting job for him, but I've got to reach him today, before noon if I can."

She smiled faintly. "I know where he lives."

"Where?"

"Near the Georgia movie house, north of Howard. I don't remember the street name. Do you want me to go find him?"

"I don't know if I can get an engineer. If not, there's no point. Do you have his address?"

"No, but I can find it. You better let me go."

"No. I can't ask you to go up there."

Anne already had the door half-open. "I'll get Verdie to take me on her bike. I'll call as soon as I find him."

"Well, let me find someone to run the disc cutter first."

She stepped back in. "Chief, why don't you tell me what you need, where and when, and trust me to take care of it?"

Calvin had always avoided looking at Anne's half-scarred face for more than an instant, but at this moment, she was making him look. "All right. I need an engineer and a Negro radio actor at the South building studio at two this afternoon."

Ann's eyes sparkled. "They'll be there, sir. Fourteen hundred hours."

"Should we synchronize watches?"

"Yes!"

Calvin paced in the control booth. In the studio, Anne laughed at Gabriel's mock sermon about the lack of humor in Ibsen's works, "the only flaw that kept him from true greatness." Calvin stepped back into the studio to check Gabriel's progress on the script. He drew in a breath, but before he could speak, Gabriel said, "I'm marking up the script, I hope that's all right."

"Oh, sure, we have…"

Gabriel loosened his neck as he spoke. "I'm glad you have a clean script without the emphasis already marked. That could lead the actor to stay on top of the character instead of working from the inside, don't you think?"

"Well…"

"The rhythms are fascinating, Mister C, you really have captured the rural idiom."

"Oh, well thanks."

"You're welcome. So, I know you're pressed for time, I'm ready when you are."

"All right. Let's do a mic check then."

Kathryn pushed through the door and went straight to the

disc cutter in the booth. Anne joined her there, and they put on headphones and swiveled in their chairs to check meters and tweak knobs.

Calvin's voice cracked as he spoke. "Ready in the booth?"

"Ready."

Calvin cleared his throat and read his first line.

Announcer: And now, it's Grandpa Sam's Woodshop of the Air. Join us again in that little woodshop in the country where a visitor has arrived and waits for Grandpa Sam and little Timmy.

Gabriel came in right on cue, reading his lines with a high nasal twang, frying the vowels like eggs in a pan.

Uncle Dan: Oh ah come frum Alabamy wid my . . . Durn, ah dun nocked ober Mr. Sam's can ob nails! Rekon ah bedda jest sit an wittle a bit til Mr. Sam gits here. Kain't jest be doin nothin!

Off script, Gabriel added his own line. "T'aint there nothin' I kin do? ...that's my motto!"

Calvin nodded and looked up at the booth. "Let me go see how that was." He scurried to the control booth door and dove through. "How was that?" The two women looked up at him, black headphones buttoning down their ears.

"We can hear you on the microphones," said Anne, "you don't need to run in here every time you have a question."

"I know." Calvin lowered his voice and nodded discretely toward the young black man in the studio. "He sounds like a hillbilly."

Kathryn looked through the glass at Gabriel underlining words in the script. "At least he doesn't act like one. Ask him to cut the nasal twang."

Calvin nodded and returned to the studio. "They asked if you could, with your voice, reduce some of the nasal twang."

"Oh, of course, the nasal twang! My fault! A stereotypical depiction of the rural Anglotype!"

Calvin smiled and gave the thumbs-up to Anne. "Okay everybody, from the top!" Gabriel looked around the empty studio for the multitudes that Calvin seemed to be addressing. Calvin felt himself flush. Behind the glass, Anne held the stopwatch in one hand, her other hand caught the overhead light. Her hand went down and Calvin snatched up his script to begin reading in the announcer's voice.

Gabriel's first line came with his voice placed in the back of his throat. He gave an arching rhythm to the vowels, pacing each word like a child counting out pennies. Calvin missed his line and held up his hand, then made slashing motions across his throat. "I'm sorry! Sorry! Cut! Cut!" He fumbled with his script as if there was something missing. "Let me check one more thing. Just…We'll get it." He strode to the booth and pulled the door after him. "God almighty, what are we going to do?"

Anne pulled off her headphones. "What's wrong?"

"Listen to him. I do a better Negro voice than he does."

Kathryn looked square at him. "Calvin, he's not *doing* a Negro voice!"

Calvin stood for a second, gave a quick shake of his head and turned back into the studio.

Gabriel arched his eyebrows at him as he returned. "Problems?"

"No, it's fine."

"Let me make sure I understand the character, Mr. Cobb.

So, Uncle Dan is a rural mountain sort with primary access to folk culture. A kindly old fellow, beloved of young Timmy's family. Neither genteel or, pardon the expression, white trash?"

Calvin was impaled for an instant by Gabriel's glare. He looked at Kathryn and Anne behind the glass, then back at Gabriel. "Sounds good."

"Sounds good," echoed Kathryn's voice over the squawk box. "But tone it down a little so it doesn't sound like you're making fun of anybody."

"Thank you, love. A tasteful treatment of our cornpone comrades! All right then. From the top!" He raised his voice and turned into the empty corners of the studio. "Everybody! Quiet please! This is a take!" Calvin looked at him as if he were from Mars. Gabriel grinned and gave his head a boxer's shake. "Ready when you are!"

Calvin said his last line and looked up to see Anne grin, pop her stopwatch, and lean to her microphone. "Timed out perfectly gentlemen, on the money!"

"On the money." Calvin reached into his vest for his billfold. "So, thirty dollars?"

Gabriel's eyes were closed and he was glistening with sweat. "Dat's wut we 'greed on boss."

Calvin glanced at him with a weak smile and held out the bills.

Gabriel took the money and tucked it into his shirt pocket. "Say, ah sho nuf likes dis here gub-mint radio. Lemme no if'n you be wantin any udder kind ob Negro down heah sum time, cause ah kin do all seben kinds ob Negro—from yo contented slave to yo exotic primitive to yo magical Negro—so you jess let me know. Mebby yo be doin sumpin on makin a lectic chair fo dem ol Scottsboro boys!"

Calvin rubbed at his left temple. "Thanks for your help today."

"Well thank ya suh, thank ya. Oh, and befo ah fogits, ah wants to thank y'all fo dat Rural Lektrfikashun. Sho is better gettin lynched by dem lectric lights den by dat smelly ol torch light! Sho nuff is. Hee! Hee!"

Anne stepped into the studio bearing two large cardboard sleeves. "Tremendous! Here's one for duplication. One for Mrs. Roosevelt."

Kathryn followed close behind. "Don't let this go to your head Gabriel Valentine but that was delightful. You sounded like an Appalachian Will Rogers."

Anne kept her eyes on Gabriel and almost dropped the recording as she handed it to Calvin. "You should have seen him in the *Wild Duck*."

Kathryn picked up Gabriel's jacket and held it over her arm. "Hjalmar the photographer — Ibsen's hackneyed symbol of the delusional bourgeoisie."

Gabriel leaned over her, eyes twinkling. "You don't play symbolism, you play the *character*."

"But Ibsen intended it symbolically," said Kathryn.

"And that's why the play is dated," said Anne.

Gabriel held open his hands as if the point was obvious. "But now with everyone doing Georgia O'Keeffe, bell-pepper-dog-in-heat photographs, the original symbolism is meaningless."

"How anyone can justify photographing rocks and trees when the world is coming apart is beyond me," said Kathryn. "Not that anybody sees them anyway. All people see is Bourke-White's imitation of…"

Gabriel tugged at his jacket. "Oh, don't get started on that again! You can't judge high culture by popular standards. You act like people don't know their Steiglitz from a Mohol in the Nagy."

Calvin looked in the record sleeve, smelled the freshly cut disc and wished he could crawl in with it.

Kathryn held Gabriel's jacket open for him. "Look. If Ibsen's constant theme is the hollow duplicity that sustains the bourgeoisie, then what's the point of wasting it on…"

"Then by your argument there's no point to *Tobacco Road* or *Hamlet* either, is there?" demanded Gabriel, giving his necktie a triumphant tug.

Kathryn answered with a tilted head and a smile.

Calvin raised his hand. "Excuse me." He bit his lip. "I've got to get this to duplication. Thank you all."

Gabriel reached out and patted him on the shoulder. "Hey, thank you, man. Sorry I was messin' with you. No hard feelin's huh?" He patted the bills in his pocket. "My lucky day! I got a pocket full of personality and two lovely ladies for lunch."

Anne looked up at the clock. "Just so I can drop your recording off at the White House on the way." She laughed. "Oh, I love saying that!"

Kathryn gave Gabriel a pat on his shoulders. "Good job, Mister V!"

"Thank you, baby," said Gabriel. He gave Anne a wink.

Calvin eased out the door.

"See you in the shop, my man!" Gabriel's voice boomed. "But don't wait up!"

The hot pavement rolled beneath his pounding feet like a worn, wobbling conveyor belt. Calvin stopped only at the cross streets to wait for streams of shadow cars driven by transparent people. The clock painter was back at work on the numerals on the south face of the tower. Maybe they had all been fired, he thought, and Washington was an entire city of Bartelbys just working on because they preferred not to leave. The sun baked in through the central skylight, making a giant hothouse of the old Post Office. He pulled himself up the eight floors of stairs. At the end of the corridor, Linda led a man from Calvin's office into the machine room. She spotted Calvin and stepped back out to intercept him.

"Chief! In here."

All four women were gathered around the rumpled chief of Radio Services. Calvin dropped back against the wall. "Mr. Hattersley. Now what?"

Hattersley looked back with sunken eyes. "Congressman Richter's office."

Ellen hung up the telephone in her lap. "They think it'll work. The cards will act as the warrants so Treasury can issue the checks. I think we can do it."

Hattersley rubbed absently at his face. "That's probably the best we can do."

Calvin pointed to the telephone. "Was that the congressman? We got a Negro actor! It's all done!"

Ellen shook her head. "Nothing to do with that. It's Social Security. They think we can refund the money by punch card check, just like they do."

"What money?" demanded Calvin. "What's going on?"

Hattersley fanned himself. "Apparently there's a statute where the government is prohibited from competing with private industry—in certain cases. Recipes don't count, but 'hobbycraft plans' do. We've been charging three cents for your measured drawings, and that puts us in violation of the no-compete statute with *Superior Woodworking* magazine."

"But the three-cent stamp was just to cover the cost of printing!"

"Calvin, Superior Publishing is in Congressman Richter's district. They put out *Superior Home* and *Superior Woodworking* magazines." Hattersley rubbed his fingers against his thumb. "I know I don't have to explain this to you."

"So, we'll stop charging."

"Stopping's not the problem. The remedy's the problem. All monies received in violation of this statute have to be refunded to the citizen. And you've got hundreds of citizens." Hattersley turned to Linda. "How many did you say?"

She looked in her ledger. "One thousand, eight hundred and twenty eight."

Calvin sat on the corner of a table. "Wait a minute, you said 'Treasury issue the checks.' You mean we have to send a check for *three cents* to everybody who sent us a stamp?"

"That's right," said Hattersley, shaking his head in disbelief.

Calvin put his hands to his head. "But that will cost much more than…"

Hattersley nodded. "Much more, but the law says you have to keep an audit trail, so the refund has to go through Treasury. Otherwise, you could just send back the stamps as they came in."

Ellen rocked back and forth in her wheelchair. "If we can use the punched cards as warrants, we can just generate a bundle and drop 'em off at Treasury."

Anne picked up the thread. "They'll automatically cut and mail the refunds, just like they do social security checks."

Calvin looked out toward the distant Treasury building. "Well, there's six programs already duplicated on discs and shipped out to stations all over. We're gonna have stamps coming in for weeks. So this applies to requests that come in from now on?"

"Yep." Hattersley smoothed the rim of his hat. "Until you get some new shows out there with a new tag line that doesn't ask for a stamp for the plans." He worked his tongue against his teeth for a moment. "Calvin, you know it might seem odd to folks that they're getting a government check in the mail for three cents. Is there a way to include some kind of explanation, maybe a personal note from you that promotes the program?"

"A note tucked in with each check?" asked Verdie, shaking her head. "How can we do that if Treasury prints and mails the check?"

"How 'bout on the check itself?" said Anne from her place by the door. "We punch the cards so they make the Treasury printer add a line or two under the address. Just, you know, something like 'Thanks for the good work, from *Grandpa Sam's Woodshop of the Air.*'"

"Can you do that?" asked Calvin.

Anne looked to Linda who surveyed the eyes of the other women. "I think so," she said. "We just follow the pattern of the social security checks. We should talk to Treasury, though, and make sure we don't cause them any problems."

Hattersley waved his hand. "Don't draw attention if you don't have to." He rose and wagged his hat towards the humming machines. "It's a good thing *Grandpa Sam's Woodshop of the Air* isn't more popular than it is, or even…"

"Little Shirley," said Linda.

"…even your Shirley machine couldn't tap-dance us out of this. So, ladies, thank you. Sorry to barge in, I know this is not your regular work."

The women chorused their goodbyes. Calvin followed Hattersley out the door and the two walked down the hall, both glancing back to judge when they were out of earshot.

"Larry, what the hell is going on?"

"It's not your fault, Calvin. It's ridiculous. Charging three cents is competition, but giving them away is a public service."

"So who's behind this idiotic business?"

"Could've been anyone. As soon as you do anything worth noticing, there's always someone ready to say they came up with it first. You've been on the air for, what, three or four shows? That's all you need to make someone jealous."

"Jealous of my stupid radio show? That's insane."

Hattersley laughed quietly, shaking his head. "Get used to it."

Calvin cradled his head in his hands and stared at the *Newsweek* photo of grinning Japanese soldiers playing baseball in China during a butchery break. *Maybe— Commodore Perry turning baseball bats in Tokyo harbor?* Calvin pushed the magazine away and pulled over the still-open Wallace Nutting furniture book, anxious for seven more program ideas. A drawing of a cradle. *Sacagawea's baby? Virginia Dare?* He flipped the page. A nice milking stool. *Mrs. O'Leary's before the Chicago fire?* The headache augered between his bloodshot right eye and left shoulder. Maybe an Adirondack chair—*Mark Twain can't write Huckleberry Finn because he needs a chair?* Seven great programs might make up for the *Box for Ben* fiasco—a sinking performance millstoned down by the receptionist's last-minute observation that Ben Franklin probably wore a round Quaker hat like the guy on the oatmeal box rather than a tricorn. And now half the scripts had to include a Negro actor as well.

The machines drummed through the wall and into his skull. He wondered if he was just stupid—and if he was, how would he know? The popular doggerel repeated in his aching head.

"See the happy moron.
He doesn't give a damn.
I wish I were a moron.
My God, perhaps I am!"

His crackers were gone, box and all. Gabriel could well use his third catch phrase on Calvin now. "He ain't much — but he's arn and we loves him!" He slowly stood and looked out the window toward the White House. The pale green of a pecan tree stood out among the deep elms. *Maybe — Thomas Jefferson needs a cracker box, or a nutcracker. A nutcracker and a bookstand so he can read and eat, or he won't finish the Declaration of Independence in time for the Fourth of July.* He sat back down, wondering why this seemed like a good idea when it so obviously was not. No, the golden Gabriel had to have a part. *The Handyman's Book* never let him down. Calvin flipped it open to the pages enfolding the noble Moor's wood shaving bookmark. There was the Library Ladder/Chair.

He rolled a new sheet into the typewriter.

Bubby signaled six minutes remaining. Calvin glanced up to the clock over the control room window. It was Kathryn's line. She had edged back into a slight southern accent. None of them could recall (if they ever knew) where Clara Barton was from.

```
CLARA BARTON: Good Morning gentlemen.
OLD REBEL:    Ah, good morning Miss Barton. Here
              you are, workin' so hard!
```

"T'aint there nuthin' I kin do?" added Gabriel in his Uncle Dan character voice.

```
OLD YANKEE:   And I have a surprise for you too!
```

"And I'd like to help as well!" added Calvin's "Old Yankee," trying to make sense following Gabriel's unexpected insertion.

```
OLD REBEL:    Ah spoke first, suh! Ah have
              priority!
```

"You jest tend to your whittlin'!" added Gabriel's "Old Rebel."

OLD YANKEE: You think you're always firstest with the mostest! Well ...
CLARA: Now gentlemen! The war is over! We must not let old animosities interfere with the work of the Red Cross in marking the graves of your fallen comrades!
OLD REBEL: Sorry Miz Barton.
CLARA: Well, my cup runneth over gentlemen! We have all been working so hard. How do you have the time to arrange any surprises?
OLD YANKEE: Oh, there's always time for makin' something out of wood! Come on in. My surprise is waitin' for you inside the office.
OLD REBEL: And mine's around back. I'll go get it!

Bubby walked limping steps in the gravel box, then opened and closed the tiny door. Kathryn was right on cue.

CLARA: Why Captain, it's a beautiful little stepladder! Now I can reach all those uppermost pigeonholes here in the office. Wherever did you get it?
OLD YANKEE: I made it m'am, you see there was this odd-looking chair, and ...
OLD REBEL: (outside) Dad blamed - dad ratted!

Gabriel was delivering his lines in full-tilt Uncle Dan voice.

CLARA: Major Davis, your language, what ever is the matter?

OLD REBEL: Some thievin' camp rat stole the chair I made for you last night. It had a special shelf for your papers. I left it right out here on the ... hey what the? ...

CLARA: It's my new stepladder. The captain made it so I could work up high.

OLD REBEL: Why that sure looks ... wait a minute! It is! That's the chair I made for Miz Barton. Why you Yanks never change! You sawed up the chair I made! Thought you'd play General Sherman and destroy ...

OLD YANKEE: Wait a minute now! What kind of chair was that? I had no idea it was some crazy thing you had made. Besides, she needs a stepladder.

OLD REBEL: She needs a chair you thievin' bluebelly!

OLD YANKEE: You cornpone corporal! She needs a stepladder and I made her one!

Bubby held up his fingers in the two-minute warning.

CLARA: Wait a minute, wait a minute gentlemen! Obviously there has been a mistake.

OLD REBEL: You're dern tootin there's ...

CLARA: Now stop it both of you! There must be some way we can remedy the situation.

OLD REBEL: Well, I suppose I could rig up some mending plates and join the seat back together. Make it back into a proper chair again, like this!

Bubby squeaked his cedar turkey call in a long, bending tone.

OLD YANKEE: Wait a minute, she still needs a stepladder. Like this!

Calvin glared at Gabriel as Bubby squeaked slowly again.

OLD REBEL: No! Like this!

Bubby squeaked. Gabriel met Calvin's glare.

OLD YANKEE: I tell ya, like this!

Calvin was shouting now, pegging the meters.

CLARA: Gentlemen, the way you're swinging it back and forth, couldn't it be ... both?

Bubby gave the finger-circling hurry-up signal.

OLD REBEL: Both? What do you mean?
CLARA: I mean couldn't we hinge it in the

	middle? Then I could have both a stepladder and a chair when I needed one.
OLD YANKEE:	You know, it might work!
OLD REBEL:	Sure it will work, and the whole thing will take up less space than both a stepladder and a chair.
CLARA:	Speaking of a hinges, Captain, couldn't we put a hinge in the middle of that wooden leg of yours. That way it wouldn't stick out when you sit down.
OLD REBEL:	Well I thought about that, but then it would collapse when I need to stand up.
OLD YANKEE:	But looking at it now, I could rig a hickory spring that would keep it straight until you wanted it to bend!

"You ain't too smart, but you's arn and we loves you!" added Calvin. Gabriel glared up at Calvin from his script. Bubby gave the one-minute warning.

OLD REBEL:	Why you ... durn Yankee, that's a great idea! "
CLARA:	Well, gentlemen, there may be hope for us yet!
OLD REBEL:	Got to agree. I'm an old shot-up rebel, but it took a one-armed Yankee to help me get the spring back in my step!

Bubby plunked a saw blade making a 'boing' sound as Calvin delivered all the final lines.

GRANDPA: So Timmy, ya see, that stepladder-chair was how Clara Barton was able to help so many people after the terrible War Between the States.

TIMMY: Wow grandpa, that's got to be the worst ending I ever heard to one of your stories.

GRANDPA: What do you mean? Spring in his step? You thought I'd end with that? Why I haven't even told you the ending! I haven't told you why the old Rebel finally quit fighting.

TIMMY: Quit fighting? Wasn't it because he was injured?

GRANDPA: Certainly. You see, a cannonball took off his leg, so he had no choice but to lay down his arms.

Bubby plunked the saw again, shook his head and dropped the needle on the recorded theme music. He glanced at his stopwatch and gave the taffy pulling, "stretch it out" signal to Calvin.

ANNOUNCER: Well, maybe that's not the way it really happened, but if you would like a measured drawing to make your own chair that converts into a stepladder, handy around

> the farm and home, just write to
> Grandpa Sam's Woodshop of the
> Air, care of the National Farm
> and Home Hour, US Department of
> Agriculture, Washington 25, DC. ~~Be
> sure to include a three-cent stamp
> to cover the cost of duplication.~~

Bubby signaled frantically to Calvin for even more stretching. Calvin ad-libbed.

> "You know, every American has
> made a contribution to American
> woodworking, and we're delighted
> to have the opportunity to repay
> our debt to you through this
> little program."

Bubby gave the wrap-it-up signal.

> This has been Uncle Sam's Woodshop
> of the Air, transcribed in
> Washington, DC, and I'm Calvin
> Cobb wishing that, as you slide
> down the banister of life — that
> all the splinters are going in
> your direction! So long!

Kathryn started to give a "*WHOOH!*" — but too soon. Bubby threw up his hand for silence. She stifled herself with her hand forcing a snort out of her nose.

Bubby crossed his eyes. "It's the snort heard round the world!"

"Oh no! Did that go on the recording?"

"Nah, I had it faded out." Bubby blew the acetate shavings off the aluminum disc. "So, congratulations, all! Let's get the studio cleared. We've run over time."

As if on cue, smiling Brockwell entered the studio followed by two guitar-clutching women in church-going clothes.

Gabriel grinned at the women and said. "Lawd, dem is some purdy git-ars, bet you gonna play some preddy songs!"

Kathryn rolled her eyes at him and became formal, straight-backed, measured in her voice and movements. "Mister Brockwell, ladies, I'm so sorry to keep you waiting. Bubby, I'd like microphones for the girls separate from the instruments."

Gabriel looked at Kathryn with big eyes. "Well m'am, don' you worry none. I'll hab dat ole dead rat outta yo place 'fo you kin say cracker-facker!"

"Thank you!" she returned his big eyed stare with a stern one of her own.

Bubby too, became conventionally professional. "We'll put the saltshaker mikes on the guitars and have them sing into the seventy-seven."

"Very good," said Kathryn. She pushed her script into Calvin's hands. "Mister Brockwell, we'll be ready to go in a moment."

"Do you want me to stay and help?" asked Calvin, knowing that Brockwell could easily devour the afternoon.

"Thank you so much Mister Cobb," said Kathryn, "but I think this is just an audition for the July folk festival, am I right Mister Brockwell?"

Brockwell nodded, set his papers on the piano and sidled over to Calvin, who was loading the sound effects back onto the cart. "Good afternoon to you, Mister Cobb."

"Afternoon Mister Brockwell. I'm so sorry to hold things up."

"Not at all." He peered at Calvin's eyes and forehead. "How is your little program going?"

"Doing fine, sir."

"And your audience response? How is that going?"

"Just a few hundred letters so far."

"Just a few hundred! Well you deserve better than that." Brockwell glared at Bubby as if the poor showing was his fault.

"That doesn't mean anything," said Bubby. "Mail from the Midwest won't be here till Thursday. That's where the big audience is"

Brockwell's gaze snapped back to Calvin. "I wonder Mr. Cobb, if you know what your own name means?"

"Not unless it's a chewed-up ear of corn."

"Hope dere ain't no corn in heah! Dats what dem rats love so much!" said Gabriel, looking wild-eyed around the studio.

Brockwell squared up to face Calvin, uncomfortably close. "No, no, no, the name Cobb is old Norse. It means — a big lump of a fellow. It means a good man to have beside you in battle! Cobb is an ancient and powerful name. A name with the fierceness of our race in it!"

Calvin squirmed under Brockwell's pale eyes. "Well, I'm feeling pretty dim at the moment, but thank you." He pushed the studio cart behind the chairs and glanced at Kathryn. "Miss Harper, I'll...see you soon." Close to his chest he drew a circle in the air with his finger and then held five fingers outstretched, indicating their rendezvous with the streetcar at Washington Circle at five in the afternoon Saturday for the ride to the dance at Glen Echo.

She smiled and nodded and held her hand up with fingers outstretched, indicating both the number five and that it was time for Gabriel and Calvin to make their exits. They walked steadily backwards and slipped out the door.

Gabriel came up beside Calvin as they walked down the hall. "Hey, wait for me! Got to have big lump like you beside me in battle!" he said, in a fair imitation of Brockwell's voice.

Calvin walked a bit before speaking. "So which kind of negro was that in there?"

Gabriel laughed quietly and affected a ghostly voice. "The invisible kind." He put his hand to his chin. "Oh, no, wait! That was the trickster, verging on the magical. Hard to tell."

"If you want to be invisible, why do you keep adding lines?"

"The catch phrases? Man, you gotta have a hook! That way the listeners carry the foundation of the character with them through the week. Makes the audience a participant. You know that!"

"Well, you really throw the timing off."

"Well if you don't like hooks, why did you steal one of mine? You shouldn't confuse characters like that. Besides, we ran short in there."

"I meant the internal timing, the cues. You really should stick to the script."

"Well if you write my hooks into the next script, I won't have to add them in later, will I?" Calvin stopped walking and turned an incredulous face to Gabriel, who responded with a grin followed by awe-struck regard. "You big old lump! I am so glad to have you beside me in battle!"

The Saturday morning newspapers in the quiet city headlined horrors from the siege of Barcelona, but Calvin was too keyed up to read the text. He bought a pack of Beechies at the 14th Street newsstand to give him browsing rights. The frightening economic news ran a close second to the international horror-show. *Newsweek* featured photographs of the police battling strikers at Republic Steel. Dorothy Thompson's column warned that the vigilantes attacking the striking steel workers could initiate civil war in America. Mustard gas in Ethiopia, bayonets in Shanghai. Jews in Berlin holding up their racial identity cards as SS men issued them shovels.

But *Life* had a feature on swimming with plenty of shots of nude bathing. *Newsweek* had a story on the history of burlesque with plenty of shots of nude dancers. The photography magazines had plenty of nude shots throughout. If only *Popular Mechanics* and the woodworking magazines like *Superior Craftsman* could figure out a cheesecake connection. *Refinishing a Burlesque Stage: Stripping in a Strip Joint* or *Old Telegraph Poles Make a Dandy Diving Float — But Watch Those Splinters!*

Back at his desk, Calvin fanned through some of the week's letters addressed to *Grandpa Sam's Woodshop of the Air*. The misspellings and grubby pencilings on chunky school paper mingled innocently with flawless Spenserian script on personal stationery. Return addresses ranged from Magnolia, Arkansas to Beaverton, Oregon—but most were solid corn belt letters; clear, polite requests for measured drawings. Letters that showed long experience in bringing blue jeans, welding rods, poetry books, marigold seeds and arthritis cures to dirt road mailboxes. Some wanted to buy or sell tools or wood or begin a new career in woodworking. He had begun a separate pile for these letters, and his anxiety grew along with it. Each letter was a problem, a little chore someone expected him to do for them—and there were dozens and dozens. He committed himself, however, to work them down one by one until it was time to get ready for the dance. Perhaps undertaking this pile of little good deeds would make up for his big mis-steps of the week.

The girls, despite their earlier objections, seemed fascinated by the letters and the problems they presented. *Was the folding ladder the same as the folding ladder chair? This letter doesn't say what drawing they want. Shall we send multiples in the same envelope? Which Springfield do you think this is? This one has a check for baby chicks in it. These stamps are stuck to the page. This one didn't include stamps. These stamps look canceled.*

Little Shirley was helping too. Thinking ahead, the girls realized that if someone asked for plans for all thirteen episodes, then they'd have to retype their name and address thirteen times. But by punching the information into a Burroughs card and asking folks to send it back with any subsequent request for measured drawings, Shirley would work like a giant addressograph machine. Now they would only have to type cards for new customers, keeping a master punched card for each individual that Shirley could update for each request. As a bonus, Shirley could quickly sort and count the cards to tell what shows were the most popular and who was listening and where, as well as generating the warrants to trigger the refund checks from Treasury.

The girls were giddy with pride in the accomplishments of their Little Shirley. A few days back, though, Calvin noticed a subtle rearranging of papers and split-second breaks in the conversation when he entered a room. By Thursday, Calvin sensed something was up. There was a tense undercurrent in their corner of the eighth floor, but Friday evening came with no surprises — just hearty well-wishes from the five women as they pinned on their hats. They teased him about his upcoming date and made fussy fixings of his hair and staightenings of his tie. He peered into the curiously vacant offices of the eighth floor as he changed his shirt. There was too much energy built up in the women for them not to be here today. He stared at the wire guts of Little Shirley, but she wasn't talking. He laid his hand against the relay bank — she was still warm. He pulled crumpled paper from the trash can — paper covered with arcs of dark letters and, at the bottom, the words "Acceleration 0 To 55 Mph, Deere Model 'E' Spiral Beater Manure Spreader." Another paper, a letter bearing the The Ford Motor Company header now caught his eye. "Beltsville experimental station hosts the most powerful tractor in existence! Our new..." He threw the paper aside and pounded furiously down the stairs to the street, shouting for a cab before he even reached the sidewalk.

"**My** God! That smell!" She slid away from him on the seat and looked around to see if the other streetcar passengers were suffering as she was. The surrounding seats had already been abandoned.

"Pig manure, I'm sorry! I changed and washed but it's persistent."

"What did you try to cover it with?"

"Lilac vegetal."

"Wooh! It's like a hot day at the Budapest zoo." She brushed at his sleeve as if to knock the smell away, evoking a wince and gasp from Calvin. "What happened to your shoulder?"

An hour earlier, the black bruise on his shoulder left by the flying chain had been as sharply defined as a photograph. "We had an encounter with the fourth horseman of the crapocolypse out at Beltsville this morning. Spreader chain broke. I was in the wrong place." He looked at her with raised his eyebrows. "They borrowed your camera for the test, so I suppose you knew about it."

She put her hand on top of his and looked down to hide her grin. "Well, I couldn't tell you. Anne made me promise. They didn't want you to worry."

"I feel like a puppy in charge of tigers."

"You're a nice puppy." She patted the back of his hand. "But you sure are due for a bath."

The hammering of the air-brake compressor echoed in the valley as the streetcar clattered over the Rock Creek bridge. At Wisconsin Avenue, more college kids piled in, the motorman eyeing them in his overhead mirror. Calvin stole glances at Kathryn. This, now, had to be about fun — not work. He drew on his long-prepared topic of discussion to demonstrate "taking a genuine interest" in her. "I once saw Margaret Bourke-White when she was shooting pictures of the Supreme Court building."

Kathryn kept her gaze directed out the window. "You know it's perfect that she's working for *Life*. Every issue is one part decapitated Chinaman, one part brain surgery closeup, and two parts Hollywood bathtub shots. She fits right in." The streetcar wheels squealed so loudly on the hot, dry rails through Georgetown that she had to speak in short bursts. "My aunt thinks Bourke-White is wonderful, thinks she's the living image of *Liberty Leading the People*."

"Well, you're more famous than Margaret Bourke-White."

"Oh, but Margaret's a social activist." They screeched down to Prospect Street where the grimy boy in the pit disconnected the electric plow connector that had powered the streetcar from below. "The duty of an intellectual is to lift the lid on the engine, to expose invisible social inequities. Not to opiate the masses with recipes and decorating tips." The kids in the back started singing *The Big Apple* and practicing steps in the aisle while the driver stepped outside to raise the trolley pole to take power from the overhead wire. "She's just too obvious. People in need get high-angle shots looking down at them, either on their rear ends, on their backs, or huddled for a hand out. But if they were factories, well, then they'd all be worshipful up-angle shots, all looking up at them." She suddenly stood and swung up to the front door. "Oh, here they come!"

As if dressed for Halloween, a half-dozen people, all in glittering national costume, came down the sidewalk. They kept up their rapid pace but straightened up as they approached. They were led by a tall man wearing a glossy frock coat, brilliantly polished black shoes and black hair to match. From under his coat, there peeked a badge of gold surrounded by ribbons. Second in command was a short Chinese-looking woman, in a black skirt with a red and white checked top with an ivory kokoshnik tiara haloing her head. A young man in tennis flannels and a deep red embroidered diplomatic sash across his chest came next. Two women wearing long skirts with vests over white blouses and inverted conical caps flanked a tall black man with in a blue coat with an elaborate gold threaded vest, wire rimmed glasses and a gold embroidered silk cap. The man was Gabriel.

"Sophie! Kippy!" called Kathryn as she swung down from the steps of the streetcar to the street.

The Chinese woman pulled herself up to her very short height. "Katrine! Protocole!" and nodded toward Calvin who was now hanging in the doorway.

"I'm so sorry!" said Kathryn, curtseying and then pulling herself into formal posture. "Count Sycherny, my friend, the Calvin of Cobb."

The count clicked his heels and nodded most properly towards Calvin. "Mister Cobb, a great honor. If I may introduce, her ladyship Sofia Goldschmidt." The Chinese looking woman made a quick curtsy. "May I also present Augusts, Krista, and Marta Balodis of the Latvian national mission to your United States." Two more curtseys and a bow followed. "And, we have the great honor of escorting his most magnificent majesty, his most serene highness, the Lion of the Zambezi, King Chepumba of the Kwambai people."

Gabriel stepped forward and the others gave way in regal respect. He faced Calvin, still hanging between the hand rails framing the door. A frown darkened Gabriel's face. "Your head…is higher than mine."

Calvin hesitated. The assembled company, the streetcar passengers, now crowded at the windows, the gaping motorman, and the pit boy leaning out from under the car — all held their breath. Catching Kathryn's judging gaze, Calvin finally, slowly dropped his head. Even the streetcar brakes let out a jet of compressed air in relief.

"That is better," said Gabriel in his deep, kingly voice. "This is your conveyance?" Before Calvin could answer, he stepped past him and up the steps of the car. At once, all the heads in the car lowered. "I shall ride among the people to the place of celebration." He regally took the seat directly behind the motorman's.

Outside, the motorman lunged forward but the Count stepped in his path. "The King is very eager to learn the ways of your nation."

"Well, there's one thing I've gotta teach him right now! You can't board here, and besides, we're going to Glen Echo."

The Count pulled a black leather portfolio from inside his coat and began to thumb through bills. "The King is very important to your country and he needs relaxation. You see, back in his country, he has many, many wives." The Count glanced knowingly at the motorman and fanned open three five-dollar bills. "I'm sure you understand." The motorman quickly pocketed the money, took his place, and dinged the footbell twice as the car hummed to life.

They swayed with the sparking car as it rollicked down the heat-warped rails. All the passengers audibly breathed out the last of the city as they crossed the rickety trestle below Georgetown University with its dizzying view over the river. Out the front window, the tracks, the brown power poles and the overhead wire framed their corridor through the woods.

The Count turned from window to window, trying to take it all in. "When I was little, in Budapest, I always wanted to ride the trams, but our governess insisted we always take the carriage."

Calvin could overhear a little of King Gabriel's conversation with a curious college girl. Gabriel pointed up at the advertisement card for Spearmint Gum mounted in the curve of the streetcar's ceiling showing a gum stick man holding a spear protecting the rest of the pack. "Your warriors seem very thin," he said to her in kingly sonority. She dissolved in giggling.

The loaded streetcar labored as it climbed the grade evidenced by the frequent locks in the canal below them. The warm wind carried the acrid bite of creosote oozing from the crossties and power poles; a smell softened by the soothing dankness of the woods and river.

As the others chattered in French, Sophia leaned in to Calvin's ear and pointed out the window to the waters of the Potomac through the trees. "I was fourteen when the fascists took Budapest. Our neighbor showed me bodies floating in the Danube and said, 'You're lucky to be Americans. Those are all Jews.'" She glanced quickly around at the other passengers and then bounced her shoulders in an exaggerated accompaniment to the sway of the streetcar, then began gagging as she caught the full sensation of Calvin's aroma.

Calvin's glances at Kathryn caught her alternately listening to the gossip from Sophie and the Latvian siblings, or stifling laughter at Gabriel as he carried on his interrogation of the motorman regarding the driver's paltry number of wives. The streetcar made its last mail stop before the amusement park.

In the relative quiet as the driver exchanged mailbags with the postmaster, a distant chorus of screams from the roller coaster drifted through the trees. The motorman dinged his foot bell for the final stretch.

They poured off the streetcar into the smell of popcorn and motor oil, the sound of carnival music, cracks from the shooting gallery and the gravelly undertone of motors turning rollers and pulling cables. The Count led the way, using his wallet like a machete to clear a path through the jungle of open mouths and narrowing eyes. As they passed through the turnstile, calling voices made Kathryn turn. A well-dressed couple waved at her from the roller coaster line and her eyes went wide. She skipped over, exchanged kisses with them, spoke in French for a moment and then rejoined the group.

The Count leaned over to her. "We must keep together, now. For the sake of the King."

"Of course." She turned to Calvin. "That was the nephew of the Brazilian ambassador. I almost didn't recognize him without his monocle. He even wears it in the pool with his bathing suit!" They moved as a group toward the candy stand and bought sacks of popcorn. King Gabriel made a great show of praising the excellence of this new world treat, light as the air! And the sugar cotton! He must take some home to his wives! They wandered through the crowd to the edge of the huge swimming pool, just filled for the season, the water still cold and clear. Spray drifting from the geyser fountain in the middle made rainbows against the trees. Calvin watched bathers slipping down the giant slide into the water and tried to hear the whispered comments of the others. He turned to Kathryn. "Who's idea was this?"

"The mice will play!" She waved again at the young man with the monocle.

Sophia overheard his question and squeezed up beside him. "The senior diplomats are in London for the coronation, so we were all ready for some fun!"

Calvin, however, could not ignore the disturbed glances and hurried conversations among the park regulars once they caught sight of the one black face among the hundreds. He sidled up beside King Gabriel and spoke quietly. "You know you're breaking the law."

"Me? How is it possible for a King to break the law — when he himself *is* the law?"

"You've already been in trouble in the last month. This would not go well."

Sophia, hanging close, had been listening in. "Don't worry, Calvin! The king has diplomatic immunity!" She laughed and the other joined in. Their procession now moved regally through the crowd to the shooting gallery where the Latvian sisters quickly won squat rubber dolls. On the Dodgem cars, they took huge pleasure in ramming cars driven by some "Witless Brits." When the cars stopped and the two scrawny men stalked off, Sophia muttered "Humorless snobs" loudly enough for them to hear.

A breeze picked up a cloud of dust and papers and carried it past them, whipping skirts up legs and sending a man's hat rolling. The carousel was just starting and they joined the line. The riders swept by on horses, lions and ostriches with intense, determined faces. The Wurlitzer band organ played *Boo-Hoo*. as the two young British diplomats passed stiffly by again. Sophia shook her head. "They dump their stupidest people in their foreign service. The world's going to hell and all the British diplomats care about is cultivating eccentricities."

Kathryn nodded in agreement, and then, as the carousel slowed to a stop, shouted "Aux lapins!" They dashed to their mounts across the quivering platform. Kathryn hopped on the inner rabbit. Gabriel reached for the pole of the tiger on the outside row. "I shall capture the brass ring." He threw his leg over the tiger and checked his grip on the pole. The two Latvian girls took up posts beside him, laughing as he tilted his hat back and mock-spit on his palms before gripping the pole with a determination that matched the carved beast. The carousel began to turn to the tune of *In My Little Grass Shack*.

Calvin climbed onto a horse behind Gabriel. He watched Kathryn savor the breeze as the world spun around them in a blur. The arm of the ring dispenser swung in, but the ticket-taker reached Calvin just as he was getting ready to lean out. He readied himself for the next pass, but Gabriel took the ring dispenser arm hard on a knuckle and knocked it swinging out of Calvin's reach. The Wurlitzer changed to *Smoke Gets in Your Eyes* in an upbeat, halting pace.

"It's brass!" shouted Kathryn, and he looked up to see the arm approaching again with a gleaming loop at its end. Gabriel was still sucking his bruised knuckle and could only watch it go by. Calvin leaned out and snagged it. "Well done!" she called as he handed it to her. She nodded congratulations as she rose and fell before a plaster freeze of cherubs and blue and crimson flowers. Her hair lifted and gathered the garland about her and then she drifted down, revealing his own happy reflection in the mirrors behind her.

They joined the Danish embassy staffers at a picnic table near the fortune teller's booth and unpacked box lunches from the old Chautauqua hotel. Sophia sat next to Calvin and gestured toward the young Latvians standing at either side of Gabriel, faithfully maintaining the kingly illusion. "You must get invited to their parties!" she said. "Their building is very hard to heat so they always have huge logs burning in the fireplace and drink whiskey all winter." She leaned toward Calvin. "They have the best parties in town. Their place is decorated with paintings of nude lesbian scenes. I'll take you some time."

"I've never been to an embassy party. I don't know if I could fit in."

"Oh, we could pass you off as some New Dealer egghead. Just chatter on about commodity compensation or something and chew your food with your mouth open."

Calvin poked at his chicken, hurrying to finish chewing before opening his mouth. "So, these Brits, they cultivate eccentricities?"

"Oh, yes!" said the Latvian man. "They devote themselves to things like eating only bear meat or always carrying teddy bears about. They think it's the equivalent of genius. They're all racialists and anti-Semites too."

Calvin looked about, trying to spot them. "Snobs and rednecks, huh?"

"Please!" said Gabriel. He leaned toward Calvin, fully maintaining his regal posture. "Lest you be thought a snob yourself! Reddened necks are earned from labor under the sun. Labor is noble, and it is most unworthy to speak of the workers in such manner."

"Well, thank you, your kingship, for pointing out an invisible power inequity." Calvin mustered his best thoughtful pose. "And I suppose carousels run counter-clockwise just to give the ring-snatching advantage to right-handed people?"

"You laugh?" said Sophie, "You are on the radio. Think. Why is Jack Benny number one on radio?"

Calvin saw Kathryn considering him with narrowing eyes as she twirled the brass ring on her finger. "Because he's funny?" he offered absently.

"But *why* is he funny? He's vain, cowardly, a cheapskate—yet everyone loves him! So why? Because the depression has emasculated American men, they can no longer be manly providers. So, Jack Benny exaggerates this—but still he is happy and accepted by friends — and you laugh because at least you're better a man than him. And King Chepumba here? He outranks all these white men, but because his superiority is displaced, they can enjoy it rather than be threatened by it." Sophie paused to look close at Calvin's face. "Don't you see?"

Come sunset, the count and his currency led the way as the king and his courtiers made their way into the ballroom and down the palm tree-lined promenade to the dance floor. Girls flounced their skirts in impatient display, practicing steps with one another. The lights dimmed and the band came onto the darkened stage. The crowd called out at the musicians and they each waved back as they took their places behind white, boxy music stands. The spotlight swung over to a gold trombone held by a man looking like a dapper storekeeper. The first five notes of *I'm Getting Sentimental Over You* were drowned in applause. Sophia tugged Calvin off into the sea of swaying couples. Calvin danced jerkily and she poked her finger into his side. "Come on Mr. C! *Le swing est une sorte de balancement dans la rhythme et la melodie qui comporte toujours un grand dynamism!*" The band went into *Stop, Look and Listen* and the rhythm of the dancers spread through the floor, growing into Calvin's heels like a pulsing vine. A lightning bug flashed forlornly above the dancers before it flew too low and was pulled under the crowd.

Dorsey promised to let the dancers cool off by slowing down a bit. Sophia pulled Calvin to join the refugees from the phantasm on the main floor. Kathryn, the Count and the regal Gabriel stood by an open window on the river side of the ballroom. They leaned out the steel casement windows into the cool air over the bluffs. The humidity was building back after the thunderstorms earlier in the week, and girls pulled at their blouses to make a bellows against their bodies.

Calvin hopped up to sit on the ledge as close as he could

to Kathryn. Sophia squeezed in beside him and surveyed the swinging dancers. "Ah, see the group dancing in a circle? Soviets. Best food, best wine, best music! The only thing missing at their parties? Party members!" She punched Calvin's leg. "You know how travelers say there is no toilet paper in Russia?"

"No toilet paper?"

"None! Not in the whole country! Everybody says it! So at their embassy receptions, they stuff you with caviar so you will be forced to use their facilities and see just how well supplied they are!" She nodded toward a man with dark black hair and a mustache led a slightly less hairy woman off the dance floor. "Belgians—all obsessed with guns, and buying and selling diamonds."

Gabriel stood regally framed by the Latvian girls as he received the overblown courtesies of each youthful diplomatic contingent. Girls approached him at intervals requesting a dance, which he gracefully refused. Boys took turns daring each other to stand before him and bow. Soon, he was making mock pairings of the laughing young couples, choosing suitable mates for them, just as he did back in his "own kingdom."

The band began playing *Once in a While* and the lights dimmed except for a spotlight on the turning mirror ball. He caught Kathryn's eye. She smiled, hopped down from the ledge and drew Calvin into the center of the room, directly under the mirror ball. Now they were turning slowly in the opposite direction of the swirling dots of light. She pushed closer and her softness touched his chest, his side. He looked at her face and her eyelids dropped, pearly jewel boxes. The room fell away in a hollow blur and they spun slowly alone. She dropped her head on his shoulder and her hair billowed into his face. Calvin reached up and slowly swept his fingers along the moist nape of her neck, carrying her hair on the back of his hand. She closed her eyes and inhaled slowly, luxuriously—before gagging and pushing laughing away from him with crossed eyes.

Suddenly, Dixieland notes struck applause from the dancers as the band began *The Music Goes 'Round and Around*. The Count, tapped Calvin on his shoulder, bowed to Kathryn and she flowed into his arms. Calvin stared at the man's cool power as they danced off. Sweat stung his eyes and now he was dancing with the energetic Sophia whose back flesh rolled over and jiggled in his hand. The band went right into *At the Codfish Ball*. He spotted Kathryn, momentarily holding her hair away from the back of her neck as the Count spoke into her ear. He watched them mirror each other's laugh, smile and glance. All the other dancers became a blur with Kathryn and the Count's perfectly distinct in their own bubble. The air was sucked out of the room.

The guitar and the drums started a halting progression. The crowd cheered. Sophia's eyes went wide. *"The Big Apple!"* She jumped up to look over his shoulder. "Thank you!" she called as she dove into the crowd. Two parallel lines of dancers stretched the full width of the ballroom in front of the band with couples jive-dancing down between the rows on a frantic conveyor belt of joy. At the end of the line, approving each couple, stood King Gabriel, surrounded by his enthusiastic court. Off to the side, Kathryn and the Count joined a circle of dancers.

Alone in the maelstrom, Calvin made his way to the stairs leading up to the jammed gallery cafe. The windows overlooking the dance floor were packed with people leaning out to watch. A couple suddenly ran off hand-in-hand and Calvin squeezed into their place at the window. The singer on the stage called "Now shine!" A young couple kicked straight legged as they bounced back to back, jump-turned, and froze with their arms and legs awry. Now they pecked like chickens, joined arms and circled while shaking a naughty finger at the ceiling.

They danced off to the cheers of the rest of their circle and the Count took their place as he came up in a "Praise Allah." Now a bottle flashed in the lights at the center of the clapping circle. It was balanced on Kathryn's head as she turned with her fingers pumping toward the floor, then spanking her hip and bouncing on the outside edge of her feet. The Count was up and down, nearly on his rear, kicking his feet out and circling her in a cartoon Russian dance.

A man, beer heavy on his breath, pushed in beside Calvin. Losing his balance, the man placed his hand hard on Calvin's bruised shoulder. The circle of dancers now made frenzied pigeon-toed apple jacks, their ten shoulders pistoning their hell-pointing hands. The man next to Calvin nudged him again and shouted to a friend. "Yeeeaah!" He pointed across Calvin, down at a corner of the dance floor where Kathryn, braced behind a pillar, her skirt pulled up adjusted her stocking. She was working the brass ring from her knee up to the top of her stocking. The Count, standing guard, stole a peek and Kathryn smiled at him. She pulled down her skirt, tossed the brass ring under a chair and went back to dance. In the center of the floor, a girl, agitating like a washing machine, spun her skirt high, exposing all her legs and underthings as she danced her way down the jiving lines toward Gabriel and his courtiers.

"Woah-ho! The king likes that!" shouted the man at Calvin's ear. "King of Spades likes that a lot!"

"He's not the king, he's the joker," muttered Calvin.

"What?" shouted the man.

"What if he wasn't a king, what if he's just the joker?"

The man looked at Calvin pityingly and leaned in to him. "No, no. That guy? He's a king, a king from Africa, and we're..." Suddenly the man went wide-eyed, his nostrils flared. "My God!" cried the man, "God! You stink!" He shoved Calvin away, punching his chain-bruised shoulder with his right hand while raising his left to pinch his nose.

The explosion of pain in Calvin's shoulder drove him back for an instant. He pushed back at the man who now punched him back in the same bruised spot. Calvin shouted in pain, rebounded and delivered the flying stroke of a long jointer plane into the man's gut. He then threw three mean scrub plane strokes at the man's jaw and stepped back to watch him drop like a bag of bolts. Now a red blur swept the corner of Calvin's vision before the meteor shower and blackness.

He heard his own voice repeatedly asking for a cigarette, even thought he didn't smoke, and he wondered at this. He stared up at the faces in the darkness. A wave of pain rolled through his head. "Kathryn?"

"I'm here."

"All you all right?"

Several people laughed — one very close to his ear. He turned his head and saw Kathryn's face through a tunnel. He breathed in and the tunnel opened.

"I'm fine. How are you?"

He turned and saw that the Count was close at his other side. "What happened?"

"Citizen claims you attacked his friend so he hit you with a fire extinguisher," said the Count.

Sophie's voice came too loud from behind him. "You'd be in jail right now if the king hadn't stood up for you!"

"I told them you had Beri-beri." said Gabriel's voice somewhere in the darkness. "It has made you crazy!"

The faces around Calvin laughed as, in the distance, Dorsey's trombone carried the faint notes of his theme song for the final dance. He realized that they were walking now. A woman spoke loudly in Danish beside them as she rode barefoot and piggyback on her red-faced date.

An open-sided streetcar rolled up out of the darkness to

carry them back to the city, with nothing but wooden armrests between them and the drop to the river. The Count pushed Calvin up into the first aisle. Kathryn climbed in past him and leaned back to quiet her laughing friends as they filled the seats behind. The driver tapped his bell twice and turned the handle that bumped the car into motion, sending them rolling back down to the city. As they crossed each bridge and trestle, the treetops, following the contours of the land, dropped below the level of the tracks, letting moonlight flood the car in synchrony with the crescendo of peeping from the frog chorus in the creeks far below.

Calvin bobbed in his chair, nodding with his whole body and shifting his eyes from woman to woman. The women's dresses, beige and mahogany, black and yellow slid against their flesh. Ellen and Verdie tried to explain the new process by analogy, while Linda worked visually, drawing intersecting circles, arrows and boxes on the back of a file folder. Back in France, as "searchers" trying to identify the remains of the men in the hospitals, they had devised a method of eliminating all the impossible answers before trying to find the right answers. Now, the punched-card system made it easy to apply this method to find order in partial and confused return addresses.

Calvin touched the lump on his head. *To hell with him. Screw him and Ibsen and Bartók and the Count.* "What?" he said in response to sounds coming from Linda.

She gave her head a tiny, disapproving shake. "I said, do you want one of us to go pick up the mail?"

"No, I'll walk over in a little bit."

"We really ought to have it delivered up here." She spoke as if she had been arguing this point for months. Perhaps she had. "It comes in next door and then goes all the way over to South building. We're giving Radio Services the demographic reports. That's all they need over there."

Calvin rocked forward. "Maybe later. In radio, you're as good as your most recent stack of letters. It looks better if it goes there first."

"I like walking over there," said Anne, "except that Brockwell guy is such a bastard."

The two other women shot glances at each other but said nothing about a nickel due to the cuss pot. Calvin had also heard Brockwell's complaints about Anne. The receptionist had relayed Brockwell's comments about "defectives" coming into the studio and disturbing his aesthetic imagination.

Worse, for Calvin's part, Brockwell had taken him on as a "project." Clippings from heritage newsletters and ancestry club registers kept arriving in brown envelopes. There were essays on purification, race, colonial revival decoration and the new Inn at the Williamsburg Restoration. Arriving separately in embossed envelopes, were invitations to meetings and dinners. All of Brockwell's missives added to the burden of the correspondence and counterweighted the good of the listener mail.

Calvin walked around the atrium and down the stairs on the far side. He stepped out onto Pennsylvania Avenue, stared at the traffic for a moment and struggled for breath. He turned down 12th Street toward the Mall. Why did the sidewalk continue rising in front of him? The tip of the Washington Monument reached above the skyline. The two red lights atop the obelisk winked slowly at him, seeing right through him. Calvin dropped his head, ashamed that his courage came only against fools and never knaves. And his stupid, stupid stories up against Ibsen, Bartók, Count Dracula… That's okay; he didn't need to breathe any more. On the grassy quad, a fake-limping killdeer labored to distract him from its nest. "I don't want your damn eggs!" he shouted back to it as South building loomed ahead. He jerked his head up at the windows. What if she was watching? "Great," he muttered, "Now I'm shouting at birds."

He walked up the stairs and then down again into the cool basement level. The pools of light reflected in the linoleum slipped under him. A meeting with Hattersley at eleven. Maybe he could find some place for them. Where was Agricultural Engineering? That's where they belonged. He could show them the research. The real stuff, not the idiotic artillery shells with radio fuses. But they might like this calculating machine. Little Shirley could keep track of farmers, allotments, subsidies — everything. He arched his back to push away from the tiled wall just as the receptionist's voice pierced the silence.

"Calvin!" She clicked new shoes on the linoleum like a deer on ice. "I thought I saw your shadow on the door. Mr. Hattersley's looking for you!"

"I'm supposed to see him at eleven."

"He wants to see you now!" She held the door waiting for him. "I'll tell him you're here…" She tapped her toe on the floor. "…as soon as you get in the door!"

"Sorry." Calvin scooted in.

"I feel sorry for those girls in your office."

"Yeah, it's hard on them."

She reached for the intercom on her desk. "He's here."

"I'm coming out," said Hattersley's voice.

She shook her head. "It's a good thing they've got that machine. They're going to need all the help they can get."

Calvin sighed. "I was just thinking, maybe one of the other sections might be interested in it. Like Ag Engineering or something."

"Other sections?" She pushed a ruler parallel with the edge of her desk. "You're still going to have to deal with this mail."

Calvin extended his hand towards the rubber-banded bundle on her blotter.

She grabbed the bundle and jerked it back, rattling her charm bracelet. "This isn't yours." The door leading in to the offices pushed open and thunked against four big canvas sacks piled on the floor. "Those are yours."

Hattersley leaned through the door and grinned at Calvin and down at the bags. "Calvin!" said Hattersley. He pushed the door against the sacks with exaggerated effort and then offered his hand.

"Larry?" said Calvin as he stared down at the sacks.

"Calvin, I don't know how you do it. First congress is after you. You get out of that. Next, the president's wife is after you. You get out of that! You've got more lives than Brer Rabbit." He kicked at a mail sack. "This is phenomenal!"

"How much is there?"

Hattersley glanced over to the receptionist. She bit her lip. "That's got to be about five or six thousand."

Calvin knelt to look in one of the opened bags. "And it's all for us?"

"All for you! It comes here sorted by first address line. Every bit of this is for *Grandpa Sam's Woodshop of the Air*, and it's five times our single day record."

Calvin stood and gave a great sigh and a laugh. "I thought we were going to be cancelled."

"Until ten o'clock this morning, you were."

The receptionist poked Calvin in his midriff with her ruler, making him jump. "Bahh, bahh, black sheep, have you any mail?"

He walked back across the Mall, the four heavy bags on his shoulders. A purple martin circled him, looking for insects flushed by his footfalls, orbiting fifteen feet away as if on a string, just inches above the moist grass. Another joined the first and the two coursed about him like moonlets. He stopped to rest the sacks on a bench and stood looking up at the old Post Office tower. He had presents for all the girls and boys. He had the magic beans. He had the bacon. He was bringing home the fatted calf.

They poured the envelopes onto tables and swarmed around them as if they were incoming wounded—opening, sorting and stacking letters and punched cards. They sponge-dampened stamps and stuck them on sheets of paper for easy counting and cancellation. Someone must have been in charge, but Calvin could not see who it was. Ellen wheeled back into the machine room with boxes of cards and a pile of flattened request letters on her lap. This was their old discipline—dealing with the wounded by the hundreds, each requiring instant decision, the onslaught requiring total concentration. No complaints, no chitchat, no jokes, no gossip, just constant awareness of the whole scene while attending to the task at hand.

Calvin counted off the seconds to himself, following the path of a letter from first pickup to flats in the sorting trays. Ten seconds. At six a minute, three hundred and sixty and hour, two thousand a day per person. Three of them could handle this lot in a day. But that was just receiving! He backed into the hallway and eased down to the machine room door. Linda and Ellen sat keying in names and addresses from unfolded letters, Verdie plucked the bent and mutilated cards from a stack. A stack was already flowing into one of the machines, causing new punched cards to drop into a hopper at an equivalent rate.

Dealing with the stamps and the Treasury warrants looked like half of the work. How many would there be tomorrow? Linda had shown him a column chart illustrating the numbers of letters received over the previous two weeks. Each X in a column represented ten letters. The columns peaked on Thursday and made a quick decline. Listeners wrote soon after hearing the Saturday show, and the letters took three days in transit. They would make it.

Calvin snapped his head back—it looked like a real office! Where was that GAO inspector now? Thousands of letters converging from far away, four women using a giant machine to fire them back. A shiver began in the back of his neck and ran down to his feet. He had to write another program, had to make another recording, but for the moment, he just had to watch these women work.

The next morning, twenty minutes after Hattersley's telephone call, Calvin heard the honk of the car horn eight floors below. He leaned out his window and watched three slim, pale-armed girls emerge from the car, their shadows racked in zigzags up the steps. The driver was already unloading another six mail sacks from the trunk. Linda's graying hair, centered on her white-bloused shoulders, bounced down the steps to meet them. Anne and Verdie pushed a hand cart up the sidewalk and spoke to the driver, who quickly set to stacking the sacks on the cart. The driver leaned to speak into Verdie's ear over the traffic noise. She turned her head up and pointed up at the office. She spotted Calvin and waved just as a mocking bird flew between them at the fifth floor level. He waved back and withdrew into the office, dropping back into his chair before his *Abraham Lincoln — with Mallets Towards None* script.

He stared at the grungy keys on his Underwood portable and jogged the M key, threatening the paper with the lower case strike. Somehow, the right combination of keystrokes would give him the story he needed. The door opened, letting in the hard, unmuffled noise of the machines. Ellen rolled in and laid two piles of unfolded letters on his desk. One pile required his personal response to woodworking questions and the others were just nice comments. The piles of letters on his desk already nagged at him. He had forgotten which pile was which and he thumbed through one to read a random penciled letter.

"Dear Grandpa Sam, Sinse father died we have not ben abel to mark his grave with respect. He was a wood worker and carpeter and showd us how to make things too. We have used youre blessings to have a stone cut…"

He pulled the typewriter ribbon shift lever up and down, then lifted the cover and stared at the ribbon. His script was still nothing more than a title. Maybe Lincoln made this puzzle mallet when working as a lawyer and gave it to judges where his cases might be heard. He stuffed the letters into his top desk drawer. Another knock at the door and a Western Union boy entered with a telegram. Calvin signed for it, tipped the boy fifteen cents and withdrew into that tight dread of wondering who had died. "TO CALVIN COBB STOP THANK YOU STOP BLESS YOU STOP FROM THE HOYDEN FAMILY SPRINGFIELD IILINOIS STOP." He turned it over. Blank. He read the message again. Nice, but he wished all these folks would just send a sentence of a story. Does he have to telegraph back? "YOU ARE KIND TO THANK ME BUT DON'T STOP" Another quiet knocking at the door.

"Yes?"

Linda stuck her head around the door with her finger held to her lips, she glanced back out and then wiggled her finger, motioning for him to follow her. He rose quietly and joined her behind a column in the hall. "Fifth floor," she whispered, "the far corner."

Calvin lowered his head enough to see under the railing. Across the huge atrium, in the corner of a floor of empty offices, two men stood quietly talking and referring casually to a clipboard of papers. Often enough, though, one or the other of them would sneak a glance up in their direction. Calvin leaned slowly back towards Linda. "Burroughs?" he whispered.

She shook her head. "Their hats aren't right for Burroughs," she whispered. "Too small."

He leaned out again; the two men were walking down the steps toward the south doors. "GAO?"

Linda smiled. "GAO's covered." The creaking of doors echoed up to them and she resumed a normal voice. "Probably just IRS stiffs from next door checking out the new girls. Anyway, I just thought it was funny."

"Well, let me know if they come back."

"Don't worry, we'll chase 'em off plenty fast." She followed Calvin back into his office, unable to see the hangdog look on his face.

The paper in his typewriter was totally blank, but Calvin pulled it out as if it were covered with errors. "What were you saying about the GAO not being a problem?"

She nodded slyly at him. "Guardian angels take the most unexpected forms." She pointed back out the door. "And those two stiffs down there? Probably just more fans of your show."

He bounced his pencil on its eraser, shaking his head at her efforts to cheer him.

She pondered him for a moment. "Have you been following the ratings of your show? The Hoopers?"

"Nah, just dealing with these letters," he said flatly. "I guess we're doing pretty good."

A breeze fluttered papers on his windowsill. Linda seemed to suddenly inflate with the summer air. "Why don't you get out of here? Go work outside for the afternoon! It's a beautiful day out there."

He sighed. "Maybe I will. I need to drop off the stamps anyway, we've got to keep ahead on the Treasury refunds."

She stuffed blank paper onto a clipboard and thrust it into

his hands. "You just go work on your script. I don't want to see you back here 'til five o'clock. Alright?"

"Alright, sure."

"But whatever you write today, I'll need to type into the punch cards tonight. So you be sure to come back before you go home. Alright?"

"Alright." He stood to attention and saluted. "Yes m'am."

She scurried him out the door.

He dropped the stamps off at the new Post Office, picked up a ham sandwich for lunch at the commissary and found a bench on the Mall under an elm tree. He sat facing the Capitol, its ivory dome merging into the hazy sky. Between bites of his sandwich, he scribbled notes and dialogue lines. Tourists walked by — bicyclists, dog-walking couples, groups of foreign tourists — all kicking up trails of dust. He wiped the nib of his pen on a fuzzy elm leaf and settled back against the splintering rails of the bench. Workmen drove stakes into the ground, setting creosote-stained snow fences around a cluster of small wooden huts. He pondered this for a moment and then realized that they were preparations for next week's Fourth of July crowds.

He stared at his paper. Wind stirred the tree and sent puzzle pieces of light dancing across the page. The dovetailed mallet was obviously a mistake. A rising dovetail joint was hard enough to understand when you could hold one in your hands and look at it — there was simply no way to describe it on radio. He looked up as a blue LaSalle pulling a streamlined travel trailer made slow passage down Constitution Avenue. Kathryn would love that. They could ride to the beach. She could take photographs of dune grasses while he typed his stories at a little table inside. Then she would come back in and he would brush all the sand from her feet.

"Mr. Cobb?"

Calvin turned with a start at the woman's voice and slid half off the bench.

"Mr. Cobb? Excuse me, are you Mr. Cobb? We're sorry to bother you, but the lady at your office said you might be out here." The voice came from a small but strikingly proportioned woman in her thirties who was standing next to a tall young man who was uncomfortable with his own height.

Calvin staggered to his feet and belched throat-burning acid. "Calvin Cobb? No." He glanced around to see who else might be watching. He looked back at them to see that, instead of disappointment, they were nodding and smiling to one another.

"Oh it is you! My son and I listen to you together. I'd recognize your voice anywhere! I know you're trying to keep…discreet…but we both wanted to tell you how much we appreciate what you have done for us!" The young man grinned dumbly at Calvin until his mother prompted him. "Tell Mr. Cobb what you are going to do, Tad."

"I'm going to Iowa State. I'm going to study to be a veterinarian, but I'm going to keep on working wood too."

"That's good," said Calvin, too weakly to be heard above the traffic. "Woodworking is good."

"We were able to come to visit his grandparents in Baltimore because of you. We drove all the way from Moline. I had no idea we would find you here. Oh, and I want you to know, Alan makes everything, he doesn't just send for the plans like you know some people must do."

"I'm glad," said Calvin, now desperately thirsty.

"Well, I can see you were trying to get some rest, but it wouldn't have been right for us not to thank you."

"Well." Calvin thought hard, breathed deep. "My pleasure. I'm glad you enjoy the show," he said finally.

"Ohhh, you sound just like you do on the radio!" She smiled, tilted her head and flashed her eyebrows at him. She offered her hand. "T'ain't there nuthin' ah ken do? I love that!"

Her son, beaming, reached out his hand. "Thank you, sir, and I want you to know that I work hard to do good work."

"That's good!" said Calvin. "Keep it up!"

The mother turned away, tilting her head back over her shoulder. "We'll let you work now. Bye. We'll let you... 'tend to your whittlin'!"

This had to be a dream. This attractive woman was flirting with him! She was now beside a taxi. She smiled again when she saw him looking. A friendly sunbeam defined her legs through her skirt for an instant. He glanced at his page with the sketches of the useless puzzle mallet.

The sunlight danced too brightly on his paper, and Calvin shifted to a shadier bench facing toward the Monument. Perhaps he should walk down to the Lincoln memorial for inspiration. He crossed the street and had just regained the grass when the blast of a duo-toned car horn made him turn. Back toward the Smithsonian Castle, an oddly streamlined car made a quick U-turn and pulled up to stop beside him. The two-tone car had light brown sides with a deep chocolate hood and trunk, the convertible top was folded down onto the back. A smiling Brockwell sat at the wheel, beside a white prune of a person with the goatee and flamboyant hair of a Kentucky Colonel, carefully adjusting his bow tie in the rear view mirror.

"How are you this beautiful day, Mister Calvin Cobb?"

"Fine, Mr. Brockwell, thank you." His gaze slid down the chrome band on the bulging hood to the chrome eagle badge between the two closely-placed headlamps. "Swell car!" In the edge of his vision, Calvin glimpsed a snort from the Kentucky Colonel.

Brockwell beamed. "You might want to pick one up for yourself, young man. It's an Adler two-point-five. The car of the future. Engineered for the autobahn, don't you know? Brought it back from my last concert tour."

"It's beautiful."

"Yes, beautifully crafted." He stroked the steering wheel. "Now, you remember our VIP soiree tonight. Don't be late."

"Oh! Yes, tonight?"

"You're our guest of honor, don't you know? I just wanted to remind you to wear your dinner jacket."

"Well, you see, that's another reason…" Calvin stopped, stunned by the sight of his own high school yearbook photograph looking back at him from a folded copy of the *Evening Star* on Brockwell's lap. Above the photograph, the headline read "Carpenter's Tales a Surprise Summer Hit."

"Is that me in the newspaper?"

"Of course it is! Haven't you seen it?" He handed the paper to Calvin. "Your show is number one in the Hooper ratings, don't you know?"

"My God! That's impossible!" He stared at the paper but could hardly read it. "How can we be number one?"

"Well, Calvin, you may start off as a pawn, but if we can get you all the way across the chessboard," Brockwell swept his eyes up and down the Mall, moving his grasping hand about as if the Monument and Capitol were chess pieces, "we can make you a king."

"Linda must have known this morning!"

"And now that you are a king, we just need to make sure you look like one." Brockwell pushed in the clutch and threw the shift lever forward. "You'll have to go to Garfinkle's, I fear." His goateed companion leaned over and spoke to him over the racing engine. Brockwell pulled the shift lever back into neutral and released the clutch. "Do you know what to get?"

"No, I…"

"Ask for a silk dinner jacket, double-breasted — maybe blue with black satin lapels. Single braid trousers. Box pleat shirt with a turnover collar and a Windsor bowtie." The clutch release bearing sang as Brockwell eased out the pedal. "It's the Mallard Club at seven sharp." Calvin stepped back as Brockwell called out, "Time for that next move! Let's make it another good one!"

Calvin stared at his photograph in the paper. Had Kathryn seen it? Even bishop Bartók Bela-Bale never had number-one position in the Hooper Radio Survey, nor had Count Dracula's castle, or even Gabriel the black king! And the girls? Nothing could touch them now! Something flushed deep in Calvin's viscera and surrounded him in a glow of well-being. He turned with a start to walk quickly toward South building — the only move a king needed to make.

Calvin strode past the receptionist heading straight for Kathryn's office. "Wait!" she called out, "Take your personal mail with you! Don't let it build up on my desk!" She handed him the bundled envelopes.

The letters slipped from under Calvin's arm and he writhed to hang on to them. He wheeled around and down on one knee so the receptionist could help him. "Thanks. Lost my grip. Are they in the studio now?"

"Who?"

"Kathryn."

"She's not on today's show. They've got a home canning scientist on instead." The receptionist glanced at a typed sheet on her desk. "And, she's not on tomorrow, not the next day, and not the next."

"What do you mean?"

"Looks like she got canned herself."

"Canned? You mean fired? Is she here?"

"Haven't seen her."

"Where's Mister Hattersley?"

"He's not here. He's gone to the party."

"Party? That's not 'til seven."

"I think they're waiting for you now. Oh foo, it was supposed to be a surprise!"

"What?"

"Just go back to your office. I'm sure he's there and you can have a nice chat."

Calvin pushed out the door.

"Congratulations!" she called after him. "Maybe you'd like her old office!"

Calvin bounded up the 12th Street steps of the old Post Office building. Hattersley was waiting for him at the top of the steps by the door, ready to offer a hearty "Congratulations!" but Calvin spoke first. "What happened with Kathryn?"

Hattersley blew a quick jet of air from his cheeks. "The homemaking segments are taking a break—at least for the summer." He pointed back up over his shoulder. "Let's go upstairs, they're waiting for you."

"So, what happened? Brockwell? Did he do this?"

Hattersley pulled the door open and they stepped inside. Cables writhed in the latticework-encased elevator shafts like zoo creatures. Black tire marks from Verdie's escape from the police still ran across the marble floor.

"Look, someone at the British embassy tipped off the papers to Kathryn's background."

"What background?"

Hattersley blew out his cheeks. "You know Harper's not her real last name?"

"No, I didn't. So what?"

"It's Neuman, or von Neuman, apparently."

"You fired her because of that?"

"Listen, you can work under a false name in Hollywood — but not here, not as part of a public trust."

"Oh, come on!"

They detoured around a patch of floor tiles that had become unstuck from their grout. Calvin kicked a loose tile sending it spinning down the hall. "So, wait! You fired her because she's Jewish?"

Hattersley turned to face him. "Listen, I think the world of Kathryn. That's why I tried to put her an out-of-the-way job until things calm down!"

"I'll tell you what's going on, it's Brockwell. I know he's behind all this."

"I was on the phone to him this morning." Hattersley looked around and lowered his voice. "Listen to me, John Brockwell is your best friend right now. Because if he wasn't, you and everyone you know wouldn't even be allowed to walk the pavement of this town. If Brockwell wasn't using his connections to keep it quiet, half the newspapers in the Midwest would have headlines tomorrow saying, 'Secret Yid at Center of Jew-Deal Radio.'"

"So let 'em! Who cares?"

Hattersley leveled his eyes at Calvin. "Look, the more this government looks like it's run by Jews, the more the America-firsters can play the Jewish warmongering card. If she hadn't tried to hide it we wouldn't be in this fix!"

"If she hadn't hidden it, she never would have gotten the job in the first place!"

Hattersley looked hard at Calvin. "I don't know if you read the papers, my friend, but there's another war on the way and we are not prepared — at all! If we let the government look like it's entirely a pawn of Jewish interests…"

Calvin interrupted with a shout. "Kathryn does goddamn cookie recipes!"

"Look, I needed her to just take some time off!" Hattersley stomped his foot. "And we have got to keep Brockwell happy for as long as we can. I know he's a race nut, but you keep that old guy happy and nothing can touch you — or those ladies upstairs. If you want them protected, nothing gets past him."

"What happens when we run outta bones to throw to this dog? What then?" Calvin wiped sweat from under his collar. "Someone was looking out for us at the GAO, you think it was Brockwell?"

"At the GAO?" He shrugged, bouncing his fist on the stair railing as they approached the eighth floor. "They're untouchable. Make no mistake, though, Brockwell kept Kathryn out of the papers just save himself from embarrassment, not out of any concern for her. He was mad as hell when he found out. And favors, like this help with congressman Richter, favors must be repaid."

"He wants me to go his party tonight."

"Well, for God's sakes, don't disappoint him!" Hattersley shook his head. "Even if he's not creating all this trouble, he's for damn sure the only one who can get you out of it."

The sudden burst of light from the machine room and the shouted chorus of "SURPRISE!" almost blew Calvin over the railing and into an eighty-foot free fall to the floor of the atrium. Now it was all laughter and squeals as people poured out the door into the hallway.

"Congratulations, Chief!" shouted Verdie.

"Mister number one!" chanted Ellen, "Mister number one!"

"We've about finished all the beer!" called Bubby from within the machine room.

Calvin rose up to look into the room. Ellen's wheelchair blocked the doorway. She had a drifting look in her eyes from a recent morphine injection, but still cheered "Hurray! Hurray for the Chief!" when she spotted Calvin. A match flared behind her, lighting Captain Valentine's smiling face as he drew the flame into his pipe. Close around him in a laughing, cheering wreath were Bubby and Gabriel.

"Come on in! I might have saved you half a beer!" called Bubby.

Anne eased Ellen's wheelchair back out of the doorway as the other women pushed Calvin into the machine room with pats on the back. "Look," said Anne, "even Little Shirley's proud of you!" She pointed up to a length of tractor-feed paper hung between the windows. In seven-inch-high letters patterned from hundreds of strikes of the same letter, it spelled out "CALVIN COBB — RADIO WOODWORKER!"

"You can't have beer up here?" said Calvin, his statement making a midstream twist into a question.

Gabriel pried the cap off a bottle and handed it to Calvin. "When the cat's away!"

Anne stood close beside Gabriel as he refilled her glass. She raised it to Calvin. "Christina would be here too, but she couldn't get a babysitter."

Calvin looked about the room at cake boxes and delicacies spread everywhere. "Who brought all the food?"

Gabriel grinned. "Latvian embassy, yah! Champagne too!"

"Yah! Yah!" The girls joined in with comic Scandinavian accents and laughter.

"The cuss-pot money paid for the beer!" said Verdie.

"Hail to the Chief!" said Ellen groggily. The others joined in her cheering.

"Hurry up!" said Captain Valentine to his son, who was slipping on his coat and hat.

"I'll be right back!" said Gabriel.

Anne grabbed Calvin's arm. "Gabriel's going to pick up his mother. You've got a big surprise coming!"

"Wait!" Calvin tugged his watch from his pocket — six-fifty. "My God! I gotta go!"

"You just got here, man!" said Bubby. "Come on, this is your party!"

"No, this is wrong!"

The room fell silent.

Ellen lolled her head and squinted at Calvin. "But we…"

"This is wonderful, but I don't deserve it. You think that goofy show would be number one if Brockwell hadn't fixed it somehow?"

They stared at him in slack-jawed silence.

"Come on! You know it's not that good! And our guardian angel at the GAO? Brockwell probably fixed that for us, too!" He looked up at Shirley's banner. "I wish I'd earned this. But, now at least there's something I can do to keep everybody here safe and happy. I don't like it, but that's the grown-up story!"

Bubby leaned down to him. "You're not going to Brockwell's party? He wanted me to come film the damn thing."

"Well we'd better hurry, it starts in ten minutes!" He glanced up at his friend and saw that Bubby had no intention of going. "You're the one who wanted me to make friends and influence people."

"No, no, Chief!" Linda grinned, shaking her head. "You think Brockwell's our GAO friend?"

Bubby tossed his empty beer bottle in the trash. "Do you have any idea what kind of party you're going to? Those aren't just blue-haired cave dwellers. These are Bundists, Free Partiers, Liberty Leaguers!"

Captain Valentine stepped forward and pushed Calvin's hands away from his bowtie and straightened it for him. "Let him go." He glanced back at Bubby through his pipe smoke. He turned back to Calvin. "You know that picture you got with the knight on the road, and the monsters callin' at him from the sides? For years I've been looking at that picture. It means a man has to…"

"…fight his own dragons." Calvin nodded his thanks, turned, and headed toward the stairs.

Brockwell's car sat parked under the dogwoods. Long chauffeur-driven cars pulled past Calvin and disgorged fur-draped women and their escorts under the insect-clouded lantern hanging from the portico. A black man in a red uniform held the door open for him and the sounds of a fiddle and cocktail chatter poured from within. A man in a tux asked if he might help him "find his name on the guest list." Calvin shook his head and was distracted by the eyelashes of one of the passing women. He gave his name. The man nodded and showed the list to another man.

Certainly people were staring at him and making comments. He checked his fly. Even the cheery bartender seemed to be hiding a private laugh at him. Handing Calvin his scotch and soda, he said in a strained and raspy voice, "A double dose ob courage, suh! Hope dats all right!" Calvin's sudden surprised stare at the bartender made the man abruptly turn to greet the next person waiting.

Windsor chairs sat on the stage where a fiddler in a stiff new pair of denim overalls played with his instrument held flat against his chest. Jewels glittered on the necks of the women.

Silver hair rose and fell like breaking whitecaps. Calvin fixed a smile and searched for someone he might recognize. Ice rattled in his drink, it was already empty. He made his way back to the bartender. Conversations, introductions, handshaking and nodding roared around him as the rhythm of the fiddler augered into his chest, building louder and louder, faster and faster. A few enthusiastic yelps egged the fiddler faster, louder until he peaked and the crowd broke into applause. Simultaneously, the curtain of hand-woven coverlets drew back and lights came on revealing an array of dining tables glittering with candle-lit crystal. The crowd flowed confidently to the tables. Calvin was in mid-gulp when a hand landed on his shoulder.

"How do you like our fiddler?" asked Brockwell.

"Good! Really good. Listen, Mister Brockwell, I know you were expecting me to be here tonight…"

"Good? He's our number-one prize winner! Number one, just like our guest of honor! Come on with me, we'll find our table!" He took Calvin's glass and placed it on a hovering waiter's tray. "The boy'll bring you a fresh one at the table."

Calvin followed, drying his hand on his jacket before remembering his handkerchief. Brockwell made introductions of the other guests around the table. Names that Calvin instantly forgot. The Kentucky Colonel was there, already seated beside a tall, black-mustachioed man, introduced to Calvin as head of the Blue Shirts Brigade of the Irish Free State. Brockwell motioned for him to sit to the left of the Irishman's wife, a rotund American woman whose bright red beret and lipstick failed to distract from her crooked teeth.

"You're the radio star! Oh, I've never sat next to a radio star before! Oh, no! I have!" She whacked tipsily at her husband's arm. "I met Father Coughlin! Do you know him? It must be so exciting to be on the radio! Tell me all about all the wonderful people you've met!"

"Well, we're just getting started." A fresh, full glass of scotch appeared at Calvin's side.

"A radio star!" squealed the fat woman. "And you're really more popular than Jack Benny?"

"Kubelsky," said the Kentucky Colonel. "His real name is Binyamin Kubelsky."

"You're Binyamin…who?"

"No, Mrs. Leary, Jack Benny's real name is Binyamin Kubelsky. This is Calvin Cobb."

The black-haired Irishman waved away a waiter who was attempting to fill his wine glass. He shook his cigaretted hand at Calvin. "Now Cobb, that's an east Anglian name, isn't it?"

"I guess so. English. Sorry."

Brockwell leaned into the center of the table. "Ah, don't be afraid Calvin! The same blood unites us all. I'm descended from the ancient Welsh kings myself. Battling brothers, we are!" He held his glass high and everyone followed in the toast. "Calvin, welcome to our table!"

"Thank you sir!" Calvin dabbed at a drip of scotch he felt running down to his chin.

Brockwell shook a butter knife at him. "You know what Cobb means in Old Norse?"

"You told me. A big lump."

"Right! A big fellow, the kind of man you'd like to have next to you in battle."

The fat woman raised her knife. "Charge!"

Brockwell lowered his own knife. "And, there's even an ancient kind of architecture, a clay building technique used by our ancestors called cobb."

The fat woman pursed her lips as she sucked them against her teeth. "If music is frozen architecture, Mister Brockwell, what would a cobb house sound like?"

"Perhaps you mean the other way around," said her husband.

"Oh, I understand," said Brockwell. "True folk architecture, like true folk music, expresses the essence of a people. So 'cobb' would sound like drums, rousing the race to battle the half-breed Romans. Drums, don't you think, Calvin?"

Calvin nodded absently. He had been trying to see the guests at other tables, but his chair was set facing away from them.

The Kentucky Colonel dabbed a napkin at his goatee. "Well, Calvin, they tell me you're drumming up quite a lot of mail."

Calvin was startled. It was the first time the man had spoken to him. "Quite a lot. It's overwhelming."

"But your machines are able to keep good track of people?"

"Well, the girls, they've made this machine do wonders!" He swung his head to look around the room. The candles caught in the crystal, tiny lights everywhere.

The fleshy lady put her hand on his wrist. "I heard it's like Siegfried and the ring, Calvin and his Valkyries up there in his castle."

Calvin snorted, spraying her arm. "The only ring I've ever gotten was on a merry-go-round." He swallowed and stopped sawing at his roast beef.

"How many characteristics can you keep on an individual's card?" asked the Kentucky Colonel.

"I don't know. Really, I tell corny stories like my father used to tell. I get to make things. And I get to look after some people." He set down his empty glass. "It's a pretty good deal."

"And these are modified Burroughs machines that you have?"

Calvin looked up at him. "They're really complicated. They're answering mail now. We had about five thousand letters come in the other day." He leaned back too far in his chair and had to jerk forward to keep from tipping.

"Father Coughlin gets a million letters a week," said the Irishman, "or he used to."

"I suppose that has a trajectory too. Rise and fall of all things," said Calvin, scooting his chair back.

Brockwell's fist pounded the table, rattling his silverware. "But things don't have to fall before their time, Calvin. We ourselves can *create* the lessons of history."

Calvin swung his head back and into the face of the pale, fat woman. The powder on her face emphasized the pores in her skin. He focused on her nose. He turned to look back at the stage. His eye muscles, having focused so closely, struggled to tug his lenses flat enough to refocus. Unheard through the racket, a woman plucked an instrument Calvin recognized as a dulcimer.

Now came applause and Brockwell was standing, speaking at the microphone. "All Americans here tonight. All here to enjoy the music that unites us, the music that defines us as Americans. Patriots may ask why we emphasize songs that can be traced back to Europe? Why not music that arose here in America? First, there is the evident artistic superiority of the music you will hear tonight."

Calvin squeezed his chin with his left hand, and tried to follow the man's words. He glanced down again and his glass was once more full.

"Second, unless we are going to include the tribal songs of the Red Indian or those of 'Homo Africans,' both of whom are Americans only by geographical accident, we can not controvert the fact that the American stock is European in origin."

The light of a candle focused through Calvin's wine glass cast a ruby spot on the tablecloth. Calvin admired the dance of the juddering ruby light as the crowd applauded. Bubby's new movie camera had to have a tiny focused light driven by the microphone to shoot the sound track onto the edge of the film. He tried to imagine the sound track—juddering dark and light spaces as Brockwell spoke at the microphone.

"Our first ballad harks back to the old England of Elizabeth and Raleigh, to the days of Morris dances and even echoes into the time of King Arthur. I'm going to ask a special guest of ours to introduce it. Two months ago, outside of some close friends, no one had heard the wonderfully creative tales of Mr. Calvin Cobb."

Calvin's every muscle locked.

"As of this week, his program, *Uncle Sam's Woodshop of the Air*, broadcast every Saturday as part of the *National Farm and Home Hour*, is now the numberone mid-day radio program in America!" Brockwell held up the folded newspaper.

Water spigoted from under Calvin's arms. The applause echoed hollow.

"He has surely struck a chord with the American people. His is a voice we're sure to be hearing more of, so let's see if we can hear him tonight. Calvin, come on up!"

Calvin's leg had fallen asleep and he staggered like Frankenstein's monster toward the podium. Brockwell pulled him up to the microphone.

"Calvin, it's appropriate that you introduce the next ballad, because it has to do with a fellow woodworker."

He handed him the script, hand-printed in big block letters and pointed to the place for him to begin reading. Calvin glanced up at the auditorium of white hair and back down at his script. A man in the back called out "T'ain't there nuthin I kin do?" Scattered laughter and quieter renditions of Gabriel's catch phrases and assorted Uncle Dan-isms bounced about the room. Calvin read, and then remembered he had to speak the words out loud. "*The House Carpenter's Wife* is one of the many folk ballads that warn of the perfidy of men. We find over fifty documented versions of this ballad, and in several texts, the tempter that lures the carpenter's wife away is seen to possess cloven feet, hence its second title, *The Demon Lover*. Here is

Campbell Wilkes to sing for us, *The House Carpenter's Wife*."

He turned to applaud the curly haired woman and her guitar as they came to the stage. The sound of the room went hollow again and he staggered slightly. She sang. He looked at his script. Had he said "perfidy" or "perfid-ditty?"

The sorrowful, modal song filled the room.

"Oh won't you leave your house carpenter
    and come and go with me?
I will take you where the grass grows green
    On the side of the salt, salt sea."

A fine looking woman in a red gown with a pile of lemon colored hair in the second row of tables smiled at him. Her left eyelid gave a tiny twitch as her chest rose gently. He smiled back and then looked down at the floor, feeling his face flush. He glanced back up.

"Oh, she picked up her sweet little babe
    and kissed her one, two, three
Saying, "Stay at home my sweet little babe,
    Keep your papa's company."

Applause. Brockwell at the microphone. "Thank you Mrs. Wilkes, thank you Calvin. Of course it's not just men that can be treacherous. This next familiar ballad, known as *The Jew's Daughter* is based on an incident that transpired in England in the year 1255. The story survives in this ballad still sung by the American descendants of the English originators. Singing this captivating caveat is our Irish tenor, James Welden of Loudon County, Virginia."

Calvin stiff-legged his way back to the table as the high voice sang.

"The Jew's daughter came to the door, all clad in golden sheen.
Come in, come in, you bright little son. You shall have your ball again."

He sat back at the table. The Irishman was speaking into the ear of the Kentucky Colonel, who furrowed his brow and said. "He's the best we have!"

The high voice sang;

"She showed him an apple as yellow as gold. She showed him a bright gold ring.
She showed him a cherry as red as blood, and that enticed him in."

The Irishman wrinkled his nose. "He won't do. Why is every Irishman is represented by these damn soprano castrati."

"She took him by his little white hand and led him through the hall;
She took him to a little dark room, where no one could hear him call."

Calvin turned to consider the high-voiced singer at the microphone. "I know what you mean," he said. "It confirms the powerlessness of the Irish people. The high feminine voice coming from a man." They turned to face him.

"I can't come in, I won't come in, I've heard of you before.
Whoever goes in at your garden gate, will never come out no more."

Calvin enjoyed a sip of his whiskey. "He's like Fibber McGee, the stereotypical Irishman portrayed as an ineffectual liar — an emasculated fool dominated by Molly."

"She pinned a napkin over his face, she pinned it with a pin,
and then she took her carving knife and carved his little heart in."

The corpulent woman broke the silence. "But I like Fibber McGee!"

Calvin emptied his scotch and set glass down too hard, rattling the silverware. "It defuses the rage of the oppressed and confirms the subservient relationship." He laughed. "Now I've got a woman who sings in my building at night. My God, she has a voice! If you could hear her…" he suddenly ran out of steam "…you'd agree."

The Irishman looked to the heavens. "He's right! I didn't

have the words for it, but he's right! It's an emasculation!"

Through the applause for the tenor and his introduction of the fiddler's medley, Brockwell shot glances at them from the stage. The Irishman shook his head at Brockwell as he sat back at the table. "I know we agreed on a ballad singer to win, but I can't have one of these high-pitched cabin-boys. Young Cobb nailed it. It's unmanly, and it's contemptuous of the Irish people."

Brockwell glared at Calvin and tapped the table. "The folk festival begins in three days. We can promise you a winner, Sean, but we do need someone who can actually sing."

Applause for the fiddlers interrupted. The curtain of coverlets pulled back revealing a dulcimer-playing lady on a platform in the middle of tables of sweets and liqueurs. The assembly rose. Men lit cigars and strolled toward the courtyard garden. Brockwell motioned for Calvin to stay behind at the table.

"Mr. Brockwell, thanks so much for inviting me. I'm sorry if I said the wrong thing there, about the tenor."

Brockwell let out a dismissive "tuh!" and shook his head. He studied their dining companions as they sampled treats from the table. "Ignorant twits." He turned to Calvin "We need them, though, the Irish, like oxen. Human progress is an endless ladder which cannot be climbed without treading on the lower rungs."

"Ah." Calvin nodded absently at the wall. "Mister Brockwell. I want you to help me. What happened to Kathryn, it's not fair and I know you…"

"Calvin, the intelligence and vigor in your bloodline makes you superior to other men, but only when you succeed in conquering your passions."

"I haven't done very well at that."

"Don't fret over that papist moron. But I'd let his dog win the contest if I thought it would help us reel in the Blue Shirts."

"I'm really not worried about him. It's Kathryn."

Brockwell smiled at the tablecloth. "Let's have a little chat." He stirred sugar into a cup of hot tea that appeared at his side. "You like technology don't you? What do you think was our people's first technological feat?"

Calvin squirmed in his seat and shrugged.

"It was when we first put yokes on the lesser species and made them subservient to our will. Just as we needed horses before we invented the motorcar, we use them until we no longer need them. That's why we need these Irish. Just a step on the ladder of progress."

"I don't think this has anything to do with me. Really."

"Oh, but it has everything to do with you. You've been set on a very big stage for a purpose. Surely you recognize that the genius of our race is finding its voice in you."

"Mister Brockwell, I don't think you're listening to me. I came here to ask for your help."

"And now the genius of our race will speak through you, Calvin. It will speak at the Festival of the True American Folk, Calvin. It will speak from the beautiful Virginia mountains among the greatest reserve of pure Anglo-Nordic blood on the continent. It will speak across the land and we'll share our beauty in the newsreels and very soon on televisors. Our race will speak through you, the new voice of our crusade!"

Calvin pushed himself up to stand beside his chair. "Mister Brockwell, I know you made my show number one somehow, but I just don't believe in all this racialist stuff. I just can't be a part of this."

"Young man!" He grabbed Calvin's wrist. "The people have chosen you, not me. They have chosen you!" Brockwell's smile never faltered as Calvin pulled his wrist free. "Your success is all your own, but your duty is to your blood!"

"You said you made me number one."

"Not at all, and I will confess I did a few things that made it harder for you, and for that I am sorry." He rubbed his chin and worked his eyebrows, struggling to rationalize his weakness. "The fierceness of the Anglo-Nordic race is a double-edged sword, Calvin. We fight among ourselves, but only to become stronger for the great battle of purification to come."

Calvin steadied himself on the table as the room tilted. "So, you had nothing to do with my stupid show and the Hooper ratings?"

Brockwell lowered his eyebrows in concern. "Your show is not stupid! In fact your success made me finally admit how much our culture has been degraded by Slavic vaudevilles and Negroid bestiality. I know now that our work must commence at a much baser level — your success is proof of that!"

"My God, Brockwell, life has given you nothing but roses! Where did you get all this hatred for everyone?"

His eyes widened in defense. "I have no hatred whatever for the lesser races, only love for our own people! Do you know what your jewess tried to do to me? She was going to carry on her masquerade and host this dinner tonight, as I have had you do. We are people who treasure our heritage. Yet here she would have been! Can you imagine the humiliation!"

Calvin stared at him for a long second, threw up his hands and pushed back his seat.

From behind Calvin came the voice of the Kentucky Colonel. "If you want to help her, then you need to stop her."

Calvin looked at them both in turn. "What do you mean, stop her?"

"She's a woman scorned, out for revenge." The goateed man tossed a yellow magazine on the table in front of Calvin. "Petty harassment of the most mean-spirited kind."

"She's there?" asked Brockwell. The Kentucky Colonel nodded. Brockwell scooted his chair close beside Calvin, reached for the *National Geographic* and flipped it open to a photograph of men in colonial costumes seated in a tavern. "Look here." He thumbed through the pages. "This whole article is on the Williamsburg restoration. They've got all this woodworking and American history and furniture and decoration. All kinds of woodworking things to inspire you! American history and heritage to inspire us all!" He pushed the magazine back at Calvin and poked at a photograph of a tourist standing with his head locked in a pillory.

"We had arranged for her to visit — before we found out what she was, and now she's gone down there clearly with the object of despoliation," said the Colonel.

"I can help her, but not if she embarks on a campaign to denigrate our founding fathers and all who have worked so hard to honor them." Brockwell maneuvered to make eye contact with Calvin. "Let this be your first assignment then."

"Assignment, hell!"

"It is our holy purpose to purify the blood of our people, and that purpose *will* be achieved through you."

Calvin stood, pushing too hard on the table, upsetting a water glass. "Mr. Brockwell, I have studied manure spreaders for most of my working life, but you and your pals — you beat 'em all."

Brockwell nodded at the mess. "Where the blood is pure the mind can be restored. Your blood might want to have a bit less whisky in it."

After the miserable, sleepless night, Calvin needed the train — needed this big friend blocking for him on his run down the football field. Now, on the train, he could hear the bumps long before they reached him — listening for them ahead as they slowly approached, passed underneath and receded behind. A northbound freight suddenly streamed past, inches from his face.

He leaned his head back against the window and saw, reflected in the window ahead of him, a peaches-and-cream blonde fixing her makeup. He watched her, calculating angles of incidence and reflection. She folded her compact and leaned toward the window, looking intently out. Her reflection created a confrontation between beautiful twins. He was no longer surprised by his indifference to such sights. This was not the face he longed to see, and he sighed in admission that his trouble was deep indeed.

He flipped open the *National Geographic* to the mammy in the kitchen photo and women in dresses wider than sofas. There was a Dufaycolor photograph of two colonial soldiers standing over two barefoot black children holding watermelon slices in front of their faces. There were more symmetrical photos of brick buildings, flowery gardens, powder-wigged men and wide-gowned women.

The train barreled across a swamp of cypresses and dark gum trees; lily pads and marsh grass on brown water. Morning sunlight flashed patches in the forest—images offered and withdrawn before he could register them. Vines covered derelict buildings like sheets pulled over accident victims. South of Fredericksburg, the landscape opened up; white farmhouses with columned porches overlooked rows of ripening tomatoes and white okra blossom towers.

The hobo camps in the woods and under bridges multiplied with the approach to Richmond. In the switching yard, lines of Standard Oil tank cars alternated with streams of pulpwood cars. A locomotive sloppily took on water. Calvin chiseled at his thumbnail with his incisor, waiting for the slow easing that began each leg of a train trip. Ahead of him, a passenger was already snoring. A man and woman toting white shopping bags from Richmond department stores rustled down the aisle and took the seats across from him. She jauntily sang *Bei mir bist du schoen* as he set the shopping bags on the rack above the seats.

The train began to move with creaking leverage, the frantic urgency of the whistle mocked by their slow progress. They crept on an elevated track between red brick warehouses held together with rusted bolts, boarded-up windows passing just a few feet from the train. Now they stopped again to let an empty westbound coal train head back up to the hills beyond Clifton Forge. Sweet tobacco from the huge tile-roofed warehouses along the river competed with aromatic cedar from a factory that made tubs for ice-cream makers.

The woman with the shopping bags pointed out the window. "Look, that is so cute!" Calvin eased high enough to see boys throwing rocks in puddles to try to splash one another. "See what those colored girls are doing!"

The man leaned over and looked. "That's dangerous."

The woman whirled towards Calvin and said, "Look what they're doing! It is so cute!" She caught him already straining to see. "See, on that coal car over there."

Two little girls in ragged overalls with long braided pigtails were standing at the top of the iron ladders on the sides of the coal car. They were reaching in and rearranging lumps of coal into little towers along the top edges of the car. Little towers already stood along the top edges of an adjacent car.

"What's going on?" asked Calvin.

"That's how you can tell you're in the South! Their mammies would whip them if they took any coal from the cars, cause that would be stealing. But they're supposed to bring home any coal they find along the tracks. So they pile up the coal on the top edges of the cars so it will fall off when the train starts and then they can bring it home!"

Calvin watched the girls for a second before they suddenly scrambled down and went running to a vine-covered hill with all the other children. The train lurched and Calvin swung back into his seat. The morning sun was filtered by clouds and the trunks of the pines glowed like pink candy canes.

"Are you visiting Williamsburg?" The woman leaned past her companion into the aisle.

Calvin turned. "Yes." He remembered to be polite. "And you?"

"We live there. My husband was even born there which is even more amazing! Are you going to visit the restoration?"

"Yes m'am. So you live there?"

"Yes. Avery here is a surgeon with the Eastern State," she leaned closer and whispered, "the mental hospital." She stood suddenly and looked at her bags in the rack. "I'm sorry. I've finally bought some new silverware and I'm so afraid of forgetting it."

The man leaned out, grinning. "Gotta replace the silver that Sherman stole."

Without missing a beat the woman slapped his hand and carried on. "We did have to bury the family silver in the riverbank when the Yankees came. But when they left, we couldn't find our own silver — so we had to dig up another family's!" She laughed and laughed.

The man's book was open to a disturbing medical illustration of a child with puffed-out cheeks and narrow, crossed eyes. He closed the book and stretched. The book's title, *Tomorrow's Children*, looked more like science fiction than a medical text. The man turned to Calvin. "I guess it's good turnabout, having the Yankees come and pay to see replicas of the houses their grandfathers burned down."

Yellow sunlight flashed on the ceiling of the train car, illuminating the bags and suitcases on the overhead rack. Calvin turned to see that the light was reflected off flat water where rows of turtles covered the top of every log.

"The Chickahominy," said the man.

Calvin nodded. He tried to remember a Civil War battle to name and demonstrate his knowledge of the region, but feared making an error. "I hope there's a few old buildings left in Williamsburg."

"There's a few, but most of the old buildings, and all the poor buildings have been eliminated by the restoration. They've built all these *new* old ones, but they're about as convincing as granddad's row of perfect white choppers."

The train passed an orchard. A huge cloud of dust was rising from the middle. Calvin thought it was a small tornado, but it was just a tractor-mounted sprayer dusting the trees. "There was a big battle in Williamsburg wasn't there?"

"Just outside of town. You can still find bullets out where they're putting in the golf course." The man's face relaxed. "Now that's something we do have. The buried silver is just a joke, but we do have something."

"Oh yes, tell him about the shovels," said the woman as she rummaged in her shopping bag.

The man held up his hand as if swearing an oath. "We have some shovels that two of the family slaves took with them to dig the fortifications around Petersburg. Well, after the war ended, they didn't come back, and they didn't come back, for months and months — because, of course, all the slaves were free then. And I guess it was five or six months later they showed up again at the family estate, all ragged and hungry, but so glad to be home. And you know what?"

"They brought their shovels back with them?"

A bit of the fire went out of the man's eyes. "Yes. And the digging ends were worn down almost to nothing, but they brought them back home, and they hung them on nails in the barn. And they are there to this day."

Calvin's nodding demonstration of satisfaction with the story reassured the man. Calvin's pleasure was genuine. He had never met a white family within a hundred miles of Petersburg that didn't lay claim to the same set of shovels brought home by the same set of loyal slaves.

On the Williamsburg platform, a black-skinned hand came down on the suitcase. "You gonna carry that to my car for me?" asked the grinning man.

The woman with him went wide-eyed. "Hush now!" She turned to Calvin with a tight smile and pointed up the platform to another baggage cart surrounded by white people only. "Your bag would be up there, mister."

"Sorry." He quickly set it down.

As he made his way around the hugging families, he heard the man's laughing voice again. "I thought he was going to carry it for me!"

Calvin pushed the brim of his hat back to let the air reach his sweaty brow, peeled off his jacket and draped it over his arm. All the cabs were gone, and he began to trudge with the rest of the walkers down the sidewalk past a brick A&P grocery store and the sour smell of overripe melons.

The steely scour of iron tires on pavement and the fast clip-clop of horses drew everyone's attention to the open carriage coming down the street. The just-off-the-train tourists ahead of Calvin fumbled for cameras and begged the liveried Negro driver to stop, but he shook the reins and hurried the horses on. In the back of the open carriage, a man in a yellowing flannel suit held a small chalkboard facing the people he passed. "Mr. Cobb?" called the man when he saw Calvin staring at the "C. Cobb" on his chalkboard.

"Yes?"

"Ho!" he called to the driver and the carriage stopped. "Oh good! I was afraid I'd missed you!" He hopped down from the carriage and offered his hand. "Welcome to Williamsburg, I'll be your guide while you're visiting."

Calvin shook his head as they shook hands. "I'm just looking for someone, not for a tour or anything."

The guide laughed. "Well, that's good, because we weren't expecting you so soon. Arrangements are a bit haphazard."

"You were expecting me?"

"They called me just an hour ago." He reached for Calvin's suitcase. "I'm in the research and education department so they always figure I can get free easier than anyone else."

Calvin pulled his suitcase back. "Yes, but I'm really just looking for someone."

"Well, it's too hot to carry your suitcase around all day. We can drop it off at the Inn." The horses tossed their heads and backed as the departing C&O locomotive released its air brakes. "Besides, if she's walking around, she'll be easier to spot from high in the carriage."

Calvin nodded, not caring how much the man knew about him, about Kathryn, about anything. He handed his case up to the guide and flopped into the seat. The driver turned the skittery team back around and rolled fearlessly through the traffic looping around a huge live oak tree at the edge of a colonial-styled shopping district.

"So, you're with Agriculture?" asked the guide, smiling, showing a genuine interest.

The jogging motion of the carriage made Calvin's head bob affirmatively. "I work with the research and radio sections."

"So you're like me, research and education, except you're in bread, and I'm in circuses!"

"Honored callings both." Calvin searched the passing crowd.

The guide pointed down the long main street of the restoration. "Notice anything?"

Calvin shook his head. "Just the nice buildings. And how clean it all is."

"You never notice it until some one points it out." The guide swept his arm down the prospect. "No power lines! First thing we did was hide the power lines."

Calvin nodded, smiling. He began to recognize buildings from the *National Geographic* article and was amused by his own surprise at seeing the sidewalks lined with tourists rather than the powder-wigged colonials from the photographs.

"See how this plan sounds," said the guide. "We'll drop you at the Inn; let you clean up a bit. Then we'll ride around and look for your friend. They're installing the trim work at the capitol, and one of the carpenters is a big fan of your radio program. I promised I'd bring you over this afternoon. Hope that was alright."

Calvin nodded with each step of the horses.

"They'll also be working at Bozarth's mill on the Raleigh Tavern replica rooms for the department stores, so we could go down there today, too. And, there's a car that leaves from here to go to Jamestown Island, where America began. You might find that interesting as well."

Calvin nodded as he scanned the crowds.

"I'm sure we'll find her," said the guide. "We'll take a loop around and come back to the Governor's green in time for the fife-and-drum parade."

Calvin kept nodding.

"What's your friend doing here?" asked the guide. "If I knew what she was interested in, it might help us find her."

"Writing an article or something," said Calvin quickly.

The guide squirmed in his jacket as he tried to let some air under his arms. "I mean, they said you're interested in woodworking. Was she writing on fabrics, or decorating or folk art?"

"I don't know." Calvin looked the guide in the eye for the first time, and they both relaxed when each saw the other's discomfort. "Listen, if it's all the same to you. I'd rather find her first, and deal with the hotel later."

"That'd be absolutely fine," said the guide and he instructed the driver to make a grand circuit of the streets. They passed a white wooden Victorian house. "That's one of the holdouts," he said. "But even they've come up in the world. Before the restoration they say the whole town was bare wood—folks were too poor to paint and too proud to whitewash!" They rolled around the scaffolding-covered reconstruction of the capitol where teams of masons were laying soft red bricks into a Flemish bond veneer against the cinderblock structure. "That's where the young fellow that's such a fan of your show is working. Do you want to stop in now?"

Calvin shook his head.

As they turned back down the road past the Olde Jail, the guide began a good-natured imitation of the olde-jailkeeper's spiel. "Same routine on every tour. He shows folks the privy seats in the cells and says, 'You've heard of "every man a king?" Well here at least every man has a throne! Here's where plumbing got its start!'"

The carriage rolled past a family taking pictures of their paunchy patriarch with his head locked in the pillory. The colonial-costumed jail keeper stood waiting as his group assembled. The guide leaned across the carriage to Calvin and said in a loud whisper, "and here's where neckin' got its start!"

The olde-jailkeeper held out his arm to the pillory and addressed his group, "And here's…and here's where neckin' got its start!"

They rolled down a back street past gardens and carriage houses. The tourists, although pausing to take pictures of the horses and carriage as they passed, were all headed down the street as well. The guide pointed at them. "You know the question they ask the most?"

Calvin shook his head.

"What time is the noon parade?"

Calvin nodded, smiling. The carriage wheels went quiet as they pulled onto the grass of a long open green bordered by catalpa trees. A shrill fanfare of fifes and a boom of drums from the far end of the green made the horses jerk, prompting reprimands from the driver. Calvin stood in his shirtsleeves, scanning the crowd of sweating, fanning tourists packed into the end of the green. A few of the tourists on the periphery of the crowd turned and took pictures of the carriage, but most wanted shots of the fife-and-drum corps with the reconstructed Governor's Palace in the background. The phalanx of red-coated, tricorn-hatted boys began a slow military lockstep march down the green as they played. The driver shook the reins and the horses pulled the carriage out of the way.

He spotted her on the far side of the parade. Her camera covered her face, brown coveralls and a blue kerchief covered the rest of her, but there was no mistaking the way she moved, jockeying her camera position to frame the uniformed marchers in the foreground with the faces of the excited audience in the background. Calvin was directly in her line of sight and he waved both arms to catch her attention. She lowered her camera and closed her eyes. He tumbled out of the carriage and ran around the crowd as they followed the parade onto the main street. "Kathryn!"

With the background now clear of Calvin's waving figure, she was concentrating on her photographs. "You came after me," she said, with only a glance up from her viewfinder.

"I did."

She swung her rucksack from her shoulder and unscrewed the lens on her camera. "That was sweet of you, but I'm fine. This is good." The carriage rolled up behind them as they followed the parade and its onlookers down the street. "Is that yours?"

"The carriage? No. They came to get me. It's all confused!"

"Who came to get you?"

"You can see better from up here," called the guide.

Kathryn sized up the camera angles. The carriage would make a stepladder-high platform moving parallel with the parade. She nodded and climbed in. Calvin made quick introductions. She stood and worked her camera, asking the driver to get ahead or slow down. The guide glanced at Calvin from his facing seat. Calvin nodded his thanks.

As the carriage slowly followed the parade past the octagonal brick powder magazine, she sat and rewound the motor drive on her camera. She called over the noise. "It's American verbunkos!"

"How'd you know that?" asked the guide.

"What? That it's verbunkos?"

The guide shook his head. "I misunderstood. What's verbunkos?"

"Military recruiting music designed to excite the young and the foolish." She screwed a shorter lens on her camera and glanced at the frame-counter dial. "What did you think I said?"

The guide shook his head. "I thought you said it was bunkum."

"Is it?"

"Well, historically it's not something that ever happened

here." He picked at some of the loose gold paint along the frame of the carriage. "Not a fife-and-drum parade ever. But it sure keeps the kids out of trouble."

She shook her head slowly, opened the back of her camera, replaced the film cartridge and reset the frame counter.

"Where are you staying?" asked the guide as their carriage rolled past a brick courthouse with a disturbingly unsupported portico.

She nodded toward an insubstantial wooden building with wrap-around porches at the edge of the green.

"That will be replaced with a more appropriate colonial tavern next year. We've demolished over five hundred inharmonious buildings so far." He pointed up the street. "Mister Rockefeller's philanthropy began the restoration of Marie Antoinette's little village at Versailles, and coming up on the left is his first major restoration project here, the Raleigh Tavern. Williamsburg was very busy twice a year when the court met in April and October. All the bigwigs from all over the colony would come in and the place really came to life."

Kathryn photographed the tavern as they passed. "So all these men, getting away from home, coming to town, this place must have been half bawdy houses."

"Oh no! No bawdy houses in Williamsburg," said the guide, grinning conspiratorially. "In fact, we just passed the home owned by a Captain Orr. You'll see in the guidebook that, although we have the Wythe house, the Lightfoot house, and the Randolph house, his house is referred to only as Captain Orr's *dwelling*."

Calvin caught his spirit. "So they didn't want to have an *Orr house* here!"

"Nope, not here in Olde Williamsburg." The guide laughed and glanced at Kathryn, but she was holding her camera to her ear, listening to the shutter as she fired shots into the air.

"So," she said, "prostitution really *was* here — but now it's not." She nodded at marching fifers and drummers. "And these crypto-fascist, pseudo-folkloric displays of militarism were *not* here — but now they are."

Calvin closed his eyes and shook his head. The guide smiled and stroked his chin.

Kathryn rummaged in her bag. "Is there a photo shop here where I can get some negatives developed?"

The guide pointed to a storefront on a corner. "If you don't need prints, the Rexall can do it overnight."

"Let me just run in then. I'll be right back." She hopped down to the street and strode into the store before the driver had the horses settled.

"I'm sorry," said Calvin. "Kathryn's kind of a negative herself right now."

The guide smiled after her. "So who's she doing this article for? *New Masses*? *Sunday Worker*? Certainly not for *Superior Home*."

"So you know who she is?"

He nodded.

Kathryn bounded out the door of the drug store and back into the carriage. "Sorry to hold you up."

"Not at all," said the guide. The carriage resumed its roll down the main street. "Let me tell you another interesting aspect of the restoration. Employees, such as myself, live in houses owned by the corporation." He nodded at a yellow-painted house with a white fence and perfect boxwoods. "I live right there with my wife, her father and my two daughters."

Calvin swiveled back to admire the guide's house. "Must be very nice!" said Calvin. "Step out the door and you're back a hundred and fifty years in the past."

"It *is* nice."

"So it's a company town," said Kathryn, "just like Ludlow,

Colorado. But instead of digging coal, you're mining good will."

The guide sputtered. "America has...does seem to appreciate..."

She patted her hand on his arm. "Just better not try to form a union — they might send in soldiers to gun down your family too!"

"Kathryn, I don't think..."

"Please, Calvin, he's given me the angle for my story! It's like Marie Antoinette's play village here, but instead of pretending to be a milkmaid with perfumed cows, here you can pretend to be a patriot with nice uniformed ranks of Anglo-Saxon youth marching up and down the streets. None of those nasty people whose last names end in vowels or Zs running around! Christian church in charge of public welfare! An America like it ought to be!"

The lock-stepping phalanx of fifers and drummers arrayed themselves on the lawn of the capitol surrounded by camera-clicking families. The carriage stopped. The cowed guide swung out the door and held it as Kathryn and Calvin stepped down. "One of the young workers here is a big fan of Mr. Cobb's radio show," he explained to Kathryn as he looked at his wristwatch. "It won't take but a few minutes. Then we can head down to the palace."

"Thank you very much," said Calvin.

"Not at all." The guide kept his attention toward Kathryn. "Listen, when you work here, it's not like you've stepped back a hundred and fifty years into the past, it's actually more like twenty years. So, perhaps, twenty years from now, by 1957, the workers will have liberated the place and they'll be running Williamsburg as a workers' collective." He rubbed his palms together. "But until that day, I hope you will try to sympathize with the position of a family man."

She smiled slowly. "Nobody'll know I got any ideas from you."

"Thanks."

She swung the rucksack onto her shoulder and walked down the brick path to photograph tourists photographing a gnarled white mulberry tree.

"I'm sorry," said Calvin.

The guide waved his concern away but would not meet his eyes. "Thanks for doing this, we'll just stop in that first room there and ask for Jimmy. He was really excited to hear you were coming."

"I'll join you in a second, okay?" Calvin ran his fingers back through his hair and turned back down the path to join Kathryn. "What was all that about?" he whispered. "He's our host! He can't answer back!"

"He's your host, not mine." She put her sunglasses in her pocket. "He's supposed to be an intellectual. I'm sure he was flattered that I was taking him seriously."

"He deserved a little more courtesy than that. Rudeness does not become anyone."

"That's right. A gentleman is never rude to the waiters. That's what makes you stand out from the rednecks, isn't it?"

"I thought you were supposed to be so damn diplomatic!"

"It's one thing to be diplomatic, it's another to play make-believe when you're an educated adult." She turned to sweep her hand down the street of colonial homes and white picket fences. "This is just a guilty shroud pulled over the murders at Ludlow! I just want to remind people of that!" She leveled her eyes at him. "Brockwell sent you, didn't he? That's why you're riding shotgun with the company man!"

"Brockwell told me that you were here. He said you might be digging yourself in deeper."

She kicked at an exposed oak root. "I'm digging myself out!

At last!"

"I came because I was worried about you."

"Worried about me, or about what I might do?"

"Mr. Cobb!" the guide called out. "I'll be inside."

"Go on and meet your fan club. You're number one now!" She gave the winding knob on her camera a turn but it was already fully wound. "Go on."

Calvin kept looking at her until she finally, reluctantly, returned his gaze. He nodded and turned to walk inside the building, unconsciously joyful at the occasion of their first real spat. Peering around the corner into a large room, he saw a half-dozen men working — some on scaffolds trimming mouldings, some tending to joints in the low wainscot around the room. The smell of pine and paint rode atop the base note of curing concrete and mortar. Four men in white coveralls were setting the casing into one of the widow embrasures. They eased the quivering tour-de-force joinery of arching, conic-sectioned panels into the deep-splayed window opening until it wedged against the furring strips and covered the coarse school-basement cinder block of the actual structure. One of the men resumed his story about someone who had beaten his hand black and blue trying to hammer a dent out of his truck fender with his bare fist. Another man picked scroll-cut modillions from a gunnysack and handed them up to a man on a scaffold.

Calvin opened his mouth wide as dripping sweat tickled his lips. It must have resembled a yawn because a man in coveralls and a dusty gray fedora looked up from his bench. "Hey, it's not that boring is it?"

"No, not at all."

"You the radio man?"

Calvin wiped his mouth with his sleeve. "Yeah, I guess so. I'm supposed to meet someone."

"Hey, fellas, here's Jimmy's radio woodworker guy!"

"Well, Jimmy ain't here," said the man on the scaffold, evoking much laughter among the others.

A nickel-plated multi-plane sat at the end of the bench next to a flex-bottomed circular plane. Calvin pointed. "We've got one of those."

"One of what?"

"A Stanley 45. Handy when you need it."

"Hear that Ed? He's got him a Stanley 45! Must be a real woodworker!"

A man fitting a walnut strip around a panel shook his head. "Must be!"

Calvin eased toward the bench and saw that the plane was a 55 and not a 45.

"Hey, I've got a problem with my brace, this hole-boring thingy," called the man at the bench with his distinctly New Jersey accent. "Maybe you can help me." Calvin stepped closer. The man grasped his brace and jabbed the screw point of the Jennings bit into his bench top. He had disengaged the ratchet so the crank spun clattering around. "I keep turning and turning but I just don't get anywhere!" He laughed and swatted at the air in Calvin's direction. Calvin shook his head and turned his attention to a man trimming the miter on a short length of walnut moulding with a block plane.

"You can go upstairs," said the man on the scaffold, "ask the fellas up there if they've seen Jimmy."

"Thanks." Calvin nodded and cranked up the wide, sawdusty stairs. Another government building—maybe they could all be stacked, all the wide government staircases stacked to climb into the clouds in chronological order. Babylonian stone steps at the bottom, the linoleum-on-steel of the new Agriculture Department at the top. At the crossover between the two wings of the building, a narrow flight of wooden stairs under construction rested horizontally on padded sawhorses—a thick lightning bolt of heart pine. Calvin squeezed past it and nodded greetings to the two men joining the heavy planks. One steadied the tread while the other drilled pilot holes with an eggbeater drill. Calvin's hand itched for the worn saw and plane handles in the open wooden toolboxes, but he just waited as the two men negotiated a tricky bit of alignment. A card perched on the chair rail behind them read:

> **WORKMEN ARE CAUTIONED NOT TO LEAN ANY TOOLS OR MATERIALS AGAINST THE WALLS OR WOODWORK.**
>
> Those not complying with this order will be immediately discharged.
>
> By order
> TODD & BROWN, Inc.

Calvin glanced around and was relieved to see that one of the men had set his wooden saw-sharpening frame against one of the window ledges, and that his files and rags sat defiantly beside it. Lunch boxes sat on the benches, hats hung on posts and coats draped over the railings. The human disarray amid the formality of the room gave the impression of careless aristocrats at their club.

"I'm looking for Jimmy."

"He just went back downstairs," said the man with the drill. "They sent him up here for a board stretcher."

Calvin shuffled back down the stairs and stepped into the courtroom. A young man held a long wooden spirit level on the bottom of a gate as an older man marked hinge points. The older man murmured something to him and he looked up at Calvin. "Hey! Hi! I listen to your show!"

The man at the bench wedged a length of walnut into the bird's-mouth stop nailed on the end of his bench. "Doing woodworking on the radio must be pretty darn tough." He stood squared off to Calvin. "Hey Jimmy, maybe someday you could be a radio barber!"

The young man his shifted his position to better support the gate. "No, it's a really swell show! He has a story about something and then you can get the plans for it. I'm gonna make that folding ladder. I've just got the plans in the mail!"

The man at the bench snapped a lever on his miter box and swung the long backsaw ninety degrees to the right. "Glad to hear my tax dollars are going to tell people which end of a nail to use! Hey Ed, you seen my screw-hammer?"

The man fitting the moulding laughed just enough to register for his comrade's joke. As he stepped down from atop a sawhorse, he steadied himself by grasping the window surround, glancing out through the glass as he did. Calvin saw him swing back to take a longer, seemingly casual look toward the street. "Shit, Dan, we got company," he said and pointed discreetly toward the window.

Calvin's tormentor stepped toward the wall and, keeping his head low, stole a peek at two men coming up the walk. "Damned if you do and damned if you don't!" The room fell quiet as the other workmen in the room set down their tools.

"I'll talk to them," said the man with the moulding.

The hall echoed with the sound of the two men entering the building. Now they were in the doorway, the man at the back glancing up and down the hall as the first man stepped into the room.

"Listen," said the workman with the moulding, meeting the glare of the man in the doorway, "I'm shop steward. We took care of all this last week!"

"Is that so?" The big man sized up the room and its inhabitants.

"Yeah! Listen, nobody's tryin' to organize nobody! We just want to finish this job and get back home."

The big man rolled his eyes and made another slow appraisal of the workmen and the tools on the workbenches as he eased further into the room. "You got us wrong, pal!" Suddenly he whipped around to face Calvin. "You Cobb?"

Calvin staggered slightly back. "Yes."

The other man, now behind Calvin, grabbed his wrists and jerked them behind him. "Federal agents. You're coming with us."

"What?" Calvin jerked around as the manacles snapped closed. "Is somebody in trouble?"

"Yeah," said the first agent as he yanked at Calvin's coat, checking for a gun, "somebody's in trouble for sure!"

The workman at the bench suddenly had a hammer in his hand and whacked its broad side against the benchtop. "What's going on?" he shouted. The other workmen, all brandishing tools were moving in beside him.

"He's with us! Leave him alone!" shouted one of the workmen.

"Yeah!" shouted Jimmy shaking his level at the agents, "You take one of us, you take all of us!"

"Back off pal!" snapped the second agent. As they jerked Calvin toward the door, he turned a withering eye to Jimmy. "Look at a map, kid. You're not in New Jersey anymore. Even if he was with you mugs, you got a brotherhood of nuthin' down here!"

The FBI men brought a small table and two chairs into the swaying baggage car and shoved Calvin into a seat next to the stacked Adam's Express boxes. The standing agent tried to demand answers faster than Calvin could deliver. "So why were you all sneaking in on Saturdays and Sundays if you had nothing to hide?"

"We haven't done anything! We always work weekends. It just seems right to."

The sitting agent shook his head as if trying so hard to understand. "But Sunday is a day off, the Department of Agriculture gives you Sundays off, doesn't it?"

"Well, yes, but..."

"Then who were you working for?" shouted the standing agent.

He had told them he needed to pee an hour ago. Now his kidneys ached. "We were just doing our job! You've made a mistake!"

"Well now, just what is your job, Mr. Cobb?" The standing agent was thrown for a moment by his accidental rhyme. He shook it off and leaned snarling into Calvin's face. "You're not in Agriculture's roster of employees, yet you've been receiving a salary of two thousand, six hundred and nine dollars a year!"

"Pretty good for someone without a job," marveled the sitting agent.

"The records were lost, they were poisoned with mustard gas!"

Standing agent slammed his fist on the table. "Cobb, don't play crazy with me!" He thrust his finger into Calvin's face. "You got greedy didn't you! Twenty six hundred a year wasn't enough, was it? Not for a smart guy like you! You got a fancy girlfriend don't you Cobb? Maybe you needed the money for her!"

"She had nothing to do with this!"

"So it was just you?" The sitting agent nodded understandingly.

"I kept us working, yes! I'm the section chief!"

"There is no section, Cobb! You set the whole thing up!" The standing agent poked him hard on the collarbone. "We've busted your whole scheme wide open, pal. A half-million dollars is enough to put you and your whole gang away for a long time!"

"Half-million? What are you talking about? Half-million dollars?"

"Dammit Cobb, you make me sick! " The standing agent threw his coat in the chair, almost knocking it over. "It's a good thing agent Ross is here or I might forget myself." He stuck his finger in Calvin's face. "I take this personally, Cobb. You've tried to swipe a half-million bucks from Uncle Sam's pocket. That's bad enough. But you tried to do it right under the director's nose, and I take that as a personal insult!" He shot a glance at the other agent and snorted out a breath. "I'm going to get some air. There's a stink in here that I can't stomach!"

Sitting agent watched the man storm out, turned to Calvin and shook his head slowly. "He's a bad fellow to have cross with you. He's sent four men to the gas chamber already."

"But I haven't done anything! I don't know what you're talking about!"

"Listen, Calvin, do you want some water?" He poured water into a glass and held it as he said, "Listen, Calvin, if you haven't done anything, then the truth can't hurt you. Am I right?"

"No. Yes."

"Then tell me the truth, and I can help you. All right?"

"Sure."

"Good." He held out the water for Calvin. "Calvin, I think you're a man who just wanted to make things right. We looked into the records of these girls in your office, they're not bad women at all."

"No, of course not!"

He thumbed through papers in a folder. "All volunteers in France during the war. All injured in some way. All of 'em medal winners, it says here. Good girls that life just handed a lousy break. Now any decent man would want to do something about that wouldn't he?"

"Well, sure."

"So you wanted to pay back Uncle Sam's debt. So you figured a way to have your machines send the money so no one would notice. And it since it was machines that hurt these women in the first place, wouldn't justice demand that machines make it right?"

"What machines? What are you talking about?"

"The Burroughs machines, Cobb! We have the same kind of machines on our side. Of course, we use ours to keep track of criminals. You, you used yours to send those twenty-one thousand checks for thirty bucks apiece to your confederates." He pushed a fan of punched-card treasury checks across the table like a winning poker hand. Calvin stared at them. The agent reached into his coat pocket and pulled out another set of punched cards. "And here, Mr. Cobb, are the payment warrants sent from your office to Treasury." He slapped each one down in turn atop its matching check. "All corresponding."

Calvin stared at the punched cards, the amounts, the addresses, the punched holes, the note from him thanking the recipient for their good work. "Oh my God!" He threw his head back. "It was Shirley! Oh my God! I told them to do it!"

Good cop reached behind himself and knocked twice on the door. The bad cop stepped back in the door.

"Oh my God. I knew it was wrong, but I thought it was the best thing to do. I told them to increase the precision on the machines by three places — just to look busy. That's what caused this! These were supposed to be three-cent checks, not thirty dollar checks! It's just a decimal-point error!"

"So how many people were in on it, Cobb?" asked standing agent.

"Oh my God! That's why we were getting so much mail! That's why we were so popular!" His laughter agonized his swollen kidneys.

"So, you think it's funny? Then help me here, Calvin," said sitting agent. "Was the cash from your accomplices better than that from the honest folks who returned the money with personal checks?"

"What? No accomplices! It's just a mistake! They just forgot to move the decimal point when we upped the precision."

"Just you and Shirley."

"No! Shirley's the brain! I mean the machine!" Calvin shook his head as the pieces of folly drifted together. He stretched with relief, closing his eyes and throwing his head back when hands grabbed him and pushed him back into his seat. Still, he was relieved. Now he understood, and knew it was just a matter of time before they did too. "It was a mistake," he said to the silent, glaring agent.

"We found some interesting things in your office, Mr. Cobb," said good cop. He thumbed through a file folder. "Diagrams for a secret radio-controlled altitude detonator stolen from the

Bureau of Standards in May. We found cross-sections of artillery shells. We found around three million dollars in disbursement warrants being prepared for Treasury. We found illegal gambling devices. We found a supply of narcotics and needles."

Bad cop had positioned himself directly behind Calvin. "We brought in the Armenian. Interpol telexed that the German police reported him fleeing the Hindenburg explosion. So it looks like you were conspiring with foreign terrorists to boot, eh Cobb?"

"Bubby, foreign? He was born in D.C., at Columbia hospital."

Good cop leaned forward in solemn intensity. "The family of the Turkish ambassador burned to death on the Hindenburg. He had the motive and the means!"

"He has nothing to do with any of this!"

Bad cop gave Calvin's chair a sudden shake. "Now, where's the Hungarian girl?"

"Who?"

"Katrina Von Neumann," said good cop.

"Kathryn? But she's from Kentucky!"

Bad cop jerked Calvin's chair hard about. "She'll be from fricking Moscow when we're through with her! Now where the hell is she?"

The windows were painted over, but from the muffled sounds of the city, Calvin figured he was being held in a room facing the interior courtyard at the new Justice department building. They gave him a baloney sandwich and switched to praise and flatter tactics, marveling over his sketches, designs and calculations. Someone else must have subverted his brilliant plan to "share the wealth." They were closing in on the Hungarian girl, they said. They knew she was active with the Popular Front. Besides, the other girls were "cooperating fully."

Calvin was breaking down from lack of sleep, but the absurdity of the FBI man earnestly stating that the women were "cooperating fully" revived him.

For a few blessed moments on the toilet between interrogations, Calvin indulged the illusion that it was all a dream. The viewing port in the door slid open. "Finish up in there. You've got company," said the voice. The door opened as Calvin remembered he had no belt to hold up his trousers. The two agents flanking him said nothing except "left here" and "down the stairs"—as if he had any other choice. Faint church bells and shockingly bright sunlight flooded the stairwell. The agents guided him around a red velvet rope suspended on brass stands and through a huge door into rooms he knew from the FBI tour that was so popular with tourists. They passed a framed wall map with ribbons and darkened light bulbs entitled "Brains, Science and Teamwork: The FBI Hunts Down the Woodridge Gang." They passed standing panels covered with hundreds of newspaper cartoons of G-men in action. They wound around guns in glass cases, arrest photographs of pug-uglies, and posters of giant fingerprints.

They turned down a long, dark side hall. "Sit here," said the agent, pointing to a dark wooden bench, visible only by the distant lights reflecting off its polished back. One of the agents handcuffed him to the arm of the bench and left. The other reached behind a red curtain and flipped a switch. The spotlights in the ceiling pooled down on a cherry-red carpet leading down the cavernously long hallway that ended in distant polished walnut and brass doors flanked by square-shouldered eagles of gold. Spotlights illuminated glass cases on either side of the hall where Calvin sat. The case beside him held a coarse death mask of white plaster, a brown-streaked straw hat, broken silver-rimmed glasses and a cellophane-wrapped cigar. Across the hall, the glass case holding a black hood and a hangman's noose still bore nose prints from yesterday's tourists. A man in a white suit joined the agent, spoke briefly and came to sit beside Calvin on the bench.

Calvin buried his head in his hand, refusing to look at Brockwell. "I knew it. I knew you were behind this."

"You seem to think that I am responsible for everything that happens to you—good or bad." Brockwell's soft voice carried an overtone of triumph. "I'd say you were a fella who needs a friend."

"I don't need your help. They arrested us for a stupid mistake."

Brockwell laughed. "Son, you haven't been arrested."

Calvin raised his head to look at him.

Brockwell grinned and scratched at a scaly place on his nose. "You're just being held for questioning, that's all." He held Calvin in his gaze and his grin faded. "But there's a train headed back from Palm Beach, Florida, right now. And on that train is the little man whose office lies down at the end of this hall. And when he gets back, you and all your gang are going back up into your little tower down the street, and it's going to be J. Edgar Hoover and his special friend who *will* arrest you." He shook his head. "And when the last flashbulb pops..." he gestured up at the plaster death mask, "...why then you and your gang can get your own glass case."

"This is ridiculous, we haven't done anything."

"I know that. But once the Director of the FBI is photographed personally slapping the cuffs on you — our little Calvin Cobb is going to be nothing less than the ringleader of a murderous gang of international Anarchists and Armenian terrorists bent on destroying the United States from within its own Jew Deal government."

"That's insane!"

"Perhaps. But the way reputations are made...well, you know all about that, don't you? So tomorrow morning, once that arrest is made, then you'll really be famous. Embezzlement, espionage, sabotage, narcotics. " He stood and cocked his head at the hangman's noose in the lighted case. "Murder's not a federal crime. So you'll have go to New Jersey for that, or, at least your friend will.

Calvin's arm jerked at the handcuffs chaining him to the arm on the bench. "So what do you want?"

Brockwell tilted his head from side to side. "I need your voice, Calvin. I told you. Speak for me and I'll speak for you."

Calvin turned his face slowly away from him, trying to

conceal his thoughts. "I don't buy it. That stupid show of mine was popular just because everybody was getting checks in the mail. There's no magic in my voice, we both know that."

"Don't sell yourself short. You're as popular as Lindbergh — and a hell of a lot more useful to us right now." He waggled his finger at Calvin. "Just like there are movie stars, Calvin, you're going to be our first television star. We'll start with the newsreels we shoot, day after tomorrow at our folk festival." He waved his hat towards the gold eagles flanking the doors at the end of the hall. "Or, if you prefer, you and your friends can be in the newsreels tomorrow morning — but with J. Edgar Hoover as the star of the show." He bent over to catch Calvin's eyes. "The choice is yours."

Calvin closed his eyes to shut out the absurdity. "So all I have to do is host your talent show and you can get this whole thing called off? You have that kind of clout?"

"Certainly! The director is another very good friend of ours." Brockwell lowered his voice. "But we want the whole package. That machine you've got running up there is able to keep track of people with remarkable efficiency. My FBI boys say they've never seen anything like it."

"If the FBI thinks that monstrosity can help them out, then they're welcome to it." Calvin spoke loudly enough for the agent at the end of the hall to hear. "We all work for the same boss, supposedly!"

Brockwell shook his head. "Pearls before swine, young man. If the Bureau didn't invent it themselves, they won't be the least bit interested. We have a larger purpose in mind."

"I'd rather take my chances with Hoover than with you."

"It would be a cryin' shame for you to turn down my offer. The genius of our race in you, but tomorrow morning, it'll all be sacrificed to a little man's big ambition."

"Which little man, Brockwell? You or Hoover?"

"You'll change your mind when your friend is on his way to the electric chair and you're sitting in Alcatraz. But then it will be too late." Brockwell eyed him for a moment, shook his head and withdrew a white envelope from his coat pocket. "I'm sorry to have to show you these. I genuinely like you Calvin." He threw the envelope on the bench and a fan of flat, black clips of thirty-five millimeter film slid out from the end. "I haven't had these disgusting things printed, but the negatives are enough."

Calvin picked up a length of eight tiny square images. He held it before the light and then before the white envelope. He recognized the dark reversed images of regimented, uniformed children with drums and fifes, the white picket fences like black bars.

"These came to me from Williamsburg. Your little Jewess left them off at the drugstore and never picked them up."

The next strip was high contrast, a deep black background and the muscular white torso of a man seen from the back, his head twisted in profile, grinning with black teeth, as if he had clown makeup over his entire body. The images were too small to make out detail on the face. He turned the next strip so that the emulsion side caught the reflected light. Gabriel's face, black now, looked out a window, arms folded across a bare chest. In the frame beside it, a black man's bare ass framed by his clenched fists. Next, Gabriel's head tossed back in blurred laughter, his hand reaching for the camera. Next, the tilted image of a white woman in a short, open dressing gown.

Calvin's office looked no more disordered than before the FBI search. They left what papers they didn't confiscate in tall piles buttressing the walls. From the hall, ebullient Brockwell glanced in at Calvin. He paced back to the machine room and exchanged quiet words with the two men dissecting Shirley. Squared-jawed, with quick narrow eyes, they asked Brockwell questions in quiet accented English, which he repeatedly answered, "Our boy doesn't know! I tell you, you'll have to talk to the women."

"You'll have to let me talk with them before they'll tell you anything," called Calvin as he stared at vaguely remembered papers unearthed by the FBI plundering.

"You can talk to them all you want after the festival. But I want those newsreels on the boat to Dublin before anything else. You go ahead and find your clothes so we can get going."

A clatter of wheels and the boom of a trash drum echoed in the atrium. Calvin stepped out into the hallway. One floor above them, diagonally across the atrium, Captain Valentine slapped a cloth around the brass railing and tugged it back and forth, shoeshine fashion. Brockwell glanced up at him too, but Calvin's eye lingered long enough to see Valentine cock his head twice at the door to the tower. Calvin nodded as he turned his head toward the men tracing connections between little Shirley's plug board and the binary relay bank. When he stole a look back up, Valentine was gone.

"My coat and hat are in the laboratory upstairs. I'll be right back."

"Laboratory?" said one of the men, looking up from his examination of the "Calvin Cobb — Radio Woodworker!" banner.

"No, no, it's just a workshop. I only call it a laboratory."

"*Werkstatt* — for the machine here?" asked the other man.

"No. No. Not at all, just my woodworking."

Brockwell rocked happily on his feet. "Why don't I go up with you?" He swept out his hand for Calvin to lead the way. "I can help you look."

He climbed the stairs zombie-like, staring ahead. Even after he had agreed to play ball with Brockwell, the FBI men had still kept him from sleeping. Brockwell chattered on as he followed behind him. "Think of the force of history that is behind every step we take, Calvin." The man was charged with triumph. "If those women hadn't been disfigured, they would have gotten married, raised their little families. Instead they created a machine, a tool that will help us ensure that, henceforth, all families are flawless and pure. That should show you that there is a force behind this." He lowered his voice. "Talking to those boys, I think there should be a lot of money coming in from Deutsche Hollerith."

Calvin stopped outside the door to the tower. "Be right back." He ducked into the corridor, but heard Brockwell close behind him. He slowed, hoping to spot whatever it was that Captain Valentine wanted him to see. The doors were torn off the tool cabinet and the planes and chisels tossed to the back of the bench. The spreader models were piled in the middle of the floor, as if someone had been preparing for a bonfire.

"Looks like the FBI has been here," said Brockwell.

Calvin didn't care about the damage.

"But the FBI is simply a rung on the ladder." Brockwell stepped around a puddle from the overturned glue pot. "It's most ironic, you know. Director Hoover began investigating you because he wanted to hire you."

"Hire me?" Calvin scanned the room for a note, a weapon, something.

"Suddenly you had the most successful program in the history of radio, and he wanted your magic formula for his own radio show. You were about to become a writer for *G-Men: The Director's Files*. You're just lucky the Treasury agents didn't get to you first."

"Why's that?" Calvin glanced up at the clock faces. Illusions of time turning backwards wouldn't help now.

"This is a struggle, Calvin. The outcome is not pre-ordained. You could have become a servant of Morgenthau, and your calculating machine — a tool of the Hebrew financiers."

At Calvin's feet lay the broken cabinet door with the engraving of *The Knight, Death and the Devil* still tacked to the panel. Was that all Captain Valentine wanted him to see? Just some absurd image? He stared at the broken pieces of the cabinet door for a second, forgetting where he was. The cheeks of the mortises joining the top rail of the door had snapped clean off — a break that couldn't be glued. He would have to make an new frame, cut new mortises through the ends of the uprights, leaving the pieces two inches longer than they needed to be, sawing them off only when everything was assembled and there was no longer any chance of splitting. He shook his head at the useless thoughts, but now his head felt clearer.

"I know you'll be happy to leave all this trivial crafting

behind." Brockwell poked at a jack plane on the bench. "Not that you want to lose touch with the working man. And we have to think about your clothing, now that we'll be seen as well as heard. You should dress just a little better than the mountain folk — but not too much."

"I'll try." He turned back to the debris piled in the middle of the room. Sticking grotesquely out from under the pile was a woman's leg. He knelt and pulled it slowly out, recognizing it as one he had modeled after Anne's perfect leg.

"The common touch is a great gift, young man." Brockwell rattled on, his back to Calvin. "For myself, the mountain folk seem to admire my cream ensemble."

Slowly standing, holding the leg at arm's length in both hands, Calvin recognized the leg again.

"But you know what impresses these hillbillies more than anything else? They all wear these clod-hoppers, and when they see a nice pair of thin-soled..." He turned and saw Calvin armed with the leg held like a baseball bat. His eyes went wide.

"'Scuse me!" Captain Valentine's face, rounded and big-eyed, poked into the light. "One a ya'll got a little brown car?"

Brockwell released the breath he had been holding. "What about it?"

"Somebody banged a little brown car out front and I said he better stay dere till I find who it belongs to. Knocked in de hood a bit."

"Jesus!" Brockwell spun to Calvin, who was now cradling the leg like a puppy. "You got your things?"

"Not yet."

"Well, find your stuff and meet me back downstairs." Brockwell pushed ahead of Valentine and hammered down the corridor.

Valentine stopped in the doorway and hissed back to Calvin, "He'll be back up here in a few minutes, so you all talk fast."

He addressed these last words over Calvin's head. Calvin spun and looked up to see Kathryn's face looking back at him from the hatch in the ceiling. His hand shot upward, reaching to her. "Oh my God! Are you alright?"

"Talk fast Romeo," said Captain Valentine, easing back into the corridor.

Kathryn eased down the stub of the iron stair and onto the catwalk suspended ten feet above the floor. "What were you doing with that leg? I thought you were going to brain him." She reached down to touch his extended fingertips.

"It was Anne's leg, her legs were in Brockwell's photographs! Negatives from the film you left in Williamsburg."

"Anne's art photos?"

"Bastard said it was you in the pictures. You and Gabriel."

"How'd you know it wasn't me?"

"It pays to be a leg man."

She pulled her hand back. "But that's why you agreed to help him?"

"No." He pulled his own hand down. "That's why I swore I'd..." He clinched his fist and rubbed it his other hand. "Hoover was going to make the arrest, and I can't get this bastard if I'm in prison."

Her voice was tired, hoarse. "Well, you've got to keep playing along. The Valentines have letters, expense accounts gifts, travel records. They can put him in a very bad place."

"Brockwell?"

"No! Hoover! J. Edgar Hoover! He writes love letters to one of his own agents!"

"Hoover? Hoover's...a homo?"

"Gabriel's mother got wind of it. She's the GAO section chief in charge of audits."

"Gabriel's mother—section chief? That's not..." He rubbed his forehead with his palm. "Oh! She's been passing! She was the woman at the GAO!"

"And Captain Valentine's piecing together letters from the burn bin at Justice. They just need some time."

"This has to happen fast. The FBI's released the whole case to Brockwell. He's got Nazis down there right now, pulling Shirley apart."

"Oh my God! We've got to go through with this, then."

Calvin sat back on his workbench and picked up a wooden trying plane. "We're going to blackmail J. Edgar Hoover."

"But you've got to humor Brockwell until they can get the word to Hoover to back off."

"The girls are on their way here. That was part of the deal. They'll know how to sidetrack the Nazis, for a little while at least." He held the plane as if ready to go to work, left thumb on the near side, fingers finding their place on the far side. "There used to be five girls here, you know."

"What?"

"I used to have five. Linda, Verdie, Anne, Ellen and Cora." He hefted the heavy plane to rest across his lap "Cora was burned too, like Anne, on her face and arms. She could live with that. But when her parents found out about her and Linda, she shot herself with a week's worth of Ellen's morphine." He stood up, shaking his head. "Brockwell's the one we have to get."

"But the truth about Brockwell won't hurt him. Too many people agree with him."

Captain Valentine appeared in the doorway. "He's coming back up. Y'all get this straightened out?"

"Yes." Kathryn scrambled up the steps to the hatchway, ready to disappear.

Calvin held up his hand to Kathryn. "No! Leave Hoover alone—we're going after Brockwell." He spun to Captain Valentine. "Your wife—she can pass as a white lady?" The

Captain's narrowed eyes were all the answer Calvin needed. "And she's the woman I hear singing late at night—when she comes to pick you up?"

"Yeah, but what the hell…?"

Calvin cut him off. "There's no time now. I leave for the folk festival tomorrow morning. I'll write everything out tonight and leave it behind the toilet tank at my rooming house." The door at the far end of the corridor squeaked. Calvin shoved the rolling trashcan back toward the entrance. "Hold him off a second," he whispered.

He turned up to Kathryn, still peering down from the hatchway. "If we can't stop Brockwell by making him look bad, then we'll do it by making him look good." She pulled her confused face back out of sight just as Brockwell reappeared in the doorway.

Brockwell down-shifted his powerful little car, accelerating out of the tight curves, throwing Calvin against the sides of the cramped back seat. The exhaust popped as they climbed in a clockwise spiral above a tidy white house set by a rushing creek. Brockwell studied him in the rear-view mirror. The Kentucky Colonel turned around and offered the latest tidbit in his didactic campaign. "When the sons of the tidewater planters moved west they always took the smartest slaves with them. That's why there's a far better class of Negroes up here in the mountains." Calvin puffed his cheeks out, crossed his eyes and turned away.

As they descended into the big valley south of Marion, the smell of the hay-making was fresh in the afternoon air and a few catalpa trees still in bloom. Cows grazed in a highland pasture amid exposed rock flats of southwest Virginia. They stopped for gas at a tiny store by a creek where white umbels of elderberry and hemlock flowers drooped over the wire fences. Calvin watched as banty hens followed a strutting rooster in the long green grass of an old peach orchard. Brockwell tapped a poster for his folk festival tacked to the wall until Calvin acknowledged with a nod.

They climbed again, winding upward until Brockwell pulled into an overlook. As Brockwell and the Kentucky Colonel walked off toward the woods, Calvin stood watching a hawk circling high above, struggling to gain altitude on the last warm updraft of the fading day. It seemed to have a large strap hanging from its leg, and he reasoned it was some rural falconry, until he realized the hawk was struggling upward with a heavy snake in its talons. A rusty green Chevrolet truck with a braided rag rug fitted perfectly atop the dashboard pulled in beside them, the driver dashed off to the woods. Brockwell nodded at the procession of cars as he walked back. "Looks like we're going to have a good turnout. Your people better leave early if they don't want to get caught in this traffic tomorrow."

"They'll be here."

They eased down the road as it followed a creek, wheeling through a curve that reeked of fresh skunk.

"Did you take note of the way they fell into line when they saw you were taking charge?" asked Brockwell.

The Kentucky Colonel turned for another lesson. "Most advanced species are the same way. Once they know who the leader is they're a lot happier."

Calvin was queasy from the curves and the skunk. "I could have brought 'em around a lot easier if you'd left me alone with 'em for a minute."

Brockwell shook his head. "They could've also brought you around. Besides, Calvin, you're a great one for coming up with clever plots." He gunned his engine to pass around a smoking bus. "Where did you hear this woman, now?"

"She's sung in some of the biggest halls in Washington."

"The ballad contest is at eleven o'clock tomorrow."

"They'll be there."

The road wound upward again through the national forest. Men collecting admission money at the start of the private road greeted Brockwell with cowed deference. They drove past rows of parked cars and homemade travel trailers as they followed a creeping procession of traffic climbing the narrow road. As the oaks gave way in patches to red spruce and Frasier firs, gaps in the trees showed the hazy valleys below.

Calvin's ears popped and he heard music. They emerged into an immense bald mountaintop where the soil was too thin for trees to take root. They jolted past dark cars inching into the parking area and climbed toward a large board-sided building. Crowds of running children distracted him from the spectacular view for a moment, but then he turned. Shadows of clouds drifted across great green valleys far below. Dark mountains shouldered one beside another in ranks stretching to the hazy horizon.

Brockwell parked behind the building and ratcheted the parking brake. Calvin stood and stretched, marveling at the multitude and the panorama of the hills below. Across the mountaintop, small groups gathered around guitarists and banjo players. Against the setting sun, groups of boys in white shirts and crossed sashes were practicing writhing dances with wooden swords. Brockwell watched Calvin take in the spectacle. "You're staying here in one of the pavilion rooms, Calvin. You are welcome to eat with us tonight."

"I'll find something."

"Suit yourself. Need any money?"

"No."

Brockwell approached him. "We have a solemn agreement and I can do without this petty hostility, understand?" He placed a hand on Calvin's shoulder. "Now when you get ready to sleep, you've got one of the single rooms at the back." He hesitated. "Calvin, I was proud of the way you took command.

If they don't show up tomorrow morning, it'll be their heads, not yours."

Calvin nodded at the ground, but knew he would not be released until he made eye contact. He braced himself and looked up. "Let's hope they trust me then."

He tossed his bag on the porch and walked around the front of the pavilion where a square dance unfolded on a wooden platform. Fiddlers whittled off constipated notes as the caller sang "eat the oyster, eat the clam," "make your basket, bring it home," "swing your partner, swing your own." Only a few dozen people sat on the benches under the tin roof — the multitude lined deep back up the hillside from the rope barricade outside. The musicians kept up their detached look until the banjo player stepped out and, holding the bottom of his vest, danced like a shaken rag doll. Laughter broke out behind Calvin, where a woman danced with a boxer dog for a moment, holding his paws as he stepped along with her.

He went looking for food, threading a path between parked cars with awnings extended from their roofs, winding around campfires and people lounging in canvas folding chairs amid webs of guy ropes. A line of people led up to a tiny cinder-block stand selling coffee and hot dogs prepared by three black cooks — the only non-whites on the mountain. While waiting, he kept surprising himself by turning and looking out over the astounding view of the valleys below. Easy to see why someone standing in this spot would think themselves on top of the world.

The sun was almost down, and he walked off to find a place away from the crowd. He stepped off the path and down into a steep meadow where three giggling teenage girls slid their bare feet across a patch of green moss, shivering with the sensation. A rock hidden in the grass became his seat where he slowly drank his coffee from the paper cup and savored the last warm breeze rising from the valley. Halfway to the horizon, he saw the faintest glow of a town. Far below were the twinkles of occasional car headlights. Clouds drifted away from an orange cantaloupe-slice moon lightly filled with earth glow.

The breeze shifted and now it was cool—incredible after the heat and sweat of Washington. At times, the music and the laughter would cease at the same time, leaving only the sound of a few peepers, or a car making its way down the mountain, or a dog barking miles away. The dog had barked seconds ago and the sound was just reaching him. Lightning flashed in clouds far to the south. He crushed his paper cup and climbed back up to the road.

Glowing ends of cigarettes dotted the hillsides. Mothers washed babies illuminated by the headlights of their cars. In the light of the campfires, faces stood out stark against the darkness. He was drawn to a large campfire and was welcomed by a smiling nod from a quietly conversing couple. Children played checkers on a folding cot. Calvin's face, hands and knees warmed, but his back was cold. He shivered and noticed a man in a felt hat and long tan coat standing next to him. Calvin nodded and said "cold." The man didn't respond. He shivered and glanced at the man again, this time realizing that it was just a coat and hat hanging on a tent pole, flickering in the firelight.

A stiff denim bundle tumbled onto the rough board porch, knocked free from the outside latch when Calvin opened his door. He toed the bundle into his tiny room at the back of the pavilion and closed the door against the morning sun. It was a pair of new bib overalls — livery for Brockwell's new servant. He struggled into the starched shell, wrestling with the tight buttonholes in the hard fabric. Through the window, beyond the porch springing dizzily from the mountainside, he watched the cloud shadows race across golden and lime-green fields in the valley far below. Whenever one of these shadows passed over the pavilion, the huge tin roof cooled and boomed and snapped with the contractions.

Suddenly the entire building shook as if it were a giant's drum. *TUM-TUMMA-TUMMA-TUMMA-TUM-TUM-THOOM!* He made his way stiffly to the end of the porch, down the board stairs and around to the front of the pavilion. Circles of clog dancers traversed the stage, rhythmically stomping as if determined to drive the pavilion into the mountaintop. *TUM-TUMMA-TUMMA-TUMMA-TUM-TUM-THOOM!* Country people sat on the ground outside the ropes that surrounded the pavilion, still held at bay by the forty-cents admission to the benches within.

His cheek burned from rubbing against a freshly creosoted timber, and he took a place in line at the central water tap with bucket-toting women and children who danced in place as they waited. He washed, and then drifted toward a trio of fiddlers, wandering slowly until he was drawn into the orbit of the next group of performers. He jumped when a mandolin band suddenly started up beside him. A hand fell on his shoulder and he spun about. Bubby's eyes were bloodshot, his lower lip blue and bulging on one side.

"Bubby! My God, what happened?"

Bubby touched his face. "FBI tried to convince me that I shot down the Hindenburg with my tubular microphone."

Brockwell appeared behind Bubby. "But we straightened that out, didn't we?" He smiled approval at Calvin's coveralls and waved for them to follow him. "All part of our bargain."

Calvin stepped in beside Bubby. "Who else is here?"

"Just Anne and me." Bubby stood tiptoe and surveyed the scene. "The others are cleaning up the mess they made of your office."

Brockwell glanced down at his pocket watch. "What about this Irish nightingale you promised?"

"She's got her own car," said Bubby. "I couldn't ask her to ride in my van on top of a pile of cables. And, she wants to be introduced as the *Widow* McCroi. She just wants a more dramatic flair."

"The more tragic the better," said the Kentucky Colonel who had appeared behind them. "Nothing'll make our little leprechauns happier."

Brockwell glanced at his watch. "Just so she's here by eleven." He surveyed a table spread with twig-log cabin cigarette boxes, turned wooden goblets and burl-handled pocketknives. "Let's commence by filming a scenario of Calvin and me perusing the handicrafts."

Bubby nodded toward the pavilion stage. "We need to position the van before the crowd gets too thick."

Calvin pointed down the hill to a grove of trees. "Why don't you back it in on the left side of the audience area, keep the sun behind you."

Brockwell pointed to the right side of the gathering audience. "I'd prefer you in greater proximity to the judge's gallery."

"We'll need to pan from the stage to you in the same shot." Calvin made a movie frame with his fingers and swung it from the stage to Brockwell's face. "We just have the one camera."

Brockwell squinted up at the sun and turned to Bubby. "Right then, you position your vehicle and join us back up here."

Bubby's right arm twitched and Calvin feared for an instant that he was going to give a mocking fascist salute, but he just turned and threaded his way down through the crowd toward the truck, the Kentucky Colonel following close behind.

Brockwell waved for Calvin to follow him along lines of quilts and coverlets billowing in the breeze. They passed blankets spread with white oak baskets, some tall and elongated with attached cards promising that they could easily accommodate a thermos bottle for auto picnicking. Brockwell stopped to listen to a boy with a gunnysack full of walking sticks and canes shyly explaining how he found naturally bent handles along road cuts and stream banks. Brockwell nodded approval and led on past corn brooms and varnished dulcimers hanging from tree-like stands.

They stopped at a table where a man in floppy straw hat carved animals from holly and cherry. Bubby rejoined them. "You shouldn't do that yourself!" said Calvin as he helped him unshoulder the heavy wooden tripod.

Bubby eased the new movie camera from his grip. "I'm fine. I wanted Anne to pull the cables to the stage microphone before the crowd packs in."

Brockwell squinched up his nose. "Is she gonna be all right?"

The Kentucky Colonel, tagging right behind Bubby, took his meaning. "She's got her hair fixed over her face. You can't see anything."

Brockwell shuddered and turned to Calvin. "We'll look at the dulcimers and the carvings first. Then I want a segment with the Morris dancers before the singing begins."

Bubby handed the microphone to Calvin and set up his camera. The woodcarver watched as Bubby cranked the spring motor that transported the film and checked the level on the batteries that ran the audio. "Nice camera y'all got," he said to Calvin.

"It makes talkies."

"Sound-on-film in a single unit like that?" The carver raised his eyebrows and nodded approval. "It's just sixteen millimeter, though, isn't it?"

"Yeah," said Calvin, I guess it is." It was the first time Calvin had seen the new camera himself. "I like your carving."

"Thanks," said the carver, glancing up. "They said you're the guy from the radio. That right?"

Calvin nodded.

"I heard your story with them pilgrims makin' the sawhorses." He grinned and went back to his carving. "I liked that 'Descartes before the horse' gag."

"Thanks!" Calvin brightened, not so much with the compliment, but with the memory of that rainy morning in the tower when Anne brought him that joke and Kathryn brought the photos.

Brockwell cleared his throat and pulled Calvin into position beside him in front of the table. "We've got an addition to your wardrobe." The Kentucky Colonel produced a leather carpenter's tool belt with hammer loops and nail pouches and handed it to Calvin.

Calvin backed off. "What on earth do you want me to wear that for?"

"It'll help establish your visual identity. Try it on. It's adjustable."

"But I'm not working, I'm introducing a music program. It'll look ridiculous!"

Bubby chortled, shaking his head. "There's not even any tools in it!"

"We could find you a hammer," countered the Kentucky Colonel.

"I need you to appeal to the working man," said Brockwell.

"Any working man will know just how stupid this looks, wearing a tool belt just for show."

Competing emotions flashed on Brockwell's face as he stared at the tool belt. His amusement at the empty gesture won out. "Perhaps it would look a bit silly." He waggled his fingers at the tool belt, and the disappointed Kentucky Colonel withdrew the offering. "Alright, Calvin. You stand beside me now, I'm gong to act *extempore* here. You just reinforce what I say. Understand?"

"Absolutely." Calvin squinted at the camera.

"Good, and after this I'll let you direct a bit."

Bubby quieted the small crowd that had gathered to watch. He put his eye to the finder and called, "Action!"

Brockwell swept back his hair and made an open gesture at the dulcimers. "These mountain *dulcimers* are all made by Mr. *Amburgey*, who learned from Mr. *Thomas*, so they are all *authentic folk* instruments."

"They're *magnificent!*" said Calvin, stretching out his arm at them.

Brockwell sidestepped to the table. "Now these carvings are

all hand done as well, and they show the mountain people's *attachment* to the land and its *creatures*."

From a double file of varnished animals marching two-by-two toward a maple and cherry Noah's Ark, Calvin picked up a pig, smoothly carved from holly. "They *certainly* do." The carver reached for a fresh band-sawn blank from a peach basket and began paring away its sharp corners.

"Below us, cities are infested with *crawling* rats. Here, we *find* noble bears, bounding *deer*, and soaring eagles! Yes, the Anglo-Saxon is always *creative*. His *hands* are never idle." Brockwell stared fixedly at the camera long enough for Bubby to guess that this was the end of the scene. Calvin set the carved pig back next to its mate, but Brockwell picked it up an put it back in his hands. "You keep that as a memento." As Brockwell hustled them off toward the Morris dancers, Calvin turned and saw the carver's wordless protest as they walked off with his carved pig.

The Morris dancers were picturesquely situated in front of a clear shot of the valley. Calvin dutifully directed the curious onlookers to listen to Brockwell, to nod with approval, and not to look at the camera. Bubby gave the cue, the dancers began and Brockwell spoke. "For two days, music and dancing take *possession* of this great mountain. Below us, mobs of octoroons gyrate with animal instincts to savage rhythms." He gestured at the dancers as they clacked their wooden swords. "Here, the true American folk becomes once *again* transported with the beauty and *grace* of its pure traditions. Every visitor becomes *instantly* part of the *whole*, and his own traditional heritage *pours* into the general *stream*."

Calvin glanced at Bubby, wanting to talk, but the Kentucky Colonel kept too close by for even a whisper to pass unheard. Bubby managed a tiny reassuring nod in response to Calvin's glances and, when he adjusted the camera to compensate for a passing cloud, Calvin saw that his fingers were crossed. He glanced at his watch—fifteen minutes to the ballad competition.

The gathering audience had already spread well back up the slope from the pavilion stage. People murmured and pointed at the odd procession threading their way toward Bubby's van. Brockwell led in his cream linen suit, followed by Calvin in his stiff denim overalls carrying the tripod on his shoulder. Bubby carried the camera and the microphone, his Middle-Eastern face glowing under a sharp Panama hat that struggled to stay on his head as the tripod brushed against it. The tool-belt toting Kentucky Colonel with his flamboyant hair and narrow black tie in cliché imitation of a bourbon whiskey advertisement brought up the rear.

Anne popped up through the hatch atop the van as they approached. She glanced at them, but quickly turned away to pull the microphone cable onto the deck and secure it with a short rope. She wore coveralls, a long billed cap and sunglasses that held her hair hanging over her face. Calvin searched for an excuse to speak with her, but Brockwell dragged him on toward the stage where the clog-dancing contest had just concluded. The Kentucky Colonel took up his station by the van to watch over Bubby as he pushed his tripod up onto the roof platform.

The clog-dancing judges whispered to Brockwell as Calvin waited awkwardly beside him on the stage. Brockwell turned to the microphone to announce their decisions and present the awards. In the boxed-in judge's gallery to the left side of the audience, as Calvin faced them from the stage, the Irishman and his corpulent wife took their seats. Beside them, a potato-faced boy worried the knobs of the amplifier powering the trumpet-belled loudspeakers on the pavilion roof.

Brockwell was content to ignore the restless mass of the

audience as he greeted special guests in the front rows. At his signal, ballad-singing contestants filed into two of the three chairs set aside for them on the edge of the stage. Brockwell looked at his pocket watch and shook his head. Calvin glanced at the empty chair, but the old man gave a shrug and called him over with a wiggled finger. "I prefer not to take a chance on an unknown anyway."

"She'll be here."

Brockwell shook his head. "Our tenor was just fine, and a cash contribution will easily make up the difference. So, I'm going to introduce you, and then you will introduce our balladeers." He lifted a pair of headphones to Calvin's hands. "Put these on during the singing so you can hear my instructions."

All other music on the mountain gradually fell silent, leaving just the sound of the restive audience stretched back up the slope in a biblical throng. Brockwell stepped to the microphone. "For the last five *years* it has been my pleasure to *introduce* our balladeers." His oddly placed emphasis echoed in a hypnotic rhythm. "But on this stunning *day*, on our beautiful mountain top, I *will* turn that privilege over to our new friend. His name is Calvin Cobb, the versatile and amusing voice of *Grandpa Sam's Woodshop of the Air*." The loud applause confirmed the efficiency of government check disbursement. "Now many of you have listened to me, and to Calvin here, on the *radio*. But if you look over there," he pointed to Bubby and the camera atop the van, "…you'll see that we are capturing this event for the newsreels, and for eventual broadcast to television receivers, both here and overseas!" The crowd cheered and waved at the camera. "That is the future, but now, we turn to our most ancient form of communication. Our balladeers are about to transport us back to times of Elizabethan *merrymaking*, to Chaucer and the Canterbury *pilgrims*, and even farther back to when our Celtic *ancestors* looked down upon our Saxon *forbears* from the mountains of Wales, Scotland *and* Ireland and found those newcomers *worthy of their blood*!" A few small groups cheered, but most of the applause was polite or impatient. "Now, I will join our judges and turn over the microphone to our friend, Calvin Cobb."

Calvin unfolded the script and read flatly into the microphone, never lifting his eyes from the page. "Thank you. I feel so at home here among you. For I am a worker in wood, kindred to you proud men of the soil, yeoman farmers, strong of back and sure of purpose!" The applause made him look up, and he could not help but smile back.

"Do uncle Dan!" cried a man at the back of the rope line. The surrounding crowd chorused his appeal and cheered.

Calvin smiled and waved, and found his place again in the script. "What a contrast to the land below us, where money changers scramble for their bits of silver! Here, thoughts fly back to *pioneer* days, to sailing ships bringing our ancestors to this New World. Through the *purity* of this music we connect with our own lives in a *mysterious* and electrifying fashion!" Again, most of the applause was polite, but with the same scattered groups cheering wildly, more inspired by alcohol than by ideology.

He introduced the first singer and grateful applause greeted the slender girl in the white dress. She sang, alone before the microphone, with a high fine voice that rose and clipped the end of each verse of *Massie Groves*, the amplifier lifting her song to echo against rocks on the mountain crest.

From the judge's gallery, Brockwell stared at him and pantomimed putting on headphones. Calvin snatched up the phones and put them on. "I need a lot more enthusiasm out of you!" came Brockwell's voice. "Nod your head if you understand."

Calvin nodded.

"I'm sending up my tenor. He's our winner so you act

accordingly, you understand?" came Brockwell's voice.

Calvin nodded slowly, but Brockwell was already leaning to speak reassurances in the ears of the Irishman and his wife. Calvin looked helplessly over at the camera that had captured him speaking Brockwell's words. Standing beside the camera tripod atop the van, Anne was mounting Bubby's wool-covered shotgun microphone on a short post. Static popped in his headphones and then Anne's voice said, "Quick, nod at Brockwell."

He did so, enthusiastically.

"Good, you can hear me! He wants more enthusiasm on the next introduction," came Anne's voice. "Turn your head away from him and say something, we're trying to pick you up on Bubby's shotgun."

He turned his head and shielded his mouth with his hand. "Are they..." but he was interrupted by the applause for the conclusion of the ballad of *Massie Groves*.

Calvin joined in the applause and found the place in his script for the next introduction. He read slowly, imitating Brockwell's emphasis. "Below us, stunted, degraded *races* cower in their unweeded garden. Here, in our southern highlands, families *grow* strong beneath the sun with blood *that* is pure American! There comes that sense that *we are the folk* and in that fact lies the *secret* of the *Golden Age to come!*"

A man in the back shouted, "T'aint there nuthin ah kin do?" in poor imitation of Uncle Dan's catch phrase.

Calvin grinned and waved back as a nervously enthusiastic, freshly sunburned woman stepped forward to sing *The Bonny Swans*. Calvin snatched up the headphones and clamped them over his head.

"Smile at the bastard!" said Anne's voice. "He says that was much better!"

Calvin grinned and nodded at the judge's gallery and quickly turned away. "What happened to the Valentines? Brockwell's going to send up his castrati!"

"Don't fret," said Anne, "we synchronized watches!"

Calvin nodded, surveying the crowd standing in the sunshine behind the rope barricade — men with coal dust ground deep in their skin, girls holding younger brothers and sisters on their hips, a woman, perfectly proud in her old-fashioned cloche hat and dress sewn from flower-printed feed sack fabric. Among the thousands, Calvin spotted the woodcarver whose missing pig now rested in Calvin's pocket. The man stood on a boulder at the edge of the crowd, his wife beside him moving her lips in perfect synchrony to the old song.

"Hang on." Anne swung the microphone around to point down the mountain road and then swung it back to Calvin. "I hear a car coming."

"Is it them?"

"No way to tell. Nod at Brockwell, not too enthusiastically."

"What does he want?"

"He's sending up his tenor."

But instead of nodding, Calvin tore off the headphones, looked at them and examined the cable. He shook his head at them as if they had malfunctioned and turned his smiling attention to the balladeer's final verse. He joined in the applause, holding up her hand as she blushed and squirmed. The Irish tenor paced at the edge of the stage, his introduction in his hand, but Calvin kept his back turned to him. As the applause died, a rumble lingered, like the background noise of a record. A few heads turned to look down at the road.

Calvin reluctantly let the sunburned girl return to her seat, and fished the script from his overalls. "The British Isles are the home to many people," he read slowly. The rumble became a black Buick that rolled up the road, passed behind the stage and pulled up behind the judge's gallery in a cloud of pale dust. "When our Saxon forebears came into England, our Celtic ancestors removed themselves to the mountains in Wales, Scotland and the emerald hills of Ireland." His voice took on power and conviction, but all eyes were on the black chauffeur in a blue uniform who emerged from the car and walked stiffly around to open the passenger door. A woman in a black crepe mourning dress with a black hat and veil stepped out and surveyed the scene. Brockwell grinned delightedly as he pointed out the new arrivals to two hard-looking men who had joined him in the judge's stand.

Calvin waved, urging her on as she walked hesitantly through the crowd to the stage, assisted by the chauffeur. "It's a fitting conclusion then, to our celebration of our Celtic, Anglo-Saxon and Teutonic unity, that we welcome to our mountaintop one of the most gifted daughters of the Emerald Isle." He walked right past the outraged tenor, took the woman's hand and guided her to the microphone. "Let's have a big southern highlands welcome for our Irish nightingale, widow Erin McCroi!" Uncertain applause mixed with the crowd's murmuring at the uniformed chauffeur and fancy car.

Brockwell now stood smirking at the side of the stage. The woman leaned to the microphone. "Thank you, thank you everyone! So many..." Her warm, southern voice was too loud and her veil brushed against the microphone. "So many of us have lost our songs, our languages, coming from homes far across the sea. But when we stand in such a magnificent place as this..." She reached out her gloved hands to the audience as the breeze tugged at her veil.

Brockwell shook his head and strode across the stage. Calvin's sweaty hand found the carved pig in his pocket and he squeezed it into his palm. Brockwell stepped to the microphone pulled it away. "I'm sorry, folks, sorry. We have a disqualification." The crowd murmured. "But all is not lost! Fear not! Our Calvin here has arranged a surprise lesson for us, a little drama that he wrote for his friends to perform for us today." He pulled back from the microphone and spoke to Calvin, ignoring the crowd. "I enjoyed reading your script. It not only brought my GAO troublemaker into the light, it brought her up here to me where we can have a little talk." He turned to the veiled woman, still standing proud and facing the audience. "Calvin's brought us an octoroon surprise. A little talk right now could do us a world o' good."

The crowd responded with scattered, nervous laughter. Calvin looked out at the unsure but attentive faces of the audience. He saw the woodcarver trying to answer his daughter's questions.

"Perhaps the veil is in the way of your voice. Let's pull back the curtain Mrs. Valentine!" Brockwell reached toward her hat and lifted it.

Calvin grabbed the microphone and called to the audience as her face was revealed. "And she is indeed a surprise! It's America's favorite home maker, Miss Kathryn Dale Harper!"

"Hello, everyone!" said Kathryn in her best radio voice.

Applause and excited women's voices greeted her. A few hundred women checked the sit of their hats and corrected their posture.

"And who loves Uncle Dan?" called Calvin.

The entire crowd roared.

"Why uncle Dan!" said Calvin, turning to the chauffeur. "We've been here working all day, and you just showed up. What have you got to say for yourself?"

Gabriel the chauffeur stepped up to the microphone. "WELL, T'AINT THER NUTHIN AH KIN DO?"

Cheers, applause and laughter coursed across the mountaintop.

Brockwell lunged for the microphone, but Gabriel leaned in, shouldering him aside. "Now, Mr. Brockwell, I think it time you learned to...TEND TO YOUR WHITTLIN!"

Laughter echoed all the way down the valley and up the other side.

The Irishman rushed across the stage and grabbed for the microphone, but Calvin turned, brandished the carved pig like a weapon and drove him back. Brockwell again reached for the microphone but Gabriel jerked it away. The cable pulled free of the microphone connector, but Bubby's shotgun mike on the van switched in and the voices continued undiminished from the speakers. The Irishman grabbed Calvin's arm and the two of them fell wrestling to the stage.

Gabriel gestured down at them. "Don't y'all worry 'bout the way they behaves now."

"Why is that, Uncle Dan?" asked Kathryn.

"CAUSE THEY'S OURN AND WE LOVES 'EM!"

A smatter of applause and a rumble of voices came from the hillside. The Kentucky Colonel had abandoned his post at the van and was now pushing his way toward the stage. Seeing him lift the rope barrier, the crowd surged under the rope and flowed around the Kentucky Colonel into the pavilion. The crowd was agitated and confused, trying to make sense of the fight on stage and their favorite radio character now revealed in the flesh. Brockwell dropped off the front edge of the stage and yelled to the Kentucky Colonel who was still forcing his way toward them. "Stop that truck!" He waved frantically at Bubby's camera van which was now easing through the crowd toward the road. Up the hill, men cupped their hands to their ears, but the confused chatter of the crowd was too loud. The applause died. Now other men were yelling and pointing at the van.

The amplification was gone, but the cursing Irishman was plenty loud enough as he struggled furiously with Calvin. A quick shove from Kathryn's foot sent him sliding off the front of the stage, but his cursing continued. Two men armed with sticks were pushing toward the stage with the clear intention of resuming the fight. Calvin staggered to his feet, grasped the carved pig and held it high. "Puh. . . ," he managed. "Puh. . . ," More men with sticks were pushing their way toward the stage.

Kathryn cupped her hands to her mouth and bellowed "Pig-pig-pig PO-O-ie, pO-O-ee, pig-pig!"

The silence lasted only an instant before a hundred voices called back in unison. "Pig-pig-pig PO-O-ie, pO-O-ee, pig-pig!"

Gabriel grinned at the audience, cupped his hands and called out. "lO-Oke stE-Er kwO-O!"

Two thousand voices called back, "lO-Oke stE-Er kwO-O!" followed by laughter and cheers.

The front bumper of Bubby's van scraped the gravel as it jounced down onto the road. "Get to the van!" croaked Calvin, and he stepped up beside Kathryn at the front of the stage.

"CO-O bO-Oss! cO-OO-O bO-Oss, cO-O, cO-O!" they called in rough unison.

In four neighboring counties, herds of cattle lifted their heads as the multitude on the mountain called, "cO-O bO-Oss! cO-OO-O bO-Oss, cO-O, cO-O!"

The horn honked on Bubby's van. Calvin tugged Kathryn's wrist, but she pulled back and stepped to the edge of the stage. "Whe-E-gy, Whe-E-gy, Pig-pig!" She cupped her hand to her ear and leaned towards the audience.

"WUtts, wUtts, wUtts!" came the finish from four thousand cheering voices.

Kathryn gave a final wave to the audience as Calvin pulled her away. They leapt off stage and ran down the dirt road flanked by salutes from folks who'd just enjoyed the best damn folk festival ever! Ahead, the open rear doors of the van waited for them to jump in, but angry men were also pounding down through the crowd.

"Go on!" gasped Calvin. "Can't breathe!" His face was exploding red.

Kathryn grabbed his arm and pulled him along. She saw the men converging on the van. "Go on!" she shouted.

"Hell no!" cried Gabriel and he jumped from the back of the van. The men, including the Kentucky Colonel who was now waving a pistol, skidded down onto the road, blocking his path. Gabriel spun about and leapt onto the ladder on the back of the van. He grabbed at the shotgun mike as he clambered onto the roof, but grasped only the furry cover, pulling it off.

The Kentucky Colonel jumped back at the sight. "My God! The nigra's got a ray gun!"

Calvin looked up and saw Gabriel lifting the spiraling array of gleaming aluminum tubes off its post. He croaked out, "My God! Don't fire that! You'll kill everyone!"

Gabriel aimed the tubes at the men. "Damn! I don't care, I'm gonna smoke 'em all!"

Kathryn screamed. "For God's sake! Think of the children!"

The men eased back.

"Idiots! It's just a microphone!" shouted Brockwell.

Anne popped her head through the roof hatch. "Yeah? Well look what it did to me!" She pulled back her hair from her scarred face.

The men gasped and staggered. Calvin and Kathryn jumped in the door of the van as its spinning wheels threw a shower of gravel. Bubby struggled to control the overloaded van as they skidded down the road. Gabriel snatched down the last of the equipment from the roof and joined the jumble below, trying to find a secure perch among the rocking piles of cables and equipment boxes as Bubby whipped the steering wheel from side to side.

"*SPLANG!*" A bullet dented in the back door of the van.

Calvin sprung up through the roof hatch. "Give me

something to throw! They're right behind us!"

"Throw the cables!" shouted Bubby.

"THWAK!" The cable bundle hit Brockwell's car and sprayed over the Adler's windshield like spaghetti. Calvin dropped back down into the van as the Kentucky Colonel took aim at him. He worked his way to the back of the van to look through the window at the pursuers. The Kentucky Colonel was now taking aim on the tire below Calvin's knees. He unlatched the rear door and slid the heavy wooden tripod onto the road. Brockwell whipped the steering wheel and nimbly dodged it, but his partner's shot went wild.

Calvin reached blindly behind him for something to throw. "Not the camera!" shouted Anne. "It still has the film in it!"

Gabriel passed him the shotgun microphone and Calvin lofted it at the pursuers. It whistled through the air and bounced off the hood, but the Adler kept coming. Another shot and the van fishtailed. Calvin grabbed the top of the door to keep from being thrown out. Gravel drilled at his ankles. Hanging on the door, he was completely exposed as the Kentucky Colonel, leaning out the passenger side of the Adler, aimed his gun directly at him. The gray horseman appeared through the dust, resolving itself into the shape of a woman on a motorcycle. As the Kentucky Colonel leveled his pistol, Verdie swung down with her swagger stick and swatted it from his hand. The Adler swerved sharply toward the motorcycle, but Verdie had already hit her brakes and dropped behind into the dust cloud.

The Adler still bounded after the van, which was braking hard, on a sharp curve. Bushes scoured the side of the van and knocked Calvin into the ditch just behind the where the van came to rest. The pursuing car also ran into the ditch and bounded toward Calvin. He closed his eyes as choking dust rolled over him. Reports rang out in the blackness. A caped figure in a campaign hat looked down at him. Linda reached out her hand to his head. "Chief! Are you okay?"

Calvin coughed and blinked his eyes. The settling dust revealed a nine-passenger Forest Service station wagon. More gunshot sounds turned out to be slamming car doors as more ghostly figures emerged. He coughed again and rubbed his eyes with his shirtsleeve. The van rested against laurel bushes on the embankment. He staggered to his feet. Verdie, still seated on her motorcycle held the Kentucky Colonel at bay with her swagger stick and yelled at him. "Well, you're in the National Forest now and under Department of Agriculture jurisdiction, so shut the hell up!"

"You have no authority here!" shouted Brockwell. "You have no authority!"

Calvin staggered up behind Brockwell, spun the man around, pulled open his jacket and yanked a bundle of envelopes from his inside pocket.

Brockwell shouted in his face. "Forest Rangers? You think a bunch of damn Boy Scouts can stop us?"

Calvin nodded toward Verdie who was pulling the ignition keys from the Adler while popping the Kentucky Colonel's hands with her swagger stick. "No, Brockwell, looks like this time it took the Girl Scouts." He extracted a sleeve of photographic negatives from the bundle of envelopes and tossed the remainder on the road.

Coughing overcame Brockwell, giving Calvin the intense satisfaction of the last word. Gabriel joined Calvin as he limped to the station wagon. "Was that your car we left behind?" asked Calvin.

"It's alright," said Gabriel, tugging at the collar of his tight chauffeur's jacket. "I bought it with some thirty dollar checks I got in the mail."

Calvin shook his head. "Oh, now the money!"

"Don't worry about the money." Linda called out. "There

was too much of it! With elections coming up, who the hell is going to ask voters to give it back?"

Verdie pulled up on her motorcycle. "Let's go! Let's go! There's more cars coming!"

Linda dropped into the driver's seat of the station wagon. Beside her, Ellen, wearing her old Signal Corps uniform, already had her hand on the gearshift. Linda pushed in the station wagon's clutch and Ellen threw the car into gear.

Kathryn grabbed Calvin's arm and hustled him back to Bubby's van. He clambered in to sit on cables beside her. Anne was in the front passenger seat and he handed her the envelope of negatives. She pulled out a strip and held it delicately to the light in the seconds before Bubby gunned the van bouncing out of the ditch.

Verdie pulled her motorcycle into the lead and the little procession rolled down the hill and onto the paved road. Out the window ahead of them, soft gray against the blue sky, the clouds had organized themselves into long rows—for no apparent reason.

The End

AFTERWORD

This is a work of fiction and all characters and organizations derive completely from the author's imagination and the stories told by his father. Many of the events and places are, however, based on historical fact.

The story of the American women volunteers killed and injured by the long-distance German shell on Good Friday in 1918 is true. You can visit the church of St. Gervais, just a few blocks north of Notre Dame Cathedral in the heart of Paris, and see where the collapsed roof was repaired with contrasting stone.

The Hindenburg disaster was captured on a Presto recorder, just as described. German agents did try to confiscate the discs. Germany did use television just as described to present the Berlin Olympics in 1936. The application of early computing equipment, much of it American-made, to further Nazi aims is well-documented.

Glen Echo Park, just west of Washington, D.C., in Maryland, was segregated up until the early 1960s. Tommy Dorsey's band did play in the Ballroom. That room was converted into the Jungle Ride when I was a kid, but it is now restored and regularly hosts swing dances.

Many of my descriptions of the 1930s Washington diplomatic community were lifted intact from the literature of the time. The humor was simply too good not to steal for your reading pleasure. I wish I had come up with "eating only bear meat and always carrying teddy bears about," but I did not.

There was a large, annual "folk festival" held in the Virginia mountains throughout the late 1930s, much as described. It was intended as a nativist celebration of pure Anglo-Saxon heritage with socio-political motives far more creepy than I could invent.

The old Post Office still stands there on Pennsylvania Avenue. My father worked there for the Department of Agriculture in the 1930s and did indeed feed the mice. The building has had its ups and downs, but last I checked, you can still visit the tower, and the cat and the dog are still there in the marble by the 12th Street entrance. The skid marks from Verdie's motorcycle, however, have long since been scrubbed away.

ACKNOWLEDGEMENTS

Thanks to Jane Underhill and Carey Bagdassarian for generous and unfailing encouragement. Thanks to first readers Ann Browning, Jim Parker, Peter Ross, Mark Olshaker, James Whitmore Andrews, John Kresge, Charles and Thomas Underhill and Sister Barbara Ann. Thanks to Cheryl Larson and Kathy Sturgeon for inspiration. Thanks to dear friend Nan Rothwell for making this story a much better read. Thanks to Megan Fitzpatrick, Christopher Schwarz and Lost Art Press for making this story a book!

PHOTO CREDITS: *Old Post Office, Old Pension Building, farms and YWCA ad (front of book) from the Library of Congress. "Marinettes" image from U.S. Department of Defense. "Farther Afield" printed with permission of the Virginia State Chamber of Commerce.*

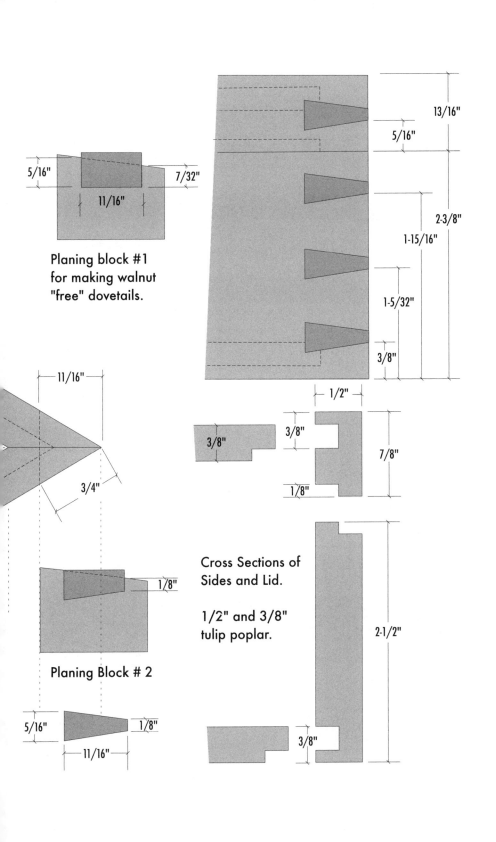

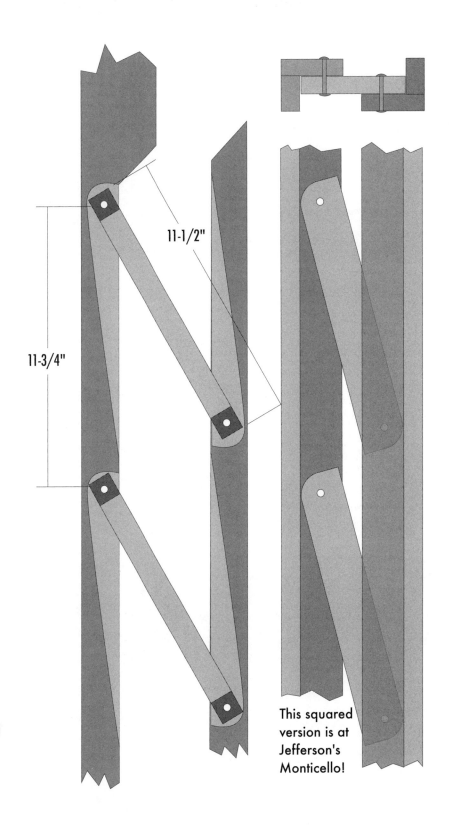

With Mallets Toward None!

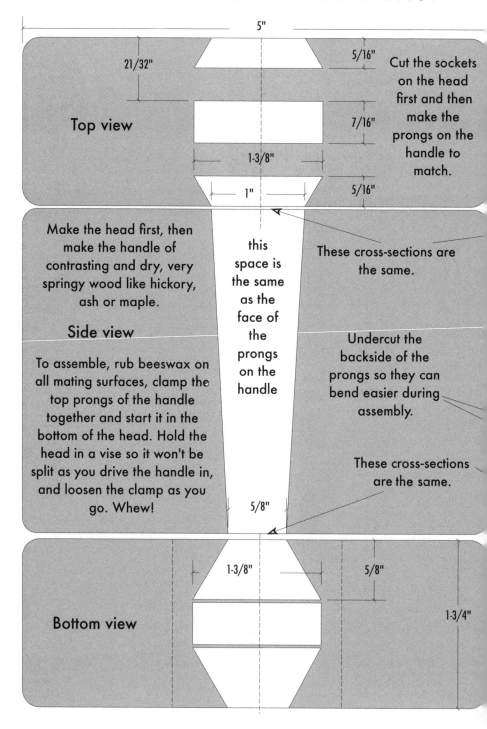

from Grandpa Sam's Woodshop of the Air

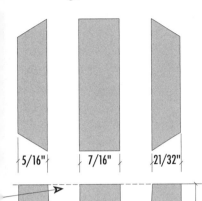

| 5/16" | 7/16" | 21/32" |

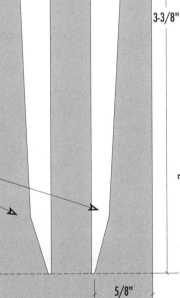

3-3/8"

5/8"

Handle, (from the view of a peg being driven by the finished mallet)

Three score...
no,
five score...
no,

Listen to Grandpa Sam's Woodshop of the Air each week on the National Farm and Home Hour, NBC Blue, with host Calvin Cobb. A production of USDA Radio Services, Washington 25 DC

The Sawhorse That Saved Thanksgiving!

1. CUT THE STOCK: Cut your 2 by 4 by 27 inch for the top and the four 1 by 3 by 30 inch legs.

What's he upset about?

There's no room at the Thanksgiving table. Better make some sawhorses fast!

Listen to Grandpa Sam's Woodshop of the Air each week on the National Farm and Home Hour, NBC Blue, with host Calvin Cobb. A production of USDA Radio Services, Washington 25 DC

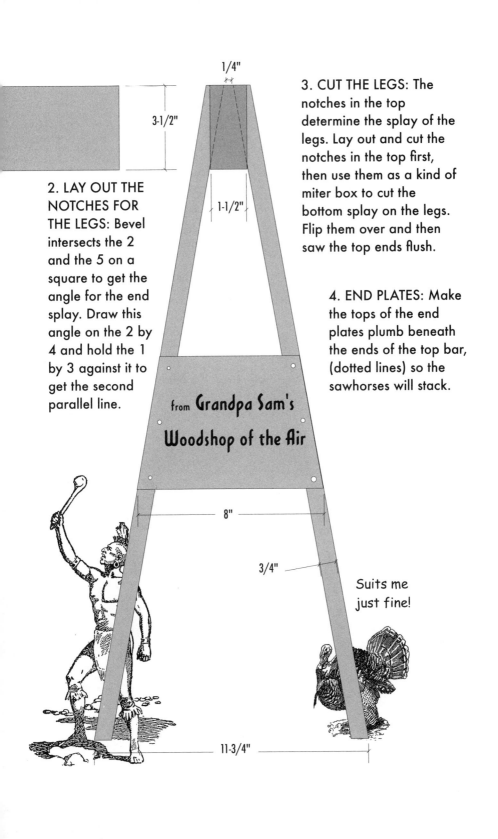